Refuge

Best,
Marci LaBarbera

Also by Nanci LaGarenne

Cheap Fish

www.nancilagarenne.com

Nanci LaGarenne

Refuge
A NOVEL

Blue Bottle Press
New York

Refuge. Copyright © 2015 by Nanci LaGarenne

For information address Blue Bottle Press, PO Box 3264, East Hampton, New York 11937

Printed in the United States of America

Library of Congress Control Number: 2015915010

Second Edition: September 2015

ISBN- 13: 978-0692523339
ISBN- 10: 0692523332

Nanci LaGarenne

Refuge

A NOVEL

Blue Bottle Press
New York

This is a work of fiction. All characters, places and incidents are fictitious and the product of the author's imagination. Any resemblance to actual persons, living or dead, events or locales is entirely coincidental

For information address Blue Bottle Press, PO Box 3264, East Hampton, New York 11937

Printed in the United States of America

Library of Congress Control Number: 2015915010

Second Edition: September 2015

ISBN- 13: 978-0692523339
ISBN- 10: 0692523332

ACKNOWLEDGMENTS

I dedicate this story to all the brave women who escaped from abuse. Your journey to self-worth and wholeness does not go unnoticed. You are beautiful warriors. Hurrah to you for standing up for yourself.

A grand shout out to the particularly compassionate who work in the Domestic Violence field, fighting for the cause of better human relationships. And for teaching women to go up a step when choosing a mate.

I salute the following amazing women I had the privilege to work with and know: Brenda, Catherine, Renata, Vindel, Myra, Ellen, Alita, Sherry, Judy, Matilda, Kathy, Rebecca, Patti, Susan, Mary, Betty, Karen, Bea, and Jen.

To M. for the butterfly pin and letting me witness your flight.

To all the children who were without a voice for what happened to you. I speak for you. I hear you. I believe you. You did nothing wrong.

Thank you James, for your help and for breaking the chain. You are my anchor and safe place to fall.

To Jen, for her in-house editing.

for Lee

Prologue

People heal. Just not on your clock. Time makes us older, not necessarily wiser. Wisdom takes work. And staying away from losers takes willpower. Doc Rain was not a fan of defeat, and she was no airy-fairy magical thinker either. She was a realist with a heart. Some of her fans liked to believe in guardian angels. Nothing wrong with that if it gets you through the day. Doc just never considered herself that spiritual or that needy. She was a therapist who helped broken women survive. You need heart and mind strength for that gig. The women she treated were not only broken in the physical sense, they had deep emotional wounds. And something called trust trauma, Doc deemed it. If they healed their hearts, the trust might follow. And one day the world will see peace. Sometimes a healthy dose of cynicism was necessary. Clicking their heels three times was not going to take anyone back to Kansas. Abuse leaves indelible scars. You just never forget, that was the plain truth.

Dr. Rain Taylor, or Doc, as she was known, came to her line of work not by chance. In most cases, social work in the domestic violence field has roots somewhere in the practitioner's psyche. Either they experienced abuse themselves or they were familiar with its ugly face.

Doc's sister, Teresa, could have been her reason. Teresa would thank her, she was sure of it. If she talked. Teresa had chosen silence and solitude. Doc's baby sister was a cloistered nun. Doc chose battle, Teresa, surrender. Not to the darkness, but for her, to God and the light. One cannot judge what is right for another and as much as Doc missed her sister, she understood. She knew why. She had seen. She had become Teresa's protector. Teresa would thank her. But Doc did not want gratitude, she wanted change. She wanted what we all want, for the abuse to end. For the abusers to be locked away so all women and children could be safe. Maybe Doc had rose-colored glasses after all.

Doc took her job as therapist seriously, basically devoted her life to it. Some might say that was digging to China with a teaspoon. Yet a small dent was better than nothing if it kept one more woman alive and one more child safe.

Doc had her own story of how she got here, but that will come later. For now her reflection remains about the women, her boarders at the Brownstone, Doc's home. And how the people in our lives can change us in very good and very bad ways. Doc wanted to focus on the goodness. The bad has a way of showing up whether you invite it or not. As for guardian angels, Doc would leave that to the heavenly realm. Most of us fly much closer to the ground.

Chapter One

Rooney

Rooney came first. Rooney McNeil, a Southern spitfire, who called Doc her guardian angel. Rooney was a force of nature Doc could not have prepared for, but then you cannot prepare for forces of nature. Rooney was a natural born fighter who pulled no punches when telling you what was on her mind. Her quirky expressions and offbeat humor were like no one Doc had ever met. She had met her share of people through the years, mainly women clients, most of them hanging on by a thread. Rooney was different. She wanted no pity and no free lunch. She wore her scars like a battle victory. She was alive. No thanks to her Cracker ex-husband who tried his best to do otherwise. Rooney was no Scarlett O'Hara. Neither was she a Melanie. She was more like the entire Civil War fighting for her life and freedom. It was safe to say with Rooney around, there was never a dull moment at the Brownstone. The day Doc found her was another lucky day for Rooney.

She lay at the bottom of the stairs in a heap. At least this time it was her fault. *Doc needs a runner on those damn stairs*. The pain grabbed her again. She heard a key turn in the front lock. *Thank God*. She let the tears come. It wasn't him.

"Rooney? What the hell? Don't move. Is it your back?" Doc knelt next to her, accessing the damage, hoping Rooney hadn't aggravated an old injury.

He'll never find me here. I swear.

"It hurts," Rooney winced.

"Sorry. Easy now, I'm going to lift you and get you over to the couch, okay?"

"Mmm, hmm," she moaned weakly. Doc lifted her carefully. She was lighter than expected. Her tough exterior belied her fragile body.

1

"Doc?"

"Got you, no worries." She went limp and Doc carried her over to the couch.

"There you go, sweetie," she used her mommy's here voice. She'd had plenty of practice at the domestic violence shelter where she volunteered.

"I'll go get some ice. Hang on."

She found empty trays in the freezer. Murphy's Law ruled in the Brownstone. Doc grabbed a bag of frozen peas instead.

"Here we are. The Green Giant's going to make it all better." She put the peas wrapped in a tea towel under Rooney's back. Rooney made a pained face, and then relaxed.

"Ahh that feels good. Lucky for me y'all came home early."

"Let's cover you with an afghan." Doc tucked the blanket around Rooney. "What happened? You get bored cutting heads?"

Rooney laughed, "Yeah, after my last haircut I threw myself down the stairs for entertainment."

"Ass over teakettle?"

"I swear. And speaking of asses…" Rooney winced and rubbed her sore bottom.

"Does it hurt? Because it's killing…." Doc began the old joke.

"Don't you dare finish that sentence."

"Was I going to say something?"

"Sure you weren't and I'm Snow White."

"There's a stretch. Where were all your dwarves when you needed them?"

"Probably out screwing Cinderella."

"I think you'll be fine, seriously. But we could go get you checked out at the ER."

"No thanks, no hospital. These peas are all I need. Maybe a hot soak later on."

"Okay. If they get warm, we've got frozen niblets in the freezer. Dory and Fiona working? And where is Mae?"

2

Doc was taking inventory of her other boarders, ever the den mother.

"Yep, the IRA are at work alright, and Mae went grocery shopping. She took Shamus with her."

"Good. Shamus would have been licking your face and barking his head off, if he was here. That dog does love you."

Doc smiled and then out a sigh. She was dog-tired, as Rooney would say. She badly needed a second wind for the night.

"Y'all have a rough day?"

Doc didn't want to depress her but Rooney was right on the money. "Oh, you know how it goes at the shelter, the usual crises. Today one of the fathers pulled a no-show at visitation again. Lots of tears when all arrived home." Rooney shook her head. "That all, huh?"

"Sometimes I wonder Rooney Bean, do we ever make a difference?"

Rooney smiled and her face lit up.

"Daddy used to call me that. I haven't heard it in a coon's age. By the way, you absolutely do make a difference, you gotta know that."

"Right, now you throw yourself down the stairs. Seriously, what is the matter with me? I'm sorry, that was insensitive." Doc felt terrible. "How about some tea? What does Dory call it? The Irish cure-all?"

Rooney patted Doc's leg. "It's all raht. At least I didn't have to fuck the hillbilly after. I'd love some. Fix me right up." She smiled the angelic smile of an imp. The old Rooney was back. Though for a minute she looked a million miles away.

"Remember what tonight is?"

"Friday?" she laughed. " 'Course, the bare-y'alls soul group. Hopefully a large pitcher of margaritas to follow directly."

"Good girl. I am definitely looking forward to the directly part. Now, you rest. Want the telly on?"

3

"The IRA is getting the better of you. What would Uncle Carmine think, hearing you talk like that?"

"He'd say I was tu se pazzo. Crazy." She handed Rooney the remote.

"I ain't touching that one...."

"Wise girl." Doc walked towards the kitchen.

Returning with Rooney's tea, Doc excused herself and took her coffee down to her office and closed the door. "Never a dull moment is there?" she said out loud. Not in your life. You took on the boogeyman and he doesn't take vacation. Membership in the Three-F Club was always on the rise. Fed-up, frightened, and forgotten women, apply here.

The name of the Friday night support group was apropos. S.A.G.A.S. Salvation & Grace & Second chances. Rooney preferred "Somebody Actually Gives A Shit." Doc tended to agree with her there. It wasn't a pretty business. The wolves were always out there lurking. At any given moment another victim would knock at her door. Distraught. Demeaned. Devoured by the wolf. Metaphorically speaking.

In nature wolves can be fascinating animals. Spiritual. Revered by Native Americans. And they can be brutal predators, like some men. Men who prey on their own species. Men who hurt women in all manner of vicious ways. The men were not her concern. They got no billing. To say they were no better than pigs would be insulting another animal species. For both slurs to the animal kingdom, mea culpa. Truth is, Doc loved her job. And it was exhausting and frustrating on a daily basis. Rooney called her an angel.

"Y'all saved us, Doc." Angel was a stretch. Champion of women? Maybe. She didn't choose her line of work. It chose her. El destino. Uncle Carmine's line. Destiny, yes. Like the day she met Rooney McNeil.

Chapter Two

"Rooney, where you at?"

The hairs on the back of her neck bristled at the sound of his voice. *Oh crap, I forgot to leave his shirt out.*

"Down here, Clyde," she shouted. "Be right up." Rooney grabbed a pressed shirt out of the laundry room and ran up the stairs two at a time. Clyde snatched the hanger out of her hand. *Mannerless Cracker.*

"What the hell were you doin'? You don't hear me calling you? Jesus."

"Sorry. I went to the store real quick. Got to talking. Y'all hungry?" *Feed the beast and he'll leave.*

"No I ain't hungry. Gotta get on the road. Can't you ever stay your skinny ass home for once?"

"I told you, I was at the grocery...."

"Yeah, yeah. Tell it walking. Do I look like an idiot? What's with the hair? Got a date?" *Careful. Don't laugh in his face, you'll pay.*

"Just tryin' out a new style. Why don't you let me cook something? How 'bout a nice bacon cheeseburger?" *Clog y'alls arteries.*

"You deaf or somethin'? I said I ain't hungry. Your mama have any children that lived?" He let out a whoop. *The sicko just cracked himself up. Remember what Granny McNeil taught you? Some questions we don't dignify with an answer. Walk away, Rooney. Walk away.*

"Where the hell do you think you're going? I ain't finished talking."

Rooney turned to him, her hand on the doorjamb. Clyde moved closer, lessening the distance between them. She could smell him. Touch him. She wanted to do neither. Unless she was ripping his heart out. Miniscule organ he possessed. She purposely adjusted her bra. Pea brain could be easily distracted. Forget his interrogation. Chance would be a good thing. Rooney sighed loudly.

5

"I'm not going out. Be nice, okay?"

Clyde wasn't feeling nice at the moment. He reached for her, caught her good. She went flying across the bed. Luckily a pile of his dirty work clothes broke her fall. She missed smashing her head into the nightstand by inches.

"Listen, hot pants, you want some Clyde, you show up here when you're supposed to. I asked you where you was planning on goin'? You remember now?"

Rooney got up slowly and rubbed her back. *Nothing broken this time.*

"I swear I'm stayin' home. Don't make up stories."

"Lyin' bitch. Right to my face. I'm gonna be workin' while y'all party your tight little ass all over town. Tell me the truth."

Rooney shook her head. *So tired of this.*

"I am *not* going out." Then under her breath, "Are *y'all* deaf?"

"Very funny. You got a real smart mouth on you. Get over here and show me how smart it is, fancy pants." He unzipped his pants. Rooney didn't move. *One good slingshot and his Johnson would be history. Hah. Okay, Rooney, get serious now. Do it and get it over with.* She couldn't make her feet move. She glanced at the clock on the nightstand.

"Y'all gonna be late...." *Was that her voice?*

"Big mistake, the sassy mouth, bitch. You don't learn do you?" Before she could utter a comeback, his meaty hand connected with her face.

"Now don't ever tell me when I gotta leave my own house. I got all the time in the world now. Get your ass over here and do what I married you for. And it ain't making pie. Cut out the whining. Do your job. All you're good for anyway. Hurry, I gotta go to work."

Rooney held her smarting cheek and swallowed some tears. *Go suck yourself off, hillbilly loser. How badly she wanted to say it. She could taste it along with the blood in her mouth. Enough, I'd rather die.*

6

"Tell you what, I'm gonna go ahead downstairs and make us a pot of coffee. I got a nice fresh pie and real whipped cream. We'll pretend we're a regular married couple, all right?" *What the hell was she talking about? She didn't know herself. Gone Stepford wife. She just wasn't sucking Clyde off and that was that.*

"Shut up about pie and get over here like I told you. Pie. Hah. Jesus, you're an idiot."

"No thank you." *Whatever happened to Southern gentlemen?*

Clyde shook his head and laughed at her. Rooney prayed he would choke on his spit.

"What? You ain't the full shilling, you know that? Just a dumb blonde is all. And you're gettin too damn skinny. It ain't attractive."

Right, I married you. I must be dumb as a rock. Thanks, Rhett Butthead. I live for your compliments. She watched him take his keys off the dresser. Good. He'll leave now. Rooney sighed in relief. A little ice on her cheek and she'd be right as rain. And get a few days reprieve from Clyde.

"You say somethin, blondie?" Clyde stopped dressing.

Rooney stared him down. *You don't look an attack dog in the eyes. That's just crazy, Rooney.* She stared right through his steel blue eyes to the other side of hell. *I ain't scared of you no more, Clyde.*

"Y'all hear me say something?"

"Fucking sarcastic little bitch. I had enough of your mouth." Clyde dropped his keys. They banged in the ceramic dish on the dresser. Rooney tried to get out of his way. Maybe he'd trip and fall, right out the window. She stuck out her foot. He was too quick for her. He grabbed her by the arm and twisted her to her knees.

"Don't mess no more, Rooney, I ain't playin."

Be smart. Do what he wants. She swallowed hard and decided she was beyond it. His threats and demands. Even the pain

7

she knew would follow. Bad pain. Maybe fatal this time. It was worth the risk, she decided recklessly. It was insane. God help me, she thought. She looked up at him, defiant. *I'm getting out. One way or another.* "Mama was right," she said calmly. Her scalp felt like it was coming away with her hair he pulled her up so hard.

"What'd you say?" He kept pulling her hair away from her scalp. Rooney saw stars. She refused to cry. *Cracker monster.*

"Mama was right. I never should have married you."

He let go of her hair. Dropped her. She rubbed her head. Waited. She knew it was coming. Retaliation. He chuckled. A fake laugh. "That right, sugar? Let's show your snooty mama how her girl likes it." He threw her on the floor. It was not a fair fight. It never had been. Rooney closed her eyes and escaped somewhere in her mind while Clyde violated her six ways from Sunday.

"No!" Rooney screamed, "Please, don't!"
Clyde just laughed and thrust harder. Rooney felt herself passing out. *I'm dead. Rooney McNeil Farrow is dead.*

"Now that'll kept you quiet." He pulled up his pants.

"Cat got your tongue?"

Rooney moved like she was a hundred years old. Her body was not her own. Her insides were like the ravages of Richmond after Grant. The nausea had passed. In its place, raw anger. *Rooney McNeil is alive and you are one dead Cracker.* What was she thinking? And yet she could not stop herself from her willpower. He would not win. You do not own me, she thought.

"You're a poor excuse for a real man. You are a bully." *She was doing it again. Telling the beast what she thought of him. That would cost her. He ain't worth it. Keep quiet. Save yourself. Nope. Not anymore. I'm going down fighting. With every last breath. Mama didn't raise no coward. Poor Mama, she detested funerals.*

"Clyde Farrow, listen to me, don't you ever tell me what I need to do again. By the way, you don't know diddly about pleasing a woman. I have more orgasms on my horse." *Nice, Rooney. You fool, girl. Prepare to die.*

Clyde's face was beet red and was that steam coming out of his ears? She'd pissed him off royally this time. *God, are you listening? How 'bout giving old Clyde one of those brain aneurisms right now. I'll owe you big time. Even get myself to Mass come Sunday. I swear.*

Rooney turned her back on him and walked out of the room. If she slid down the banister she'd be home free in no time. Out the door, hop in the truck and get to a public place. Leave town when he went to work. *You're a dreamer, Rooney Bean. Yeah I know, Daddy. Bury me next to Granny.* One hand on the banister, Rooney could almost taste freedom. *Nice warm bath, ice-cold beer on my cheek. Cursing Clyde to Hades.* The image was snatched away before she could properly enjoy it. Her head jerked back. Her feet left the ground. *I'm flying, Mama.* Her face met the wall and she slid down to the hallway rug like a discarded puppet. She couldn't hear anything. Was Clyde gone? She turned her head. Something huge was coming at her. Her world went black.

Chapter Three

Doc stopped by the shelter on her way home. It had been a sad day in the news. Nicole Brown Simpson was found murdered, allegedly by her ex-husband, O.J. Simpson. The house was as quiet as a morgue. Children were long asleep. Even the television was turned off for the night. She could see the women gathered outside by the open living room doors, smoking and drinking coffee. They spoke in soft whispers. Every one of them had red eyes from crying. Doc said a quick hello and left them to their private wake. She knew they related to Nicole Simpson because she was a victim of domestic violence. Though they did not live in her affluent world, victims are victims and violence is violence.

Self-esteem is not inbred though it is every woman's right. But it has to be taught. You have to believe in your worth. Whether you mop floors for a living or sign the lunch check at Mezzaluna, if a man hits you and you tolerate it, there's a common thread. Somebody failed you long before you iced your first bruise.

Aurora, the shelter manager, was gone for the day. One of the night staff asked if Doc would grab the other hotline phone. "No problem," she said, clicking the other phone for line two.

"Hello. Rain speaking…."

The desperate Southern drawl on the other end sent chills up and down her spine. Crying and breathing into the phone. The sounds of desperation. Nothing new to a crisis center. It was the business they were in. The extent of the viciousness didn't shock her anymore. Thankfully, it still disgusted her.

"Please…can't stay…need to get out…he'll kill me…no, I can't, no police, please, they will tell him…."

"I'm here. I'll help you. What's your name?"

"Rooney," she said weakly. Doc scribbled it down.

"Ok, Rooney, where are you?"

10

"Hallway. Upstairs."

"Where is home?"

"Mission, um, Georgia, maam."

Imagine, Doc thought, manners when you've been beaten to a pulp. *Georgia*? "Okay, stay with me, where is he now, your husband? Is he in the house?"

"No… gone… work… I can't see right… my eye… blood, um, feel sick…." She went quiet. Lying in a hallway somewhere in the South in God knows what shape. Doc scratched her head with the pen.

"Rooney? You hear me? Now listen. My name is Rain. I can help you."

"Rain? That's nice…can't stay awake… head hurts… my friend's here…."

Doc heard nothing. Rooney must have dropped the phone.

"Rooney? You there?" She shouted, repeating her name. The line was open. No response. Annie, the night manager came over.

"Trouble, Doc?" She realized what she'd said. What else?

"I lost her. She's hurt badly. Line's still open." *Pick up the phone, Rooney.* Doc heard another voice. "Someone's in the house with her," she said to Annie. "Hello? Rooney? Pick up the phone. Hello? Hello!"

"Who the hell's this?"

A woman, thank God. Doc let out a breath.

"My name's Rain, at the hotline. I was helping Rooney. She called me. I know she's hurt. Are you her friend?"

"Yep. And hurt don't describe it, maam. Sister here is fucked up. Husband beat her to a goddamn pulp. Blood all over the godforsaken place. On her cell phone, on the damn rug, on the wall. Oh Lord O' Moses, it's real bad, real, real bad."

"Okay, I understand. Did you call an ambulance?"

The friend was crying. Time was of the essence.

11

"Hello? Listen, you've got to pull it together and let me help Rooney, okay?"

The woman blew her nose. "Name's Vonda, maam. Sister here in bad shape, Miss Rain. Bad shape. They all working on her now. I told her to call y'all. Thank the good Lord you answered. Y'all gotta help her."

"Yes, Vonda, I will. Are the EMTs there?"

"Yeah. They all here. You gotta help Sister get away, Miss Rain. You hear me?"

"Rooney said you were in Georgia? Is that right?"

"Right as rain. Hah. Sorry. Don't mean any disrespect, maam. Yeah, we are in the deep dark South all right. Sister on her way to the hospital. Pray those doctors can sew that eye back together. Don't look good. No, maam. Where you at, Miss Rain? Up North, I reckon. My cousin up there gave me ya'lls number. That a New Yawk accent? "

"Something like that. Is she gonna make it? How badly is she hurt, Vonda?"

"Sister is one hurtin' unit, Miss Rain. Pray for her. Up to God now."

"I will. Take my number down and call me from the hospital, okay?"

"Yes, maam, all right. Sister don't deserve none of it."

"I know. I know. Call me. Promise?"

"I will. Thank you, Miss Rain."

Vonda hung up and Doc leaned back in her chair and let out a deep breath. She was reaching for a hotline form when Annie walked over.

"Coffee, Doc?"

She nodded and kept on writing. She had no information about Rooney other than what state she lived in and that she was in dire straits. The rest she would have to get from Vonda when the immediate crisis was over. Not much they could do from New York. Rooney was going to the hospital that was the main thing. Doc said a silent prayer for Rooney to live.

Annie returned with fresh coffee. "It doesn't get any easier, does it?"

"No. Wish I could tell you differently." Doc sipped the hot coffee and closed her eyes for a second.

"The bastards never quit, do they?" Annie said. She got up and turned on the radio. A soft ballad was playing. Something about broken hearts. What else?

"Hey Doc, I bet you didn't eat, am I right? Let me rustle us up something from the kitchen. I know there's leftovers from dinner. Interested? We're gonna be here all night anyway."

Doc wasn't exactly hungry under the circumstances, but guessed she should eat something. Keep up her strength for the next crisis. She was running on coffee nerves. She wished she still smoked. She could go for a cigarette right about now. "Okay, food. Good idea. Thanks, Annie."

Annie headed for the kitchen and Doc closed the office door gently, kicked off her shoes and put her feet up on the coffee table.

"What's got your heart feeling heavy, tonight?" the radio host was saying. "Call me, Delilah, and we'll talk. I'll find just the right song to ease your burden for awhile." Doc listened to her soothing voice. Therapy over the airwaves. Did Delilah get many takers, she wondered? Got a song for losing an eye, Delilah?

"Here we are. Let's chow down." Annie handed her a generous plate of baked ziti, salad and garlic bread.

"Thanks, I believe I could eat after all. Smells great." They ate their midnight supper serenaded by Sarah McLachlan. "...*in the arms of the angel may you find some comfort here...*"

Doc thought of Rooney McNeil and mentally wished her luck. She had a feeling she was going to need it.

"What do you think? Not bad? I know you know the real deal Italian."

"Even my mother would have to admit this isn't half bad," Doc said, biting into a crunchy piece of bread.

13

Annie laughed. "We've got some great cooks this time around. They do it all. Jamaican, Spanish, Indian. It's like the United Nations. Plus good old American comfort food. I swear I gained 10 lbs. last month."

The phone shrilled interrupting their short reprieve from reality. "I got it, Doc," Annie said, putting down her plate.

"Yes, she's here. Hold on, please…" Annie motioned for her to pick up the other phone. Doc leaned towards the end table and pressed line one. "Rain here…"

"It's me Vonda. Sisters in surgery. Gonna lose the eye." Vonda was sobbing loudly. "How's she gonna take that when she wakes up? Who's gonna tell her, Miss Rain? I surely am not able for it. What in the Sam Hill are we gonna do?"

Doc took a deep breath. "I'm so sorry. That's awful. Try to breathe, okay? There you go. Easy now, take your time." Rain waited, thinking while Vonda blew her nose.

"Don't think ahead, Vonda. Stay present. She's going to need you to be strong. You can do it. I know you can. You got her this far. You saved her life."

"But Sister is gonna lose her eye. Y'all hear me? That is not right. No, maam. What am I supposed to say to her? Can't make it better what that motherfucker did, excuse my language, but that's the truth. This here is one huge mess."

Vonda was right, they couldn't make it right. But they had to do something. Or what were they here for?

"Okay, listen to me. You're her good friend and Rooney is depending on you, right? When she's ready for some hard truth, you'll be there for her, I know you will. She will be okay in time. You have to believe that."

Right. Cue the rainbow. Pass the mushrooms. Alert the Seventh House. Whatever happened to love?

"Vonda?"

"Yeah, yeah. I'm here. Maybe, if she stays away from that sonofabitch dumbass mean redneck loser. Man oughta die. Good for nothing, since he drew breath. Lord, this is a terrible thing. Terrible. What's Sister gonna do now? You got that answer, Miss Rain, cause I sure don't."

Doc swallowed a mouthful of cold coffee. There were no answers. None that would fix Rooney.

"Okay, here's what I know, Vonda. Rooney's husband left her for dead. She didn't want the police. You know why, don't you? She called for help a long way from home. I'll help her, I promise. We can make exceptions under certain circumstances. You understand what I'm saying?" Rain was committing herself. She felt compelled.

"You mean y'all can hide her? Good. Just get her the hell out of this godforsaken town. Cops ain't gonna keep Clyde's ass in jail. Never do. No, he's comin' back home lookin' for Rooney. Sister is dead then, for sure. You understand me, Miss Rain? This here's the Deep South. Big white men stick together. Ain't no good ending. So tell me what I can do to get Sister the hell out of here and I'll do it. I ain't afraid of that big 'ol wife beatin' Cracker. Let him bring it. Vonda Jones stepped on better."

Doc smiled. "That's the spirit." She gave Vonda instructions. They couldn't do much while Rooney was in surgery. But they could prepare for her escape. She explained to Vonda how the underground worked in general details.

"I know a bit about that idea, Miss Rain. Sister gonna steal away in the night like a damn slave. Like my people did. Sister is a true Sister after all."

Vonda was up for the job. She gave all the necessary information on Clyde Farrow. Doc thanked her, assuring her she would not let Rooney McNeil fall through the cracks.

"She's my best friend, you hear that? Better than her you ain't gonna find. She was wasted on that Cracker. Shame."

"We'll get her out, try not to worry. It's a little complicated since we're way up North. But not impossible. You on your end and me up here, we're a team, yes?"

Vonda sighed. It sounded like relief. "Yes, maam. Sister needs a change of scenery, big time. You get her out of here, there's a place in heaven for y'all. A lifesaver that's what you are. This is one nightmare, Miss Rain."

"I am only doing my job, but thank you. You are being very brave."

"I like you, Miss Rain. Ya'll are one righteous woman. You sure y'all are from New Yawk?"

"Never said I was." Doc smiled. Shelter personnel cannot give out any information. First names only. "Chin up, Vonda."

"Y'all are an angel." With that Vonda hung up.

Doc clicked off the phone and glanced out the shelter office window. A full moon lit up the backyard. She walked back into the other room where Annie was doing the night log. Doc's discarded dinner sat on the coffee table. She had no appetite anymore. What she could use was a stiff drink. Annie looked up from her desk. She started to say something. Doc held up her hand.

"Give me a minute, Annie, ok? Then I'll fill you in on whatever you didn't hear."

Annie nodded. Doc took their plates and walked out of the office into the shelter house. There was a light on in the kitchen.

"Hey, Doc, doing some overtime?" One of the clients was standing at the microwave heating up a baby bottle.

"A little extra work, yes."

The microwave beeped and the sleepy mother removed the baby bottle.

"Night, Doc."

"Sleep tight," she said.

The woman padded down to her bedroom softly humming a lullaby. Doc washed the two dinner plates and set them in the drain board. She checked the kitchen door lock and shut off the overhead light. The stove light gave off a dim glow. A new bulb would go on the Wish List for supplies. Tomorrow was another day.

"Doc, why don't you go home?" Annie asked, when she returned to the office. "I can handle anything that comes in. If it's urgent, I'll ring you at home. Or Aurora will."

"Thanks, I think I will. I'm bushed. Are we full by the way?" Annie knew she wasn't talking about their stomachs.

"No. There's one bed. Think Georgia will fill it?"

"That's up to Aurora. Maybe we can at least place her somewhere far enough away from her husband."

"Where's that? On the moon?"

"Good point. Call me if you hear anything on Rooney. Good night. Hope the rest of the night is quiet for you."

" 'Night, Doc. Have a drink for me."

Doc smiled at her and walked out the shelter door.

Chapter Four

Rooney McNeil spent the next three months at the new shelter in Brooklyn Heights. Aurora approved her relocation to New York. Luckily it went off without a hitch. Rooney went back to her original name and began a new life. She was happy just to be alive. Some might say she was lucky to have escaped the abuse. Doc didn't consider her lucky. Rooney had a glass eye and scars that would take years to heal. Some would never completely vanish. The nightmares would last a lifetime, or feel as if they could. But she was free. That was an undeniable fact. Free and alive.

Rooney made it abundantly clear that she was never returning to Mission, Georgia. Not for any reason on earth. Her Granny was dead. Her parents she didn't speak to. As for Clyde Farrow, she planned not even to lay her glass eye upon him ever again. Everyone at the shelter took her at her word. If she could survive a 250 lb. man leaving her for dead, New York wouldn't frighten this Southern girl one bit.

Rooney fit right in at the shelter. The camaraderie among abuse survivors is uncanny. They understand each another in a way that one who has not been in their shoes cannot. The playing field is level concerning battered women. The unique details unimportant. They had all suffered needlessly. Their poor choice of men and their shame cost them a regular life. In the shelter it was simple. He beat me, I left, I'm alive.

Rooney had one big advantage. She had only herself to worry about. There were no small victims in her horror story. Children were the true helpless and unprotected fallout. The inevitable pawns in an unbalanced family court system that had more cracks than a city sidewalk. It was ironic that it was the women and children living behind locked gates.

Doc fought a constant battle to keep her emotions separate from her work. That was next to impossible. She was a mere mortal, not Mother Teresa. The burnout rate was high.

The work not easy, though rewarding at times. Not high paying. No deals to celebrate. You don't do it for the money.

The childcare worker at the shelter told Doc it was the only job in her life where she was applauded when she arrived at work. The small children waiting for her every morning outside the office door in the living room of the shelter house, jumping up and down, clapping their little hands, made her day. You don't get that on Wall Street. But you don't get bonuses either. Yet if one woman was saved from the wolves, one child went to bed without nightmares, then they had accomplished something at the end of the day. A small miracle.

It got hairy when the shelter was full. So many different personalities and cultures under one roof. Women who otherwise never would have crossed paths. Shelter life was an equalizer. And a very rude awakening. Many abused women owned their own homes. Tried for the normal life bit. Pictures on the walls. Milk in the fridge. Coffee on the stove. Family. Friends. Pets. Cars. Their own clothes. Hobbies. They just got the life mate all wrong. At the shelter they were issued a toothbrush, shampoo, a set of sheets, donated clothes and a shared room. Shelter children left behind their toys, their pets, and their childhood.

Clients were assigned chores and a rotating cooking schedule. Suddenly a whole lot more people than a woman normally had to worry about were sitting at her dinner table. Not to mention the noise. There were often over a dozen children of all ages at any given time. But yes, the women were free. No longer did they allow a man to beat and control them. Anytime they wanted, they could choose to leave the shelter. Nobody ever did. Not voluntarily. Most had nowhere else to go.

Doc had a chat with one of the clients after Group. Epiphany was a beautiful kind woman with a little boy her spitting image. She had escaped to the shelter with only one of her three children. Her husband got to her other children first. He took them from school and hid them. Unless she

19

came back to him, she would never see them again. Epiphany had a difficult choice. Save one child and herself or go back to the abuse. She chose freedom and a new life for herself and her small son. Heartbroken didn't describe how Epiphany felt. Part of her was now missing in those stolen kids. She fought hard for them in Family Court. And lost. Her husband had money and power. No contest. Justice is unbalanced.

Doc gave her a small ceramic angel to hang in her room after her grueling day in court. Epiphany thanked her, tears falling down her fair cheeks. "You know Doc, I used to have a lot of angels. I collected them, had them all over the house. The ones he didn't break. I had a real pretty house, even with three kids. I miss it but not him. He turned ugly after each baby was born. He was jealous of the kids. I don't miss his yelling at everyone every night and the beatings. What drives a person to be that mean?"

"I'm sorry, sweetie, I wish I knew. There is no simple answer. And no excuse."

What else could she say? Epiphany was a mother and now she would only see her other children under controlled visitation if and when her husband decided to show up with them at the police station, the usual meeting place. Eventually the visits would dwindle, once the kids were good and brainwashed by their father to hate their mother for leaving. It happened all the time. It was the harsh reality. The system sucked but it was the only one they had. Doc had been witness long enough to know the drill. The women lose. The system doesn't back them when they leave home. Some archaic minds still thought it was the woman's fault she was beaten. That old "he's a good guy," routine. Tragic, people's ignorance. Unless a body bag is dragged down the front steps, no one really gives two shits what's going on next door.

The conversation Doc had with Epiphany that day shed a brighter light on what was often overlooked in cases of domestic violence. The women's exodus from their homes. No war or natural disaster prompted their action. They just picked the wrong man. The blue dot theory could be the answer. If all men who liked to beat up women had a blue dot permanently tattooed on their foreheads, women could steer clear of them. Life should be that simple.

Chapter Five

Rooney walked slowly upstairs to run herself a bath. While the tub filled she sat in the big old overstuffed chair in the corner of her bedroom, listening to the quiet of the brownstone. A few creaks and groans in the old house were a comfort. They reminded her of another old house way down South. A happier time when she was a youngin' playing under her Granny McNeil's weeping willow. Without a care in the world. She added comfrey powder to the bath. For bruising. A sprinkle of lavender to relax. Switching off the taps, she swished the steamy water around and revisited the past in her mind.

"Why in blue blazes did y'all go to New Yawk City, Rooney Earl? Of all places on God's green earth, child. I never." Beulah McNeil, her mama. Her way or the highway. Rooney had inherited her mama's stubbornness. Mama could pretend differently all she liked, until the godforsaken cows came home for all Rooney cared. But Mama knew well and good why Rooney left Georgia behind. Mama could say, "But shug…." It didn't matter a fig. What mattered was Rooney being miles away from the monster that left her for dead and half blind. That poor excuse for a man would never get close enough to hurt her again, Rooney had decided. *Never again.* She soaked her sore body and thanked God she survived that marriage. Barely.

Hey, Doctor Jekyll and Mister Clyde, you don't get to touch me anymore. There ain't no hell hot enough for you. Not after what y'all did to me. Rooney ran a light finger over her eyelid. Funny, she thought, she'd lost her eye the same night her eyes were finally wide open. She'd gone for broke knowing she couldn't stay with Clyde a minute longer. It nearly killed her. But she was free of his cruel hands forever.

Her folks did not want her marrying Clyde Farrow. *Mean-spirited, that boy. Y'all can see it in his eyes. Careful, darlin', don't be fooled by the sex and romance.* Mama's words verbatim. A bit shocking, coming from Mama. Daddy, too, would not cotton to the idea of Clyde in the family at all. *Don't do it, Rooney Bean, you will be disinherited, child. Think on that."*

Rooney was refused their blessing. She became defensive of Clyde and downright pathetic, now that she looked back. She'd pleaded with her folks. "Y'all, he's got a job...."

Clyde drove a poultry truck for Chicken Georgia. Not the kind of life Beulah and Kell McNeil envisioned for their little girl. Rooney defied them and everything they stood for. Ruffled their proper Southern feathers and married the loser from the wrong side of the proverbial tracks. It wasn't that he was simply white trash. "Purely evil is what he is, shug," Those were Mama's last words on the subject. Well next to last. "Don't y'all come home crying when you find out the god awful truth. You'll see." Those were Mama's true last words on the subject.

There was no wedding present. No mother daughter shopping for gowns. No reception at the Club. Rooney was an outcast. Could she ever have eaten enough crow to return home? No, she was a McNeil. Stubborn to the core.

Rooney finally called her folks after she moved into the Brownstone. She told Mama she'd stayed in a domestic violence shelter. Beulah McNeil was predictably horrified. "Rooney Earl, Lordy day, shug, y'all did not stay in one of those filthy places. What about bedbugs? I do declare."

Rooney laughed, remembering how the conversation went. *Sure I did, Mama. I had little choice. I wanted to live.* Mama wanted her to at least have considered coming home. *Home to Tara. Fat chance. Beg y'alls forgiveness for marrying down? I'd rather eat snails.*

Rooney knew Daddy was not afraid of Clyde. He would have loved nothing better than to knock Clyde on his ass any day of the week. Daddy despised bullies. Rooney never gave him that chance. Too bad, she thought now, that's a show she would pay to see. But her mama just couldn't let the New Yawk thing rest. It was a slap in her flawless Southern face. Her only daughter was a traitor living amongst Yankees. The horror. "Seriously, shug, the crime...."

"It's fine," Rooney assured her. "I've got two attack dogs and a SWAT team in the front yard."

Beulah McNeil wasn't amused. But she was fairly gullible. "I suppose the dogs are a good idea. Now when are y'all coming home, child? Seriously now, shug."

"I am home. Tell Daddy I called. Tell him his Rooney Bean is safe and sound. Snug as a bug in a rug." That got to Mama. The steel magnolia started to wither.

"Aw raht, shug," Beulah McNeil drawled, thick as honey dribbling down a biscuit. "Have it y'alls way. Can we send you some money? For your New Yawk life? How about a packet of decent grits? What do they all eat up theah anyway? I shuddah to think. Good Lawd."

Rooney swallowed her Southern pride and agreed to let her folks send money. Why not? She was poor, not stupid. Her brains remained intact despite Clyde's frequent bashing of them. But that was all over now. Clyde was out of her life forever.

Rooney stepped out of the tub feeling much better. The fall earlier had been merely an accident. And praise the Lord she did not have to service Clyde afterwards. Or dread footsteps on the stairs when he came home late. Mean and ornery and drunk. She was safe in Doc's Brownstone. She wished Vonda could see her. Good old Vonda. *One day I'll see y'all again, to thank you proper for saving my life, girlfriend. Yes I will.*

Rooney hummed an old country song her Granny used to sing to her and threw on some jeans and a loose sweater without a bra. Small and perky had its advantages. She inhaled a delicious aroma from the kitchen that wafted its way upstairs. "*Don't sit under the apple tree with anyone else but me....*" she hummed and took the back stairs down to the kitchen.

Chapter Six

"Umm, smells like heaven. Where's Mae?"

"On a date. All I had to do was heat and serve. There's cornbread too. You okay?"

"Yep. The tub was the thing for it, all right. I'm famished."

"Good. It's just us. The IRA are doing doubles." Doc ladled chili into two bowls. Rooney laughed at Doc's use of Rooney's nickname for her two Irish boarders.

"Right, so they are. I suppose we're gonna need large glasses of water, hmm?"

"Knowing Mae, yes. That girl loves her spices."

"Now that's one place she and I can agree."

Mae and Rooney did not agree on much. Night and day those two. Rooney wasted no time slathering up two pieces of cornbread. She took a healthy bite and rolled her eyes. "Purely heaven."

Doc tasted the chili and grabbed her water glass. "Mae overdid it on the chili powder. Whoa." She fanned her mouth.

Rooney laughed, got up and went to the fridge.

"Here, try this." She spooned a dollop of sour cream into Doc's bowl. "RX for sissies. Down South we call this five alarm chili. No self-respectin' Southerner would eat it any other way."

"Well, go ahead and call me a sissy then."

She watched Rooney. The girl could eat. You wouldn't know it by looking at her. She was petite. Lithe as a ballerina, minus the dainty and demure bit.

"Remember you're first night here?" Doc sliced herself a piece of cornbread.

"I do. My height in the Heights. After the shelter it was like dyin' and goin' to heaven. Not that I wasn't grateful for the bed there."

"I know. When I first found it, this place was a shambles. About to be condemned, I'm sure. Lucky for me Uncle Carmine indulged my vision. Bless the ponies for running in his favor. You know he never missed a race. He would read me the scratch sheets for a bedtime story. I'd forget my times tables but I knew what horse was running in the first race at Belmont. It didn't please my mother one bit. Or the nuns."

Rooney laughed and helped herself to another bowl of Mae's killer chili. Doc was in awe of her. Not just her appetite but of what she had overcome. She couldn't help but think what a long road they had all traveled to arrive here.

"Goes to show you, as Uncle Carmine would say, 'It ain't over till the fat broad sings, Lorraine.' Politically correct he isn't, but his heart is in the right place." I must call him soon, she thought. They were overdue for a chat.

"Yoo hoo, *Lorraine,* want me to put up the coffee?" Rooney looked back at her from the sink.

"Very funny. Yes, coffee. I'll go turn on the front light. The women will be here soon."

"By the way, Rain suits you much better."

"Why do you think I changed it?"

Chapter Seven

"Come in, welcome to SAGAS. I'm Dr. Taylor. Call me Rain," Doc told the woman standing under the stoop light.

"Hi. I'm Lauren…" she hesitated.

"That's fine, Lauren, first names only. Come on in." Doc took her coat and hung it on a hook in the hall. "Lauren, this is Rooney, Rooney meet Lauren." The two women shook hands. "Hey. How 'bout some coffee?" Rooney offered.

"Sure. Thanks." Lauren followed Rooney over to the sideboard where they had set up a coffee station. "Nice house," Lauren said, helping herself to a cookie.

"Thank you, make yourself comfortable." Doc excused herself to answer the doorbell.

"Sugar and milk?" Rooney asked Lauren.

"Black, please."

Rooney looked up. "Ya'll are not from New York, I reckon?"

Lauren smiled, accepting the cup Rooney handed her.

"Um, no. Kentucky originally. Why?"

"Everyone up here drinks their coffee with half and half or those fancy lattes and cappuccinos. We Southern girls take our coffee straight up, am I right?"

"Yes, maam." Lauren seem to relax. "So where 'bouts are y'all from, Rooney?"

"Oh, down in the bayou. Somewhere between here and there and no damn place at all, if ya'll know what I mean. Another life I'd rather leave behind." Rooney sipped her coffee.

Lauren nodded. "I understand. I surely do."

"Okay, ladies, have a seat after you help yourself to coffee," Doc announced. "Welcome to SAGAS." Her voice filled the room as the women settled into their seats. "I'm Dr. Taylor. Please call me Rain. I'd like to congratulate all of you for coming here tonight. Your first and most important step, admitting there's a problem and wanting help. Now let's get acquainted. Starting here to my right, please introduce yourselves."

A slight dark haired woman started, "I'm Camey. I'm here 'cause my mother won't babysit my kids no more while I work if I don't leave my boyfriend. She knows he beats me. He always says he's sorry. Like I feel sorry for him then and take him back. I know I gotta stop doing that."
Doc nodded and the next woman continued.

"Hi. I'm Evie. I came tonight because my husband hits me. I'm was afraid he might find out I came here so I told him I was joining a book group," she laughed nervously, letting her long straight black hair fall in front of her face, covering the fresh bruise on her cheek that Doc had spotted immediately, at the door.

Another woman cleared her throat. "My name is Sybie. I just moved to the city. Trying to start over. My boyfriend thinks I went out of town to visit my sick grandmother. Last month he knocked me unconscious when he found out I went to a friend's bridal shower. There was a male stripper. I didn't know about it beforehand. He didn't believe me. I have hearing loss in one ear because of how hard he hit me. I threw him out but then felt sorry for him and took him back. But I don't love him anymore."

"Hi, I'm Lauren. I left my husband down South. Came up North with a girlfriend. Her sister told us about ya'll's group. My husband was really jealous. I mean he thought every guy in the world wanted to fu...um sleep with me. He has a bad temper. He hits me then apologizes and cries about how he's so sorry later. I knew he was jealous before I married him. Then it got worse. He threatened to kill me if I ever cheated on him. I never even looked at another man. He just doesn't trust me or what we have. Which I guess isn't much of anything."

"Hey, ya'll. I'm Rooney. Doc Rain helped me get away from my no good husband after he raped me and beat me almost to death. Lost my eye over it. I lived in a shelter for awhile and now I live here. On my own terms." Rooney looked at Doc. She smiled.

"Thank you, everyone. You have each spoken your truth. You know now if you didn't before, that you are not alone. You obviously want a better life. You deserve to be respected. You deserve to be loved. Most of all, you deserve to feel safe." As if on cue, Shamus, Doc's big Irish wolfhound, bounded into the room, taking up residence at her feet. The women laughed.

"Everyone, meet Shamus, our protector. As I was saying, you came here for help. Good start. Point is you must help yourselves. I will guide you and you can pull yourselves out of the shadow of abuse. And please call it abuse. Don't pretty it up and say you are treated badly, ignored, dissed, etc. You are *abused*. Period. It is the ugly truth and it has to stop. Keep that in your head and you'll follow through. Accept less and you will be a victim forever. One slap, one punch, one shove, one humiliation, one forced sexual episode, is one too many. In your case, you have to decide: do you go back and chance another smack, another fist in your face, another night living in fear? Or do you put an end to the horror? I am going to teach you that you are worth so much more. This is not a fight you take on yourself. That will get you killed. Tools are what you need. Mental preparation. Everyone follow?"

They nodded eagerly. She had their rapt attention. There was still lingering terror in the eyes staring back at her. Except for Rooney. She had already faced her demons. She was a good example for the other women. Been there, done that, survived. And she was hardly shy about her story even if she kept her origins guarded. There is residue with abuse. Time does not heal all wounds.

"Okay. Let's have a question and answer exercise," Doc said, "You can shout out your answers and I'll write them on the chalkboard. "How can you tell a guy is an abuser when you first meet him?"

"You can't" someone yelled out, "They're usually on their best behavior."

29

"Yeah. Presents, flowers, all that nice stuff at first. They want to make nicey nice to get what they want," another woman added.

Rain wrote a few words on the blackboard then turned around quickly. "So why stay after you get hit the first time?" Silence. It was a provocative question.

Rooney spoke up. "He said he was sorry. He seemed to mean it. He'd been drinking. I blamed it on the booze. He loved me, how could he hurt me, right?"

Someone else spoke up. "I was too embarrassed to tell anyone he hit me. I was afraid to leave. I knew he wouldn't let me run away from him. I knew another girl whose boyfriend hit her too. I didn't think it was that strange. Even though I felt so bad, so worthless."

"He promised me he'd get some help. He lied," Lauren shook her head.

"He told me I got him all worked up," another voice added, "He was tired from work, the baby was screaming, he was stressed out. 'A man can snap,' he told me. I believed all that for a long time. Not anymore." She wiped her eyes. Someone passed her a tissue.

Satisfied with their honesty, Doc filled the chalkboard with words in two columns. Positives on the right: Trust, respect, love, safe place, consideration, security, fidelity, shared dreams. Negatives on the left: disrespect, fear, pain, sarcasm, silent treatment, humiliation, lies, jealousy, control, infidelity, rape, broken dreams.

"Thanks for your honesty, everyone. When we can see in black and white how the reality of an abusive relationship looks, we can no longer kid ourselves that we are going through a rough patch or someone we live with has had a tough time in his life. There is no excuse for abuse. Say it with me nice and loud. There is no excuse for abuse!"

The voices rang out in the living room and for a brief moment Doc felt there was hope. One of these women would walk away from her prison. One woman was a victory. All four of them a bleedin' miracle, as the IRA would say.

"Great. Now let's take a short break. Bathroom is down the hall. Coffee, cookies, and cold water on the sideboard. Help yourselves, please. We'll start back up in ten minutes."

Rain walked over to get a fresh cup of coffee. So far so good, she thought. They were a chatty bunch. If they showed up again there was a chance of saving some lives. She watched Lauren and Rooney. They seemed to have found common ground. Their Southern roots. And the abuse. The tie that bound all of them in this dark world.

"So, how do ya'll like it up North?" Rooney asked Lauren.

"All right, I guess. People are sure in a hurry. It'll take some getting' used to." Lauren sipped her black coffee.

Rooney laughed. "Sure, I know what you mean. New Yorkers are a nervous bunch all right. I met some real nice people through Doc and my clients."

"Oh? What do y'all do?"

"I'm a hair stylist. Back home we just called them beauticians. Anyway, I've been doing all right for three years so far, knock wood." Rooney tapped her head.

Lauren laughed. Rooney thought she had the thickest and most beautiful hair she had ever seen. Flaxen and curly. A good shaping and cut would do her fine. "How 'bout y'all?"

"Well, I guess you could call me an artist. My passion. I really just do a little painting. I waitress to pay the bills. I should have finished Art School, but my husband wouldn't let me get financial aid. He just didn't want me out at night on my own. My aunt is willing pay my tuition now, if I promise to divorce him. Been stalling for no good reason. Well, other than I am afraid. He's got a stinking temper. I have an Order of Protection, in case he shows his face at my aunt's or at my job. It's just a precaution. He's too lazy to come after me. Likely he's already moved on to someone else by now. He needs someone to boost his ego and take care of him. He is a needy bastard. Good luck to her, whoever that poor soul is."

31

Rooney nodded. "Boy, do I know what you mean. I got a feeling about you. Things are gonna turn right around, darlin.' Listen to that aunt of yours. She sounds like a wise woman."

Doc was calling the group back together. The women took their seats again.

"I want to talk a little about myths and stereotypes. Where could we start? Anyone want to try?" She urged them on. She had a feeling they were stoked.

"You mean like he must be a drunk to beat on a woman?" someone volunteered.

"Good. What else?" Doc kept writing on the blackboard.

"How 'bout it only happens in white trash or minority families?" Lauren said.

"Right," Rooney piped up, "Like truckers beat their wives but lawyers don't."

Doc smiled. "Keep going, we're on to something." She purposely didn't turn around. It was easier for them that way.

"We make them do it? They can't control themselves or their anger," a voice shouted out.

"Excellent. The classic myth." Doc was proud of them. They were getting it.

"What about the scary mind-game stuff. Like making you feel like you're the one out of control. Because you cry or get emotional. Or call them on their lies."

"Right and it's never their fault," another woman said.

"Yeah, like you'd think a man who hits his wife or girlfriend would be obvious to everyone," another woman called out. "But they have two different personalities. Street angel, house devil. In private you pay for however you react in public, even when you didn't do anything wrong. You are constantly walking on eggshells."

"I think most abusers are male chauvinists, don't you?" Someone who hadn't spoken was finding her voice.

"You know, they turn away from you while you thought you were in the middle of a conversation and look right at another woman passing by. What is that all about? So rude. And God forbid you say anything about it. They get mad at you and show more disrespect by flirting and touching women while you're sitting right there. I swear, if I did that, I'd be dead."

"They have affairs and deny it to your face, even when you have proof. Or they give you a sexually transmitted disease." The woman looked down into the coffee cup in her hands.

Doc turned around. She met the woman's pained green eyes and nodded in appreciation of such honesty. It wasn't easy to share personal shame. It took courage to speak up and name it.

"Good work. Thank you, everyone. You're brave and honest." She motioned to the blackboard. "This is your truth. It matters and it is important. Take that to heart. You matter. You are meant to be treated kindly and valued as women. Anything else is not acceptable. If you have any doubts read the poem called The Desiderata, framed on the wall on your way out. There's a copy of it in your pamphlets. It says, '...you are a child of the universe, no less than the trees and the stars, you have a right to be here.' One more thing, remember, the violence is not your fault. But only you can put an end to it. You might have to leave your home if he won't. Your life may depend on it. Do not take that lightly. I don't. The people who can help you don't. We are here for you. You aren't alone. Be safe always. Trust your intuition, your gut. When you feel unsafe, call someone, call the police, or run for your life. Do not live with the secret. That will get you killed. Please come back next week. And feel free to call me in the meantime, if you need anything."

The women gathered their coats and papers and headed out into the night. Doc locked up and headed for the kitchen. Rooney followed with a tray of cups and cake plates.

She set them on the counter and opened the dishwasher. "Good meeting, don't you think?"

"Yes, I'd say it went very well. Nice bunch. It could have been a Tupperware party if you looked at it from a distance."

"Yeah, hah, a Tupperware party. If only."

Shamus barked and ran out of the kitchen to the front hallway. The front door opened and closed. Voices and laughter came from inside

"Cooee, do I smell margaritas? And don't they smell brilliant?" a beautiful Irish brogue sang out.

"Don't be shy with the tequila now," Rooney lined up the glasses. Doc laughed.

Dory and Fiona came bursting into the kitchen.

"Howyeh, IRA?" Rooney asked.

"Here you go, first dibs for the hardworking café crowd," Doc handed them a drink.

"What, no umbrella? Thanks just the same," Dory laughed.

"Thanks a heap. My dogs are killing me," Fiona plopped into a kitchen chair.

"Where's Mae?" Dory asked, sipping her drink like it was the last elixir on earth.

"Date," Rooney said. "Here's mud in your eye, IRA."

"Cheers, bayou girl," Fiona said, kicking off her sneakers.

"Tunes, we need tunes." Rooney hopped up and headed for the living room. The rhythms of Bob Marley filled the rooms. They all joined her by the still toasty fire.

"Busy tonight, girls?" Doc asked, adding a few pieces of wood to the fire.

"We've full pockets, all right. Worked our arses off for it." Dory shook her red curls out of her hair band. "Isn't that right, Fee?"

" 'Tis. I wouldn't mind a 'tall if some of this arse actually fell off," she laughed.

"Stop complaining," Dory said, "You've a right grand bum. What is it they call it here? Ah yes, thong worthy."

Rooney whistled, fingers in her mouth. "Sizzlin' is what we call it down South y'all."

Dory hooted. Fiona gave her the backward peace sign in motion.

"Nice. That's very ladylike now."

"On a serious note, I think I might have a new customer for your 'somebody gives a shite' group." Fiona said, dipping a blue corn chip in some guacamole. "One of the waitresses lives with some wanker. Likes to push her around so. She's scared to leave him. Thinks he belongs to a gang. I can't see what the attraction is in the first place. He's creepy if you ask me. It's desperate."

"Be careful," Doc said, "If he is hitting her, you could be in danger if he gets wind of you helping her leave. Talk to her away from the restaurant. Or simply write down our meeting time and pass it on to her. Let her commit the address to memory so he can't find out. Or she can call us when she's ready to come."

"I know what you mean. She may not be ready anyway. He buys her all this jewelry, ugly as sin, gaudy shite, probably stolen, and she gets all lovey dovey about him. It's pathetic," Fiona scowled.

"It's sad to watch somebody lose their self-esteem. Nothing we can do but be here when they fall." Doc drank her margarita and watched Fiona. She likely had more invested than concern for her work mate. One day Doc might learn just what that was.

Chapter Eight

Rain

Her given name was Lorraine. Before she reinvented herself. Loraine Nino. Half Italian, half Irish. She grew up in Gravesend. More than a stone's throw from the Heights and light years away compared to today. The Wonder Years, Brooklyn style. Same kind of innocence. On the outside. Small houses, simple lives. Lots of neighborly contact, wanted or not. Extended families for better or worse. Churches with attached convents and rectories, the eyes of God and their families and neighbors, watching their every move. They weren't wealthy and they weren't poor. Middle class. Her father was blue collar. Literally. He was a mailman. He pushed his three legged cart from house to house, chatting up the residents, all of whom he knew. Lorraine's mother stayed home, always impeccably dressed despite her infinite domestic obligations. She took great pride in her appearance, her children and her house. In that order.

Supper was on the table at 6 p.m. religiously. Home cooked. They didn't eat out or take away. Nobody did. Birthday parties, baptisms, communions, graduations, and funerals were a home catered affair. The only time they saw the inside of a restaurant, was if someone was getting married. Except Lorraine's Uncle Carmine, her father's bachelor brother, who lived upstairs. He ate all his meals with them, entertaining all with his risqué jokes and betting tips. Much to her mother's disapproval.

Kids ran free, within reason, inside the neighborhood. For 25 cents you could buy a Pensie Pinkie and play Stoop Ball, Sewer Tag, and Monkey in the Middle. Or melt crayons into old bottle caps and play Scully. Olga's candy store was the local hangout. Olga was as cheap as dirt, unless you were willing to earn free candy or a soda by putting out the flag in the morning or stacking comic books in the afternoon. Most of all, Olga wanted company.

She was lonely. She lived alone in a smelly firetrap at the back of the store. Wide as she was tall, she could barely fit behind the old manual cash register. If you insisted you wanted licorice roll-ups, Olga would sigh and step aside, letting you shimmy behind the old wood and glass display case and help yourself. It would have been suicide for Olga. But she had a big heart. As big as her whole body, which filled out the tent-like housedresses she favored. Lorraine imagined the gold star she wore around her chubby neck part of a lost galaxy swallowed up by her enormous bosom.

Everyone liked Olga. The entire neighborhood went there for cigarettes, newspapers and local gossip. She loved the gossip. Had her nose in all of it. Put her two cents in whether you wanted it or not. You'd get more than your RC Cola when you stepped inside the musty store, the odor of the past and leftover Chinese food hitting you head on. It was the only candy store where you could buy cigarettes by the smoke. Three cents apiece. A Parliament, a chocolate Ice Cube, a chew of Bazooka and you were only out a nickel.

If they ventured out, a bus ride away was Nelly Bly, a miniature Coney Island. It was heaven on a Saturday afternoon. A roller coaster complete with screaming repeat customers, cotton candy, french fries, games of chance and a fortune telling machine that spit out tiny scrolls of predictions. The calliope on the merry go round droned on relentlessly as its tireless horses lifted riders up and down while their reflections gazed back at them from mirrored pipes.

Lorraine's favorite ride was the helicopters. What a thrill to see above the whole park, almost reach out and touch the storybook figures painted on the brick wall. They're all that remain of the park today. All dismantled before she had the chance to buy an old horse from the carousel or a small tugboat out of a pretend lake. When she was small, the tugboat ride was her thing. She would ring the bells on a string madly as the boats went round and round in about a foot of water. Across the way goldfish in bowls sat on a shelf swimming in circles and dodging ping pong balls and waiting for a new home.

Life didn't get much better. Unless she was playing Bonanza. She and her best friend Colleen were torn. They couldn't decide if they were go-go girls or cowboys. Cowboys definitely won for awhile. Flying down the center of the street on Schwinns, they were riding the range. Both wanted to be Little Joe, so they had to take turns. There was such freedom in those rides. They were simply kids, neither girls nor boys. True innocence untouched by society's roles. A mere moment in time.

Until time interfered and they turned into full-blown girlie girls. It was bound to happen. All their role models were glamorous. Tomboys didn't fare so well in good old Brooklyn. Besides when boy-crazy hits, there's no going back to Little Joe.

It started with young wolves. Lorraine and Colleen were trusting and naïve. To wolves, that is dinner on a platter. Shy and unassuming doesn't rule out curiosity. We all know what happened to Little Red Riding Hood. They were something else too, obedient. Thanks to the Dominican Sisters who had their rapt attention and sore knuckles, since the innocent age of six. Lorraine came to despise the word obedient. It smacked, literally, of the physical humiliation and pain endured at the hands of the good Sisters.

One day, she and Colleen were riding their bikes, and a few boys called out their names. They stopped to talk and noticed an older boy they didn't know. He had to be at least sixteen or seventeen, with facial hair and muscles.

"Wanna play a game?" he asked, his deep voice way passed the awkward squeak of adolescence. He dragged on a Marlboro like he meant it. The girls were hypnotized. Colleen was as quiet as a mouse, her foot nervously tapping her bike pedal. Lorraine could not stop staring into his dark brooding eyes. It was like staring into black.

"Come on," he said. "Follow us."

They shrugged, and rode their bikes behind him.

"Bring your bikes into my garage," he said, "So they don't get stolen."

That should have been their first clue. Bikes were never stolen from their block. It was a safe neighborhood. Every kid owned a bike, even if it was second hand. Old Mr. Beeker fixed all the kids bikes on the block, so they lasted longer than they probably should have.

The big garage door slammed shut. Their eyes adjusted to the dark. He switched on a lamp perched on top of an old wine barrel. The dust swirled around settling on a tattered couch and a few odd chairs arranged like a makeshift living room.

"Nice, huh? I stay here sometimes. When my mother gets on my nerves, and that's a lot. So, the game…."

They stared at him and looked around. There were no game boxes in sight.

"Here's the way it works. You take down your underpants and let us see your business. Then we'll show you ours."

Just minutes before Lorraine was thinking she would pair up with him in a game of Clue or Monopoly, because he was probably smart. Boy, was she stupid.

He casually strolled over to the garage door and snapped the lock closed. No chance to change their minds now.

"Let's go, do what I said…."

He told the other boys to sit down and he directed the girls to the middle of the garage.

"I can help you if you want…." he said.

They dropped their jeans and slid their panties down to their ankles. They rotated like a two girl vagina carousel, their flowered underpants discarded on the dirty floor. The boys watched. Without as much as a touch, they could feel themselves being stripped of something unnamable at the time.

"Who wants to go first?" He asked.

Nobody answered. He grabbed Lorraine and led her to the dusty couch.

"I'll show you how it's done," he said to the two boys. "Lay down and open your legs nice and wide," he was talking to Lorraine. She obeyed. He was in charge and he wasn't about to let her get up. Colleen continued to rotate in the center of the garage, her pale freckled cheeks and strawberry scented hair out of place in the dingy garage.

"Don't be afraid, you're gonna like this...."

He slid his finger into her very gently. He probed and explored while she held her breath and prayed for him to stop. He started to rub, faster and faster. Lorraine bit her lip, rather than scream out or cry because he told her not to. She felt her face get flushed, as her body shuddered, her own vagina betraying her. Tears fell down her cheeks.

"See? You liked it," he declared.

Lorraine could not speak. She felt dirty and cold. She didn't know if he was through with her. He pulled her up to her feet.

"Come on over here, Blondie," he called to Colleen. "You two switch places."

Colleen walked slowly and shamefully over to him and took her turn on the couch. Lorraine stood in the center of the garage again. The boys watched. She wanted to spit at *him*. She wanted one of the boys to get up and punch him in the jaw and then hand her her clothes. She wanted to rescue Colleen. All of that happened in her mind. But not in that garage. One day, she thought, he is going to be sorry. Very sorry.

Pleased with himself, he let Colleen get up and they both put on their clothes as he watched and smoked, blowing smoke rings up to the garage roof.

"Don't even think about breathing a word to anyone about this, you get me?" His voice was smoky and feral.

They nodded. He flung open the door and they rode out of there like they were on fire. At Colleen's backyard they threw down their bikes, not stopping to use kickstands and preserve the paint. They ran into Colleen's house and locked the kitchen door behind them.

"Oh my God!" Colleen screamed. Her face bright red, her freckles standing out like exclamation points.

"I know, I thought we'd never get out of there, either," Lorraine held her as Colleen burst into tears. They were both shaking. They looked at each other. Colleen found some tissues and they blew their noses.

Nobody had ever touched them that way. They were confused. It had felt good, while making them feel bad about it feeling good. They felt betrayed by the boys who knew them. They were supposed to be their friends, not look at them naked. They felt different. Bad girls did things like that. Went into dark garages with boys. *He* knew that. *He* had done this thing, this game before.

"He tricked us," Colleen snuffled. "Didn't you think we were gonna play Monopoly or something?"

"Yeah. Oh God, why did we follow him?"

"We made a big mistake. You gonna tell Uncle Carmine?"

"Are you crazy? No! We can't tell anyone. They'll just think we wanted to go with the boys. They'll blame us. We'll get in trouble, not them." Lorraine didn't know how she knew that to be true, she just did.

"Are we tramps now?" Colleen's big blue eyes searched her friend's face.

"No. We're still us."
Were they tramps? Lorraine didn't think so. But people would, if they knew. They would say they were asking for it.

Colleen looked like she had just been given a sack full of Christmas gifts. " Right. We're good girls. Us, still."

"Yep. We're Little Joe, always."

"Promise?"
Lorraine held out her hand. "Pinkie swear." They locked fingers, innocent once again.

"Let's take showers," Colleen said. "You can borrow clothes and we can wash these…."

41

Lorraine followed her up to her bedroom. Colleen's house was quiet, her parents at work. They were safe. She kicked off her Keds and sat on Col's bed reading Teen Beat. She heard her singing a Monkees song in the shower. She was okay. They were both okay. A half hour later, they were dunking Sugar Wafers in hot chocolate with triple marshmallows. They escaped into the world of Dark Shadows until dinnertime.

Lorraine's next run-in with the wolves was a few years later. At a sleepover at her cousin's house. They went out for a walk one Saturday afternoon to the neighborhood candy store. As they turned the corner, a voice from above called out to them. "Hey girls, look up here…." They followed the voice. As plain as day in broad daylight in front of an open window, a naked man was rubbing himself with a vengeance and grinning like a fool. He had long golden hair that shone in the sunlight illuminating every God given inch of him. Beatific is what strangely came to mind. If he had been praying instead of what he was doing, he wouldn't have looked out of place in one of those Bible epics. Like in the baptism scene.

They screamed bloody murder. That only egged him on with increased fervor. He strummed that organ of his like it was a prized guitar that would burst into flames at any moment from the friction. They ran for the candy store, nearly falling in the door breathless and laughing in nervous relief for their swift escape. Not that "Jesus" seemed intent on doing them bodily harm. Nonetheless, they had Sweet Tarts and Jawbreakers on their minds that morning, not penises.

Her first encounter with a naked man was closer to home. Lorraine burst into her parent's bedroom one morning, and stopped stone still in her tracks. She looked at her startled mother in bed and whispered in her three year old voice, "Shh…there's a mouse on daddy's leg… don't move, here's a shoe…." Her mother quickly covered the "mouse" and told her to go back to her own room and she would take care of it.

She was promptly instructed to knock next time, and her mother tried to break her father's habit of sleeping au natural.

"Kids should learn how to knock," he said.

She had a history of sudden entrances. When she was two, running into the living room, she had taken a sharp turn in their tiny apartment, and broken her father's big toe as he lie napping, like a snoring giant on the small zebra striped sectional. Gulliver never used language like her father did that day.

Her third encounter with the male anatomy happened at a friend's house. The girls ran down to the basement to use the toilet. The bathroom door was unlocked, so they burst inside. Her friend's father stepped out of a steamy shower to a chorus of screaming banshees. Their hasty retreat was the end of that. Harmless. The guy in the window beat all, pardon the pun. So far it would seem she had managed to keep the wolves at bay. But before *him*, there was another dark garage.

Lorraine was six. She had gone downstairs from their second floor family owned apartment to the backyard to get her doll carriage. She opened the big creaky wooden door of the garage. As her eyes adjusted to the dark, a hand pulled her inside. Her screams were caught in her throat. She looked up to see who grabbed her. She knew him. He smelled like cheese. It was the old immigrant grandfather, who lived next door, no relation of hers.

"I just want my carriage," she said in a little voice.

"Thisa what you want? A carota?" he spoke in his broken English, baring his rotten teeth. He took her little hand and put it on his exposed penis and rubbed it up and down. She felt sick.

"I just want my carriage," she whispered, grabbing her hand back and running out into the light, dropping Thumbelina on the cement. She could hear his filthy laugh all the way out of the yard.

She scrubbed her hands twice in the bathroom when she got upstairs. She told her mother, who was busy cooking, that she had changed her mind and didn't want her carriage

43

after all. She took out her sketchpad and drew quietly in the other room. She never did tell her mother or anyone else, about the old man in the garage. She did not know how to or have the words to say it. She did say something when it happened to her sister.

Teresa was five. Lorraine was nine. They were playing outside, a game of Hide and Seek, with the kids on the block. Teresa was suddenly gone. The game was over and she was still not coming out of her hiding spot. Lorraine heard crying at the back of the alley by the house where the old man lived. It was Teresa. Lorraine followed the cries, shouting her sister's name, announcing her presence. The old man had Teresa in the basement. He saw Lorraine and let Teresa go, disappearing down his dark cellar.

Teresa sobbed as Lorraine soothed her and carried her up the stairs and out of the alleyway. They got safely upstairs to their mother. Teresa would not let go of Lorraine. Their mother asked what happened but Teresa wouldn't say a word. She stopped crying and went completely silent. She let Lorraine wash her hands and carry her inside to the living room. Lorraine brought her milk and cookies, Vanilla Thins, that she loved. She ate two and sipped her milk and stared into space.

"Will you tell Mommy later?" Lorraine asked her, smoothing her baby fine bangs. She nodded her little head yes and handed Lorraine a book from the table to read to her.

Teresa never said a word about it. Not later. Not ever. Lorraine did. She told her mother. And later her father was told. An aunt and uncle were told, who lived next door. No one did a thing. Maybe the grown-ups talked. She had a feeling Uncle Carmine wanted two minutes with the old man but was probably stopped. Carmine had a temper. Too bad they didn't let him loose. Lorraine and Teresa did not hear about it, until years later, when the girls were adults, and their mother oddly brought it up, with Lorraine. She said she "felt guilty that it happened. I was not there to protect you," she said. "It was not right, looking back. I knew it then. I'm sorry."

Lorraine figured that their father blamed her mother for it. Everything was her fault when they got hurt. But at the time it happened, no one did anything. The adults asked the old man what happened and he lied. He was brought to a family doctor. Not a psychiatrist. No one called the police. As small girls, no one defended them, and some did not believe them. There was no retribution. No justice for Lorraine and Teresa. No help. No therapy. No nothing. It was simply not talked about, ever again. In a quick-tempered Italian family there was no display of the usual hotheaded emotions. Oddly enough no chairs were flung, no punches thrown and no punishing silence to anyone on the girl's behalf. They were little girls and nobody fought for them.

The old man was not sent packing to the old country. He remained a smarmy toothless presence they had to endure at every backyard birthday party and barbeque with relatives, to follow. Their mother was all the more vigilant of them but the damage was done. Teresa started to stutter. And wash her hands obsessively. She was nervous. She was brought to a regular doctor and the his advice was "ignore the stuttering and she will stop." Eventually, the stuttering and constant hand washing stopped. And when Teresa was of age, she stopped talking altogether, on purpose. She joined a Carmelite Order of nuns and never had to speak again.

By the time high school rolled around, wolf sightings were more obvious. They were thrust into the real world, well, semi-real. Lorraine still attended Catholic school. An all girl's high school, way out of the neighborhood. She was exposed to different cultures and new religions. Hasidic Jews strolled the block of her high school. She and her friends stared at the little boys with their peyos (curled sideburns) and the boys stared back at them, in their plaid skirts and weskits. One alien to the other.

There were free spirits roaming around. On a

45

particular day, one of them drove a yellow Volkswagen. He had a flaming red Afro and a nice smile. Lorraine and her friends ran right over to his bright yellow VW Bug, eager to give him the directions he so sweetly asked for. They looked on in stunned horror as he bopped the bishop, his face as innocent as a choirboy.

Sister Hildegarde heard their screaming and abandoned her door post. She ran over to them, rosaries swinging and face beet red. They got detention for being outside during classes and for walking up to a strange man's car. Not before Sister gave "carrot top" a hell and damnation speech. Probably ruined his stiffie. Or in Sister's words, "the rod of Satan." They were lectured as well. "After all, this is not Galilee and you don't always have to be Good Samaritans." They wondered if Sister had seen many wolves in her day. She was very cool about the whole thing, for Sister.

Colleen started going steady with some jerk who liked to push her around. She met him on Kings Highway at the pizza parlor after school. He was a tough, too good looking for his own use type. The first time Colleen had sex with him, she cried. She couldn't stop. The boy slapped her face a good hard one. Enough to leave an imprint. When she told Lorraine about it, she said she thought that was cruel. Colleen said, "You know nothing about sex." Colleen was right about the sex part. But the slap, Lorraine knew, was just not on.

Eventually Colleen wised up and was rid of him. She got married soon after high school, to a kind and gentle man who let her rule the roost. They had twin girls they named Joey and Candy and moved to a log cabin in Pennsylvania Dutch Country. Lorraine sent her a housewarming gift. A sign that said Ponderosa. In memory of their Bonanza days on the block.

Lorraine went to Brooklyn College and earned a BA in psychology. It was the late sixties and she was restless. Some college friends were heading out West, to Berkeley.

46

She decided to join them. Get out of the neighborhood and see another part of the country. Lorraine Nino, she decided, was over. She needed a rebirth. Rain Taylor, was born. She changed her name legally, choosing from the second and first names of her two favorite authors, Samuel Taylor Coleridge and Taylor Caldwell.

She joined a women's rights group and embraced transcendental meditation. She was on her way to reinventing herself. There were no wolf sightings for a while. The only howling came from inside.

Chapter Nine

San Francisco brought interesting people, from across the globe, many passionate and intent on changing the world and some going nowhere fast. Hippies and flower children and wine and hash induced philosophers were a dime a dozen. She experimented and had her share of intense love affairs. Was there any other kind? She decided what to do with her life, help women who had fallen prey to the wolves. Do her part in ending the senseless violence against women. It was a heady goal.

She attended workshops on rape prevention. Her thesis in graduate school was titled, "Women and their struggle for independence in a male ruled society busting out of its ill-fitting clothes of Puritanism." She earned her PhD in Psychology. She became Dr. Rain Taylor, savior of women. She counseled clients in a dilapidated Victorian she shared with a few colleagues and ran free group therapy sessions. Her eyes were wide open, witnessing the casualties of the travesty called domestic violence. They used to call it wife beating. Semantics. Call it what you want, it's the same ugly thing.

Her parents back in Brooklyn were proud of her, though her mother would have been quite happy had she settled down with a nice guy and given her a few grandchildren to feed. Her father didn't quite know what to make of the whole thing. That thing, being her life. Living out in California, that crazy hippie place. He never came right out and asked, but she got the distinct impression he thought she might be a lesbian. Not that the word would ever pass his lips. He knew she wasn't nun material, so what other possible conclusion could there be for her single status? Unmarried liberated female was not in his vocabulary. Feminine liberation was a lot for some to swallow back then. Radical. Militant. Those were the connotations. We've come a long way, baby.

California was no Brooklyn. But it had its charm and benefits. Rupert was one. Rain met him at a symposium for therapists in San Francisco. He was a charming Aussie specimen of manhood. She fell for him like a ton of bricks. He cooked dinner on their first date. Rupert loved to talk and he loved old movies. She couldn't have been happier. He was an attentive lover. A one-woman man. A rare find. There was only one flaw she could find with him. Rupert was a free spirit in the end. He loved her, but he needed a quest. Alone. Unencumbered. He said he had to find his true purpose. He feared becoming ordinary. That was one thing he would never be. Therapists often need therapy the most. Rain was the first one to admit it.

"I do love you madly, Rainey love," he told her, "but you can't paint a suit on a fish. He's still after all a fish." On that note, Rupert and his incredible Australian ass took off for Bali. She never heard a word from him and mourned his departure like a death, throwing herself deeper into her work and medicating herself with far too much chocolate. But there was work to be done.

She believed one solid truth. Women needed help but they were not helpless. Men wanted power and control. The very reason why they abused their wives and lovers. Aside from the purely violent sickos. Some people contended that if women allowed the violence against them to continue, they were condoning it. Some persisted they asked for it. Nobody asks for it. And staying in an abusive home is not an option. If the woman herself or the police couldn't throw him out then she must leave. Otherwise the message 'mister can't keep his hands to himself' gets is, "it's okay to beat her, she will forgive me, she has no place else to go."

The clients were coming in droves. So much for peace, love and brotherhood. The wolves were in high season. Rain could easily have become jaded if she let her work dictate her feelings. She had to keep them separate. There were good men out there. You just had to be willing to sift through the mix. Like finding the prize in the Cracker Jack box.

Shelters were the key. With an escape plan a woman could be saved. Choose differently next time. Like patterns in abusers, women too, unfortunately choose what is familiar. Her mission was to educate, empower and enlighten and not become case hardened in the process. The most pressing issue next to getting women out of violent homes and harmful relationships was the children. Unwittingly they were being taught that abuse was normal. It was what they knew. It was grassroots back then. It is still a fight today for funds and shelters and to change the laws that don't properly protect women. Children are always the victims. They are not given a choice. Resiliency? Not to abused children. To any children really. Children are not rubber bands. Resiliency is a lie people tell themselves to ease guilty consciences or pretend a broken system works.

Women leaving their homes is not an easy task. It's dangerous. Often it has to be as secretive as the abuse. There is a domestic violence underground to this day. In gang situations, it is critical. Giving up your town and identity far outweighs being dead. The choice becomes easier when looked at in cold harsh terms. The number of rehabilitated violent men is very small. Abusers remain abusers. They find another woman to smack around when one leaves. Jails are too full to incarcerate wife beaters. There was a time when men were actually protected under the law to beat their wives. Their wives were their property. Chattel. Sadly not that long ago if you read your history books. Yes, in this very free country, not in some third world dictatorship.

Rain was in the trenches and she had a long way to go. She had her mind set to go to London to meet a woman called Erin Pizzey, who opened the first domestic violence refuge, as it was known. Rain was impressed with her work in the field and her moxie to say what she felt no matter the resistance she came up against.

Rain was tossing the idea of travel arrangements and a much-needed vacation around in her mind, while she sipped an espresso in her favorite Haight Street coffee house. She was engrossed in her reverie when the table moved and her cooled down espresso wound up in her lap.

The woman was obviously embarrassed. "Oh what a clumsy ox I am, so sorry. Here…." She handed Rain a bunch of napkins. "Now let me order you another cuppa, after we get you cleaned up. Ah, don't mind me, please, I'll be right back. Sure you don't mind if I leave my case here?" She dropped a Mary Poppins like carpetbag on the other chair across from Rain.

Rain stared at the woman who breezed by her, leaving behind a scent of vetiver and lavender, after she scooped the espresso cup from Rain's lap. She soon returned with two fresh espressos. Her hair was flaming red, her eyes like emeralds and her brogue distinct and lovely. She was a vision.

"You don't mind if I join you? I promise not to spill anything." She smiled. Enchanting. "I'm Orleigh Teelon. New to San Francisco, originally from County Wexford, Ireland." She sipped her espresso and took a bite of a chocolate cookie. "Have a bickie, er…."

"Rain. Rain Taylor. Not new to San Fran. Originally from Brooklyn, New York, County Kings, USA." Rain helped herself to a cookie.

Orleigh laughed. "How delightful. And what is it you do, Rain Taylor, in this exciting city?"

"I'm a therapist. For women. Mostly in abusive relationships." Rain thought a cloud had crossed the woman's face. She was sure of it. She watched her toss back her fiery mane of hair, as if to brush a disturbing thought away.

"A Shrink is it? Very interesting. I am in oils myself."

"Perfume? Or the healing arts?"

"Very good. Right, remedies for the body and soul. We could be quite a team, you and I. Healing the entire woman." Orleigh laughed again. A melodious sound. There was a back-story on this Orleigh Teelon. Rain was curious.

"Are you on vacation then, Orleigh?"

"No, not quite a holiday for me. More like a transitional journey. First and foremost, a place to live would be grand."

Rain was getting a strong feeling about this Orleigh Teelon. A good feeling. She decided to help her, mostly because she was enjoying her company and wanted to learn more about her. She was fascinated. She hoped curiosity wouldn't kill the cat.

"Turns out we have an empty room at the house I am renting with a bunch of other therapists. If that doesn't frighten you off...."

"I've lived with tinkers in caravans back home, not much scares me. I would love to have a look at the room. I mean I am sure it's quite lovely, looking at you. Besides, I need a place now. Beggars can't be choosers."

It was Rain's turn to laugh. "I guarantee this is an upgrade. Not that there's anything wrong with a caravan. But, we have better heating for one. And no wheels to change. And a lease. Come by this afternoon, if you like. I'll write down the address."

"Hah, that's gas. Or wheels to grease, as it were. Anyway, lucky for me I spilled coffee on the right person today. I am so pleased we met, Rain Taylor."

"Me too, Orleigh. A happy accident, yes? I have to run now, I have a client coming soon. I'll see you at the house later. Thanks for the coffee."

"Cheers. And the bath?" Orleigh laughed. She watched Rain walk out of the coffee shop. "I've made a good friend," Orleigh thought. "A very good one." She just had a good feeling.

Rain would miss Orleigh when she decided to return to Ireland. She had stayed at the San Fran house for a good year or so. They got along like salt and pepper, or as Orleigh insisted, rashers and eggs. A formidable pair no matter.

Around the time Orleigh made her decision to return home to face her past, Rain was feeling a sea change herself. London, however, was not in the cards for her. As much as she wanted to meet Erin Pizzey and see her refuge, it was not to be. Instead, she went home at Christmas and met her husband.

His name was Henry Miller, like the writer. Born and bred in Brooklyn, like she, but he had stayed. He had not caught the wanderlust that drove Rain out West. Henry was a Bay Ridge boy visiting a college friend on her old block. There was an open house next door to her parents and she met Henry at the punch bowl. He poured her an eggnog and smiled an irresistible smile. He had the gentlest and most amazing green eyes. Rain was captivated. Their conversation cinched it. Henry was exactly what she needed, an honest and interesting man without a huge ego. Plus he was hot. And he listened. Was he real she wondered? Anyway, it was quite refreshing after all the charming blarney, as Orleigh would say, that she had encountered so far. Henry was in it for the long haul. Was Rain ready for that?

He invited her to dinner over the Christmas holidays and she gladly accepted. She could think of little else until the night arrived. They went to Stella's restaurant on Flatbush Avenue, a quiet intimate neighborhood gem. They chatted easily about their work. Henry taught English at Boys High School in Williamsburg. A bachelor, he dedicated himself to underprivileged youth in his spare time. Though he had his share of dates he had never met quite the right woman. He told Rain that he believed, "Timing is everything. When we are ready the one shows up."

Henry was an amateur poet. Rain loved poetry. He loved art. Rain spent time at the museums regularly. They were kindred spirits. She told him how she spent her days and lately most of her nights. Therapy sessions and broken women. He said she was doing God's work. She fell in love before the dessert came. Considering that Stella's had the best tortoni in Brooklyn, Rain decided it was kismet.

They went back to his apartment and spent the rest of the night talking and laughing like old friends. And kissing not like friends at all. Henry made love to her, slowly and tenderly, with the passion of a man that knows how a woman should be touched. Henry was well schooled. Tall and lean with olive skin and river green eyes. Strong and kind. Sexy as hell. The picture of a college professor with his wire rimmed glasses and buttoned down shirt. Under the chamois and minus the loafers was one smoldering man. Rain could have heated her waterbed with Henry alone. His temperature always ran just a bit higher than normal. Maybe it was his Hungarian blood. Full lips and dreamy eyes. And he was quite the chef. Funny, she thought, how she found another man who could cook. But Henry was miles apart from Rupert, a mere schoolboy in comparison.

His cooking was sensational. And Rain knew good food, having been raised in an Italian kitchen. His cooking was more exotic. Henry's dishes had all the aromatic spices his nagymama, (that's Hungarian for grandmother) taught him to make. They ate chicken paprikash and goulash in front of the fire, surrounded by the books Henry loved which lined the walls. Antique furniture from his nagymama accented the cozy apartment and transported them to another era.

Henry promised to take Rain to Budapest one day and show her the birthplace of his dear nagymama, Magda. She was intrigued and inspired to learn all about this dear man who set her heart aglow. Sappy, but true, and she didn't care if she sounded like a teenager. She longed for him when she returned to California and her daily grind. She was preoccupied with thoughts of Henry. For serious work minded Rain, this was new territory. She welcomed the change with open arms.

Henry came out West in the spring. They visited vineyards by day and went to poetry readings in Frisco coffeehouses at night. By candlelight over Chianti, Henry professed his love. She was in lust with him for sure. It was more than that. Henry was her heart. He thrilled her and fed

54

her soul. She asked herself how it was possible to find such a man. How did he exist when the women she counseled were used as punching bags by their men? Perhaps Henry was fed something different as a child. A steady diet of love and tenderness. A solid and kind father who spent time with him. A mother and grandmother who loved him more than life itself. Lucky for Henry. And lucky for Rain. Her love life and work were worlds apart. She relished the distance between them, almost feeling guilty she was so saturated with love.

By summer's end, Henry proposed. Rain said yes without a breath of hesitation. It was now a question of my town or yours? Rain decided to return to her roots. Her work was needed everywhere, unfortunately. Besides, she loved Henry's apartment and couldn't wait to move in. And she truly missed the seasons. Henry assured her that he would be willing to relocate if that's what it took. Rain said thanks, she was coming home. The only souvenir she was keeping from her California days was her name. Dr. Rain Taylor was taking a husband.

They were married in June, exchanging vows by the lake in Prospect Park. A reception followed at Gargulios in Coney Island. Uncle Carmine insisted on giving them the party as a wedding gift. They accepted graciously. Rain knew better than to argue with her godfather. Not to be outdone by his brother, her father gave them first class tickets to Italy for their honeymoon.

What a time, eating their way across the beautiful Italian countryside. They ended their stay on the picturesque Amalfi coast. Henry was as sweet and sexy as a man could be and Rain loved him completely. By the time they returned to their humble abode in Brooklyn, they were even more in love.

Rain opened her practice in a small office down by the Promenade in Brooklyn Heights. Clients came in no time. The wolves were never at rest. Henry had the rest of the summer off so he made it his job to spoil her rotten. He cooked and shopped and generally loved the daylights out of Rain. She was blessed.

55

On weekends they would go to concerts under the stars in Central Park. Sundays they brought picnics to the Botanical Gardens. There was plenty of good jazz in the Village after they wandered through museum exhibits. With Henry there was an easy momentum to life. They set the sheets on fire every night. It was newlywed heaven but they didn't neglect their friends. Dinner parties were a common occurrence. Colleen and Joe would come down from the Ponderosa and they would laugh about the good old days. Colleen couldn't have been happier for her. "You lucked out, Rainie, Henry is a keeper."

Colleen was right. And she was wrong. Sometimes old sayings make sense. Too good to be true or don't spit into the wind. Only hindsight is twenty-twenty. They had talked about having children someday. When Rain's practice was less demanding. When they were less selfish in wanting each other all to themselves. Rain knew Henry was game whenever she was ready. Easy, no pressure. That was Henry. What was the rush?

Henry often stayed late after class to cheer on his students at their basketball games. That Thursday night was no different. As he crossed Flatbush Avenue to catch the 6:30 bus home, a speeding car rounded the corner. It plowed mercilessly into Henry. He never had a chance to get out of harm's way.

She got the call at her office. She had just switched off the lamp on her desk and was grabbing her coat when the phone rang. Probably Henry calling from school to say he'd be home shortly to start dinner, she thought. "Get your sweet fanny home to me," he would say. She didn't hear those words. The ones she heard instead were not part of her world, because after all, she was blessed.

"There's been a terrible accident, Lorraine," Uncle Carmine sounded hoarse, stricken. Not like himself at all.

"No, Uncle Carmine. Please, no." she repeated, the room blurred through her tears.

"I'll come and get you, bella," he said softly.

She dropped the receiver on the desk and ran out without a coat. There's been a mistake, she thought, as she started her car. She didn't wait for Uncle Carmine. She could think only about Henry. He must be okay. He has to be. Henry loves me, she thought. He loves life. He has to be okay. He must be okay, she was blessed.

She shot over to Methodist Hospital, driving like a demon and praying like a saint. "Hang on, Henry. I'm on my way. We'll fix you up as good as new. A few scratches and bruises to make life interesting. A story to tell the grandchildren someday." She was rambling out loud, frantic, her adrenaline pumping. If there truly was this merciful God that her mother said her endless novenas to, then he would let Henry live. "Please, dear God, let my Henry live. I'll go back to church. I swear. I will sit there and listen and be Catholic again. Please. Have mercy on my Henry."

Henry died in her arms in the wee hours of a cold gray Friday morning. Rain kissed him goodbye, stood up as the nurse led her out of the emergency room, and collapsed on the floor. Later there was screaming and cursing God. She was not a calm stoic widow. Her passionate Sicilian blood coursed with anger and denial. Rain wanted her husband back. She wanted it to be yesterday morning when he brushed her lips with his before he walked out the door to work. "See you tonight, Doc…."

"You bet, Teach." Their last words to each other. Coffee and bagels and work and death.

"Why couldn't one of those abusive scumbags be sent to kingdom come instead of my sweet Henry?" Where is the justice in the world? Why my Henry?" she yelled to no one in particular and anyone who would listen. When she woke up the next morning, she was in their bed, alone. She reached across the bed to Henry's pillow. Empty. No smooth face to touch. No river green eyes looking at her the way only Henry could. Gentle and kind and seductive all at once. "Breakfast in bed, love?" he would ask with a wink. "Oh God, why did you take him from me?"

There standing by the window was her mother. She turned to Rain, who had exhausted herself crying and with the help of a pill had slept out of exhaustion. Her mother's eyes were rimmed in red and her face was blotched with dried tears. It was true then. Henry was gone. Rain wanted to be dead.

Her mother told her how she fainted in the hospital and later had to be sedated, she was so beside herself with grief. She could not be consoled and would not stop yelling and keening for Henry. Her mother related it all in a non-judgmental way. She understood Henry was Rain's life. What she didn't know was that her daughter decided there was no need for her to go on without him. Rain looked at her mother and waited, pleaded with her eyes for her to say it was all a bad nightmare. She watched her mother's tears fall and closed her eyes again. You cannot survive this, Rain, she told herself. It is too much to bear. You don't have to. Let go. Just will yourself to die.

Rain inhaled the steam from the strong hot coffee her mother brought her in bed. She let her mother smooth her hair like she had done when she was a child. Lovingly touching her cheek. Soon she would feel nothing. Blankness. Death. You cannot fix this, Rain, her mind told her. Fresh tears flowed from her heart into her cup. She couldn't swallow the coffee she should have been drinking with Henry. Her mother took the cup and set it on the bedside table. Rain leaned into her as she cradled her in her arms and rocked her like a baby. She hummed softly while she stroked her hair. "Shh, that's all right, Rainey, you cry love, Mommy's here," she cooed to her. Rain cried herself back to sleep, unable to accept the cruel light of day. In her dreams, Henry was alive and all was right with the world.

She woke to a heartless sun bursting through the space in the drapes where her mother had not completely closed them. Stupid cheerful sun having the nerve to shine when her Henry was lying lifeless on a cold slab. She did not want life to go on, business as usual. Not when her dear

Henry was dead and her soul was bled dry. She did not want sympathy cards and casseroles. She did not want Mass cards. She wanted to be left alone. She wanted numbness. Nothingness.

She spent countless days in a fog and nights in a medicated sleep. She buried Henry. People came and paid their respects but she remembered none of it. Her parents handled all the details. She was shut down. Useless. A zombie woman propped up in a parlor chair. She had no face for guests. No stiff upper lip. Tragedy robbed her of her best friend and lover. Protocol be damned. Forget niceties. Henry was a goner and this was her grief and it wasn't pretty and she wasn't brave and she didn't care. As far as she was concerned, the game was over. What was the point anymore?

She had no child to grieve alongside her or try and live for. No sweet little face to look upon and glance into the eyes of his or her father there. Nothing. She damned herself for that. She had been selfish. Why didn't she want Henry's child right away? She should have gotten pregnant when she had the chance. Now she would be bitter and alone. She had no right to live. It was an insult to Henry. He was the nice one. He deserved to live a long life. She should have the decency to slit her wrists and bleed for him. Feel the pain viscerally. Just like Henry did when he was thrown onto that cold unforgiving street.

She poured another bourbon to numb her grief. Coward, she thought. She liked to drink now when she was alone. It kept her company. She was a good drinker. The bottle was her new best friend. Reliable. Like Henry. Liquor was her new lover.

She heard his voice in the room with her one night. Even smelled his cologne. She dropped her glass of bourbon on the rug and looked around suspiciously. She picked up the bottle and poured the remainder of shiny brown liquid into her glass and drank deeply. Again she heard it. Henry's voice in the room.

"Rain? Are you there?" Henry was speaking to her. As plain as an ordinary day. What was that like, she wondered? How much bourbon had she drank? Who was counting? Certainly not her.

She sat down across from Henry's favorite chair. If he was there, she didn't want to sit on him. Well not until she freshened up a bit, dabbed on a little perfume. She laughed out loud. What the hell was she thinking? She was a crazy widowed lush. What if Henry really was there? She was not a pretty picture to see when he made his first haunting.

"Sorry, Henry. I've gone straight into the shitter since you croaked." Nice talk, Rain. Henry would be so disappointed. "My husband is dead," she spoke to the chair. "Dead. Morto."

"Henry, is that you?" she pleaded to her lonely parlor. "Henry, it hurts," she sobbed into the chair, on her knees.

"Fight, Rain. Get back to the business of life. I will love you for eternity, darling. You won't forget me. But you must live. Love yourself for me. Now put the damn bourbon down and get into the kitchen and eat something!"

Chapter Ten

Henry had snapped her out of it. Even in death he was her hero. In their little apartment she felt connected to him again. Among his treasures and books she could feel him near. His innate goodness and his tender heated touch. Her ethereal husband. The Ghost and Mrs. Muir, that was them. Except he was no dead sea captain. She cooked his favorite Hungarian dishes and set the table for two every night. Candles and good dishes. Even if it was take out Chinese. She was quite sane really, merely trying to heal the gaping wound Henry's death left in her life. The booze did not win. Miraculously, Ophelia had been overruled.

The paprika tin would occasionally fall down from the spice rack into whatever pot she was stirring. Henry saying hello. Giving his blessing for Rain to go on. Reminding her to rejoin the living. Do more work with the women. For a spirit, Henry was very persistent. And because of him, Rain chose life.

A new domestic violence shelter was about to open its doors in the Heights near her office. She was invited to the ribbon cutting ceremony since she had been part of the grass roots campaign to get the shelter started. There were mixed feelings about its completion. More women would have a refuge. Sad that they needed one at all. We had not progressed as much as a society where it counted most. The way some men still treated women and what was tolerated by the masses. How we often turned a blind eye. When would all of that change? That was a wonder for a longer day.

Rain donated her time at the new shelter several times a week, running group sessions for the resident women. Her days and nights were filled with work. She slept soundly out of pure exhaustion, no longer needing to self medicate. She said a wistful goodbye to her old pal Southern Comfort, dug out her walking sneakers and hit the park. She missed Henry but she was back in the crusade. Colleen called often from the

Ponderosa. She urged her to find some socializing time. "Come up and visit us," she begged. Rain wasn't quite ready to witness happiness and wedded bliss and children. She made excuses. Colleen didn't push. Rain loved her for that.

"How about getting a dog?" she suggested.

Rain knew she was worrying about her becoming an all work and no play person. Not healthy. A dog? She thought about it. But the poor dog would be alone all day and sometimes half the night. Not fair to coop up an animal that way, Rain decided. So, no dog. Not right now.

She bravely made some calls to friends she had been avoiding since Henry passed. She forced herself to accept a lunch invitation. They all met up one Saturday at a favorite restaurant near the Promenade. They were her and Henry's old gang. It wasn't awkward at all. Lunch was enjoyable, everyone made her feel like her old self. Rain didn't even feel guilty that her appetite returned.

Henry was included in their topics of conversation instead of sidestepping around the mention of his name. And no one told her how to grieve. In fact they gave her no advice at all. Just their company. What a relief. Rain was glad she came. Why do people make death so hard? Separating it from life like we do? As if we can escape its very presence. We can't. Someone's always being born and someone's always dying.

Rain wandered around the Heights the rest of the afternoon, taking in the lovely neighborhood that she took for granted lately. It was alive with possibility and renewal. She felt a presence there that she hadn't before. So quickly had she passed through each day, busy inside her office and then quickly back to Henry's apartment. Barely noticing the gem of a neighborhood all around her.

The brownstones were romantically historical. Beautiful aged brick. Ornate embellishments along the roofs. Cherubs, winged lions, egg and dart molding set in stone. She gazed up at tall windows and wide stoops and beveled glass double front doors in awe. "I will live in one of these mysterious buildings," she decided. She would make the home she and Henry dreamed of once. A germ of an idea was gestating in her brain. She found herself in a real estate office making an appointment to see a brownstone. The reality of mortgages and where the money would come from, were secondary to her at that moment. Rain Taylor was back and that was that.

When her group session at the shelter finished for the night, she had a chat with the shelter manager. "We're dealing with a difficult situation, Rain." Aurora looked very worried. "There just isn't enough affordable housing for the clients who have completed the program. We can't keep them beyond their extension dates because we're filled to capacity at all times. Yet how can we throw them out on the street?" Rain sipped the welcomed cup of coffee Aurora handed her and pondered the shelter manager's words.

"I may have a solution, believe it or not. I'm going to look at a brownstone to buy."

"Sorry? And that solves what around here?" Aurora raised her eyebrows.

"A house," Rain said, as if that explained everything.

"Right. That's great for you, a fresh start. But what's that got to do with this situation?"

Rain laughed. "I'm being unclear. I mean to take in boarders. Women, former clients if need be."

"Oh, now I get you. That sounds wonderful. But clients? It would probably be unethical, no?"

"They won't be clients anymore, will they? Not once they leave. They have to live somewhere. Any reason they couldn't live with me?"

Aurora scratched her head. Her silky silver hair fell forward on her cheek. "None I can think of at the moment. I can look into this further, if you're serious."

"I am. Very." Rain sipped her coffee, pleased with herself. The seed was planted. All she needed was a water source.

63

Walking into her apartment an hour later, she took a deep breath and looked around. How was she ever going to leave? The wind was knocked right out of her sails as she inhaled the familiar smells of her and Henry's little Shangri-la. The amazing love she shared with him was kindled here. Nourished and satiated. On this very rug, many times. How could she abandon all that? It was nothing short of dishonorable to their love for her to leave.

She poured herself a glass of Portuguese Port and kicked off her heels. She lit the fire and curled up in a fireside club chair. The firelight shone on the intricate pattern of the old Oriental that circled the cozy parlor. The very rug Henry had laid her down on to make sweet love. Even in her California days of sexy Rupert, she had not climbed to the heights that Henry took her to each night he held her. The song Magic Carpet Ride took on a whole new meaning. Before she met Henry, she had been merely preparing for a man who would unselfishly take her on a journey of bliss. She sighed, sipping the ruby Port. Reminiscing was getting her quite fired up and there was nothing she could do about it. "I miss you Henry."

Maybe there was something for her mood, after all. She got up and lit the candles around the room. She turned the lights down low and clicked on the stereo. She set the needle on the Coltrane record that Henry had practically worn out. Henry and Coltrane, a delicious combination. The saxophone wailed as she undressed. Slowly and sensuously as if she had an audience. She lay on the carpet in front of the fire. The light warmed her bare skin and she was aroused and ready. She started from the tip of her nose and worked her way down, making herself ache for it. She arched her back. "Henry baby, this is for you…."

The real estate agent phoned her the following morning.

"I don't mean to be a pest Dr. Taylor, but you seemed very interested the other day. If you want to have a look at our recent acquisition, there's no time like the present. Is today too soon for you?"

Fair enough, Rain thought. Jump in. "Today works for me."

"Good. Meet me at my office at 3:00. Today is your lucky day, Dr. Taylor."

The realtor stopped abruptly in the middle of the second block. "Well, this is it. Home sweet home." She held her hand out to the building they stood in front of and Rain thought, no way. She looked up at a sadly neglected brownstone. She followed the realtor trustingly up the cracked stoop. Oh brother, she thought, what have I let myself in for?

"Well it is large enough for boarders…." she tried to sound convincing, mostly to herself. She wanted to turn and run back to her safe apartment. The realtor turned the key and creaked open the front door and they stepped inside a dismal foyer. The smell of abandonment hit Rain between the eyes. Chin up, Rain, she told herself, waving her perfumed wrist by her nose. She could feel the dust settling on her clothes. Won't kill you to look, she thought, watching for loose floorboards.

"There are three floors," the realtor sang out, as if taking Rain on a tour of the Royal Palace. "To the right we have the very spacious living room. Formal parlor if you like, complete with large marble fireplace, which I'm sure, a chimney sweep will have working in no time. Next is the dining room, complete with old fashioned pocket doors and plenty of room for a wonderful table and comfy chairs. And a sideboard or dry sink perhaps….

Voila! Another fireplace in here as you can see. And notice the turn of the century chandelier. Comes with the house, as do all the fixtures. Can't you just imagine the beauty you could restore in here?"

"I'm sure it was stunning, once," Rain said, admiring the hanging crystals and velvet cord, holding back a dusty sneeze.

"Okay, let's take you to the kitchen, shall we?" the realtor chirped gaily. Rain wondered if a singsong voice was a requirement for the job? Rain was trying to be optimistic. That was a lie. She was simply not very encouraged so far. The house was a wreck. No wonder no one had snatched it up, even at such a reasonable price for a brownstone. Someone let the old house go straight into the crapper, as Uncle Carmine would say. And he would be right.

Rain stepped across the threshold into the kitchen and felt her senses change dramatically. There was a good feeling in this room. It had been a happy place at one time. Rain sensed it, and a familiar smell of Hungarian cologne. Did ghosts haunt with a dab of rosemary oil? And why would Henry be here? Ghosts haunted familiar surroundings.

Rain walked across the worn out linoleum and straight to the hearth. A real kitchen hearth. She was transfixed to the spot. Dirt could be whisked away. Bad energy or ghosts, if you believed in them, not that easily. The energy was good. Okay, a positive.

"Dr. Taylor? Is everything okay? I know it needs a major overhaul, to say the least." She pointed gingerly at the old sink and gas range.

"I'm fine," Rain said, "I think this could be a charming room. I was daydreaming, well, imagining what it was."

"What say we venture upstairs to the boudoir?"
Rain laughed and followed her lead. The banister was oak. Solid as a tree. A good rub of Murphy's Oil Soap would reveal it's natural beauty in no time. The staircase was grand. No other word for it. The carpet was threadbare and grungy but the effect of the winding steps left the climber to wonder what was around the bend. This was a house where stories lived. A little mystery made these old brownstones the sellers they were. Each an original.

"As I said before, there are three floors. Four bedrooms on the second level and two more on the third

66

floor. The larger one on the third floor has the turret window. You're going to love it." Were realtors psychic as well?

They had a quick look at each bedroom on the second floor. The rooms were surely lovely in their time. Rain had to envision them that way. Imagine a roaring fire in each of the fireplaces, the dreary wallpaper fresh and clean, and beds plump and ready for sweet dreaming, windows squeaky clean and draped with flowing curtains, sunlight peeking through.

They climbed the shorter set of stairs to the third floor and entered the larger room first. Rain had arrived at her destination. She felt it in her gut. This was her room. No question. The turret sold her. A fairy tale come true. Every little girl imagines such a room. Every woman desires a room of her own at some age. Here was Rain's. Her very own Velvet Room, the book she read as a girl came to life before her eyes. She could already picture it decorated. She wouldn't even mind the climb. The exercise would keep the glutes in shape. This room was worth every step. Rain shook her head as if to wake from the dream. You would think she was going to spend her days reading blissfully by the fire in a satin robe. It did no good, she just knew she would sleep in this room. And sleep well. Like a flipping queen.

The realtor had become oddly quiet. No fool was she. You don't interrupt a dream. They walked downstairs and Rain had another quick gander at the living room. The mirror over the mantle was an old beveled rectangle framed in a crackled wood finish. Or was that just cracked wood? The mirror glass was a bit pitted but that could be replaced. Shined up it would be lovely. It spoke to her in a strange way. She pictured someone standing there, boot leg up on the fireplace ledge, saying her name. Smoking and talking.

"Daydreaming again, Dr. Taylor?"

"Sorry," Rain apologized. "Do houses ever speak to you?"

"Of course, all the time. This is truly an enchanting house," she said.

She was good. Enchanting was pushing it.

67

"It is a handsome house all right. It must have been gorgeous once. I think it has possibilities."

Did Rain just commit? Her palms were sweating. She felt warm suddenly. She looked around. No need to change the layout, the design of the house was perfect. Full of character. She would let it reveal its spectacular uniqueness to her after its very wounded state was tended to, poor neglected house. Her house. Uh oh. Had she made a decision? Was she crazy to get herself involved in a restoration project? She had a full plate already. Without Henry to see it through with her, was it even a rational thought? He would think so. Move forward, Rain.

"You don't have to let me know today, but I wouldn't wait too long. I'll have to show the house if others want to see it, you do understand? You see when these babies are in tip top condition, the prices go through the roof. This brownstone, at this price, is a rare find."

"Right, I know, yes," Rain agreed. Then she remembered the ancient bathrooms. New plumbing is no joke. Thankfully the original wiring had been replaced and the lights were all working. Including the charming one that lit up the front stoop. That was something to consider. She took a last glance into the kitchen and they turned to walk down the hall. Something dropped onto the floor behind Rain. She swung around, startled. There on the red and white linoleum in front of the stove, was a tin of paprika. She picked it up and smiled.

"Dr. Taylor? What have you got there?"

"Paprika." Rain turned the grimy container over in her hands.

"Oh?" The realtor looked concerned. "You've gone a shade pale, but you look oddly delighted. Thought it was a mouse, didn't you? Can't blame you…."

"It's Henry. My dead husband. Do you believe in signs?" Rain thought she'd probably believe in aliens if she wanted to sell the house badly enough.

"Actually I do. I love paprika. It's a childhood

familiarity. My nagymama, that's Hungarian for grandmother, used it on everything. Why are you smiling?"

"Henry was Hungarian. I'm familiar with a nagymama, all right. His read tea leaves like a gypsy."

"They all do."

"Amazing. Are you wearing rosemary oil, by any chance? By the way, I'll take the brownstone. And please call me Rain."

"Great. And yes, I am wearing it. I have the oil sent to me from Budapest. Did you think your husband was doing a fly by? Fantastic. You won't be sorry about the house. Call me Angie. Anjelika is my given name. Anjelika Magzda. You can see why I go with Angie Madison, for work."

"I'm familiar with name changes myself. And Henry was not a Miller by birth either. I cannot even pronounce his real surname. By the way, I'm going to have this paprika tin framed and hang it over the stove when I move in. You'll come for coffee, Angie, how's that?"

"Sounds great. I'll bring the beigli."

Rain's mouth watered just thinking about the scrumptious Hungarian pastry she and Henry shared at his favorite bakery in the city.

"You made the right decision, Rain. You will be very happy here. This house is a beautiful place to start fresh. Now who are you going to call to celebrate?"

Only one person came to mind.

Chapter Eleven

Uncle Carmine suggested Gargulios for dinner. Where else? Rain told him she would met him there after work.

"Take a cab. I'll bring you home," he said.

He hugged her tightly and when they were seated at his favorite table, she filled him in on her current plans. He loved the brownstone idea.

"Anything to see my Lorraine smile again. You scared the hell out of us for awhile, bella. Glad you're back in the race." He squeezed her hand. She looked up at him.

"Sorry. I was in the twilight zone all right. No need to worry anymore. I'll be okay. I just miss Henry, that's the thing."

"I know, bella. Henry was a good guy. Sorry you had to lose him. No more tears now. Let's drink good wine and eat good food."

Rain followed his lead and sipped her Chianti and dug into a generous portion of eggplant parmigiana. Uncle Carmine entertained her with tales from the track. The ponies were doing right by him again. Over espresso and Anisette he told her he was going to take care of the brownstone renovations.

"Case closed," he said.

Rain opened her mouth to object and decided that was a waste of time.

"Listen, I got the money, so what's the problem?"

"You're always so generous. I appreciate it, you know that, but...."

"But what? You rich or something all of a sudden? Henry leave you piles of cash? He was a school teacher, nothing wrong with that, but it didn't make him rich. Don't be proud. I got it, it's yours, capisce?"

"Capisce. Thanks. I love you."

"I love you too, kid." Kid. She was 45 years old. But that was Uncle Carmine. To him she was still his little niece. A person could have more genuine complaints. They sat and sipped their Anisette and toasted the brownstone project.

"Okay, I got carpenters, plumbers, whatever you need. Let me know... I make a few calls and you're in business, you hear?"

"Yep, got it." Rain could tell him the money was enough, but who was she kidding? There would be no discussion. He wanted to help so she would let him. It was his joy in life. Helping his family. That and betting on the ponies. He didn't drink much and he was a good guy to have in your corner. So why not?

His life was simple. No wife, no kids. Rain and Teresa were his only nieces and he couldn't give her sister a thing. She had God and solitude and hopefully peace of mind. Not a bad trade for a robbed childhood, Rain thought, but it still made her sad.

"I gotta spoil somebody, bella," Uncle Carmine touched her hand. They both knew he was talking about Teresa without mentioning her name. Did he fight for them, back when it all happened? Rain never asked him. Her father and the others would have stopped him. He had a temper. But you wanted him on your side. Rain knew it was no secret he did not like the old man next door. Just knowing her uncle might have tried to do something on her and Teresa's behalf made Rain love him all the more. Maybe one day she might ask him. Not tonight. She was just enjoying being happy.

Uncle Carmine was a good guy. A war veteran and an ex- narc that had seen the seamy side of life and loved to talk about it. A long time ago he got himself jammed up and had to earn himself back into the good graces of the Police Department. But he was a stand up guy. Only harm he'd ever done was to himself. He would swing for whoever needed it. Rain was lucky to get him by blood. Plus she was on the top rung of his affection. Lucky her.

"Remember, Lorraine, oops, sorry, that Rain name I can't get used to, bella. But that's your business. Anyway, I got cops who can watch the place. Noon and night. No problem. I got a few favors coming to me. You know, if those broad's husbands or boyfriends come looking for trouble. We take care of it right away. Long as you don't worry. You get wrinkles that way." He laughed hard. He was an original, no doubt about it.

Rain laughed. "Okay. I'll keep that in mind. Thanks." She wasn't about to get into a debate with him. She knew the abusers wouldn't know where their wives or girlfriends had relocated. It wasn't public information. But it was hardly necessary to get into all of that with Uncle Carmine. He worried enough for both of them.

He wasn't finished. He would drive his point home some more. He leaned in and looked at her. "You get what I'm saying? I know about these things…."

Rain didn't have to ask how. Of course he did. You cannot be a cop in a big city and not see the ugly side of life.

"Yes," she said, patiently. He looked at her sideways.

"Yes, I understand. I do. And I know how to shoot a gun, remember? You taught me yourself. I still have it. If that fails, I'm Sicilian. I'll stab the motherfu…."

"Whoa, easy there, cowgirl. Where'd you get a mouth on you like that? Oh yeah," he laughed, "Your fucking Uncle Carmine." He laughed harder and toasted her with his glass of Anisette. He was an original. They broke the mold after him. He paid the check and they walked out to his car.

"Pasta Fazool is still going strong, I see." Pasta Fazool was his car. A beat up cocoa brown 69 Chevy he refused to upgrade or replace.

"Yep, the old broad's great. Mind if I smoke?"
He already had a Camel planted between his lips.

"No, go ahead, they're your lungs." Rain laughed at his choice of an ashtray. An old tin can affixed to the dashboard with duct tape. Pasta Fazool mortified her parents.

"Carmine, for Christ's sake, why don't you buy a new car?" her father would ask him. "You win all that money from your damn horses," her mother would tell him. "Buy yourself a car, it's a disgrace." Rain's mother did not think highly of his gambling or his car. Uncle Carmine wouldn't budge. Pasta Fazool was staying.

"Something wrong with this car? It gets me around," he would say to them. And that was the end of that.

Now he sang along with the big band music he loved. The only station that came in on his ancient radio. Rain watched him push a thumbtack back into the roof upholstery that was coming loose. She stifled a laugh and inhaled the cigarette smoke that mixed with the cool air as they crept along the night streets at thirty miles an hour. He finally pulled up in front of her apartment building.

"Thanks for dinner. And everything. I can never repay you for all you do, not that you'd let me." She gave him a good hug and kissed his cheek. "What would I do without you?"

"Shhh with that crap. I do what I want to do. Take the money and be quiet about it. Please, bella. I know you're grateful. Basta, already." He meant no disrespect. It was who he was.

"Okay. I love you. Ciao."

"Ciao. Lock the door behind you and let me see you at the window. That's my girl."

She blew him a kiss and walked into the building. Safely inside the apartment, Rain flicked the lights twice and pushed the curtain back so he could see her. Satisfied, he drove off, chugging along in Pasta Fazool. Rain kicked off her shoes and threw her coat over a chair. She was wired from the espresso and toasty from the Anisette. She put the kettle on for a cup of decaf Earl Grey. That and a good book and her lavender candle and she would be sleeping in no time.

It was a good plan but it proved useless. Her mind was too busy thinking about the brownstone project. She walked around the apartment letting her eyes sweep over every beautiful thing she and Henry had shared together. His Nagymama's paintings and furniture, and artifacts he collected on foreign trips he'd taken before they met. Rain's collection of baskets from San Francisco markets. Souvenirs from Italy on their honeymoon. She turned off the screeching kettle and reached instead for the bottle of Frangelico. She threw in some ice cubes and sipped. Grabbing a pen and pad from the counter, she walked to the French doors in the living room and threw them open. She stood on the balcony of the small terrace and watched the twinkling fairy lights in the garden below. Henry had strung them their first summer together in the apartment. All that was missing now was Henry beckoning her for a dance below. How could she ever leave here?

She sat in one of the wicker chairs on the terrace and started to write. She couldn't concentrate. She walked back inside and put on a Billy Holiday record. Billy's sad voice floated out to the darkness. "*My man ...*" Rain toasted Henry.

"Salute, my angel, I miss you." She closed her eyes and pictured Henry holding her. She picked up the list and began again.

The Brownstone Project, she wrote across the top of the page in capital letters. First, the practical and necessary. Overhaul kitchen and bathrooms, have chimneys cleaned, restore wood flooring, and install new locks and a security system. Ah yes, Henry, the times they are a changin'. She sipped her Frangelico and tapped her pen on the pad. Furniture, lamps, a desk for her home office. She could hit the sales for bedding and linens, maybe take a ride out to Englishtown in New Jersey for some antique beds and dressers.

Next, a wish list:

1- Boarders.

She supposed they should go on the necessities list.

2- Big dog.

It was a big house after all.

3- Aga.

Henry told her his Nagymama cooked on one. It seemed fitting for the Brownstone. From here on in The Brownstone would be its proper name. Where would she find an aga in Brooklyn? No doubt Uncle Carmine would have that answer. Or Angie the realtor.

4- Garden.

There was room in the small backyard for roses and herbs and maybe tomatoes. Definitely a cutting garden. Gorgeous flowers for all the rooms. Rain laughed. When was she going to find time to garden, no less snip pretty roses to put in vases? Oh well. That's why it was called a wish list.

Perhaps there would be a boarder interested in tending a garden. Growing vegetables even. Good therapy digging in the dirt. Maybe she should find the time. Speaking of boarders, what would the first one be like? Would they click? How would they all get along? Sure, they'd have a commonality among them, healing from abuse. Reclaiming their dreams. A collective restoring of souls. Thoughts of emulating Sylvia Plath gone from their heads.

Rain crossed out the word Project from the top of the pad. She wrote again in capital letters: Restorative. Yes, a Brownstone Restorative. She finished her drink and let her mind float along to the music, with Billy's pain. "*The very thought of you…*" Satisfied with her planning for one night, she decided to hit the hay. She locked the terrace doors and padded down to bed.

The sun was shining brightly the next morning. Rain took it as a good omen. She poured strong coffee and steamed milk into a travel cup and headed out the door. The weather was crisp. A perfect fall day. She drove over to the shelter with minimal traffic. A good day so far, she thought, sipping her coffee. Umm, delicious. Just a hint of cinnamon. The way Henry always made it. Henry. Always right there at the brim of her thoughts. Familiar and comforting. The shelter was coming up on her right. She set her coffee down in the cup holder, and buzzed the intercom and waited.

Before she could say, "Yes, it's me, Doc," a small bark beat her to it.

"Got a cold, Doc?" the shelter manager asked, laughing. She could see Rain's car through the window.

"No. It's me, and a friend, apparently." She opened her car door as the gate started to open. The puppy jumped right in beside her. She closed the car door and drove inside the gate. She looked over at her passenger. He barked again, in a friendly way and they locked eyes.

Rain was done. Instantly in love. She disengaged herself from the seat belt and the puppy that was now snuggled in her lap. She set him gently on the ground, climbed out of the car, grabbed her briefcase and coffee and walked towards the back entrance of the shelter. Her new friend followed. No sooner had Aurora opened the door, the puppy trotted inside like he owned the joint.

"Sorry, I was ambushed, I'll find out who he belongs to. Must be a neighbor."

Aurora chuckled. "No worries. He's a regular lately. Doc, meet Shamus. He just has his days confused. He's usually here on Wednesdays with Connie." Connie was the shelter's legal advocate. "The kids love Shamus. He seems smitten with you though."

Shamus was licking Rain's stocking. Then he noticed activity in the house through the office window and ran inside to the outer office to have a closer look. She hung up her coat and went in search of a water bowl for her new friend, who wouldn't let her out of his sight for very long. Aurora handed Rain the client list for Group.

"Aurora, any chance Connie might sell the little booger?" she asked her, petting him on her lap behind his soft tan ears.

"A very good chance. She has eight just like Shamus. Why don't I give her a call and let her know he's here. She might not have noticed he snuck out of her yard. You can talk to her then if you like."

"Okay, thanks." Rain looked up from the night log she had started to peruse. I think I just committed myself to becoming a dog owner, she thought. She went back to the log and waited for Aurora to finish her phone calls. She returned a few minutes later, smiling. Uh oh. You did put a dog on your wish list, Rain, she remembered.

"Connie said he's all yours if you want him. Now for the real world. Sari is leaving. Today." The office phone rang. "She... oh excuse me, Doc, I'm expecting a call from her case manager. This must be it." Aurora went back into her office, leaving Rain with a question on her tongue to which she sadly already knew the answer. She drank her coffee and read over the notes from the night log. Aurora came back into the staff room and sat down on the couch.

"I swear I got zero sleep last night. I am sick with worry for Sari." Her face was filled with sadness.

Aurora and Rain had been down this road before, many times. Aurora poured herself a cup of green tea. When a client leaves before their allotted time is up, it is never a good thing. Something or someone had failed her. The system. Herself. But Rain knew there was more to it in Sari's case.

She watched Shamus slurping up water from a Tupperware bowl on the floor. Would Sari ever know such simple pleasures? A cup of coffee with a friend or co-worker. A puppy. A life without fear. A new beginning?

Sari was their miracle case. Originally from Saudi Arabia, she had been a resident of Queens living with her husband and three children and mother-in law. The beatings were a daily occurrence. The Department of Children and Families got involved after Sari stopped showing up for parent teacher meetings. Sari's little daughter started wetting her pants in school and crying and pulling out her eyelashes. Her brother told her he was going to tie her up like their mother because "that's what girls get."

Sari was found locked down the basement, her hands and legs bound with chains, her face swollen from her last beating. On further examination in the hospital after the

77

police were called, it was revealed that Sari had been raped by her husband. She was terrified. But the evidence on her slight traumatized body spoke for itself. Sari's husband had disappeared before the police arrived and her mother-in-law, who had been witness to Sari's torture, denied being an accomplice but was not about to help her.

Sari was placed in the shelter with her children until she could say she didn't want to be there. She never said so. She knew she was safe and she believed her husband would not know where to find her. Aurora told her about the underground and how she could change her identity. Relocate. She explained about pressing charges. Filing for divorce. Sari refused. But she didn't leave the shelter. She chose to stay. It was probably the first real choice she ever made in her whole life. Even her marriage had been arranged.

Sari took to the shelter program like a duck to water. She was the only woman there that dressed in her native country's traditional garb, long thick gauze embroidered dresses that she sewed herself. Underneath she was just the same as any other client, only quieter and more private. She was not used to talking about her life with strangers. To their credit, the other shelter residents treated Sari no differently. Eventually she wore pants and sweaters. A little make-up. Not that she needed any; she had a naturally beautiful face. Emerald green eyes, dark complexion and perfect pearly white teeth. She wanted to become more Americanized, like her children. Yet she always maintained her modesty, careful to keep her legs and arms covered. Religion and culture were ingrained in her.

She made clothes for the other clients. Ornate cotton blouses with trimmings donated by volunteers in the community. Her progress was an inspiration to the shelter residents. If Sari could do it, they could too. She was by far the most hopeless case at the shelter. It was her background and oppressive religious beliefs coupled with her abuse and her self-loathing from her suicide attempts. It was against her religion to take her life under any circumstances. She was an outcast and a fugitive. Sari remained at the shelter. That was no small accomplishment. Women in her community did not ask for help. And they did not leave their husbands. No matter what.

Sari had only a few weeks to complete her stay and then be placed in a house where she could live a normal life. Wherever she chose. A place where she would be unharmed. Rain listened now as Aurora told her the devastating news.

"It happened only yesterday. Sari called a close friend. Someone she trusted and kept in touch with on a regular basis who would never tell Sari's husband anything. The calls were always placed when the friend was at her job. Never when she was at home. Just in case. As you know Sari's is a tight-knit community. The women are often the men's property. Sari's friend didn't believe in that nonsense, she is a free Muslim woman. She practices her religion without the stereotypical 'woman is lesser' mentality. Anyway, she and her husband are educated people who tried more than once to convince Sari to leave her husband. But she wouldn't. Of course they didn't know the extent of her suffering until DCF got involved. She was always very covered up of course. You already know from her file that her husband is a powerful man in his country and was feared over here as well.

She knew this friend through her children at school and would see her friend at school functions, when allowed. Their parents are from the same village back home in Saudi Arabia. Sari asked her friend yesterday about her family back home. As she always did. Her mother and father and sister. Her friend had bad news. She asked to meet outside the shelter. Somewhere in the city, where she would be one of many in a crowded place. It was not something to speak of over the phone her friend said. Sari agreed only after her friend swore an oath not to tell a soul about the meeting. She felt sad that Sari had asked her to swear but she understood her friend's terror. It was a little thing to ask in light of the situation.

So she left the children here and went into the city with her case worker to meet with her friend. She wore a disguise a few clients helped her put together. To blend in. Even her friend did not recognize the tiny woman in the Yankees cap and boys clothes sitting at a corner table in a pizzeria drinking a can of Diet Coke and eating a slice of Sicilian. Until Sari winked at her and smiled her sweet smile. Her friend clapped her hands softly and they hugged like old friends.

Sari choked back tears as she listened to what her friend said. It seems Sari's husband had issued an ultimatum. A fatwa against Sari's family. If she did not return home within the month, he would see to it that her family in Saudi Arabia were killed. She would have proof of their deaths. He would take pictures of their executions to show her. Before he ordered the murders he would make sure Sari's sisters got married off to controlling despicable men he chose for them. Unless she returned to him with the children. It was all up to Sari. Her friend wished she were not the one to bring such news. Sari asked her how she came to know. She had a gut feeling who would speak of such cruelty with pleasure. Her friend confirmed her suspicion. Sari's mother–in-law was only too glad to let her son's fatwa slip out. She was an evil woman, but far from stupid. She knew it would get back to Sari.

The friend urged Sari to run. 'Let the shelter people help you. Go far away and never return. The children will be better off. Be a free woman. Not some man's slave and punching bag.' She herself had not suffered the indignities that were Sari's reality. But she alone could not help Sari. She took a huge risk going to meet her and Sari knew this and loved her for it. 'Sari, stay there,' her friend pleaded, 'stay in safety at your shelter and let these wise women help you for your future and the children's. Your papa and mama will be warned properly. You cannot protect them anyway. He will likely do what he had planned even if you return to him. He is a liar. Do not be a fool. It does not say in any prayer book for you to be tortured by your husband. You must end it. Remove his power over you. I will find you a lawyer, you can divorce him and move on.'

But Sari could not risk her family suffering that way back home. She knew too well that her husband would carry out his threats. No one could warn her family in time. He would find out and carry out his promise of violence and death. Only her friend would dare speak against him and she was no match for his rage. Who would believe her anyway? There was no proof of his threat. Nowhere was it written down. Sari knew instinctively that she should stay in the shelter and let them place her safely underground. But she was heartsick with thoughts of her murdered family back home. It would be her fault. She must try to prevent it. She could not sacrifice her family and live with the knowledge that they had been tortured and killed because of her. She would have to return to her husband. There was no other choice.

He would not hurt her children. And her parents and sister would be spared. If he beat her for leaving him, so what? It was nothing that she hadn't endured before. Her friend would be very disappointed at her decision but it was hers alone to make. Perhaps she could help Sari find a way to leave her husband for good. Outside the shelter. Sari was kidding herself. The shelter and its support system were her only hope.

Her friend's words replayed in her head. 'Tell the shelter people. They will help you. Pray on the right answer. For the strength to take care of yourself and your children. It is the only answer. Your parents would not want their daughter to live in shame and humiliation and pain every day. You must continue your fight for your freedom and your children's.' Her friend held her tightly before they parted. Would she ever see Sari again, alive? And that is it, Doc, the whole sad truth. I wish it weren't."

Aurora got up to refill her tea. Rain wiped her fallen tears from her blouse. The childcare worker came in to make her notes for the day. She excused herself and walked back into the house after one of the children called her name. She was gone for a little while. When she returned her face was wet with tears.

"I just spoke with Sari. How can this happen, Doc? You can't let it, we have to do something." She sat on the couch and accepted the cup of coffee Aurora handed her. She fiddled nervously with her notes and tried to gain composure.

"Aurora, please, can't somebody help? I was making such progress with Abu," she said, her voice cracking. Doc's heart broke for her. "You remember what he was like when Sari first came here, a very angry filthy mouthed little boy. So mean to his little sisters, calling them 'he' all the time refusing to say 'she.' He doesn't do that anymore. It will all go back to how they all were when they first came here. This is awful. Please do something for her." She sniffled and looked from Rain to Aurora. Neither one could give her any hope.

"I know how you feel, sweetie," Rain said gently. "It is very, very sad. But we cannot force Sari to stay. It is her choice to leave. Hard as that is to hear. Listen to me, your shift is almost over, when you get in your car, turn on some upbeat music nice and loud, and when you get home divert yourself with something that will make you smile. We cannot fix this, sadly. I wish we could. You have a big heart and you suffer for it. But look at the great job you do and the difference you make with the children. While Sari was here, you gave her and the children joy. That is not erased. I understand how you feel. We all do. Truth is, it sucks, plain and simple."

Rain drove back to her office with such an intense feeling of gloom and doom. Sometimes this line of work was the pits. Sari's leaving was akin to handing a helpless child over to the Anti-Christ. Though she made her own decision to leave the shelter, it still felt like they had failed her. What would become of Sari now?

The phone was ringing intrusively disturbing her thoughts as she entered her office. She picked it up and took a deep breath. Could the day get any worse? "Hello?" It was Connie, the shelter's legal advocate and Shamus's owner.

"Hey, Doc, heard you saw my boy today. He's yours if you want him. Wish I were calling with better news though. Like Sari changing her mind for instance. I did what I could. Frustrating as it is, legally it was her decision. We can't prove the bastard means to do her any more harm even with his track record. Plus he still gets to see his kids even if she stays. He could run with them and she'd never see them again. She couldn't live with that. It's a complicated mess. The system needs a lot of work yet."

"You're right. Dead right, unfortunately. I know you did your best. It just doesn't feel right. Like throwing her to the wolves. And yes, I'll take the dog. I need some time though, to get into the Brownstone. The apartment's too small and I'm gone all day and half the night."

"No hurry. You can see him at the shelter and take him to the park when you feel like getting out for a bit. Do you good. He'll be a fine runner one day and a protector. Did I mention he's Irish wolfhound and Australian shepherd? Fine mix. Gorgeous breed as you saw for yourself. Very loyal. And protective. Now have yourself a nice strong cup of tea or better yet, a whiskey, and try not to feel too bad about poor Sari. It stinks, that's the stinking truth."

"It sure does. God help her, poor thing. Oh, what about the price? For Shamus?"

"He's a gift. I insist. Think of him as a housewarming present for your Brownstone."

"You're a doll, Connie. Thank you." Rain hung up the phone and had to admit her mood had lifted a tiny bit. She had one more client to see, she needed to focus. She jotted down some quick notes and plugged in the electric kettle.

She sipped her Earl Grey and thought about Shamus. Wasn't he perfect? The wolf and the shepherd. All she needed now were a few boarders when the Brownstone Restoration

Chapter Twelve

Rain had her first official boarder in the Brownstone. Rooney McNeil left the shelter, her husband's name and the state of Georgia behind. She cooked, cleaned and attended a beauty school a bus ride away on Church Avenue. Each day was a forward step into a new life. The nightmare of Clyde Farrow a horror from her past.

They hit it off like old friends. Rooney's quick Southern humor kept Rain laughing. She had an easy smile and a face like those adorable cherubs in a Botticelli painting, but a mouth that would make the devil blush. It was her eyes though that grabbed you. One as blue as Dresden china, the other a fair man made indigo replica. A blue marble that never moved. But Clyde hadn't won. Rooney was still beautiful. In low lighting, a few loose tendrils fallen forward and the scar on her face was nearly invisible.

Rooney found Rain's next boarders. Two Irish waitresses working in a café down by the Promenade, currently sharing a small apartment in a dicey yet affordable neighborhood. They loved the Heights and would give anything to live in one of the brownstones. Rooney mentioned the Brownstone and they were more than interested. Rain went to the café the next morning and met them herself.

She spotted both immediately. Two very attractive redheads bustled around the café obviously no strangers to hard work and hospitality. Dory had the thicker brogue and the chat came easy to her. Rain got the feeling she could talk to a statue and get a response. How refreshing in a big cynical city. She was charming. Her brogue fascinated Rain with its lilting tone. Her bouncing butterscotch curls and her very full C cup, had likely gotten her a good bit of attention and a fair bit of trouble. Dory was a truster, Rain could tell. A giver. An easy mark. Women didn't get off easy in this world. If you

85

think pretty women have it any easier, think again. Load of shite, as Dory would say. Everybody pays.

Fiona Monahan was a Celtic stunner. Her deep chestnut hair with glimmering copper highlights compliments of nature, would make any woman envious. She moved like a gazelle up and down the restaurant aisles pouring coffee and smiling. A young Maureen O'Hara on the back of a horse riding through a green field. Whatever she was pouring you were having. She did more than justice to the boring waitress attire of black pants and a starched white man-tailored shirt. But Fiona was not born to serve. She reeked of class. To the manor born. There's a story here, Rain thought. Fiona shook her hand and met her eyes. She looked away a second too soon. There it was, clear as a bell. Fiona was a good actress. Rain would put money on the fact that she'd had to be at one time. Very good. And Rain knew instinctively that Fiona was not very proud of that fact.

"So you girls are running back and forth to the city between shifts on modeling auditions, yes?" Rain asked them, sipping her coffee when they'd finally taken a break.

Dory hooted. "Good one, Doc. You don't mind if we call you that? Rooney told us that everyone does."

Rain smiled. "Not at all. But I am serious, you are both gorgeous."

"Hear that, Fee? Models is it? That's gas." Dory laughed again. "But thanks very much for the compliment. Cheers."

"You're welcome." Rain smiled at Fiona. She smiled back.

"We hardly possess the teeny bums and flat chests necessary, or the magazine looks, but you're sweet to say so, Dr. Taylor. Now I wouldn't mind their money. Actually Dory and I are interior designers back home. We haven't had a go at it here as yet."

"Oh. I see," Rain said, thinking of the Brownstone. It could use an experienced touch. And she was right about Fiona. Proper formal language. Silver spoon for sure.

"Yes, the money here's been grand," Dory piped up, "So we haven't done much to organize our portfolio. When can we come have a gawk at your Brownstone then? I'm chomping at the bit meself," she laughed. A lovely sound. Like happy children. Rain was entranced. Not a blemish between them. Though she noticed a dime-sized scar under Dory's bangs when she moved her hair.

"Anytime, really. Rooney works at home during the day. Or you can call me at my office and come by after your shifts. I'll give you my card." Rain reached for her purse.

"Grand, thanks," Dory said, studying the card. "Is there no Mr. Doc, then?"

"Dory, don't be such a Nosy Morgan. Dr. Taylor's personal business is truly none of ours." Fiona was apparently appalled. One had attended charm school and the other basically spoke her mind. Rain liked them both. Rooney's instincts about these two were right on. It was turning into an interesting Brownstone.

"No problem. I don't mind the question, honestly. My husband Henry passed away last year. I don't plan on remarrying so the Brownstone is a man-free zone. Except for my Uncle Carmine who drops in occasionally to see me, and he's harmless. By the way, he loves redheads. And the ponies. Not necessarily in that order.

"Can't blame a man for that," Fiona said. "We're single ourselves and plan on staying that way. As far as we're concerned, men can be awful shites, pardon my language. Unless Jesus Christ himself comes down in a pair of Calvin Klein boxers, we're not going near any bollocks anytime soon." Fiona set her coffee cup down. Purposefully, like a gavel. Court was adjourned on that subject.

"So, it's settled then," Rain said. "The Brownstone seems right up your alley. Give me a call and we'll set a time for you to come over. The sooner the better." She got up, put on her coat and reached for the bill. Dory slipped it away from her grasp and put it in her pocket.

"No worries, Doc. We can buy your cuppa. You didn't touch your muffin. Would you like me to wrap it up for later? Can't go without a brekkie now."

Rain smiled at her Irish slang. "Thank you. That's very considerate."

"Nonsense. 'Tis our pleasure," Fiona said. "We're grateful you took the time to come in and meet us. I come from a long line of horse betting men myself so I'm familiar with strokes of luck. I'd say we just had one."

"Thank you. That's very kind. And please, call me Doc." Rain took the brown paper muffin bag off the table and put it in her purse. She looked up at Dory's shining blue eyes and her heart clutched a little.

Dory studied the card in her hand. *Dr. Rain Taylor. Therapist for women. Facilitator of Friday night support groups for Domestic Violence. Abuse is no secret to keep.* Rain's telephone number was underneath. She passed it to Fiona.

"Right. We'll call, Dr. Tay… Doc," Fiona said, from the next table she was clearing.

"Ah, we will so. Cheers, Doc. All the best," Dory added quickly, slipping Doc's card in her apron pocket.

Chapter Thirteen

Mae

Sometimes a client came along who seemed tailor made for the shelter. Life there was not a far cry from how she lived most of her life, under supervision in a group setting. Without privacy and among women. Mae West was that client. The shelter children loved her. She was tiny; they could easily assume she was one of them. Who better than Mae to understand their fear and confusion? Though of course they didn't know, Mae had a nightmare story of her own. She was elected unanimously by the other clients, to be the unofficial babysitter/playroom supervisor.

Most of the shelter's young children couldn't verbalize their distress. Only their immediate needs. Like hunger and cold. An urge to go to the bathroom. Another cookie. One more minute to play. You only had to spend a little time with these kids and you knew a piece was missing. Robbed from them early was a sense of joy, a carefree spirit, trust, easy laughter and the quick smiles of childhood. Somebody had messed badly with these serious children. Many were victims of physical abuse in addition to being small witnesses to the crimes against their mothers. They were traumatized. Somebody had left a mark on the innocent.

Mae brought them happiness. A little bit each day. She taught them how to be children, maybe for the first time. Not protectors of their mothers. Not miniature worry warts and go-betweens from abusive men. Mae played games with them. Sang to them. Rocked the babies. She got on the floor and crawled in and out of tents. Made trains out of cardboard boxes the children had painted bright colors with finger paints. Mae lightened their small heavy hearts.

She had to tread carefully with the children. Not get too close and keep the affection at their comfort level. She learned to cope with their mood swings and tears and gave gentle instruction and reprimands when necessary. They listened to her most of the time because they craved her attention. Mae did her level best to be their champion. She knew she was no Mary Poppins. Some of the moms took to calling her Nanny Figalilly. Mae just laughed. "Seriously, Mae, you have great patience with them," they told her. How could Mae tell them that the children were in fact healing her? If the mothers had an hour of peace and quiet, it was her pleasure. They could go to a class or an appointment by themselves. Take a shower. Go exercise in the fresh air. Read a magazine or a few chapters of a book. That was a big privilege in a busy noisy shelter. One filled with children the women were solely responsible for. No luxury of babysitters to hire, no grandparents to step in and help. But Mae was just a client herself after all. It wasn't her job. It was her generosity.

The kids were not easy. Some were hyper. Others skittish and withdrawn. They were extra needy, leery to leave their mothers alone without reassurance that the women would be okay. Their role as children had been compromised. Constantly on the defensive, the older children and teens could be extremely argumentative and dramatic. More so than average teenagedom. They were suspicious of everyone, other clients or counselors and staff talking to their mothers. It was risky for them to trust anyone. Understandable. Look what happened when their mothers had.

In those mother/child relationships gone awry, they blamed their mothers for taking them out of their homes, away from their friends and schools, hobbies and sports. They were angry and hurt. This was acted out constantly. Someone was always having a fit about something. There were extreme cases where an older teen had to be removed from the shelter. Sent off to a teenage facility in the area. A boy had started to behave as an abuser himself. Now there was danger within the safety zone. Unacceptable. Defeated the whole purpose of the shelter. The dynamics of the children were complicated.

Each child was special. Each needed to be saved. Staff did their best. Sometimes that was just not enough.

Little Martie was one of Mae's charges. She was a tough little challenge. She kept her distance from Mae and the other children, hanging around the edge of things. Looking into the playroom but not committing to join a game or a coloring fest. She avoided eye contact. Not unusual for a child who suffered or witnessed abuse. Martie was adorable. A real little angel. Tiny framed with wispy blonde hair and enormous blue eyes swimming with sadness. It slid across her sweet face, a shadow of fear, when you tried to catch her attention.

Her mother Rita was a nervous wreck. Reed thin with nails bitten down to the quick and thinning brittle hair from stress. She wore it drawn back in a loose ponytail. Her eyes popped at you when she spoke, darting sideways like a chameleon. A woman on constant alert. Shell shocked. When she laughed, and that was rare, it was a soft nervous laugh. As if someone might hear and punish her for it. Rita seemed to trust Mae. She would watch her with the kids in the playroom from the kitchen. Drink her coffee and stare into space every once in a while. Keeping one eye peeled on her little girl the whole time. Mae gave Rita a paint by numbers art kit. Unicorns on velvet. You'd have thought Mae had given her the world. She shared her chocolate bars with Mae. Rita was addicted to chocolate and cigarettes. She wasn't alone. Small vices considering. Simple pleasures.

The other clients kept their distance from Rita. She was too much work. She didn't share herself and came across as odd. She'd stand off to the side and smoke in silence, staring at the other clients. Indifferent to join their circle and commiserate. Was she shunning them, they were apt to wonder? She wasn't. Not intentionally. Mae could tell. Rita was just somewhere very distant in her mind. But the other women had their own problems. Chores to do. Dinners to prepare. Kids to mind. Court dates for visitation to dread. Rita was on her own if she couldn't engage. Tough luck. We all got troubles. You want to act weird, the day ain't long enough.

Mae couldn't be that way. She always had time for the underdog. The outcast. The abandoned. She knew if you went ahead and opened yourself up to people, they'd do the same eventually. Later you might be sorry you didn't walk away to begin with. Leave the people to their own torment. That was the risk of getting involved. Mae took it.

One day out in the small playground behind the shelter Rita started talking. Very unusual for her to initiate conversation. Mae gave her her undivided attention. *What could be worse than my own story?*

"Little girl over there," Rita said, pointing to little Martie, "She's a damn survivor, that's what." Mae looked over at Rita's daughter playing on the swings.

"He *cut* her. Cut my baby from stem to stern. Like he was gutting a deer for Christ's sake. She's got a scar on her little body from her chest down to her privates." Rita shivered. Mae wanted to scream. She swallowed hard and kept her eyes on Martie. Rita continued.

"Bastard told me he'd do something I'd remember if I ever tried to leave him. I thought I could outsmart him. Wasn't like he was no genius or nothing. He caught me packing. I was gonna leave. We didn't get out before he took her into the bedroom…."

Rita lit another cigarette and inhaled deeply waving to Martie who kept Rita in her sight at all times. "He wouldn't open the bedroom door. I called the cops. If you'd heard the way she screamed… my baby was screaming so loud. I still hear it in my head. That don't go away. I couldn't break the door down. Cops came fast. Wasn't the first time they'd been. Even they were shocked. There was so much blood. How she lived is a miracle. Or maybe it ain't. I don't know. Maybe it's my lesson. To always remind me to protect my baby first."

Mae drank her coffee and kept her eyes on the children. Rita went on. "The emergency room team was incredible. They knew time wasn't on my baby's side. The surgeon who sewed her up is a god to me. He wasted no time. It was hours before she came out of surgery. I blamed myself. That fucker was bad. But I let him in the house, didn't I? I saw him watching her. I had to watch her like a hawk when he was there. Imagine such a monster? Right under your nose and you don't see it at first."

Mae took the cigarette Rita offered her. She didn't smoke but under the circumstances she needed to do something. Breathe fire. She felt the urge to scream again. She smoked instead. *Keep it down, Mae.* She smoked and listened to Rita. Rita who never talked to anyone and who today would not shut the hell up.

"I'm reminded of my baby's horror every time I give her a bath. She didn't bother nobody. Why did I let it happen, let him into our lives? Not like he was her father. All for what? Love? That wasn't love. It's pathetic. I'm so ashamed. I know people here got their own stories. I just figured they couldn't be as horrible as mine and Martie's. I was ashamed to tell the other women. Doc knows. But she's Doc, ain't no judgement from her."

Horrible I'm familiar with, Rita. Horrible I know real well. Mae wanted to tell her that. She didn't. Rita had finally broken her silence. Shared her shame. God help her, Rita would never forgive herself for what happened to little Martie. Mae turned and looked into Rita's eyes. For a second she let Mae connect there without looking away.

"Know what's pathetic, hon?" Mae asked her. Rita shook her head. "These men who are supposed to love us. Protect us and love us. We love them with our trusting little girl hearts and they distort the whole thing and…" Mae now had Rita's rapt attention. It must have been the look on Mae's face and the way her voice changed from its usual soft tone. Mae wasn't known to go off on a rant like the others could.

Rita waited. Mae looked at Martie on the swings.

"I'll tell you what's horrible, hon. Fathers who have sex with their daughters. And mothers who look the other way." Mae crushed her cigarette under her sneaker and picked it up and put it in the ash can by the door.

Rita coughed. "Man. Sorry. I didn't mean to go on and on. I'm sorry about...well, I'm just sorry. We all got ghosts, huh? It ain't like my ghost is meaner than yours, right?" Rita looked like she was about to cry. Mae couldn't handle that. She had to push it back down her throat or she would scream and scream and never stop. She had to stay angry for the moment.

"Fuckers deserve to die. Your boyfriend. My father. You don't get to be redeemed after you harm little children. I don't care who believes otherwise. There's evil in this world. Martie's scar is proof of that. I need to go inside. Got some laundry to do." Mae started to turn away. Rita touched her arm.

"Can I say something? You're an angel. Like my Martie. You showed the world that they didn't get you. The bad ones. You help the children. Anyway, thanks for listening. I ain't got no friends here. Only you."

"No problem. I've been called a lot of things, Rita. Angel was never on the list."

Chapter Fourteen

Mae felt like crawling out of her skin. Little Martie's story had affected her. Brought back buried nightmares. Were they ever really buried? The shelter was closing in on her. It had gotten noisier in the last few weeks. A full house. And the language barrier among new and old clients was causing problems. The women at the end of their stays were resentful of the new client's refusal to follow the rules. They believed the newbies to be feigning ignorance at the posted rules. A conveniently uttered "I no understand," just wasn't cutting it. Tension was mounting.

The case worker and secretary both of whom spoke fluent Spanish worked day shifts. They were absent during the hectic dinner hour when the air got thick and patience ran thin. Kids home from school. Babies overtired. The witching hour. Television blaring and often inappropriate. Messes left in the kitchen with no one claiming responsibility. Bathrooms and bedrooms in disarray. Limited night staff were busy taking hotlines in the office and preparing materials for Night Group. Meanwhile, they were also running to supply closets to give out toiletries, diapers and grocery items. Running back to the office to answer calls, deal with an unexpected crisis, calls from the main shelter office and therapists and/or volunteers on their way to the shelter. They had to dole out and record medication to clients, which was kept locked in the office for good reason. At any time, back out in the house again to referee children or clients. Or both.

During Group, Mae was encouraged to talk about her feelings. Whatever was bothering her. Out with it, she would feel better, they told her. But she just didn't feel like sharing. Hard work baring your soul. Exhausting. Talk. Cry. Talk some more. Listen to other women talk. Hear them cry. Buzz words thrown around all over the place. My *abuser*. His *control*. Your *empowerment*. And the endless list of initials in the system. D.S.S., D.C.F., S.S., C.S.W. Section 8, WIC. The

Social Service agencies probably had a hard time remembering who did what for whom. In the end, for the clients it was a pure waiting game. B.S. is what they felt like yelling. Where's all the red tape around the bastard who put me here?

Mae was tired of all of it but her stay was almost over. Another client wasn't that lucky. Frustrated, the client broke a cardinal rule. Made a phone call to an ex- boyfriend and told him the location of the shelter. Clients were free to make outside calls on a pay phone inside the shelter with their own calling cards. Supposedly to talk to trusted girlfriends and family members. The calls were not monitored and maybe they should be. In some cases it was a dangerous privilege. In a weak moment after a particularly grueling day, a woman could forget. Develop temporary amnesia. Maybe she was sick of the curfews they had to adhere to in the shelter. Tired of being told what to do. After all they were grown women. And so very human. Forgiving. To a fault. No client ever came to the shelter after her first beating. Or slap, or shove or verbal battering or rape. It takes in some cases something like seven times before a woman leaves for good. Women just don't give up that easily. They are generous with their second chances. And their hearts.

One client met her ex out on the street a little distance from the shelter house. Apparently not far enough away since another client saw her get into a strange car with a man. The client was foolish. Careless. And shocked when she returned later that day and was told to pack her things. But there were no exceptions. She'd broken a major rule. A much needed one to protect all the women at the shelter. And the children. It was supposed to be secure at all times. Shelters are always a secret location. A safe house. A sanctuary. The client had compromised that. Her options were two. Leave and go wherever she chose or complete the remainder of the program in another D.V. shelter. She chose to be relocated. Mae felt sorry for her yet she knew she had to start thinking of herself first. Where would she end up?

Around this time, Rooney had opened a small haircutting salon in the Brownstone basement. A veritable cellar that she transformed with good old Southern elbow grease and a few sheet- rockers and painters, courtesy of Uncle Carmine. Rain had a full client load at her private practice and usual Group at the shelter. Someone who could cook and clean would be a dream come true. Before winding up in the shelter, Mae lived in an orphanage run by nuns. She knew quite well how to keep house. She also knew how to get along with others. The other boarders would love her.

While Mae moved into the Brownstone, Rain went back to planning an idea. Holding a Friday night Group at home. Women who were in limbo, in between fleeing their homes to a shelter and admitting they were living with domestic violence.

Rain had the day off and planned to relax for a change. Long overdue. It was busy days and nights lately. She was queen of her castle for a few hours at least. Everyone was out. Rooney had gone into the city for a hair expo at the Javits Center. Dory and Fiona were doing their usual shifts at the café. Mae had taken Shamus for his annual flea dip and was going to do the grocery shopping while she was out.

Rain poured herself another cup of coffee and headed for the back door. She grabbed her gardening gloves off the hall table then remembered the pruning shears were on the kitchen counter and went back for them. The front door clicked shut. Mae's home early. But she didn't hear Shamus. Or Mae for that matter. Maybe it was just the wind. Knowing Mae, she probably ran out quickly earlier and forgot to close the door properly. Rain turned around and walked down the hall towards the front door. Her gardening clogs made a squishy sound on the bare floor. She had an uneasy feeling all of a sudden. Silly. It was broad daylight. She shook her head at her foolishness and turned the dead bolt. There. Now she could get to her gardening. She walked back towards the kitchen. A low deep laugh stopped her in her tracks.

She held on to the banister and looked up the stairs towards the bedrooms. "Mae? You up there? If you think this is funny, it isn't." Silence. The Brownstone wasn't haunted though there's always that possibility with old houses. Henry was their Brownstone guardian, on the spirit level. He still spoke to Rain, but he would never scare her. There it was again. A low guttural laugh. Rain zoned in on the sound, her hackles rising. It came from the living room. Please let it be Uncle Carmine. I'll give him hell, elder or not. But he never just dropped by. And all his workers were long gone. Months ago. None of them were given keys. They all respected and feared Uncle Carmine, in a healthy way.

Rain looked around for something to grab. A weapon. By now she was convinced it was a stranger. Her pruning shears! She reached into her back pocket. Nothing. They were in the kitchen. She could run. Towards the front door. Or up the stairs. No, then she would be trapped. Back door? Too far away. *Move, Rain*, she chided herself.

He was in front of her now. The voice in her Brownstone. He took her by the hand into the living room. Pulled her with him. Like they were a couple late for a party he was anxious to attend. He urged her down on the couch while he took the chair in front of her, dragging it closer. His legs quickly twined around her. She was a corralled child. His eyes bore into her. They were dark. Black. Empty. He studied her. She suddenly knew those eyes. She broke eye contact and noticed the black tip of a gun sticking out of his jeans. He watched her watching him. He let her look him up and down, enjoying it. He was something women looked at. Maybe he got his jollies frightening the sheer hell out of people. Wolf in sheep's clothing. But he was no vagrant. No bum who happened upon an open door. Why the hell was he in *her* Brownstone? She wanted to scream but nothing came out of her dry throat. Who would hear her anyway? Neighbors were at work. Doors and windows closed nice and tight. Her mind started racing. *Are you going to let this wolf trap you? In your own Brownstone? Become another statistic? Use your brain,*

Rain. Oh that's rich. You're about to die and you're playing rhyming games.

"Hey! Pay attention. *Lorraine.*" He clapped his hands.

Rain looked at him. Her intruder was addressing her by her old name. How odd.

"Cat got your pretty tongue, Lorraine?" he said as sweet as pie but with a smoky harshness he couldn't remove if he tried. He smiled and lit a cigarette. Dragged deeply. Kept one hand on the gun handle. She knew if she moved it wouldn't do any good. Why was he calling her *Lorraine*? No one called her that anymore, except her parents and Uncle Carmine. And this is no friend of theirs. Did she know him? She thought hard. No, it can't be. Impossible. She refused to accept it. The reality of that was insane.

Talk, Rain. That's what you do for a living for Christ's sake. Talk to the man in your house. He can't be that bright if he robs people for a living.

"You need money?" Her voice was shaky. *Get a grip, Rain.* His eyes traveled up and down her body. Obviously he was in no hurry. To rob her. Or kill her. Or…. He stopped on her eyes. Smiled. He had nice teeth. *Better to eat you with….* She concentrated on his mouth. *Don't say my name again. You.*

"Where is she?" he growled. Mr. Mood Swing was obviously pissed. "Where's Mae?" *Growl.* "I heard you call her." That voice. It hit her between the eyes. Jarred her brain. The movie of her life on rewind. Was it the way he blew his smoke rings? But Mae? What could she be doing knowing the likes of him? Rain blinked, on purpose. His voice came at her again. Angry. Echoed in the big room.

"I know she lives here, and you know that I know." Big grin on his dangerous handsome face. Inappropriate. Diabolical. He might as well have had fangs. And he should have been ugly. Had a scar on his cheek or a broken nose at least. But not him. He knew how to survive. One step ahead all the time. *What we have here, Doc, is a macabre reunion.*

Welcome to the dark side. So much for your therapy- speak. You don't have a prayer with this one.

"Know what? Forget Mae," he said, soft spoken again. He touched her face. Bizarrely gentle. She started thinking how recently she had come to dislike the term full circle. Was that what this was? Victim of the wolves. Defender against the wolves. Now lone wolf comes calling. He sat back and watched her. He knew now that she *knew*.

Rain could hear the words again. *Lay down on the couch, Lorraine....* God help me, she thought.

"Sonny?" Her voice was small. Like a whisper. She moved back further in her seat on the couch. Could she make a fast turn and grab a heavy candle holder on the table behind her? He leaned forward, closer now as he spoke. She jumped like a skittish girl at his sudden move. This struck him as funny. He laughed. It sounded dirty.

"Surprised to see me?"

She nodded. He stroked her face with his long fingers. Nails like a woman's. Soft hands for a tough guy.

"How nice. *Hiss*. I know you remember me."

She started to shake her head no. He stopped her and breathed into her ear. His breath was hot. "Wanna play a game?"

Chapter Fifteen

Mae parked the car in front of the Brownstone. She laughed to herself. "Only in Brooklyn, Shamus, only in Brooklyn...." she said to the shiny clean dog beside her. Mrs. Rigaletti, their neighbor, was scrubbing the sidewalk with a push broom. Suds from her bucket splashed soapy water down the curb. The old woman looked up at Mae and kept scrubbing. She shook her head.

"Morte," she said to Mae, "Righta here, aghhh, terrible!" She pronounced it *te-ree-blay.*

"*Who's* dead?" Mae asked her, holding on to Shamus.

"Go inside, Mia, ask Doctor Raina, shea tell you... policia here, now everybody go away. Aghh, terrible...." She went back to her scrubbing.

Shamus was pulling toward the gate.

"Thanks, Mrs. Rigaletti. Gotta go. Okay, boy, let's go see Doc."

Mae ran up the stoop behind Shamus who was barking his head off. Not like Shamus. He barked for a reason. "Stop, that, boy. Doc's here, shhh...." Mae pushed open the unlocked door and unfastened Shamus's leash. He took off towards the living room, barking. "Easy now, boy, maybe Doc's resting." It was Doc's day off. She was entitled to some R&R, Mae thought. Why was the front door unlocked? Was that flute music? It was eerie.

"Doc?" Mae's voice carried in the large foyer. She walked towards the living room. The shades were down and it was dark except for the firelight. Doc was there in her robe sitting by the fireplace. She looked different. Not herself. Staring into space. Was she stoned? Not Doc. Mae walked over to her.

"Doc? Are you sick? What's with the music? You get into Rooney's stash?" Mae laughed. Rooney was known to roll a joint on occasion. Doc stared back at her. No response.

Mae noticed the empty glass in her hand. Was that whiskey she smelled? It sure wasn't wine.

"Zamphir. The greatest pan flutist you'll ever hear. Lonely Shepherd, so beautiful." She shook her glass at Mae. *Doc was drunk.* At this time of day? Alone? It made no sense. This was not Doc having a glass of wine before dinner. Something was wrong.

"Um, Mrs. Rigaletti is washing the sidewalk. She said somebody died? Police were here? Is she crazy or what?"

Mae hoped she would say: "*I've no idea. She's a crazy old cleaning nut. I've been gardening all day and felt like tying one on, that's all.*"

Doc stared back at her. Looked into her empty glass and hit the stereo remote. The same eerie song came on again.

"You're scaring me, hon. Please tell me, what's wrong?"

"Let's not talk. Let's drink." Doc held out her glass.

Mae got the chills. "Did someone come here? Was it one of the wacko men of one of your clients? Did you get bad news? The groomers took their sweet time with Shamus and then the line at the grocery was... anyway I should have been home hours ago...what *is* it? Who was here? Please talk." *Something very bad happened in this Brownstone today. And it was still lingering.*

"I... never mind..." It was an effort to speak. So Rain didn't bother trying. Mae's eyes were wild. Frantic.

"Oh God. Someone hurt you, didn't they? Oh God, hon..." Mae started to bawl. "Not you..."

The girl was way too emotional. Rain hadn't said a word yet. She looked down into her empty glass. *That sweet ole Southern Comfort in my soul...* She shook her last ice cube around. Held up her glass. *Stop the damn crying, girl. Please.* Rain waited. Licked her chapped lips. Mae stopped bawling. *Good girl. Give the Doc a drink. Good girl.*

Mae took the glass and walked over to the dry sink. She came back with two half full snifters of bourbon. Not too many rocks. *Smart girl.* She placed the glass in Doc's waiting hand and sat down in the other fireside chair. Doc's legs were crossed and she swung one back and forth nervously. Rain swallowed a generous mouthful of the delicious elixir and cleared her throat. "Sonny was here today." Rain drank again. Played with a string on her bathrobe. Where were her clothes? *You have to stay naked for me, Lorraine. Remember the game?*

"What? What do you mean? *Here*? Why? He can't know where I am. Please don't tell me that. I'll kill him. Where is he now? Did *you* kill him? Good. He deserves to die. How dare he come here. What was he thinking? He doesn't think of course, he just takes. Hurts people and takes. Damn him to hell, filthy bastard. The utter nerve of him, imagine him…"

Mae was going on at a pace. Silly girl was ruining Rain's drunk. She turned up Zamphir. That's better. Nice. Soothing. Mae was sniffling now. Rain was not able for her tears.

"Stop it," Rain said quietly, but sternly. "Drink up and get it together. He's dead. You're right, his being dead is a good thing. And I can imagine only too well. You have no idea."

Mae looked at her. Rain shook a cigarette out of the open pack of Marlboros on the side table. She ceremoniously lit it and blew out a thin stream of smoke. It curled up the chimney. A look of shock came over Mae's face.

"You don't smoke."

Sweet Mae. As if she was reminding Rain of an important fact she had forgotten. Rain continued to smoke, enjoying her discarded habit.

"I do now. Be still for a moment. Drink. Have a smoke. I'll give you the blow by blow in a minute." Rain threw her head back and laughed. "Poor choice of words, under the circumstances…" The poor girl looked horrified. Oh great, she was going to talk again. Damn her.

"I should have been here. He wanted *me*. He'll burn in hell for this. It's my fault. I'm so sorry. I want to die."

103

"That's nice. A bit over the top though. Actually Sonny was delighted to find *me* home. Let me explain… give you the gory details. Shhh, now, Shamus. I know, boy, you can smell the devil on me, can't you? Could you give Shamus his dinner? I'll wait right here. Go with Mae, love." Shamus wouldn't budge. He would not leave Rain's side.

"He won't come with me, hon. It's no use." She sat down again.

"Never mind then, I'll feed him in a bit. I *knew* Sonny. Yes, your Sonny. Years ago. And he knew me. Imagine his lucky surprise today. He found out you lived here somehow. Must have been following you for awhile. He is cunning."

Mae shook her head. Poor tortured thing.

"I know, I know, you didn't give him our address. Relax." If she shook her head back and forth anymore it would fall off. "It's okay, I believe you. He told me he followed you for weeks. You had no idea. He likes his games, our Sonny."

Mae grimaced. *What the hell was Doc talking about?*

"He's not *mine* anymore." *And he's certainly not yours*. Mae looked at Rain strangely.

Rain took another belt of bourbon. "He raped me."

Mae gasped. Rain drank some more.

"It was a reenactment of a scene in his garage back in the day. Only this time he indulged his full fantasy." Rain rubbed her jaw. Drank some more. It burned her throat. She liked that she could feel it. "Afterwards, he shot himself. In the head. Bang. Just like in the movies. Right on Mrs. Rigaletti's sidewalk. I watched his life bleed out onto the cement. But I'm getting ahead of myself…." Rain sipped at her bourbon and lit another cigarette. She was Bette Davis in the four-thirty movie. "Where was I? Oh yes, we spent the afternoon in bed. The guest room. For obvious reasons, I told him it was my room. He liked that." Rain smoked like Bette would. Hard and purposefully, without the red lipstick.

Mae's face was priceless. Poor Mae. She was horrified. Rain's behavior must have seemed off the wall. Rain was being cruel. She knew better. She was a therapist, for crying out loud. They all depended on her. Well how *does* one act when they've been violated? Emily Post, any ideas? Martha? You were in jail. Get anything funny up your hooch? *And today we're baking large zucchini up the hooch cake.*

Poor Mae. She couldn't handle it. Tears fell down her cheeks. She reached for the Marlboros, stopped and looked up at Rain for approval. She seemed reluctant to touch the pack. Dirty cigarettes. Smokes of the damned.

"Are you kidding? Go ahead, Mae. At the very least, we can smoke his damn cigarettes. He doesn't need them where he is." Rain leaned back in her chair and inhaled deeply.

Mae smoked in silence. She was trying to figure out what to say. Rain could see her mind working. Mae hadn't seen this side of Doc before. Hell, neither had Doc. She wasn't proud of herself, but Mae would have to deal with it. *Forgive me, Mae. All my orifices are sore and I'm piss drunk. Isn't that what the IRA call it? "Doc's pissed," they'd say if they were here. "A right piss-up she had for herself."*

"Doc? Should I call someone? The police were already here, I take it? You should go to the hospital, shouldn't you? Why didn't they take you? He didn't hit you, did he? I mean I don't see any bruises."

Of course you don't, Mae. Now if my cunt could talk....

"Shhh. I'm fine. Call me hon, like you always do. Know what Sonny calls me? Lorraine." *Kiss me, Lorraine. I won this game, Lorraine. I always win."*

Rain held her glass up to the firelight. She swirled the amber liquid around and took the last swallow. She flung the empty snifter into the fireplace, where it crashed against the bricks and fell into the fire.

Mae was in shock. Poor Mae. Poor Rain. The Doc is out. They sat quietly in the firelight as darkness descended on the Brownstone. Mae came over and put her arms around Rain. Rocked her like a baby. Cried for her. After a minute or so, she helped Rain out of the chair and they walked together, Rain leaning on her, into the kitchen with Shamus leading the way.

Mae turned on the lamp above the table and settled Doc in a chair. Covered her with a blanket she'd brought from the living room. She clicked the other lamp on the counter on. She knew Doc hated overhead lighting. Too harsh. Cold. She lit a fire in the kitchen hearth. Put the kettle on and fed Shamus. Dear Mae. Their little Brownstone mommy. How ironic, after all. Rain watched her, thinking how lucky they all were to have Mae.

Sonny wasn't Mae's fault. She'd suffered at his hands, badly. Doc knew it better than anyone. Mae's story was beyond a nightmare. And part of that nightmare was dead.

Rain let Mae carry her tea and help her walk up the back stairs to her bedroom. Mae knew Doc wouldn't want to pass the guest room. She propped up the pillows for her and went inside to run Doc a bath. Shamus was on the bed, never leaving Doc's side for a minute. Rain rubbed his back. Mae helped her out of her robe and eased her into the tub. Mae closed the bathroom door halfway. "I don't want you passing out in the tub, hon. You've had a lot to drink."

Rain nodded. "Thank you. I'm sorry."

"No. You have nothing to be sorry about. Just soak. Think of angels on the wall and nothing else. I love you, Doc."

Rain sipped her tea. Shamus stood guard beside the bathtub. She sunk the soap with her toe. It sprung back up again. Ivory Soap. Mae's favorite. Mae and her soap and her angels. Good Mae. Rain smiled as the tears fell. Raining in the bath. *You're okay, Rain. You will be okay*. The wolf has gone to slaughter. Zamphir played on; she could hear the flute faintly from downstairs. She sank down and let the water cover her head. *That's you, Rain, The Lonely Shepherd.*

Chapter Sixteen

Mae lit a candle in her bedroom and got undressed. She lay in bed fingering the scar on the inside of her wrist. She had cut herself on purpose. Sonny told her to. At the orphanage. She remembered the day he arrived.

Sonny sauntered up the brick stoop of the Sisters Of Perpetual Mercy Orphanage, hit the doorbell with the back of his hand and lit a Marlboro. Mae watched him from the living room window seat. She was hidden behind the heavy drapes, chewing her oatmeal raisin cookie thoughtfully, savoring each bite. *He's like James Dean. Only darker. Cool. Aloof. Bad.* His full lips mesmerized her. The way he dragged on his cigarette, he made it look like a sin. Mae was way out of her league.

Sister Devora heard the front bell ring. She walked briskly down the long hallway. *Must not keep Monsignor waiting.* Monsignor liked his tea served on time. He could be very persnickety if he didn't have a cookie in his gob by tea time. Sister Devora needed his support to keep the orphanage going, so she aimed to please him whenever she could. She adjusted her veil and smoothed down the front of her habit. *Thank goodness Sister Beatrice baked her oatmeal cookies this morning.*

To Sister's surprise, Monsignor was not her caller at all. *Well well, Devora, what do we have here?* She looked at the young man on her doorstep. *Perhaps he's lost, Devora.* She gave him a cautious smile. He glared back at her. *The epitome of the angry young man is it?* His surly dark eyes moved up and down Sister's body in a most uncomfortable way. *I haven't felt that kind of sexual arrogance in years, God forgive me the thought.* Sister Devora mentally blessed herself. *Memory has so much to do with the flesh and so little to do with the soul, Devora.*

The young man continued to puff away on his cigarette while he studied her. Unbeknownst to Sister, Mae's eyes were riveted to the visitor at the front door. If this was a stare-down, this guy has met his match. Sister never lost one yet. Endless patience was her strength. He'd surely blink first.

Sister Devora let him finish his cigarette before she spoke. The aroma of smoke surrounded her and she inhaled remembering a time long ago when she enjoyed a good smoke. Sister extended her hand to the young man who flicked his butt into the gutter without so much as a glance behind him. *Impressive.* But Sister didn't let on. She had an excellent poker face. Another vice Sister hadn't thought of in years.

"Good afternoon, how can I help you?" she addressed the man-child before her. This one's tough, she thought. She kept her cool. Mustn't be harsh or hasty. "I'm Sister Devora. The director of the orphanage. And you are?" A cold stare is all she got back. Manners were in short supply these days, Sister thought. A generation lacking in grace among other virtues.

"Sonny." A voice filled with sex and smoke.

God help me. Sister's radar was going off in loud alarms.

"I'm here for the job. I saw the ad in the paper…" He was looking at her as if she were slightly off her head.

Think, Devora, think. The ad. Oh dear. Her own doing. She desperately needed a handyman since the demise of the last one who died of old age on the job. The parish had not come up with a replacement since. Sister could wait no more. She wondered when the young man last saw the inside of a barber shop. She could whack off a good four inches of hair without a second glance. That mop will need tying back if he intends keeping that style, she thought.

"Have you had much experience, Sonny?" *Oh Lord, Devora, that was a loaded question. You're out of practice.*

Sonny licked his lips in response and jammed his hands into the front pockets of his rather fitted jeans. "Yeah, Sister, you could say that…." I wonder what she's hiding under that getup? *Love to get my hands under those rosaries, show you where heaven's really at.* She wasn't bad looking for an older lady. The outfit wasn't exactly a turn-on. Bet she's a natural redhead. *Bet you're no stranger to a hot night, huh, Sister? The priests show you a good time? Like they did my mother. Boy, Ma could moan like a cat when Father Fingers was giving it to her. Eat your cookies, Sonny. Mommy will be right out. Father is hearing my confession.* Yeah, right. And pumping you full of redemption. *Whore.*

He's trying to charm me, Sister thought. Seduce me, if I didn't know better. Which I do, God forgive me. A dose of hard work will keep his idle mind busy. And he wouldn't charge too much, she imagined. Sister saw no work van parked on the street. So he worked alone. Fine. Get him to do the work cheap and get rid of him fast. Too much temptation about.

"So there's painting in the kitchen to be done, Sonny. Cabinets and the like. Some floors need sanding. And the basement is very damp and could use new insulation. Can you handle that, son?"

"Yep. No problem." *I ain't your son.* "I do it all. Won't charge you an arm and a leg either. Go ahead and get another price for the job after I give you my estimate. Guaranteed mine's the better price. I got referrals if you need one." Sonny knew he sounded confident. The nun would hire him, no doubt. He hadn't lost his touch. Women couldn't resist him. "Can I come in, Sister? Take a look at what you want done? Then I'll let you get back to your holy work."

Sister Devora nodded and was about to push back the door when Sonny's attention moved from her towards the front window. Sister followed his gaze. There as bold as brass, was Mae. Precisely what I was worried about, Sister thought. Better nip this in the bud. "Right. Yes, Sonny. Do come in," Sister said, raising her voice a good octave.

"I must let you know that we run a very strict school here. I forbid any contact with our students, you understand. They are all in classes now of course, where they *belong*. Or studying in the library. So you won't see any of them. But in

109

future, keep in mind, no contact. And they will know to stay out of your way."

Mae froze behind the curtain until Sister and her new handyman were out of sight. She hightailed it from the room and back up to the library. She had been on a library assignment an hour ago when she snuck down to the kitchen for a snack while the Sister on kitchen duty was in the chapel. She knew there were cookies baking earlier. Mae could smell them. She had a mad sweet tooth.

Sister Devora would have words with her later. But it had been worth it. Mae recalled the way the guy at the door looked at her. The way he licked his lips. She imagined feeling them on her skin. Mae felt her cheeks go hot at the thought of him. She buried her nose in the library book she grabbed off the shelf and started to read.

Sister Devora led the new young handyman out towards the front door. She was relieved Mae had the sense to get back to class. "Now Sonny, you can come back tomorrow morning. Start anywhere you like. May I suggest the basement, as it is the biggest project. Again, I must stress that you mind my rules. And I will see the children do not bother you. Do work up an estimate for me so I can look it over."

"No problem, Sister. You're the boss."

Sister Devora found his obedience a tad bit condescending. His tone. Those eyes. Trouble. *Oh Devora, perhaps this is a mistake.*

"I'll be a good boy, don't worry, Sister. I need the work." Sonny smiled his sweetest smile.

A mind reader, was he? Sister sighed. A choirboy he's not, she thought. But for now he would have to do. He was within Sister's budget. She would watch him like a hawk. And Mae too. Wasn't Mae just the most brazen girl in the window earlier? Sister Devora gathered herself.

"Yes. Very well then. I'll look forward to seeing you in the morning, Sonny."

You do that Sister. Have a nice little dream about me tonight. Bet you'd like that. Sonny stifled a laugh. This one's no virgin. She came late to the nunnery. I'd bet money on it. *Like a good poke in the whiskers, Sister?*

"Well, thanks for coming by, Sonny." Sister Devora looked at her watch. "Almost time for afternoon prayers."

Sonny stuck a Marlboro between his lips and stepped down a step on the stoop. "No problem, Sister. Say a prayer for me." Sonny turned around and walked out of the gate whistling an old hymn his mother would sing after the priest left. "Oh come, oh come, Emmanuel…."

Chapter Seventeen

Mae West was the oldest of a dozen discarded children who lived with the good Sisters of Perpetual Mercy. She was sixteen and had spent most of her young life behind the convent walls. Sheltered from the big city outside, Mae attended classes the Sisters taught inside the orphanage, thus she remained an innocent. Her size added to the effect. Mae was a tiny wisp of a girl with enormous brown eyes the color of espresso and a shiny jet black pixie haircut. Dubbed "little elf," by Sister Devora, she was the Sisters' favorite. A pleasing little thing who never gave any of them a lick of trouble. Mae hoped that Sister would remember that tonight and forgive her the small transgression of snooping at the window during study hour.

Mae smelled roast beef cooking when she found her way back downstairs near supper time. She knew she'd better get to her chore of peeling potatoes before Sister decided it was time for a discussion. Mae set the potatoes in a large pot of water and turned on the stove. She hurried into the big dining room and lifted a stack of plates off the sideboard. She felt the angels watching her as she passed the mural on the wall. It was her favorite room. She counted out napkins and made sure the silverware was spotless. Sister would be proud of her. She looked at the clock. Five-thirty. A half hour until supper. The "banquet of megrims," Sister Devora called it. Mae wasn't sure what that meant. Only that Sister always smiled wistfully when she said it. "Something like a table of sadness, Mae," Sister had explained. Mae understood sadness. She had been sad for as long as she could remember.

Mae was five years old when her mother dropped her off at the Sisters. She didn't shed a tear. Nor did she cling to her mother's leg. What was the point? Her mother hadn't come to her rescue before. Not each night when Mae cried softly in her bed. Not when Mae asked her if she could tuck her in instead of her father. Her mother was too busy running to the store to buy that awful smelling whiskey her father liked. And more bars of that horrible perfumy Cashmere Bouquet soap Mae hated. Her mother would scrub her down every morning until her skin was practically raw. *God washes away our sins, Mae. We have to be clean for Him.*

Why didn't God know what she had to do every night with her father? There wasn't enough soap in the world to wash that away. Mae couldn't say that to her mother. She might never come home from the store. Mae said nothing. In fact she didn't speak at all when her mother took her to the good Sisters. She just listened. To her mother asking Sister Devora's forgiveness for giving her child away. To her mother saying "I'm sorry, Mae," as she walked out of the orphanage forever.

Mae felt safe at the orphanage for the first time in her small life. The Sisters let her eat pastina for breakfast instead of the lumpy oatmeal her mother force fed her. At night she was given her very own nightlight. She could burn it the entire night never fearing the dark again. Never dreading the sound of drunken footsteps on a creaking wooden floor.

The Sisters gave her bars of Ivory Soap. Mae loved the clean fresh smell. Like the Sisters themselves. Mae could play in the bathtub with her floating boat of pure white and dream of angels protecting her. The angels painted on the Sisters dining room wall. Mae pretended she was Madeline from her favorite storybook. And Sister Devora was much kinder than Miss Clavel. Soon Mae was ready to talk. Sister Devora taught her prayers and old folk songs. The other Sisters let her help with household chores. She was so eager to please them. These holy women didn't think Mae needed to be cleansed of her sins. They just loved her. She didn't know it, but the Sisters all thought it a miracle how she came out of her shell. The day little Mae laughed out loud was a day for rejoicing. Everyone had chocolate cake for dessert in Mae's honor. Sister Devora was nearly brought to tears at the sight of Mae's beaming face full of chocolate frosting. But that was all before Sonny.

113

Sonny did his jobs around the orphanage. He fixed everything that was broken and offered to do more work without pay. He kept his distance from the children as he promised. He was determined to have Sister Devora trust him. He didn't move a muscle in the wrong direction. He didn't have to.

Mae made it easy for him. She sought him out. Followed him around without Sister noticing. Mae was very good at hiding. She used to hide from her father. But he found all her hiding spots. Sonny knew she was there. He didn't let on. That made Mae more determined. She wanted him to notice her. Find her. Hidden under the basement stairs, she would watch him nailing sheetrock. Or wiping his sweaty brow. Or smoking a cigarette. To Mae it was all a harmless game. A child's game. Except Mae was no longer a child.

Sonny could smell her. Ivory Soap. Pure and innocent. So ready for him to teach her. He had to be careful. This one was special to the boss. And that made her all the more a prize. One day he had his chance. Mae came walking into the kitchen as he worked on the cabinets. He pretended not to see her as she plainly sat in his line of vision at the table eating her sandwich.

Mae watched him. He could feel her big eyes on his back as he painted. He said nothing to her. Maybe Sister was watching him. Mae told him everyone was out. On a field trip. Including Sister Devora. Only Sister Beatrice was left behind with Mae. And she was in chapel. Mae was supposed to be confined to her room with a head cold. Sister Beatrice would bring her soup after prayers. Mae was hungry now and Sister's prayers were taking too long. Mae counted the bells ringing in the courtyard. Sister had a lot more prayers to go.

Sonny went down the basement stairs to get more paint. Mae followed him. She went to her spot under the stairs. Sonny came over to her. He touched her hair. Her face. He held out his hand. She took it. He gently ran his hands over her pajamas. Mae liked the way it felt. Sonny smelled

114

like paint. Not whiskey. He asked her if she wanted to touch him. She said no. He didn't force her. Mae liked that best.

She met Sonny in the basement under the stairs whenever she could. When it was safe. He didn't ask her to touch him again. He just touched her each time. Sonny seemed to like touching her. He was very gentle. Mae felt good every time she met him under the stairs. The next time she was ready to touch him. He kissed her on the lips. Told her she was doing it nicely. Mae wondered why he didn't force her to do other things. But he didn't. So Mae kept returning to the basement. She had a new friend and he was making her feel special. Like the day he asked Mae to cut her wrist with him. They rubbed them together and Sonny put Band-Aids on both of them. He told her they were going to be together forever. Mae liked that idea. Sister Devora wouldn't always be there. That was okay. Now she had Sonny.

Chapter Eighteen

Mae spent two more years with the good Sisters. At eighteen she was ready to tackle life on her own. Sister Devora suggested an all girls Catholic college upstate. Mae flatly refused. She felt as blessed and studious as she needed to be. No more prayers or textbooks. What interested Mae was some breathing room. Experience. A life out among the people. The big city. She knew Sister loved her and meant well. She loved Sister too. But sometimes love could smother you.

Sister Devora understood Mae's need to spread her wings. Still she worried about her little Mae out beyond the cloistered life of the orphanage. Sister Devora had spent a good few years on the outside herself. Long before finding her sanctuary with God and her calling to help the children who needed her. *Perhaps Devora, you could use your influence and Mae would be safe.* A phone call to Sister's widowed cousin in Greenwich Village would do the trick nicely. To Sister's relief, Mae agreed to the arrangement. She would board with Sister Devora's cousin. The rent would be minimal. Mae could do the grocery shopping and help with the cleaning. Mostly the old woman was lonely and loved to cook and fuss over someone. She wouldn't impose on Mae for anything, Sister promised. Certainly she would mind her business where Mae's social life was concerned. Sister Devora laid it all out for her, and Mae was grateful. She had no other plan except to leave the orphanage. Why not give Sister's idea a shot?

Sister Devora handed her an envelope she removed from her office safe. Mae opened the old tattered flap and found a substantial sum of money inside. There was a small note wrapped around the money.

For your freedom, Mae. Forgive me my weakness. You did no wrong, child. I did what I thought best bringing

116

you to the Sisters. I'm sorry I waited so long. Be happy. Don't let us have taken that from you too. Mommy

Mae folded the note and looked up at Sister Devora who sat quietly at her desk. Sister saw no sign of tears. She knew none would come. Mae had given up on her mother a long time ago.

Mae smiled warmly at Sister Devora. The woman in front of her was her real mother as far as Mae was concerned. Her protector. Her champion. Her teacher. Her soft place to fall. Mae's life began when she came to Sister Devora's house, as Mae liked to call the orphanage. It had been her home and she never felt misfortunate to live there. She felt lucky. She had lived among angels. Sister Devora had sung to her each night and combed her hair. The other Sisters baked her favorite treats. That was the childhood Mae would choose to remember.

Grownup Mae was in the mood for celebration. The money left to her would come in handy. Fashionable clothes for her curvy new figure. Make-up. Mae hadn't had those luxuries at the orphanage. She would indulge in the latest bestsellers. Mae loved books. Now she could buy them all at once. Why not be good to herself? The money was for her after all. Her mother's guilty conscience money. Fine. Mae earned every penny. *No, I don't forgive you, Mommy. You can't buy back what you stole. My innocence. My trust. I was your little Mae.*

Sister thought Mae had the oddest expression on her face. "Something on your mind, Mae?" *That, Devora, is quite the understatement.*

Mae smiled an angelic smile. "Just thinking how much chocolate I could buy." Mae's eyes were wide as she held up the wad of bills. "Hmm, Sister?"

"Well, yes, I suppose you could. However I know you'll spend it wisely. Save for a rainy day and all that," Sister Devora smiled. "Ah, a wee dose of chocolate now and again never hurt anyone."

Mae laughed. "What I am going to do is buy all the Sisters something beautiful. A new couch. A painting. A television that actually works. New pots and pans for Sister Beatrice. Wouldn't she love that? One of those fancy mixers for her breads. New shoes. Yours look very worn out, Sister. Oh, and toys and pajamas for the children. And new slippers. Brand new books. Instead of those used ones. Let's see what else…."

"Slow down. You're making me dizzy. It's all very generous of you, but that money was meant for *your* future. I promised your mother."

"Well promises are broken every day. I'm sure she promised *me* when I was born that she would protect me. So I wouldn't worry about any loyalty to her."

Sister didn't like this tone in Mae. It was harsh. Bitter. Very out of character. Maybe she should have destroyed the note and just given her the cash. Still, the girl had a right to her opinion, Sister thought. Lord knows Mae was a helpless wee victim of a horrendous sin. The ugliest of all. But Sister believed in forgiveness. For the victim's sake, to keep the heart open and let in the light. Bless Mae for wanting to give her money to the Sisters and the children. She was not a hardened heart, thank God. But Mae would always want to please, God help her.

That was exactly what Sister was worried about regarding Mae's leaving. She wouldn't be there to protect her. But what could she hope for? That Mae would join the Order and remain at Perpetual Mercy forever? *Yes, Devora, that's exactly what you'd like. That your little elf never be harmed again. Was that so wrong?*

"Sister? Are you daydreaming? Please don't refuse my gifts. I want to give something back. There's plenty of money to save for later."

"Right, dear, okay. Books for the children. Sister Beatrice would be over the moon with a new set of pots. Year of the Flood, her old ones."

"And a TV and couch. And new shoes for you. No argument, please. One more thing, a case of Ivory Soap." Mae was grinning from ear to ear, quite enjoying her new role as Santa Claus.

"Soap? You know we get our regular soap delivery. But thank you anyway." *God, you better keep her safe.*

"The soap is for me. I want to make sure I always have my Ivory Soap. You were the first to give me my very own bar. I'll never forget that. Or you for..." Mae swallowed hard. How was she going to walk out of Sister's life? She had been the one constant for her. The pure loving kindness that Mae craved before she came to the Sisters. The world was a scary place. But Mae was ready to tackle it. She had to have her chance. Sister Devora would be here if she needed her.

"Oh, dear, how I'm going to miss you. You are the light of my life." Sister was crying. Poor Sister Devora. Her heart was breaking.

"Thank you," Mae managed. That was what she would remember most. Being worth something to somebody. Knowing she mattered.

"I love you, my little elf," Sister said, coming around the desk to throw her arms around Mae.

Mae laughed. "I love you, too. Thank you for everything. For saving me. For loving me. For giving me a nightlight. And most of all for letting me be a child again." Mae leaned into Sister's chest and sobbed like a baby. She had saved up all her tears in her own private cloud. Today it rained for Mae alone.

I would light the very sun in the sky for you Mae if I could, to take away your nightmares. Erase what was done to you, child. "You cry, Mae. It will always be the happiest day of my life the day you came to me. And the saddest when you leave."

119

Chapter Nineteen

Mae was enjoying the warm spring day as she strolled along Fifth Avenue. She never stayed indoors on her lunch break from Saks. Years spent inside the orphanage left her hungry for the sky. It didn't matter if the day was cloudy. As long as Mae could be outside she was happy. It had more to do with freedom than the outdoors. She had hardly been deprived of fresh air at the orphanage. There were field trips to museums and zoos and botanical gardens, and daily backyard play with the other children. Mae knew how to throw a ball and she built her share of snowmen with the Sisters. On sticky summer days she had run under a sprinkler that drenched her and the other squealing orphans running around on the wet concrete. She hadn't been a prisoner by any means. Yet there was confinement. Seclusion. And of course, religion.

Now she was finally free to go and do as she pleased. No rules, only her own. No chaperones, no afternoon prayers. No afternoon chocolate cookies either. You can't have everything. She could make her own cookies if she wanted homemade. Or ask Sister Devora's cousin to bake some for her. Her elderly roommate loved to cook and she adored Mae. Miss Dee was just happy for the company. She cooked a feast every night hoping Mae would never leave. Just like Sister Devora had wished.

Mae liked Dee's cozy warm apartment. Dee was a dead ringer for Sister Devora. A natural born nurturer too. Mae did long for a bit more privacy, if she had to tell the truth. Not that she ever had it. You can't miss what you never had. She considered moving into her own place. But what would she tell Dee? The old woman needed her. Or is it me who needs her? Mae wondered. Maybe I don't really want to be alone? *A big girl like you still afraid of the dark? Shh, little Mae, daddy will keep you company...* Mae shook her head and picked up her pace down the bustling street.

The buzz of the city excited Mae. She was like a tourist in Manhattan every day. She got drunk on the electricity. The busy vibe. The smells of the different foods, the noise of the traffic, the hurried pace, the preoccupied expression on people's faces. When they weren't looking down at their cell phones or gesticulating into the air like mental patients. Mae supposed some of them actually were. Everyone was in a hurry, racing along en masse like an unhappy parade. One direction or the other. Choose quickly or get sucked along with the crowd. Rush hour? Every minute was a rush here. Mae never rushed. Her co-workers called her "snail girl." Mae didn't take offense. How could she argue with the truth? No one had to remind Mae to live in the moment. Her moments were huge. Now she had a whole hour to herself. Among hordes of people. If she walked for forty minutes she could still enjoy a yogurt and cup of coffee and be refreshed for the rest of the work day. She stopped to browse in a bookstore window and thought about the children at the orphanage. Mae sent them books every month. Sister Devora told her they had so many that she had to request Monsignor hire someone to build more bookshelves.

"You can never have too many books, Sister," Mae told her.

"Hey there, beautiful," a man sitting on a bench near the street called out in a loud voice. Mae could see his reflection in the window. He caught her eye and waved at her. He can't be talking to me, Mae thought. She continued looking at the books on display and ignored him. The city was full of kooks.

"Hey, beautiful, yeah I'm talking to you in the red skirt."

Mae felt herself blush. How cheeky, as Sister Devora would say. And no manners, obviously. Talk to my back, Mae thought. *Buzz off.* She decided to go inside the bookstore. Maybe he'd be gone by the time she came out. She took out a list of books she had jotted down from the Book Review in the Sunday Times. She had her hand on the door when she felt someone very close behind her. Too close for comfort. Mae caught a glimpse over her shoulder. Him. Bench boy. Damn. *Get away, jerk.* I'll elbow this clown right in his solar plexus and he'll think twice about harassing people, Mae thought. She was going into her warrior mode. A girl can't be too careful in a big city. She was inside the bookstore now, safe.

Mae didn't feel him behind her any longer. Good. She breathed a sigh of relief and started perusing the New Fiction. She looked down and saw a pair of work boots moving closer to her. She let her gaze move up the boots and jeans. She turned sideways. There he was again. Persistent. I'll move away quickly, she thought. He was not taking the hint. Mae studied the book titles. She chose one to look over.

Bench boy was studying her. Mae was getting annoyed. She snuck a look at him. He didn't look like a bum. Or a psycho. What do psychos look like? Maybe he was a druggie. Or one of those internet porn weirdos looking for a victim. Oh Mae, you are a drama queen, she thought. Maybe he's just a regular guy who thinks you're cute. Could be he's killing time on his lunch hour too. Now she knew why she didn't date much. Much, hah! At all was more like it. Maybe she should have become a nun. Oh, no, bench boy wasn't exactly looking at her so much as her breasts. What nerve. *Okay, weirdo, take a hike.* Mae held the book against her chest and moved down to the next display.

He was still standing there watching her, his legs crossed, leaning against a table of books like he owned the place. He held a bestseller in his hands. As if. He was devouring *her* instead.

To hell with this, she thought. She looked straight at him, ready to tell him off. *What's your story, bench boy? Looking for trouble probably.* He was good looking, no doubt. Not Wall Street. More like the Village. But straight. Definitely straight. Hardly lacking for dates, so what was this? His pick-up deal? His jollies? Or was he a psycho serial killer on the prowl? Now you're being dramatic, Mae, she thought. You spend too much time with old people and kids. Maybe you should just be flattered. Or maybe he is a stalker after all. Bench boy was talking to her. Oh God, breathe, Mae.

"Excuse me?" Mae said, her hands were shaking.

"I said, do you wanna dance?" He put the book down and leaned back, both hands on the stack of bestsellers behind him. He casually ran a hand through his long brown hair. It fell in shiny waves to his worn leather jacket. *Dance?* Was that the current line these days? Mae wouldn't know a line from a tomato. Okay, Village boy, did you fall out of the Romance section? Gorgeous men don't approach you in bookstores. Maybe he escaped from an asylum. Bellevue was in the city. He's escaped, that's it. *Walk away, Mae. Now.* He was still grinning at her. *Help.*

She was about to tell him to go somewhere and dance with himself and not exactly in those words. She took a second look at his face. Studied him right back. A huge shift occurred. Her smile reached her toes. She was struck mute.

"Cat got that gorgeous tongue of yours?" he said.

Oh my God. Mae thought she might faint. Talk more, Village boy, she pleaded mentally, while she gathered herself.

"You are one hot looking chick. I saw you walking down the street. When you stopped I got a real good look. Long time no see, Mae."

No way. Could it be? "Sonny?"

"In the flesh." He moved closer.

"I knew I'd see you again. I prayed every night at the orphanage." Mae was embarrassing herself but she did not care.

"On your knees, I bet," he said.

Mae blushed. She couldn't stop smiling.

"Still a sweet little thing, aren't you? And *may* I say you've filled out in all the right places. Wow. Hey, don't be embarrassed, women pay a lot of money to get that kind of body. You're hot."

Mae would normally feel very uncomfortable with that kind of talk. But right now she was so happy. Sonny had returned to her. She couldn't care less if he went on and on.

"So you didn't forget me. How long has it been, little Mae?"

"I left the orphanage five years ago. When I turned eighteen."

He smirked. Not exactly what he meant. *Careful, Sonny. Timing.*

"A lady of independence, huh? Got a boyfriend?" He bet not. Nuns, that was the extent of Mae's social life.

"I've been kind of busy. Working and going to school at night and doing some volunteer work with kids on the weekends. I don't have much time to date."

"You're like a real live saint, aren't you? You probably could've become one of those nuns you lived with. What a waste."

Mae laughed. "No. Even I'm not *that* good." She blushed again. He had that effect on her. "I mean…well you know what I mean. Not perfect. Besides I liked…."

"What did you like, Mae? S-E-X?" he whispered. "Is that what you were gonna say?"

Sonny was so close to her she was getting dizzy. She could smell him. Not paint like she remembered. Mae had an excellent sensory memory. Sometimes she could still smell that awful Cashmere Bouquet soap her mother bought. She shivered at the thought of it. Sonny smelled like patchouli, her favorite incense. She had goose bumps. Good ones.

"You cold, Mae? Too much AC in here, if you ask me." He put his arm around her.

How can this be happening? she thought. To her, of all people. Thank you, God. I owe you one.

"Yeah, I guess it is a little cold. Want to go outside and talk? I don't really need anything in here. Do you?"

Was she kidding? Like he came in for a book. Sweet Mae. He shook his head. She smiled.

Sonny held his hand out and Mae walked in front of him out the revolving door. They walked up the street talking like old friends. She told him she worked at Saks. He told her he still dabbled in carpentry and painting when his other ventures fell through. Mae didn't ask what those ventures were. She'd been a teenager when she had her mad crush on Sonny at the orphanage. He had been in his twenties. That was seven years ago. Now they were both adults. Not strangers if you count history. Sexual history.

Mae might have been a kid back then, but she was an eager student, Sonny recalled. A natural. A female who liked sex as much as he did. He wasn't fooled by the blushing innocent bit. That was just Mae being raised by nuns. This little girl could sizzle better than a pro when you got her going, he remembered. How did he ever let that nun stand in his way? He should have kidnapped Mae when he had the chance. That hawk of a nun got rid of him when she got wind of Mae's little hideaway under the basement stairs.

Now here she was again. Little Mae with the full mouth and now very grown-up body. Still so sweet. And obedient. That was ingrained in her. *Yep, you're every man's wet dream, little Mae. And mine just came true.* He smiled at Mae and held the door to Sak's open for her. She thanked him. She kept her eyes on him so he wouldn't vanish into thin air, in case she was dreaming. What if she never saw him again? She couldn't bear that pain twice. No, Sonny was here to stay.

"Dinner tonight, Mae? My apartment? Bring your pajamas in case you want to spend the night. Just kidding. I'll behave. Where can I pick you up? You don't have plans already, do you? Saving the world tonight? Lost children and dogs or something? Old nuns?"

Mae laughed. "No. Tonight is great. You can pick me up here at 6:00. I have everything I need with me. I'll call Miss Dee and let her know I won't be home for supper."

"Who's Miss Dee? Another nun?" Sonny laughed. Christ, the girl had amazing tits. *Nun shmun.*

"No. She's my roommate. A lovely old lady who dotes on me. I'm very lucky," Mae said. "But tonight I think I'll be luckier...I mean...oh God, I didn't mean that how it sounded," Mae was almost stammering. How was she going to get through the rest of the day?

Sonny laughed. *You're in high fucking cotton, man.* "You're adorable, Mae. You do what you have to. Square it with Sister Dee. I'll be here to get you at 6:00." He leaned in and gave her a soft kiss on the lips. *Control, Sonny, control.*

Mae wanted to undress right then and there. "I'll see you later, Sonny." She stepped on the escalator and watched him below. He licked his lips and watched her ascend to the second floor. He winked at her. She was undone.

Chapter Twenty

It wasn't exactly candlelight and tablecloth like Mae had imagined. But Sonny was there and Mae was with him. That was the only thing that mattered. She helped herself to another piece of takeout chicken from the cardboard bucket and Sonny handed her another beer.

"You drink much beer with those nuns? Because you're doing all right there. Damn."

"I'm a little nervous. No, we never drank beer. Only a little wine at Mass." Mae dipped a french fry in some ketchup. She felt good. Tingly all over.

Sonny lit a Marlboro, rolled one towards her. She shook her head and rolled it back. "I don't smoke."

"Of course you don't. How about this kind of cigarette?" Sonny put a neatly rolled joint on Mae's plate. She picked it up and held it to her nose. The smell was familiar somehow. The basement at the orphanage. Sonny's smell. Mixed with paint.

"Pot?" She slid her finger up and down the smooth thin cigarette.

"Yep. Good too. Wanna try some?"

"Okay. We are celebrating…." She handed the joint back to Sonny to light. He took a good strong pull, handed it to her. She imitated Sonny, and coughed her brains out. Sonny laughed.

"You don't swallow it."

She took a swig of beer. "Oh. I thought I was supposed to swallow."

Oh, man. Don't touch that one, Sonny boy. "Um, no. Just inhale the smoke. Hold it in and then blow it out."

"Oh, right. Silly me," she laughed. "Let me do it again."

Oh, yes, Mae, you'll be saying those words a lot. Sonny laughed.

"What's so funny?" Mae asked.

127

Nanci LaGarenne

"Nothing. You're adorable, that's all." *Fucking A. High cotton, man.*

He watched her sleeping now. It was hard to admit it, but the girl had exhausted him. She was one hungry little piece. The pot made her as horny as a cat in heat; she couldn't get enough. She must have been touching the hell out of herself in that fucking convent. Poor Mae. She'd had a brief taste of it and then nothing. Until tonight. She'll be sore tomorrow. When the pot and beer wear off. All mine, Sonny thought. Little Mae you got a lot of Sonny to catch up on.

Sonny dropped his cigarette butt into the beer bottle on the nightstand. He watched Mae breathing. He couldn't keep his eyes off her tits. Now that's fine art, he thought. Not those stupid pictures his mother used to have hanging in the house. Every goddamn saint known to mankind on the wall. Creepy martyr eyes. Halos and wings. Lights shining on them at night. Scary fuckers always watching you. No wonder he'd had nightmares.

Mae smiled in her sleep like a contented baby. *That's right, Mae. Keep that sweet mouth where it belongs and your nose out of my business and we'll get along just fine. Cross me and you'll be praying you were back in Hells Kitchen with your daddy in your bed.*

Chapter Twenty-One

Mae moved the last of her stuff out of Dee's apartment. The sweet old woman was sad to see her go but wished her well. Mae thanked her, counting the minutes when she would see Sonny again. They already had a routine. He'd meet her at Saks. They'd stop off at the grocery store, get some beer or wine and the night would unfold. Mae loved cooking for him. She had a fair share of recipes from the convent plus the ones that Dee gave her bound in a little flowered book. Sonny would be on the phone as usual. Mae would set the table and run inside to change into something sexy for him. While dinner simmered or roasted or baked, Mae brought Sonny a beer and gave him his oral appetizer. After the dinner dishes were done, Mae was ready for the rest of the night. Sonny would sometimes offer to do the dishes while she took a shower and changed. Mae got a good discount at Saks and her lingerie collection was building. She knew exactly what Sonny liked. The less covering her the better. When Mae returned to the living room Sonny would be waiting. He'd click off the TV. Mae knew it was time for the music. She'd hit the stereo button and start dancing for him. Then a little lap dance. Sonny was obsessed with her breasts. He couldn't get enough. If Mae didn't come and she knew better than to fake it with Sonny, she would go into the bedroom and wait. Always a game with him. Mae didn't mind. She'd yell when his hand came down on her tender cheeks. "Mercy!" she'd say. Sonny loved when she said that. It really turned him on. "Beg for it, Mae."

"Please, Sonny, make me come...now..."

On her back, she closed her eyes and waited. Seconds later she'd feel his tongue, darting and searching and then expertly hitting its mark. She would sigh in delight as she raised her head, cheeks flushed, body on fire. Stars and angels danced before her. Every time she came, she was in heaven. Mae wondered if everyone felt this way when they had an orgasm. If not, she felt very sorry for them. The poor Sisters, Mae thought, they never get this pleasure. It was a sin for them to touch themselves like that, even in secret. But it was their sacrifice when they married God.

Religion has odd rules, Mae thought. Men have sex with their daughters and go to church on Sunday and priests molest little boys and serve communion. But masturbation is a sin? Sex for pleasure a no-no? Crazy world. She might have lived with nuns but she knew some things made little or no sense at all. What was it Sister Devora said? *It's a man's world, Mae. Even in the church.*

"Something funny, Mae? Or does fooling around make you smile like you just heard a good joke. What?" Sonny was lying next to her, smoking.

Mae giggled, "Sorry. I didn't realize I was thinking out loud. Just wondering if I'm lucky. Do all people feel so good after they have sex?"

Sonny laughed. Dragged slowly on his cigarette. She was priceless. "No, you are definitely blessed."

Mae liked his answer. She smiled and leaned over to kiss him. "I think I am."

Chapter Twenty-Two

Mae took the icepack off her face. Her cheek felt numb. She held her hand on her cold cheek and licked her swollen lips. The tears were welling up again. She swallowed them back. "It's your fault, Mae," she told herself. She looked around the bedroom. When did she turn on the lamp? Did she get herself ice? She couldn't remember. It didn't matter. Her head pounded, she needed aspirin, some water, and a hot cup of tea. She swung her legs down to the floor and stood up. Stars floated in front of her eyes. She walked slowly, baby steps to the kitchen. Her back hurt. On one side down low. Must have banged it when I fell, she thought. *You didn't fall, Mae.*

If she could get to the kitchen and eat something, she might feel better. Cereal, maybe. A piece of toast. A chocolate graham cracker. Four Tylenol. Well three for sure. The rest of the apartment was dark and quiet. She hit light switches as she walked, illuminating her way. Sonny must have gone out for smokes or beer. He'll apologize, Mae thought, and we'll start over fresh. I'll explain that I'm not used to living with a man. Sonny will forgive me for butting into his business. I'll offer him his oral starter. But right now the thought of it made her lips hurt and her stomach queasy. The tears were fighting to surface again. She willed them back down. She felt ashamed of herself. Small. Invisible. Worthless. Alone.

She settled for chocolate chip cookies and milk. She didn't have the energy or steadiness to cook anything. It took too much energy to even boil the kettle. She grabbed the Tylenol and put it in the pocket of her robe, stuck the cookie bag under one arm and reached for a glass in the drain board. A container fell out of the cabinet. Oatmeal tumbled out of a half open box and covered the counter sprinkling down onto her feet, like snow. She looked down unfazed and opened the refrigerator. She poured herself a large glass of milk and walked through a dusting of oatmeal. It was soft on her bare feet. She sat at the kitchen table.

Mae dunked and chewed and felt a bit better when the sugar kicked in. She swallowed three Tylenol with milk and picked a few nice sized chips off a cookie and ate them. Some oatmeal was stuck between her toes. She drew her thick fleece bathrobe tightly around her; she was chilly now. The kitchen clock tick tocked in a comforting rhythm. Old fashioned schoolhouse clock. Must have come with the apartment. She couldn't imagine Sonny buying it. Mae ate another cookie. A bath would be so nice, she thought. She wiggled her toes; a few oat flakes fell to the floor.

She carried her glass to the sink and put the cookies away. The oatmeal box sat at her feet. She stared down at the man with the hat and the cheerful face. She kicked it and it rolled under the table. *Another bad dream last night, Mae? Eat your oatmeal. It's a new day. Yes, Mommy.*

Chapter Twenty-Three

Sonny didn't apologize. It wasn't in him. He'd have to admit he was wrong. His ego prevented that. He was in charge. That's what they told him when his father left. His mother and that priest she worshipped. *You're the man of the house now, boy.* Bad advice for a kid who blamed his mother for his father leaving. Bad advice, period. Sonny interpreted his newfound responsibility as power and he liked the feeling. He preyed on his mother's guilt and wore her down. She was convinced it was her fault her husband went away. Despite the fact that he smacked her around on a daily basis. Had affairs with women. Generally showed her no respect. Her lack of a backbone did nothing to help her son. Unconsciously, she was breeding an abuser.

Sonny learned that women were to blame. They asked for what they got. *A man doesn't need to explain where he goes and what he does to no dame.* His father's words verbatim. Sonny memorized them. Took them as gospel. That legacy was his guidepost to manhood. A guarantee he would become at the very least, dishonest. In all probability a womanizer, a misogynist. A wolf.

When he got in trouble at school, it was never his fault. His mother made excuses for him. If he failed to keep a job, they had it in for him. His mother believed him every time. She was afraid of Sonny. There was a certain look in his eyes that frightened her. If she hadn't given birth to him she would have thought the devil himself was standing before her.

"God help you," she said to him one day at the end of her patience. "You cannot lie all the time, Sonny. God frowns on that."

"What God?" he spat back at her. "The one that priest you love works for? Give me a break, you sanctimonious whore. God, my ass."

His mother blessed herself. Started a Hail Mary out loud. Sonny burst out laughing. "You are a piece of work, Ma. You pray after you and the priest do it?"

His mother screamed. "Shut up! It's a sin to talk about a priest that way. How dare you."

"Yeah? But it's not a sin to have the Holy Father coming around here with a stiffie? You're the sinner." He walked away from her. She followed him, screaming.

"You are the devil! Shut your filthy mouth. Father helps me. Say you're sorry for talking that way. Say it!"

Sonny laughed in her face. She raised her hand to smack him. He took it and twisted it hard and brought her to her knees. She looked up at him, her eyes bulging and her breathing heavy. She gasped for air. "Help me," she pleaded with her only son. He watched her. She held her chest and slumped to the floor.

Sonny went out to get beer. When he returned Father Fingers was sitting at the kitchen table. His mother was nowhere in sight. "Where is she?" he asked the priest.

Father looked at him, lowered his eyes. "Your mother has passed on, Sonny. I'm very sorry. She had a heart attack. I found her in the dining room. I guess you were out. I called an ambulance. It was too late."

Was this dude serious? Was his collar too tight?

"What'd you do? Give it to her real good, Father? She collapsed, huh? She ain't no spring chicken you know. You gotta go easy on the older ones...."

Sonny didn't get to open his beer. Father's fist caught him square in the jaw. The bottle fell and crashed on the linoleum.

"What the hell?" he rubbed his face.

"Have some respect or I'll be the one to teach it to you. Your mother was a lovely woman. She was a lonely and devout Catholic. People need comfort in hard times."

Sonny held a new beer to his cheek and glared at the priest across the kitchen table. "You waiting on me to apologize? Forget it. Yeah, my mother was devoted to you all right. You and your visits. Now what happens, Father? How you gonna call bingo tonight without your afternoon love fest?"

When Sonny came to, he was on the couch with an icepack on his other cheek and an aching jaw. Father Fingers was gone. He sat up and shook his head. Grabbed a smoke out of his pocket and lit it. "Fucking priest knows how to throw one. Shit," he said out loud to the dark room. He turned on a lamp. He heard a voice coming from upstairs. Someone was humming. Maybe he'd just had a bad dream. Maybe his mother wasn't dead. He hollered from the couch. "Ma? You up there? Ma?"

"No, honey, I ain't your ma. It's me, Aunt Nina." His aunt stood in the doorway. "Poor baby. What happened? When Uncle Nicky got the call about your ma, we came running over. The priest called us. Who hit you, baby?"

"The priest," Sonny said, taking in the wonderful view. His Aunt Nina was hot. Her tits walked towards him first. His face felt better already. She stood so close he wondered if she could see his erection. She bent over and touched his face.

"The priest hit you? Why would he do a thing like that? You got ice, that's good." She sat on the arm of the couch and crossed her legs. "So sad your ma dying and all. Terrible. So sudden." She smoothed his hair. "Can I get you something? Tell Aunt Nina what you need."

Sonny smiled at her. "Could you hold me?"

She lay next to him, wrapping herself around him like he had just returned from war. Sonny slid a hand up her leg and found a nice warm place to land. She didn't flinch.

"Uncle Nicky won't be here until after 6:00. He has to make the arrangements for your ma and check on the restaurant. Come, let's put you to bed. You must be overcome with grief."

Sonny looked at her and nodded. He kept his fingers where they were. She moved her hips on them. "You want me

135

here or upstairs?" she asked, as casually as if she'd said angel hair or linguini for supper?

"Upstairs," Sonny said. He had enough bruises for one day. He didn't want any surprises. He untangled himself from his aunt and went to make sure both doors were double locked. Uncle Nicky would have to ring the bell. Perfect.

Sonny lit a cigarette and wondered if his father ever got a piece of this action. His aunt was one hot tamale. He looked over at her. She was watching him.

"You finish your cigarette and I'll take care of you one more time, Sonny. Being you're grieving and all. Uncle Nicky will be here in an hour or so. I gotta freshen up before he comes."

"And I gotta come before you freshen up."

Aunt Nina laughed. And gave him a full rear view of her perfect ass while she went down on him.

The party was over. Aunt Nina and Uncle Nicky were moving to Florida. Sonny didn't take it personally. Not worth it. There was plenty of action in the city. Uncle Nicky had already put the house up for sale. The money would go towards funeral expenses and the rest to the church. His mother's will specified that. Sonny scoffed at that to his aunt and uncle. They were all sitting around the kitchen table eating pizza from Spumoni Gardens.

"Fucking priest," Sonny said between bites. "She sleeps with him and then leaves him her money too." Sonny shook his head.

Uncle Nicky stopped stuffing his face. "Don't talk like that. It ain't right. Have some respect for the dead. Your mother was a saint."

"I'm telling you he was here all the time." Sonny drank his beer. "Horny bastard," he said under his breath. He wasn't about to get Uncle Nicky all riled up. Aunt Nina wasn't shocked. She was too busy rubbing Sonny's groin under the table with her stocking foot. But she was listening.

"Terrible, those priests. Not very Christian, is it?" she said. Sonny stared at her. He didn't dare move. She took a

136

ladylike sip of her Pinot Grigio without stopping the subtle motion of her foot between his legs. Sonny lit a cigarette like nothing was happening. As if he didn't want to throw Aunt Nina on top of the pizza box and hump away like a jackhammer. Uncle Nicky had his jaws around a fourth slice of Sicilian, oblivious. Sonny thought his rock hard erection would rip through his jeans. He pictured Aunt Nina riding him while Uncle Nicky devoured a large pepperoni pizza.

"Your mother had religious loyalty, Sonny," Uncle Nicky said, coming up for air. He pushed his empty plate away and belched loudly. "Personally, I thought it was over the top, giving the church her money. I'd rather put my money in Vegas," he laughed, his jowls shaking. "But that's me. Your mother, she didn't care for gambling. Or my brother's fists. He was a loser my brother. Sorry, kid, that's the God's honest truth."

No, Sonny thought, my mother liked priests. His uncle stood up. His aunt removed her foot from Sonny's lap.

"You gotta go already, Nicky?" she asked, voice dripping innocence.

"Yeah, duty calls, doll. I'll see you later. I got business at the restaurant. Sonny, you keep Nina company. And no more talk about no priests. You hear? Listen, you don't worry about money. I got more than enough. You'll be okay. You gotta work anyway. You're young. It'll keep you honest. I'd take you to Florida but that's for old people. You got oats to sow. We'll get you squared away before we leave."

Sonny wanted to laugh in his uncle's face but he knew better. "I look worried, Uncle Nicky?"

His uncle laughed. "Good. You're a tough guy. That'll be in your favor. Nina, gimme a kiss sweetheart, I gotta go." Sonny watched his aunt strut across the room and throw her arms around his bloated uncle.

"Take care, Nicky honey. We'll watch some TV until you get back. Will you be late?" What an actress. She kept her arms around his uncle and nibbled his ear. Sonny wanted to puke. But he had to give her credit. She was good. *In more ways than one, Uncle Nicko.*

"If I'm gonna be late I'll call you, doll. Enjoy yourself. Make some coffee. There's cannoli in the fridge. The kids too thin." He lit a cigar and headed out the back door. Aunt Nina locked the door after him and walked over to the coffee maker on the counter. She stuck the glass pot under the tap. While it filled she rubbed one long leg on the back of the other. Sonny took his eyes off her ass for a minute and walked out of the kitchen. He stopped at the front window in the living room. He slid the curtain back and looked down the street. Not a soul out tonight. His uncle's car was long gone. He walked back into the kitchen.

"Coffee's on…" Aunt Nina chirped.

Sonny smiled at her. She laid a manicured hand on her chest as if she was straightening her gold heart necklace. She let her hand slide further down into her cleavage keeping her eyes on him

"Oh let me get the cannoli," she said suddenly, walking over to the fridge. She bent down searching the lower shelf. "I think Nicky must have hidden them," she laughed. Sonny had a primo view. Her dress rode up her hips, her red thong dividing her perfectly delectable cheeks. Sonny's mouth watered.

"Can you believe it? They're all the way back here. Oooh..." Sonny pushed her panties down and slid inside her.

"I guess we can eat them later," she said, holding onto the fridge shelf.

"Good idea, Aunt Nina." He pumped her a few more times and slid out of her. He helped her up and she turned to face him.

"Maybe we should go into the living room?" she asked, stepping out of her thong and her dress. Her perfectly purchased breasts spilled over the top of a lacy red bra. Dark red nipples peeked out through the lace. "Sonny?"

"Not yet," Sonny said, tracing Aunt Nina's full lips with his index finger. She licked his finger with her tongue.

She looked back and grabbed the dish towel from the fridge door handle. She folded it into a padded square and placed it at Sonny's feet and knelt down.

"Let me show you how to eat a cannoli." She was teasing him with her tongue. Before long she had his entire erection in her mouth. Sonny dug his hands into the counter top. He wanted to rake his nails over her back. Leave marks. But he had to be careful with Aunt Nina. Their little secret had to stay that way. Sonny sighed. She was working him like he was the last pastry in the world. He was almost ready to explode, but he held himself back. He wanted her someplace else when he did. He tugged at her hair gently.

"Wait, Nina...." He was breathing hard. She released him from her jaw and stood up.

"You were almost there, I felt it," she said, sounding disappointed. "No cream in my cannoli today?" she teased him.

"Come with me, I want you where the saints can watch."

"We going to church?"

She followed Sonny upstairs. He went into a bedroom. She stood at the door, hesitant to go in. Sonny looked back at her. She watched him remove his jeans and shirt and boxers. His body was hard and glistening.

"This is your mother's room, Sonny. That ain't right. We shouldn't be here. Bad luck, God rest her soul."

She stared at the glass candles burning on an altar at the foot of the bed. A small statue of the Madonna and child at the center. She gazed up at the crucifix that hung above the headboard. She felt like she was in church. It gave her the creeps and turned her on at the same time.

"Come on in, don't be afraid," Sonny urged her. "So what? It ain't her room no more." Sonny held his hand out to her. She stepped into the room and stood in front of him. "Now turn around," he said, holding her by the shoulders. She turned. Her eyes went wide.

139

"Mother of God." The wall facing her was covered with framed pictures of saints. Every inch of it. There was a light above them illuminating their saintliness. Sonny unhooked her bra. It fell on the rug and he cupped her breasts pinching her nipples just hard enough to make her moan.

"Guess what we're gonna do now?" he said, spinning her around to face him.

"Give the saints a show?"

"You know, I always liked you." Sonny took the candles and statue off the altar and put them on the nightstand. "I want you up here now."

Aunt Nina climbed up on the bed and lay down on the altar. The wood was warm from the candles. "Ooh, hot."

"You said it. Let's give the martyrs a nice show," Sonny said, lifting her legs high in the air as he entered her. He slid in and out of her until he had emptied himself completely.

"What about me?" she asked him. Sonny laughed climbing down.

"Open wide. Say amen."

Aunt Nina laughed. "Amen."

Chapter Twenty-Four

Sonny got off the train in Little Italy. His buddies would be glad to see him. With any luck they would have some business for him. Numbers to run. A sure thing on a few ponies. A bag of good Columbian weed. Prostitutes. He needed to chill. Mae was starting to piss him off. He stepped onto the subway platform and mixed in with the flow of people running up the stairs. Nobody strolled. Everyone was in hurry. Only the tourists took their time. And Mae. She could make a walk last. Goddamn Mae, he thought. Why did she have to ruin everything? Maybe she learned her lesson. Otherwise he'd have to hurt her again. He thought Mae would have known about obedience, living with nuns. If not, he was ready to school her. She had potential. But if she even tried to leave him, she would only begin to know real pain.

Mae didn't leave. Which convinced Sonny he was right. *You gotta keep the dames in line.* His father's line. Mae would get the hang of it. Learn not to ask questions. Keep her trap shut. Except when she had something useful to do with it. Aunt Nina knew when to shut up. Sonny thought about Aunt Nina on the altar. A prime memory.

Mae felt small and powerless. Everything had changed. Sonny had disappointed her when he was supposed to be her hero. *How could he hurt me?* The question haunted her. She wanted to ask him. That would be a death wish. Maybe she should tell someone. Who? If Sonny found out her life wouldn't be worth a dime. She couldn't count on much. Even her job didn't make her happy anymore. The end of the day only meant going home to Sonny. Being a robot. Making his dinner. Giving him oral sex. Letting him do whatever he wanted to her. Being afraid. Faking it. I can't even count on an orgasm, Mae thought. Her nerve endings were numb, like her emotions. If she complained, she knew dying was the only thing she could count on.

It was no way to live. But where could she go? Sister Devora would be crushed if she knew the truth. It would probably kill her. No, let Sister go on thinking I'm doing okay. Like her co-workers at Saks. None of them knew her life was a battle zone. Mae knew how to expertly apply make-up by now to camouflage any bruises. If she was too swollen, she didn't go to work at all. She told her manager she had a recurring sinus infection due to her time at the orphanage. All those sick little children. Mae made up the time so she was never in danger of losing her job. Plus every one loved Mae. They loved her, but they were not naïve or blind. When one of her co-workers asked her point blank if she had been beaten by her boyfriend, Mae feigned shock.

"That's ridiculous," Mae said.

"No it isn't, Mae. I know the signs. The long sleeve blouses, the nervousness, the sadness in your eyes. Somebody put that hollow look there. You're different now. And by the way, all the Clinique foundation in the world isn't going to cover it. It shows. Don't bullshit a bullshitter. I've been there. Had my face used for a punching bag. Don't look so shocked. I'm not proud of the fact, just being honest. But I'm not the one in denial, am I?"

Mae started to cry. She quickly excused herself for a bathroom break to fix her make-up and apply fresh lipstick. Her co-worker handed her a new lipstick sample from the drawer below the counter.

"Go get yourself together. Admitting it is the first step out. At lunch we'll talk more. I'm not giving up on you, girl."

Mae was touched. Besides Sister Devora and Dee, no one cared about her. Not Sonny. Not anymore. She was under his thumb. Not special. She felt stupid. Sonny had used her.

That's all you're good for, Mae. She looked at herself in the employee bathroom mirror. *Get in the tub now, little Mae. You need a good scrubbing. Aren't you just daddy's little pleaser?* Mae used to choke on the bubbles she had swallowed while her mother wiped her mouth again and again

142

with the rough washcloth. She shook her head now and applied the new lipstick.

At lunch the conversation gave Mae hope and some much needed balls. She felt for the first time that she could make it on her own, without Sonny. She had a friend after all. Someone she could trust who didn't want anything from her. Not sex, not money, not even love. She agreed to go for a drink after work with her new confidante. A simple decision a grown-up makes. Mae was a grown-up but so far hadn't been treated as such. She was always little Mae, someone's property or cause.

What she truly desired was to just be herself. Who is that, she wondered? With her new friend from work she could at least attempt finding out. She ordered a beer and felt happy making another small decision. A beer and a burger seemed quite harmless. In an ordinary life, it would be. For Mae, it would be the beginning of her undoing.

She was relieved when she found the apartment in darkness. That meant Sonny wasn't home. She breathed a sigh of relief and snapped on the living room lamp. A cup of tea and a book were on her mind. Followed by a nice long sleep. Tomorrow was her day off. So this is what normal is, Mae thought, kicking off her shoes. She headed for the kitchen to put on the kettle. The night's fun drained out of her instantly. Sonny was sitting in a chair by the window. He dragged hard on his cigarette and stared right through her. Mae shivered, realizing what she was to him now. The enemy. She smiled at him anyway. *Please God, don't let me die tonight.* Feigning business as usual, she slipped off her coat and hung it on a hook. She walked slowly towards him.

"Oh, I didn't expect you to be home already. I thought it was your late night with the boys. I went out with one of the girls from work. We just talked about the job, you know…girl talk." Mae was rambling. She sat down on the couch. Sonny hated small talk. Mae would pay for that. But she was so nervous and a little high from the beer that she kept talking. Mostly because he wouldn't speak at all.

143

"So, did you eat dinner? I could fix you something real quick, like some eggs or a steak…I think there's leftovers too." She waited. No response, save his dark stare. She was frozen. Sonny stood up and walked over to the couch. He leaned over to Mae as if to kiss her.

"Liar." He spat the word at her. "Red-faced slut. Who the hell do you think you're dealing with?" Sonny had his two hands on either side of Mae's shoulders on the back of the couch. Mae could feel her breathing getting heavier. *I'm trapped. Again.*

His breath was making her nauseous. Pot and Tequila. She held her breath and concentrated on strategy. She would have to back pedal. She had nothing to be guilty about but it was the necessary thing to do.

"I only went to a restaurant," she began, her voice soft but audible at close range. "You know it, the small café we ate in once, remember? It has the red striped awning. I just had one beer. And a burger." Mae realized her voice was pleading. Begging. Defensive. She was ashamed of herself. Desperate. She would do what she had to do and than she'd leave him. For good!

"Shut your stupid mouth. I don't want to hear it. Who did you fuck tonight? Who?" His voice was booming in her ears. She flinched and shook her head.

"Don't be ugly. Please. I went out with a girl from the store for one beer. That's it. She's nice. She works with me at the cosmetics counter. She is a nice girl. I have a friend."

"Shut up. Liar. Who was he? I'll rip his head off."
Mae closed her eyes. This was not going well. He had to be distracted somehow. Maybe he was horny. Maybe a blow job. It wasn't what she wanted to do for him anymore, but it beat the hell out of getting her brains knocked in. Pride be damned.

"Sonny…." Mae touched his leg. "You want me to make you feel good?" She kept her eyes on him while she moved her hand up to unbutton her blouse. He watched her. Mae was glad she hadn't worn a sexy bra to work. He would

144

find a way to turn that ugly. She let the blouse fall away onto the couch. She took one breast out of its plain silk ivory cup and ran her fingers over it. He was paying attention. Getting hard. Mae could see the bulge in his tight jeans. She offered him her breasts with both hands. He drew his hand down to her erect nipple. And slapped her hard in the face. Mae saw stars. She was crying. Fumbling for her blouse.

"So," Sonny said, "You like showing off your tits? You and your girlfriend suck each others tonight? You like girls now?" He was laughing. It was demonic. Mae wanted to throw up. He grabbed her blouse and flung it across the room. "Don't cover up. I'm just getting started. I want to hear all about your carpet munching." He squeezed her breasts. Sucked meanly on her nipples. Mae gritted her teeth and looked into his eyes. The physical pain was not as bad as her humiliation.

"Please, Sonny. I don't like this...I didn't do anything like that."

"Like what? Show me. Open your legs." He stuck his knee between her legs and forced them open. He ripped her stockings and hiked up her skirt. "This how she did it to you?" He shoved two fingers inside her roughly.

Mae started to cry. "Stop, Sonny. I didn't do...no one did anything...please don't...."

It was no use. He wasn't hearing her. He kept fingering her like a madman on a mission.

"Tell me her name, your girlfriend. Say it."

Mae tried to ignore him but he was hurting her. "I told you, she's not my girlfriend. Please. Can't we go to bed?"

He stopped for a minute. He let her get up. She smoothed her skirt down over her bare bottom and stood up. She walked away from him.

"Where the hell do you think you're going? I'm not done."

Mae sighed and kept walking towards the bedroom.

"Get the hell back over here. Don't make me drag you. Get your ass into that chair." Sonny snapped and pointed to the chair he was sitting in earlier when Mae walked in. She sighed. Crossed the floor and sat down in the chair. Crossed her legs. And her arms. He walked over to her.

"Cute, Mae. Now take off the skirt and blouse and get on your hands and knees."

Mae did as he ordered. The quicker the better and then she could sleep. He was standing behind her and she knew that was never a good thing. She took a deep breath. Sonny unzipped his jeans. Mae felt his skin on hers. Than nothing. She braced herself. He cracked her hard on the ass with his hand. She yelled. That's what he liked, his little games.

"Now say her name while I fuck you. Keep saying it until I come. Go."

Mae wanted to laugh in the midst of this insanity. She knew she'd better not. What the hell was she supposed to say? Surely not her friend's real name. Sonny might find her and beat her up too. Think, Mae. Think. Sonny cracked her other cheek and jammed himself inside her. She screamed again.

"Say it!" His breathing was heavy. *The end was near. Hallelujah.*

"Chloe." Mae shut her eyes. Chloe was the name of a perfume at the store. He wouldn't know it from Adam.

"Say fuck me, Chloe." Sonny demanded, breathing heavy. Mae knew he was close. She wanted to laugh, but she held back in the interest of survival.

"Fuck me, Chloe," she repeated. He came.

146

Chapter Twenty-Five

Mae related the incident to her co-worker the next day. They laughed about it. Mae could now. For that her friend was grateful. But she wasn't fooled by Mae's cavalier attitude. Not for a minute. She knew that humor did its job disguising pain. Mae had a bonafide abuser on her hands. It wasn't going to get any better. Mae West, her friend feared, was on borrowed time. She needed to get away from that Sonny character while she could still draw breath. Her friend shivered. She had a premonition. Something awful was about to happen.

Mae left the store that night in a lighter mood. Sonny had been bizarre last night. Maybe it was the drugs. The drinking. Mae hoped tonight would be a much different story. Could they spend some time just talking? Go to bed with a pizza like they did in their early days together? Sonny could be gentle. Like at the orphanage. Mae forced herself to remember what was fast becoming a very distant memory.

Sonny wasn't there when she got home. Mae spurred into action cleaning up the apartment he'd managed to mess up in just one afternoon. Guess he figured he had a live-in maid. Why pick up after himself? She put on some music. Melissa Etheridge. Sonny couldn't stand her. "Fucking dyke," he called her. But he wasn't home. Mae turned it up. She lit incense and candles and dimmed the lights. She put a chicken roaster into the oven and peeled some potatoes for mashed. A nice dinner. That's what they needed. Mae searched the cabinets for a bottle of wine she'd hidden when Sonny was polishing off far too many for his own good. She located it way in the back and dusted it off. Now wine glasses and a tablecloth, some fresh lipstick and she was ready. Mae had talked herself into a good evening. If only life would cooperate. And Sonny. She remembered to lower the music. She switched CD's. Why borrow trouble? The strains of Bon Jovi's Wanted Dead or Alive filled the rooms as Mae applied

147

her lip gloss in the bathroom mirror. The apartment door slammed and she heard his keys drop onto the glass end table. Mae ran a hand through her short shiny shag and prayed for peace. Normalcy. *Just one night to live like other people.*

Sonny was drunk. And stoned. Lovely, Mae thought. What a turn-on. She hid her disappointment and the wine, shoving it back into its hiding place behind a huge sack of flour. She quietly put the wine glasses away and replaced them with large tumblers of ice and filled them with water and lemon slices. She placed a few cans of Coke on the table and went in the living room to give Sonny a proper greeting. Not that he deserved one.

"Well if it isn't Chloe's little girlfriend, the carpet muncher. "Sonny lit a Marlboro and sneered at Mae. He wasn't going to be nice. She kissed him anyway. Like an obligation. On the cheek. He grabbed her arm.

"Hold up. What the fuck's that? Am I your priest or something? What kind of a kiss was that?" he looked up at her. Mae kissed him on the lips. She reeled with the alcohol on his breath. He cracked up laughing,

"S'matter, do I offend your delicate senses?"

"No. I'm just a little tired. Are you hungry? I'm making a big dinner." She sat on the end of his chair because he wouldn't let go of her arm.

"Such a good girl, aren't you? Did I ever tell you how the priest used to come over every day for his fix? Yeah, he and my mother used to do the nasty right on the bed under her crucifix. Father Fingers couldn't get enough, man. You ever carpet munch with those nuns, Mae? Bet there was fierce diddling under the covers, huh? All you little girls and them horny nuns. Come on, tell me...."

Mae refrained from rolling her eyes. She wanted to be able to work tomorrow. Without bruises. No sense being stupid. He's drunk. There would be no reasoning with him. She spoke in her soft sweet way, "Stop that talk now. There was no such thing at the orphanage. Do you want some coffee before dinner?"

148

"Don't patronize me, Mae. It's fucking true. They were screwing their brains out. That church-going hypocrite and her pimp priest. Don't tell me no, I was there. I was a goddamn kid. That priest and her, all moony eyed, every time he stepped foot in my mother's house. That ain't normal. My mother couldn't get me out to play fast enough." His eyes were glaring. He really is the devil, Mae thought. And he was drunk and fuming. Mae had to get him off this subject. Fast. She lowered her eyes. No matter what she said it would be the wrong thing when Sonny was in one of his moods. So she said nothing. And that was the wrong thing.

"What? Cat got your tongue? Thinking about your girlfriend. Bet you never run out of things to talk about with her. For me you got nothing." He was going to be mean tonight. Mae could feel it. Make it right, Mae, she told herself. Diffuse his anger. Feed him and then he'll fall asleep.

"Time to check the chicken," Mae sung out cheerfully. "Than I'll listen to all your stories, hon, how's that?"

"Choke the chicken, ha ha, now you're talking," he unzipped his jeans. Mae sighed and stood up.

"Put that away," she chastised him like he was a child who had taken out a lollipop before dinner. "First we have to eat dinner." She smiled a charming smile though her stomach was tying itself in multiple knots.

"You refusing to do it, is that what I'm hearing?" he was absently stroking his penis while he looked at her. Good, she thought, he can play with himself all he likes while I mash the spuds and pretend his penis is getting squished by the blades of the mixer. Mae walked towards the kitchen. She almost made it before he grabbed her by the hair. "When a man asks you to suck his cock, you don't walk away. Unless you got something better waiting in the kitchen, hmmm?" Sonny pushed her from behind until they reached the kitchen. Mae sighed.

"Go ahead, check your goddamn chicken, Mae. Than get busy on me."

149

Mae opened the oven door. Sylvia Plath came to mind. One of Mae's favorite poets. No wonder. Victims relate to one another. Even posthumously. Mae didn't know if Sylvia's husband beat her. He did cheat on her. Sylvia kept loving him with a passion that drove her right out of her mind. To the oven and out of the pain. Mae could feel the heat burning her cheeks. She was frozen there.

"Where are you, Mae? You blowing that chicken?" Mae startled and took her head out of the oven. He was going on at a pace. Talking to himself.

"Licking girls, blowing fucking poultry, you can't keep your mouth shut these days, can you?" Sonny was laughing like a fool. Mae wanted to strangle him with the dish towel. Or stuff it into his mouth until he couldn't breathe. Yes, I could murder, she thought. And than sit down and eat chicken and potatoes and green beans afterwards. Have a nice glass of secret red wine.

The chicken was dried out by the time Mae gave Sonny his oral appetizer and served dinner. He didn't appreciate a nice dinner one bit. He barely tasted the food, washing it down like a juvenile with glasses of Coke. Drowning each piece of chicken in puddles of gravy and eating like he was going to the electric chair.

Mae managed to eat her own dinner in a semi-normal state. There was no conversation, merely animal sounds from Sonny. Pigs make less noise when they eat.

Mae finished drying the last pot and was looking forward to a movie when Sonny's baseball game was over. She went inside the bedroom to change into her pajamas. When she returned to the living room, Sonny was gone. Probably ran out for smokes. Mae breathed a sigh of relief and turned on the Lifetime channel. Now this is heaven, she thought, propping her feet up on the couch. She thought about a nice cup of tea but hated to move she was just so comfortable. Maybe Sonny would stay out the rest of the night. Could she be that lucky? Halfway through the movie

Mae thought about going to sleep. She was beat. She got up to make herself a cup of herbal tea to take to bed.

The apartment door opened and banged shut. Loud voices barged in on Mae's short-lived tranquility. She took her cup of tea and made a beeline for the bedroom. Maybe they wouldn't notice her. Sonny and his disgusting friends. You couldn't call them lost boys. They looked more like thugs. Who else would Sonny be friends with, she realized? Birds of a feather. She nearly made it to the bedroom door when his voice penetrated her being.

"Don't be rude, Mae. We have company. The boys are thirsty. Get us some beers. What's with the getup? Who the fuck are you, Mother Teresa? Put on something sexy. Hurry up." Sonny and his friends stood there laughing at her. Mae stared bullet holes of hate through him, ignoring them. If she was nobody to them, they were less to her.

"Excuse me?" she said, like she had encountered a stranger on the street. A crazy rambling stranger. And a band of idiots with him. "Are you talking to me?"

"Cute, Mother Teresa. Now go get the beer." Sonny plopped himself on the couch, flicking through the channels on the TV until he found the ballgame.

Mae sighed and walked into the kitchen slamming her teacup on the counter. She flung the fridge door open and grabbed a six pack. She left her untouched tea and shut off the kitchen light. She put the beer on the coffee table and moved towards the bedroom.

"Hey, where the hell are you going?" Sonny barked. "Be sociable, say hello to the guys."

"Hello, guys." Mae started walking away.

Sonny grabbed her robe and pulled the tie open. Mae tried to retrieve it from him but it was no use. She let him keep it and held her robe closed.

"Stop, silly. I'm going to bed. I have work in the morning."

"That so? I got money. You don't need to work. You can party with us."

151

Mae sighed. "I like my job. I am going to work tomorrow. So please, I need to go to bed."

"Shut up with that. Go get those goddamn pajamas off and come back and entertain my friends. Do it, Mae." Sonny opened a beer and put his feet up on the table. "Make it snappy, we ain't got all night."

Mae thought about climbing out the bedroom window. But there was no fire escape and three flights down was too high to jump. Though a few broken bones would be more welcome than more of Sonny's shenanigans, she thought. She reluctantly changed into a skirt and short top and put on her high heels. Sonny and his stupid games. One dance and then she was done. *I'm never doing this again.*

Sonny muted the ballgame when Mae walked into the living room. She blocked out the wolf whistles and hit the CD button. The music of Enigma pulsated. She stood in front of Sonny so she didn't have to look at his moronic friends. She wasn't used to an audience. The guys were leering at her; she could feel it. Even with her eyes closed, she was degraded. Sonny slapped her on the ass.

"Get in the middle of the room, Mae. Dance for all the guys, go ahead."

Mae obeyed. Just to get the thing over with. Dance. Then sleep.

"Take something off… come on, show us those great tits…" Sonny's voice again. The others didn't dare suggest anything. He was the boss and they knew it.

"I'm not a stripper." Mae protested, continuing her dance. And dying inside.

"You're a whore. You forgot? Whores don't refuse."

Mae wanted to cry. *I hate you, Sonny.* She could see herself stabbing him in the heart he didn't have. Usually she abhorred violence.

"Sonny, please, I am not a…."

"Do it, bitch. Now." Sonny's voice boomed in the room. He would not be humiliated in front of his friends. Mae tried her best to transcend. She lifted her shirt a little but found she couldn't go through with it. She had limits.

"No, Sonny. I'm sorry, this is not right. Make them go."

"Oh really? You don't tell me what to do. Ever. How about we pretend nobody's here. Get over here and hike that skirt up for me. Do what you like to do."

"Sonny, don't do this, please."

"Isn't she precious, guys? A real tease, huh? And what a natural, man. You have no idea. Do it. Show me your sweet ass." He spoke through gritted teeth. He would not lose face. The bitch would suffer badly for even trying to refuse him. Who the hell did she think she was all of a sudden, the Queen of Sheba?

Mae walked slowly over to where Sonny was now standing. His favorite chair. "Lean over, skirt up, let's go...."

Don't, Sonny. It's me, remember? Your little Mae.

Her silent plea went unheeded. She did as she was told, digging her nails into the upholstery and preparing for his cruel chance to show off. When he was finished with her Mae sighed a small sigh of relief. Suddenly it wasn't Sonny she felt. Strange hands were on her breasts. *Not this*. What was Sonny up to? She screamed as the strange body forced his way inside her. *You have no hero, Mae. I'm dead, Sister Devora.*

Chapter Twenty-Six

It was daylight when Mae came to. She was on the bed. How she got there she couldn't remember. The sun attacked her eyes and face. It hurt. Why? Suddenly she remembered. Sonny hurt her again. She turned her aching head to look for him. *Him*. He was the enemy now. Mae strained to hear any sounds coming from the other rooms. She heard nothing but her own breathing. *Please let him be gone.*

There had been four of them. They used her all night. Mae closed her swollen eyes. She tried to get up, her stomach roiled. She was nauseous. *Need a bath.* Was there time? A shower would have to do. *What you need is a good scrubbing, little Mae. Than you'll be a shiny new girl. Fuck you, Mommy.*

Mae forced herself to move. Time was of the essence. He would be back. She fought the sick waves rocking her empty stomach. Swung her legs to the floor. *God, I'm a mess. Look at the state of you. Like Jesus on his way to the crucifixion. Step lively, Mae. Your oatmeal is getting cold.*

Mae stood up, holding on to the dresser, avoiding the mirror. She grabbed her cell phone out of her purse. She walked like an old lady to the bathroom. Turned the taps in the shower on full. While steam started to fill the tiny room she sat gingerly on the toilet seat. She yelled. It burned. Hot vinegar on a cut. *No more, please, whoever you are. Sonny, make them stop.* She grimaced and punched in the number to Saks.

"Cosmetics…" Her co-worker's friendly voice on the other end. Mae took a deep breath and swallowed her tears that were rushing forth. Like a flood when the dam breaks.

I'm all broken. "Trudy, it's me, Mae."

"Are you feeling better? You have a cold? That son of a bitch called in for you this morning. Said you had a bad toothache and you took to your bed with Codeine."

Mae blew her nose. "Sorry. No, that's not what…."

"Stop apologizing and tell me what's going on."

I'm broken, Trudy. Mae swallowed hard. Her throat ached. *She can give a blow job like nobody I ever met, boys. Have at it. I hate you, Sonny.*

"Um… Trudy? We have to be quick."

"Talk."

"I need you to come here. Hurry. Tell them anything you have to. I can't make it downstairs alone to a cab. I'm a mess. Weak. They put something in my drink. Don't call the police. Just come. I'm about to shower. Bring that nice big guy, the security guard on 2. In case Sonny comes back. You have to hurry. The address is…."

Mae clicked off the phone and stepped under the hot water. The pounding water assaulted her tender bruised body. She didn't care. It was only water. Warm. Healing. She grabbed her bar of Ivory Soap and held it to her nose and inhaled. Sobbing like a child, she lathered her broken body and thought of Sister Devora.

"Why do people hurt little children, Sister?"

"I don't know, Mae. Perhaps they are missing a piece, a necessary part of themselves."

"Like a broken wing?"

"You're thinking of the bird in the garden?"

"No. The angel on the dining room wall. She has a missing wing. Did you paint it that way on purpose?"

"Yes. For you and all the children. For our banquet."

"The banquet of Mae dreams?"

"Yes, my elf. Close enough."

Chapter Twenty-Seven

Rooney was the first one up the next morning. She'd had fitful dreams about Clyde all night. She had not thought of the bastard since she came to live at the Brownstone. In the Friday night groups it was as if she were discussing another woman's life. She had mentally and physically moved away from Clyde. He was just a ghost who lived in her subconscious. Lately he had came out to haunt her. What power could he have over her now?

She sat in the quiet kitchen sipping her strong coffee. She imagined Clyde dead. The sonofabitch wasn't of course. She'd have heard. Mama would love nothing better than to share that news. Let Rooney gloat over it. Even Mama knew she deserved that. Paid for the right. With flesh. Blood. Humiliation. An eye.

The oven timer buzzed and she jumped. Laughing at her skittishness she inhaled the sweet aroma of blueberry muffins. Closing her eyes she pictured another kitchen. A red and white gingham tablecloth blowing in the breeze on the front porch.

"Will you teach me how to cook muffins like y'alls, Granny?"

"Ah surely will, child. One day y'all can serve them to your own guests, Sugar. May the good Lord allow me to be there to see it, darlin' girl."

Granny's good Lord didn't see fit for that to happen. *Had ya'll been witness to my life, it would have killed you for certain, Granny.*

Rooney filled the milk pitcher and willed her mind back to the present. Someone was coming down the back stairs. For a second she felt a quick flash of fear. The footsteps got closer. Rooney whirled around.

"Oh, it's just you, Doc."

"And you were expecting who? The Brownstone ghost?"

Rooney forced a laugh. "Something like that. Coffee?"

"Thanks." Rain sat down and watched her pour. Rooney had that look on her face. Mind gone somewhere bad. Everything was not okay. If it was, you'd be out of business, Rain.

"What's up?" she asked easily. Rooney could get worked up in an instant.

"Me? Nothing major. Bad dream is all. About Clyde."

Rain sipped her coffee and buttered a muffin. Sometimes the wolves just won't stay dead. Rooney sat down at the table.

"I got this gnawing feeling in my gut."

"What do you plan on doing about it?"

Knowing Rooney, something would have to be done. Rain sipped more chicory coffee, Rooney's special high test. She took a bite of muffin and waited.

"Gonna call Mama. She'll set my mind at ease. Hah, now there's a laugh, ya'll. Mama easing my mind. But she'll know if the bastard's on the loose or what. Maybe he got the notion to come lookin' for me. God forbid, cancel, cancel, cancel and knock wood." Rooney tapped the kitchen table three hard knocks and nonchalantly drank her coffee.

"What was that all about?" Rain asked.

"Scare ya'll, Doc? Just one way my granny would get rid of the demons."

"Does it work?"

"Like everything else. Only if you believe."

"Gotcha. These muffins are delicious by the way. Granny's recipe?"

Rooney smiled. She was beautiful. And she had no earthly idea.

"Yep. Her guarded one. If she told you she'd have to kill you afterwards. She left it to me in her will. Granny won first prize every summer at the Mission County Fair. 'Bout drove Mama crazy. Her pickled watermelon rind always took second."

"Hats off to Granny. They are outstanding. If you ever get tired of heads, you could open a bakery." Rain stood up to put her dish and cup in the sink. "I'm off to the cemetery. Think happy thoughts today, okay? You are safe here. And remember we always have Uncle Carmine looking out for us."

"Right. Hey, you still miss Henry something awful huh?"

"Always will. He was one of the rare ones. I was lucky. I treasure every moment I had with him. His spirit is like my compass. I feel like he is always with me. My ritual visit and chat on his birthday. Silly really. Maybe one day I won't need to do it anymore."

"That's the most charming thing I ever heard. And it explains a lot too."

"Meaning?" Rain asked, immediately sorry she did.

"Just that you don't ever date."

"Oh. Well. True, true. My work comes first. It's what got me through after Henry passed. You know, helping the women. I'm so busy..."

Rooney shook her head. She wasn't buying it for a second. Rain's pithy answer wasn't gonna fly.

"My daddy has an expression. "Don't piss down my back and tell me it's raining."

Rain laughed. But Rooney's serious face stopped her in her tracks. It asked for the truth.

"Okay, I'm afraid. Big therapist is afraid. Scaredy cat. Wuss. The poor widow playing it safe. Satisfied?"

"Horseshit." Rooney crossed her arms.

"Now there's an underused expression."

"Seriously, why the monk routine?"

"We're not gonna leave this alone, hmm? No chance?" Right. When pigs fly.

"I loved *well*, Rooney. I was loved well back. Why top that? Why even try? Can't that be enough in one life?"

Rooney got quiet. That was either trouble, Rain thought, or she bought what Doc said. Uh oh, the doubting look. Trouble.

"What about sex?" You had enough of that to last a lifetime?"

And the gloves were off. No flies on this Southern belle.

"Got a secret life we all don't know about?"

"Very cheeky of you to ask. But no. No secret life." Rain was in deep. Called out on her own carpet. And she didn't like it one bit. Rooney made a good argument. Rain was pathetic. Therapist shmerapist. *Fact: You have no life outside your clients and your Brownstone*. She was getting a headache. Classic defense mechanism. *You vill talk...Vee have ways...*

"So I've pissed you the hell off is that it? Shucks, I didn't mean to...."

"Did you say, *shucks*?"

"Don't change the subject. Not like I'm Gomer Pyle, okay? It's an expression. I'm not some dumb hillbilly."

"I wasn't implying that. Easy, cowgirl. I happen to think it's adorable. Really. And no, I'm not angry. I've got nothing juicy to disclose, that's all. Sorry to disappoint you."
Now get out of the room, Rain, before she spins around twice, taps thrice, or turns over a broom or whatever she's got up her magic bayou sleeve.

"Having fun without me? What's so funny?" Mae waltzed into the kitchen. A ray of sunshine. A diversion, more importantly. Bless her. Rain owed her one.

"Morning! Try the blueberry muffins. To die for." Rain started to make her exit. Two more steps to the stairs and she was home free.

"Actually we were discussing Doc's love life, if you must know. Or lack of one." Rooney had this tiger by the tail and she wasn't budging. Can you badly want to strangle someone you genuinely care about merely because they were pushing all your buttons? Freud? Jung? Anyone?

159

"Oh I love blueberry muffins. So are you in the market, hon?" Mae looked at Rain while she bit into a muffin. Not fair. Now she was being double teamed. Rooney winked at Rain. Very funny.

"No." She glared at Rooney. "Thanks just the same, I'm fine."

"How 'bout you?" Mae directed that one to Rooney. At least the heat was off her, Rain thought.

"Eat your breakfast, darlin.' I'm all raht."

"But you told me the other day that the last time you had a decent ride, as Fiona calls it, you'd been on the back of a horse." Quit while you're ahead, was not in Mae's vocabulary either. Rooney wanted to pour hot coffee on her; Rain knew it. She filled a mug for her instead. Set it down ever so gently. Leaned in real close.

"I wouldn't tell it. Now eat up, girl."

Can you tell someone off and drip sugar at the same time? Apparently so.

"Okay. Fun as this has been, I'm going now." Rain whistled for Shamus. He appeared at her side, tail wagging, loyal and without an inquiry. She stroked his fur and looked at her boarders. "By the way, Hungarian goulash for dinner. It's Henry's birthday."

"I'll make a cake," Mae offered, looking up from her newspaper.

"Bye. Say hey to Henry for me." Rooney called out. Rooney watched Mae cut open another blueberry muffin.

"These are great, hon. You should market them."

"Raht. Rooney's Just Desserts, I'll call it."

"I like it. You going to open a bakery?"

"No. Never mind."

"So how about a double chocolate cake tonight? For the birthday? Doc's dead husband. Hellooo?"

"What? Great. Double chocolate cake. Whoo hoo. What else? I've got work to do. My first head should be here any minute."

Mae could sense Rooney was very preoccupied.

160

"Then carry on, catch you later."

"Hey, you ever think about the past?"

"What for, hon? Not like we can forget. But we don't need to go shining a light there either, you know? There's a reason tattoos have to be surgically removed. The ink goes into the skin."

"I hear you on that. You're a profound woman. Anyone ever tell you that?"

Mae laughed. "Never. Did you just give me a compliment?"

"Don't go advertising that."

The doorbell rang and Rooney went to greet her customer.

Chapter Twenty-Eight

Rain put a bunch of lavender on Henry's grave, sprinkled the earth with paprika and lit a new white candle and set it atop the headstone. Shamus did his usual ritual sneeze and settled down on his haunches. "Good boy, isn't he Henry?" She patted Shamus. Her routine visit wouldn't be the same without him. Henry would have loved Shamus. And vice versa.

Rain sat cross-legged on the ground next to her dog and on top of her dead husband. The two men in her life.

"Happy birthday, my love. I'll be cooking your favorite tonight. Goulash. Just the way you taught me. Wide noodles. Can it be five years already? I still miss you madly. Keeping busy though. You know me, always trying to keep the wolves at bay. The women at the Brownstone are terrific. I wish you could meet them. They have been my salvation. I know what you'd say. Why haven't I moved on? Truth is, Henry, I didn't have the juice for it. Know what I mean? Not for the love stuff. It takes too much... what's the word? Investment. Risk. You're laughing at me, aren't you? I can just picture you and your crinkly river eyes.

"What happened to you, Rain?"

"I'm still me. A bit wiser. A bit sadder."

"Are you content, Rain?"

"Henry, here's the thing... I thought I was fine. What more did I need? I had you. You were the great love of my life. A person only needs one great love, right?"

"Oh my sweet Rain, you have a right to be happy again."

"I don't understand this weird feeling that is happening to me, Henry. I don't know what to do about it."

"Oh, Rain."

"Oh Henry! Remember how I loved saying that?"

"You're stalling, darling."

"Okay, I'll get to the point. I think I might be in love again. There I said it. Are you still there?"

"Go on…"

"I can't tell you…" Rain could hear her own breathing. She touched the mound of grass on top of Henry's grave.

"Still here. Seems your father was right after all…."

Rain burst out laughing. "Oh my God! What are you saying? My father was right? Traitor."

"I've never known you to be a coward. What are you afraid of? You don't need my permission. I insist you be happy. You deserve that. You have my blessing, though you never really needed it, my love. Go have a love-filled life. I love you."

Rain stood up, kissed Henry's headstone and blew out the candle. "Say goodbye to Henry, Shamus." Shamus gave a farewell bark and they were off. She felt so much better now. Relieved. A huge burden lifted from her mind. The twinges of guilt about disloyalty to Henry were gone. Driving away from the cemetery Rain's thoughts were not the usual ones after her cemetery visits. Waxing nostalgic about her life with Henry. Today she could think only about new love.

"Seriously? You are acting fifteen."

"Henry, I'm nervous. I feel… what does Dory call it? Gob smacked." She pulled over in front of a liquor store to get wine for tonight's birthday celebration.

"Only in your life Rain, do people have parties for dead men they once loved."

Ah, but Henry was supposed to be a keeper. Colleen said so a long time ago. Oh God, Colleen! She hadn't considered what she might think about all this. Hang on to your horse, partner. Little Joe has a big surprise. A real bonanza. She laughed to herself and opened the door to tinkling bells and aisles and aisles of wines. Her head was spinning. Just pick some wine. Don't be a drama queen. She decided on Shiraz, Cabernet and a new French Rose with a bicycle on the label. She paid quickly and headed back to the car and Shamus. A gorgeous vase of sunflowers caught her eye in the florist shop next door. She stopped and stared. *Her* favorite.

"A sign, Rain. A sign."

"Shhh, Henry, I'm trying to keep it together," Rain whispered. She realized she was acting odd, but odd seemed to be the least of her problems.

"Fill out a card if you like," the cheerful shopkeeper suggested while she wrapped the sunflowers. Rain looked at her. "Well I mean if you want to…unless they're for yourself?"

Did she give her a petrified stare back? You're an idiot, Rain. She forced herself to smile normally.

"Oh, yes, thank you, a card would be nice." She chose one and started writing. Than she noticed another card with a red balloon on it. The word Surprise! Written boldly across the top. She ripped up the other one. Under the red balloon she wrote simply: Love, Rain.

"Doesn't get much more personal."

"Shh!"

"Pardon?" The shopkeeper said, holding out her hand to attach the card to a gorgeous orange ribbon.

"Nothing. I thought my dog was barking in the car. No, I'd rather not attach the card, if you don't mind. I want to write something else later. But thanks." Rain was nearly stuttering.

"You got it bad, Rain."

"Shh, I said."

The shopkeeper looked up while taking her credit card. "Your dog again? What's his name?"

"Henry."

"Henry is a good name. Like Oh Henry! The candy bar?"

"What?" Rain took her credit card back. "No, his name's Shamus. Oh, can you add these daisies too?" Mae loved daisies and she was baking a cake for Henry after all.

"Sure. No card on these, either? How about a nice red ribbon."

"Yes. Thanks."

"No problem. Women just love flowers, don't they?"

"What?" Rain signed the receipt and nearly ran out the door.

"You have got to calm down. She's a woman, not a saber toothed tiger."

Rain switched on the radio, once she was settled in the car. Dionne Warwick was singing. *The look of love is in your eyes...*

"Well, Shamus, all we need now is a mysterious thunderstorm to descend upon this glorious day." She turned the car onto Grand Army Plaza and home as dark clouds moved across the disappearing powder blue sky. "Very funny, Henry."

Chapter Twenty-Nine

The house smelled like chocolate and Nag Champa incense. Shamus beat Rain to the kitchen heading straight for his water bowl and than plopped himself at Mae's feet. She stopped what she was doing and leaned down to pet him, a biscuit for him in her hand. "You are just the best boy, aren't you hon?" she cooed. Shamus ignored the treat and was licking the chocolate off Mae's face. It was a precious sight, Rain thought. She laughed.

"You are creating some masterpiece there, Mae. It must have passed the taste test? Shamus certainly agrees."

Mae giggled. "You know me and chocolate, hon. The Sisters used to let me lick the spoon at the orphanage. Every time I bake a chocolate cake it takes me back there."

"That's such a nice memory. Food for the soul, right? I can't wait to eat a big piece tonight. Is that fresh coffee I smell? You are an angel."

"I have my moments. Help yourself, hon." Mae picked up her icing bag and continued decorating the cake.

Rain set the shopping bag on the table and walked over and poured herself a big mug.

"Goodies?" Mae asked, looking up.

"Wine for tonight and look at these beauties." Rain unwrapped the bouquets of sunflowers and daisies. "Couldn't resist them. After my talk with Henry I was so... well in a very good mood, let's just say."

"That right? How is Henry?" Mae wiped her hands on her chef's apron and sipped from a cup of coffee she had on the counter. Only Mae could ask that with a straight face.

"He's just fine, thanks. I wished him a happy birthday. Well I should go see what messages await me in the office and than I'll start dinner, when you're through in here."

"Right, hon. I'm about to finish. You want me to put those flowers in some water?"

166

"Oh would you? Appreciate it." Rain took her coffee down the hall to her office and closed the door. She could see the light blinking red on her answering machine. She sat down in the big comfy chair behind her desk and pressed play. Requests for appointments and shelter Group time changes. Nothing urgent, thankfully. She jotted down some quick notes and turned towards the window. The rain was coming down in sheets. Good for the garden. She heard breathing, coming from the corner of the room. She walked over to the puffy swivel chair facing away from her and peeked over the top.

Curled up in a ball, was Rooney. No wonder she smelled green apples when she walked into her office. There she was, sound asleep. Her soft blonde curls framed her angelic face. Her long natural lashes brushed the very tops of her cheeks. In sleep no one could notice that one eye was a different color and never moved. The scar on her left cheek was not visible the way her head lay. Just a peaceful angel taking a nap. If Rain could erase the pain of her past she would. But that's not the way life works. You get the full package, bad and good. Why Rooney chose her office to take forty winks Rain didn't know, but she didn't mind. She reached for a light comforter on the couch and covered her.

She sat at her desk to make tomorrow's schedule. She couldn't concentrate for beans. She watched the puffy chair and listened to Rooney's breathing. She could go start dinner. Or stay here and watch the rain. Dinner won't cook itself, Rain. She forced herself to get up and started to tiptoe out of the room. Silly. She hadn't tiptoed in. And she'd played the messages and Rooney had slept through it. She was about to close the door when she heard a voice.

"Doc?"

"Yep." She walked back in. "You okay? Comfortable chair, isn't it?"

"He's dead." She turned around to face Rain. Her face was plump with sleep.

"Who's dead?" She then realized, who else?

167

"Clyde. They found him in a truck stop motel. So Mama said. Seems he beat up some poor waitress pretty bad and her brothers came after him. Clyde shot one of them, grazed his arm. The other brother shot Clyde. He wasn't grazed. He's dead as a doornail."

Rain let out a breath. "Oh boy. Sorry." She knew that wasn't what she wanted to hear. She knew Rooney was relieved. The looming threat of Clyde harming her again died along with him. That was a good thing. For everybody.

"Well I ain't a bit sorry. The man was only harmful. Not one good intention in him. It jus' knocked me for a loop is all. Can't say why for certain. I sat here waiting for ya'll and fell asleep. 'Course I wanted to tell you first. Ya'll understand, raht?"

"Sure. Now how about I make you a nice cup of tea laced with a little bourbon? You've had a shock. I may just have a splash myself."

"Already had one, thanks. Mae's got a heavy hand with the bourbon. Put me raht in dreamland. I'm fine now, really. Rather not dwell on it if you don't mind. We don't need to have a session here, do we? Personally I'd rather celebrate."

"Then that's what we'll do. Celebrate. Henry's birthday and Clyde's demise. How's that for a combo?"

Rooney got up and hugged Rain. "Thanks. I knew you'd get it."

She held Rooney by the shoulders and met her eyes. "I'm always here for you." She kissed her forehead. It was maternal.

"You sure about that?"

"You getting all sentimental on me? It was the cemetery visit and all, huh?"

Rain let her go. She was suddenly tongue-tied. Her heart was racing. She walked over and leaned on the desk. She was sinking and needed a buoy.

"Doc? You look in worse shape than me if you don't mind me saying so."

168

"I suppose I am a bit tired. The visits take a lot out of me, emotionally."

"What crock is this, Rain?"

"I should go start dinner...."

"Yeah those one-sided graveside conversations are exhausting. You want some help with supper? I cook a mean wide noodle."

Rain laughed. "You're hired. Mae's already baked the cake of the century. You should have a lick before she devours all the frosting. She and Shamus."

"Doc, you're staring. Do I have a booger or something?"

Rain shook her head. "No booger, no. I.... did you ever feel like all you've ever known is suddenly about to shift in a major way?"

"Ya'll are beating around the bush. You got something to say, just say it."

Rain gathered herself. The wall was coming down. On her head. Help.

"No, I just feel weird today. Henry was messing with me, that's all."

"Sure, blame the dead."

Rain inhaled. Green apples. "Time to make the doughnuts."

"Is that a hint? Sorry to be a bother."

"You are not bothering me. You've had a shock."

"Call me crazy, but it looks to me you're the one who's had the shock."

Rain cleared her throat, smoothed down her skirt. "I'm fine. I think we should crack open that wine and start the goulash."

"You're the boss. Meet you in the kitchen, I need to go splash my face." Rooney went upstairs.

"It's lonely at the top, Rain."

"Keep it up, Henry, and I will change the menu to pizza," she muttered to herself.

"Lady Willpower, you can let down your guard a little."

"Very funny." Rain walked down the hall towards the kitchen. Mae had the Shiraz opened on the counter.

"I'm letting it breathe, hon."

Rain poured herself half a glass and drank it down.

"Okay. Guess it's done breathing."

Rain laughed. "Sorry, I needed that." She could still smell green apples.

Chapter Thirty

Dinner was ready. Rain lit the fire in the dining room and poured herself a glass of Cabernet. Everyone was upstairs showering or getting changed. They had decided to dress up for Henry's birthday dinner. While she waited Rain had a private toast to her late beloved. "To you, Henry. To every moment we shared." She set her wineglass on the sideboard and carried Nagymama's antique soup tureen into the kitchen. What a day, she thought. So fraught with emotion. And weirdness. She ladled fragrant goulash from the pot and thought of Henry. She hoped she'd gotten the spices just right. She had certainly gotten the man right. She smiled at the framed tin of paprika on the kitchen wall.

Her boarders were gathering around hub and hearth, falling effortlessly into various tasks. Fiona tossed a red leaf salad with her secret vinaigrette, Dory carried a tray of empty paprika tins with tapers stuck in them to the dining room. Mae drained wide noodles into a colander. Rooney was inside arranging dinner music. No one said a word. It was as quiet as a cloister. Rain thought about Teresa. Her sister the Sister. She would have fit right in at this moment. Rain hoped she was happy. She heard Etta James' smoky voice from the living room. *At last...my love has come along...my lonely days are over...* She sighed and carried the soup tureen into the dining room. When they were all seated and Dory finished pouring the wine, Rain raised her glass. Her eyes were moist. "To all of you, awesome women that you are, for celebrating my Henry with me."

Dory patted her leg. "Hip hip for Henry!" she clinked Rain's glass. Rain laughed.

"We feel like he's ours so, Doc, after all this time," Fiona said. Everyone nodded.

"You've certainly heard enough about him," Rain said, "You've gotten the right impression. He was an angel. And he led me to the Brownstone to meet all of you. So

171

here's to him. Happy Birthday, Henry." Everyone cheered and clinked glasses.

"Thanks for the grub, Doc. Let's eat so," Dory said.

They dug in with gusto. Rain looked around the table. Her boarders glowed in the candlelight. Each woman so beautiful. So different. Yet the same in one respect. Survivors all. She savored the goulash and reminisced about Henry. Her boarders were eating like they'd been starved for days. It was a refreshing sight. No diets tonight. It was a moment for indulgence. The stomach, the heart and the soul. Satiated, they all got up to stretch, digest and clear the table for dessert. Mae put up the coffee and Rooney changed the music. Cassandra Wilson. Somebody was in a sexy mood. Rain rinsed the dishes and swayed to the sexy beat. She had a nice buzz from the bicycle wine. Good choice. She hadn't felt this aroused in well too damn long to wonder how damn long. She sang along to the tune and reveled in the way the warm sudsy water felt sliding between her fingers.

"Fired up, Rain?"

"Shh, Henry."

"Doc? You say something?"

Rooney was in the room now. Rain smelled her. Green apples. She took a dishtowel out of the drawer beside the sink and started drying.

"Just thinking out loud."

"Um hum."

Dory blew a pretend royal horn with her hands announcing Mae's chocolate cake. Mae set a three layer confection of sinful heaven in the center of the table. Rain added five candles. One for each year Henry was gone. Mae lit them. Fiona hit the lights. They sang a rousing rendition of Happy Birthday and Rain blew out the candles. Mae served the first piece to the place set for Henry. Next to Rooney. The second slice was for Rain. When everyone had theirs they all tucked into their sweet like happy children. Eyes rolled and moans were heard all around the table.

"I'm about to have an organism, as me mam would say," Dory said.

"Thanks, hon, no one ever came to my cake before," Mae laughed. "I'm flattered. Maybe I should open a bakery, huh, Rooney?"

"Yeah, The Angel's Devils Food Cakes, you can call it."

Mae laughed. "I like that."

Stuffed, they all collapsed in the living room and put on Henry's favorite movie, Fanny, with Leslie Caron. Mae fell asleep first.

"She's full of chocolate and wine," Rain said, covering her with an afghan.

"My bed is calling me as well. I'm knackered," Dory said.

"Yes, I'll bid you all adieu if you don't mind," Fiona added. "Adieu." They started to collect cups and wine glasses from the coffee table.

"Leave it, girls. You're not working. I'll get it later," Rain told them. "Go up to bed. You must be exhausted. And thank you for the candle holders. Henry would have loved them."

"You're very welcome," Fiona said.

"Come on, Mae, get your arse up," Dory said, shaking her gently.

Mae moaned. "Okay, hon." She got up and followed.

" 'Night, hons. See you in the a.m."

Rooney and Rain sat in the dark and watched the fire. The music swelled as the movie credits rolled. Rain looked over at her. Rooney was reclined on her side on the couch. A Renaissance painting come to life in the firelight. Shiny blonde curls framed her face, lips pouty and inviting. Scars vanished. Freckles sprinkled her delicate shoulders, her sheer white peasant blouse dipped down to its laced opening. The tops of her breasts teasing with their creamy arcs. Her long deep blue velvet skirt revealed one firm thigh as it peeked out from a bold slit.

173

"Penny for them, Doc…" It came out a husky whisper.

"You have a date later? You look beautiful. I love the outfit."

Rooney laughed. "No date. But thanks."

"I just meant…"

"I clean up nice for a hillbilly?"

"You're messing with me, now, aren't you?"

Rooney's smile widened, her dimples revealed. Her good eye filled with longing. The other catching the firelight creating an illusion of sight. Rain beheld the beginning of a soft pink nipple. She took a sip of wine. What was happening to her? Maybe she was in peri-menopuase. Maybe she should lay off the wine. Henry this is your fault, she thought. I was doing just fine being a workaholic.

"Relax, Rain. You're being seduced, not sacrificed as a virgin."

"I know, Henry. But she's a woman. I've never done this. How does it work?"

I'll forgo the joke though you left yourself wide open. Sit back and let her show you. Enjoy yourself. Life is fleeting. I'll say good night now.

"Henry? What kind of advice is that? So I'm on my own here, hmm?"

The fire crackled loudly. Rain jumped. Rooney laughed and started to change position.

"No," Rain said. "Don't move."

"I need a sip of wine is all, and darlin,' my tongue ain't that long…."

"Yeehah!"

"Shut up, Henry."

Rain picked up Rooney's glass. "Here. You look so comfortable." Rooney licked the rim and sipped.

"Cowabunga!"

"Henry, knock it off. Do you hear me?"

Pop! A piece of stray log shot out of the fire. Rooney laughed. Rain turned away from her to retrieve it before it burned a hole in the rug. Rooney watched her, with the most impish look on her face. Well save for Mae, who had imp down to a science. But this was a close second, bar none. Rooney's blouse was unlaced. Her pale and perfectly pert breasts shone in the firelight.

"Touch me...." Her voice was warm molasses dripping its way into a hot bowl of creamy sweet potatoes. Rain couldn't speak. Her tongue would not cooperate. Rooney spoke for her.

"Come here, darlin,' you've waited a long time."

Chapter Thirty-One

Colleen came down from the Ponderosa for the wedding. She brought along her husband Ben and their two girls, Joey and Candy. Young ladies by now. The Brownstone garden was in full bloom on a gorgeous Midsummer's Day, bursting with fragrant lavender and honeysuckle.

Rooney and Rain exchanged vows under a grapevine arbor draped in morning glories. Epiphany, a former client at the shelter, now an ordained Reverend, performed the ceremony. She was delighted Rain had tracked her down after learning of her successful reentrance into the mainstream. Epiphany had even reunited with her older children. They had learned for themselves how wrong their father had been in mistreating their mother.

Rain and Rooney wore floor length white silk dresses they found in an antique shop in the Village. Their heads were adorned with wreaths of baby pink roses and sweet pea. For fresh starts and joy in relationships. Rain's new friend at the flower shop made them especially for the occasion. Rain no longer hid her cards in her pocket when buying flowers.

They had two matrons of honor. The Brooklyn contingent, Colleen in a pale blue lace sundress carrying a bunch of white daisies. And Vonda, Rooney's Southern angel, a dead ringer for Billie Holiday. Slinky dark blue dress, magnolia behind her ear, her smile for Rooney and Rain was radiant against her warm brown skin.

"Wouldn't miss Sister's wedding for the world, ya'll hear that? Not for the world. Sister did it raht this time. I liked ya'll on the phone. Knew you were one righteous woman. Ya'll saved her. And look what happened…." Vonda laughed. "Bet you had no idea what the Lord had in store. A blessing's a blessing, Miss Rain. I don't suppose that's lost on you?"

Rain hugged her. "Not in the least, Vonda. I am blessed for sure. And I was certainly surprised." They both laughed.

Colleen's daughters were junior bridesmaids, two young lovelies in lavender. They sprinkled tea rose petals as they glided down the garden path in white ballet flats. They were Rain and Colleen a lifetime ago. One dark curly haired and olive skinned. The other a clone of Colleen, a freckled strawberry blond. Rain said a silent prayer that these two angels would be spared the wolves.

Mae came behind them. A vision in vintage red satin. She held five roses wrapped with a matching silk ribbon. One for each woman at the Brownstone. She beamed a smile at Rain. Rooney gave her a thumbs up. The past was absent today.

Fiona and Dory did a little jig upon entering the garden. Rain would have expected no less. They held huge single sunflowers as high as batons. Humor was the Brownstone glue that kept them all from shattering. It made them stronger. Unjaded. Rain blessed the day Rooney found the IRA. Their Brownstone luck. Both Irish beauties chose pale peach chemises setting off their fiery hair and milk and honey skin. Fiona's auburn curls spiraled like shiny corkscrews down her back. Dory's newly straightened copper tresses gleamed sleekly down her shoulders.

Last but never least was the man of the house. Shamus strutted proudly as Mae coaxed him down the bridal path. He wore the wedding rings on an emerald grosgrain ribbon around his neck. Now he sat at the couple's feet as Colleen's Ben strummed "The Water is Wide," on his guitar. When the appropriate time came, Rooney untied the ribbon from Shamus who promptly licked her face. She laughed. Rain believed she had never heard a more delightful sound. Rooney handed Epiphany the rings. White gold bands encircled with tiny amber stones. For love.

Uncle Carmine was there, dressed to the nines in a navy pinstripe suit with a red tie. He stood tall and handsome next to Rain's parents and Beulah and Kell McNeil.

"You know you're getting old when there's two brides at the wedding and no damn groom," Uncle Carmine kidded. Than quietly to Rain, "What the hell, Lorraine. You're happy, that's all that matters. Salute, bella." That was all the blessing she needed. Leave it to Uncle Carmine to break the ice and make everyone relax.

Rooney's parents and Rain's were instant friends. Southern Italy meets the Deep South. Rain's mother told Beulah McNeil, "With one daughter in the convent, I was just happy Rain was getting married again. Who knows, they could adopt."

Without missing a beat Rain heard Rooney's mama reply, "Better a woman, sugar, I told Kell, than a tomcattin' ne'er-do-well, darlin.' "

Rooney told Rain what her mother said when she broke the news to Rooney's father. She imitated her mama's voice, prim and proper and thick as swamp water. "Shug, I sweah' your daddy nearly fell clear off the porch when I told him you were aimin' on marrying Rain in New Yawk. No darlin', his name's not Ren, I told him, it's Rain, and he is a she. I handled it right quick, I did, yes maam. Laced his sweet tea with a good dose of Jim Beam and he was most agreeable, yes he was. Your daddy would surely die for you, Rooney Earl, you know that."

Rain's father was another story. Not that he wouldn't take a bullet for her. He was more or less convinced now that he had been right about her all along. Even with Henry thrown in the mix. He never quite recovered from her whole San Francisco phase. If he wanted to believe his daughter was a late blooming lesbian, so be it. Rain wasn't trying to prove him right or wrong, just trying to be happy.

Rooney and Rain spent their wedding night at the Brownstone. The next morning Rain made everyone pollichinkas, Henry's recipe for Hungarian crepes. They got rave reviews. The newlyweds said their goodbyes and Mae drove them to the airport. They were off to their destination honeymoon, England. They had thrown a bunch of countries into a hat and Rooney chose one. Neither of them had been there and Rain would finally get to visit the site of the first domestic violence refuge started by the pioneer, Erin Pizzey. It seemed fitting for Rooney to be with her when she did.

Colleen was over the moon for them. Rain suspected she might be. She was her dear best friend from the beginning. They don't turn on you, the old ones. History counts. They were joined together forever, like two old bottle caps in cement.

"Love is love, Rainey," Colleen told her. "You deserve happiness any way you get there. Rooney is one lucky lady in my book."

"Little Joe, you're the best," Rain hugged her and she cried.

As for Rain, when she wondered how she wound up at this juncture, Rooney was there with her own brand of wisdom. A Southern parable if you will.

"Look, Doc, (she still called her that), there was an angel who thought she was done with love. Then fate and a broken bayou girl whispered in her ear one night. That's us, plain and simple. Nice as toast with a dollop of honey."

How can you argue with that?

Part Two

IRELAND

*"I am a man upo' the land,
I am a Selkie in the sea."*

The People Of The Sea, David Thomson

Chapter Thirty-Two

Dory Teelon was in a nostalgic mood. She lit a cozy fire in the Brownstone kitchen hearth and brewed a pot of Barry's tea. One of her regular customers at the café had brought a box back for her from his vacation in Ireland. The strong Irish tea seemed to have a magical effect. Dory hadn't thought about home in ages. She'd shut the door nice and tight when she came to America. "Don't go there," as Mae would say. Normally, Dory was in agreement. But home was pushing against the door like the persistent Irish wind. Demanding her attention. Teasing her with memories.

She pictured Mam. The queer way she had of rhyming everyone's name. Fiona Meona. Dory Glory. She and her sisters had to be the only rhyming triplets in the whole of Ireland. "Nory, Dory, and Jury, come get your tea…." Mam's lilting brogue as she'd sang to them, as they played carefree out back below in the field. Mam had cats now. Three. Cara, Dara, and Tara. What else? Surely not Whiskers or Morris.

Mam was gas. She could be brilliant fun when she let down her hair. Dory suddenly missed her. Nobody could quite tell a story like Mam. When she reminisced about her dancing days and Da playing in the bands, you felt you were right there with them. "Those were the times, Dory love. Your da put a spell on me, he did. That rich tenor voice of his and himself so handsome and talented with the guitar. Every now and again he'd get a twinge of jealousy, he would. When I danced with a friend of his while he played. I'd calm him straight away. 'Eamon,' I'd say, 'aren't you the center of the universe up there on stage in your dickie bow for all the girls to swoon over so?' That would quiet him down. He'd smile at me then and admit there was no argument there a'tall. That's your da. A man who could admit his shortcomings."

Dory smiled thinking about her da. He was always putty in her mother's hands. She could almost smell the turf burning in the sitting room. The kettle screeching on the old Aga. Mam and her occasional fags. Silk Cut, her brand of cigarettes when she fancied the odd one. Wooden matches kept in a glass jar on a shelf over the sink. Ah, the romantic memories of home. Before Declan Mahoney turned her heart to stone.

"Your tea, sham, gone ice cold I'd say…." Fiona said, rousing Dory from her reverie.

"What?" Dory looked up at her friend. "Where'd you come from?" Dory handed her teacup absently to Fiona and rubbed her eyes.

"From me mam, originally." Fiona stuck the kettle on to boil.

Dory laughed. "Ah, Fee."

"What's up? A million miles away you were."

"What if I told you I was thinking about home?"

"Home is it? A stinking cup of Barry's and you're jelly? You're a cheap date, sham. What'll a shot of Irish Mist get you talking about I wonder?"

Dory smiled. What would she do without Fiona? Only she could slag her like that and make her feel better.

"Wouldn't you like to know? Seriously, I was thinking it might be time to go home. For a holiday. Is that pure lunacy or wha'?"

The kettle screeched. Fiona walked over and shut it off. She poured hot water over loose tea in the ceramic teapot and covered it to steep. She carried it back to the table with two clean cups and sat down.

"A holiday is it? What brought this on?" She studied Dory's face. This was the last thing she expected to hear today. I hope I'm not next for excavating repressed memories, she thought.

"*Am* I crazy, imagining I can actually go back? Things wouldn't have changed. 'Tis a pipe dream."

Fiona poured tea through a strainer filling their cups. She added milk to her own and handed Dory the pitcher.

"Hang on now, don't dismiss the idea altogether, yet. Besides, you're the one who's changed. Fuck the begrudgers." Fiona took a chocolate Kimberly from the tin. "God, I've missed these." She chewed in ecstasy. "These from your man at the café? I'd say he fancies you."

Dory laughed. "He's an old man. You suppose he has a bad cough? So about home, do you really think I have the balls? Ah, I suppose I do. They need a good bit of polishing so."

Fiona nodded. She got up from the table and returned with the Lemon Pledge.

"Start polishing. You know we could do with a bit of the old craic and a decent pint of Guinness. You'll be flying it. Let's bring Mae with us. She's a bleedin' fairy herself. Now you've got me going." Fiona was strangely excited. It was like old times. Before the men left their mark. Gobshites.

The front door slammed. Shamus came running into the kitchen and nearly slid out the back door. Mae had used a bit too much wax on the linoleum.

"Well Shamus of the Brownstone, if it isn't yourself," Dory reached for a treat from the jar on the counter. "And where's the fairy?" she asked him, stroking his fur while he munched.

Mae came into the kitchen on cue, took one look at Dory and Fiona and perched herself on a bar stool.

"So what's afoot here? I smell something brewing besides tea. I'd love a cup. This boy ran me ragged in the park. So what's the news?"

"What'd I tell you? A bleedin' fairy." Fiona got up to get a cup for Mae.

"What?" Mae looked at both of them.

"Nothing. Perfect timing," Dory said, "We're planning a holiday."

"Good for you. And that concerns me how, hon? Where are you going? The Caribbean?"

"Ireland," Fiona said, setting a cup of tea in front of her.

"Thanks. Chocolate bickies too? What's the occasion? Did you say Ireland?" Mae bit into a Kimberly and moaned. "Yum. Brilliant."

Dory shook her head laughing. "You're an original, Mae West."

"See, Dor? She's got the lingo down and all." Fiona pushed the cookie tin closer to Mae. "Here's your *bickies* now, Miss. What about it? Have you got a passport?"

"No. But I know someone who can get me one fast. When are we leaving? Do I have time to pack?"

"What are you like?" Dory hadn't laughed this much in a month of Sundays. The craic had already begun.

"Whatever you're taking, please share the elixir," Fiona said to Mae. "Don't you even want to know why we're going home out of the blue?" Fiona looked over at Dory. Dory looked at Mae. Mae gave them her big brown wide eyed innocence.

"Nope. That's your business. Some of us don't need to talk about home. Whatever that means anyway. Talk or don't talk. Doesn't matter a fig. Count me in, though. Think of all the chocolate bickies I can bring back."

Do you enjoy drowning those little Schoolboys as much as you like biting their heads off, Mae?

I just like the chocolate melting in my tea, Sister Devora.

Yes, Mae, I see that.

"Good. It's settled so. We are officially going home. Bar the plane tickets and your one's quickie passport," Dory said.

"Grand. You're in for a treat," Fiona added.

"I haven't been out of this country in me whole bloomin' life." Mae grinned.

Dory and Fiona nearly split a gut laughing.

"You are priceless," Dory said.

She had to hand it to Mae. She had a knack for putting things into perspective. Ireland would eat her up with sprinkles. *Hundreds and thousands,* Dory corrected herself, thinking in Irish already.

"All we need is a date so." Fiona said, rinsing the teacups at the sink.

"Is a fortnight too soon?" Dory asked.

"How long is that again, hon?" Mae asked. "A bit rusty on my Shakespeare."

"Two weeks."

"Sounds good to me," Mae said. "Now should I make corned beef and cabbage for dinner? You know, get us in the mood. Danny Boy and all that jazz."

"We don't actually eat that in Ireland," Fiona said.

"Bacon and cabbage, now that's another thing altogether. Nothing a'tall like your bacon here. More of a cooked country ham."

"Okay. Then how do you feel about pesto and spinach pasta? It's green."

"What are you like? Ah now, don't answer. 'Tis a rhetorical question."

"I *know*, hon. I'm not a bollocks." Mae's poker face made the IRA howl all the more.

Chapter Thirty-Three

Dory stayed up late trying to get her mind around going home. It was only for a holiday as Fiona pointed out earlier. But what was it they said, you can't go home again?

She had to think about calling Mam. There was no getting around it. Dory showing up unannounced could do Mam serious damage. The shock might kill her. *I'll ring Orleigh.* Dory liked that approach much better. Let her closest cousin do the dirty work for her; pave the wave nice and smooth. Mam would love hearing it from Orleigh. All dramatic and animated. "Dory Teelon is coming home, lads. Home to Ireland. Home to the bosom of her family. Blah, blah, blah…." Orleigh would make it out to be like the second coming of Christ. Yes, She was the very ticket, Dory thought. The one person bar Fiona who knew the whole truth.

"Settled then," Dory said out loud to the empty kitchen, an enormous load lifted off her mind. She put the kettle on to boil and went inside to the living room for a book. *Let's see, what am I in the mood for tonight?* She took an Ann Rice novel off the shelf and perused the jacket. Perfect. The kettle whistled. Dory tapped the picture on the book jacket. Vampires fascinated her. For no particular reason. She wasn't afraid of them. Ireland had its share of superstitions. Pishogues, they were called. Vampires weren't one of them. She carried her tea and book upstairs. Snuggling under the covers, she flipped to Chapter One.

"Howyeh, Lestat?" she said aloud.

Orleigh didn't seem the least bit surprised by Dory's phone sudden call the next morning. "Sure I've only been counting the days till you would call," Orleigh sang out. That was Orleigh. She always *knew.* It was the witch in her. Dory felt an instant calm hearing her cousin's voice. Orleigh had saved her. Back when Dory thought there was nothing for it but to fling herself off the moors into the sea. It seemed ages ago. Still, she could recollect the very day she decided that dying was the only way out. Orleigh had interjected her own brand of wisdom. Laced with humor ala Orleigh.

"Sure that's been done. Not a'tall original, sham. And much too Wuthering Heights if you ask me. Chin up, Dory. You're a Teelon. We don't cave in, we endure. So we can get our own back, for one. And we certainly don't leave messy corpses."

Dory smiled, thinking about it now. *I was hardly spoiled for choice.* Her cousin had been right. Dory owed her a debt of gratitude that she could never pay off in one lifetime. Luckily Orleigh didn't keep a running tally on her good deeds.

Orleigh's secluded cottage in the Glen had been Dory's safe haven. Countless nights she had ministered to Dory's wounds. The ones she could bandage. Others were soul deep. The rest was up to her. Not even the strongest spell would help her if she didn't want help.

"Leave him, Dory. He's hell bent on killing you. He'll succeed one of these days." If Orleigh said that once she said it a hundred times. Dory wasn't hearing her. People only listen when they're ready to take action. Orleigh was pissing in the proverbial wind.

Dory was stuck. She kept going back not believing him to be the monster he showed her he was. Every day of the week. Hoping against hope for another end to their story. None came. *Why do we keep trying to change people? They are what they are.* Dory would spend valuable time looking for an answer that would not come.

"Don't you love me, Declan?

"How can he love you, Dory?" Orleigh would ask her time and again. "He's hurting you physically, breaking your heart, keeping you away from your family; for fuck's sake, sham, will you tell me what is worth loving about him?"

Dory had no defense. Declan Mahoney was a lost soul way before Dory shared a bed with him. Or the back seat of a car. Or pressed against a cold stone wall behind the dairy at night. He had a way with women. His brooding good looks lured them in. *"Charm the knickers off a nun,"* people said. Bad boy. Forbidden fruit. Must be *some* good underneath, Dory had surmised. He had a tough home life. Right. Get in line.

His mother was as mad as a hatter. His father went out for cigarettes one day and never returned. Poor boy just needed someone to love him. A good girl from a normal family would be like Christmas coming early. But what was in it for Dory? Nobody asked that. Not even Dory.

It was Declan who wanted to get married. But there was no coupledom, like Dory imagined. No romantic nights of newlywed bliss. They merely shared a house. She worked her job, came home and played the good wife. Declan worked when it suited him. It didn't suit him regularly. They got by. Dory worked hard. Declan partied any wages he earned. Bought himself toys. Motorcycles. Amplifiers. They ate silent dinners when he had the inclination to grace their table. Uneaten dinners went into the bin more than not. They had sex if he felt like it. He was detached, indifferent. Like he was doing her a favor. Not like a husband she had married for love. He liked sex when the mood struck him. And he liked it rough, and his women compliant. Dory complied. She made a habit of it after she learned what making a fuss meant. A fat lip cost her a day of work. A punch in the arm could be hidden under a blouse. Humiliation was par for the course. Another day another put-down. You get used to it. Disappointment makes you numb.

Declan's sluts were a dime a dozen. Barflies he saw at the pub. Dory knew. It was a small town. It became an effort to care. How did I wind up here? A question she constantly asked herself. Who is Dory Mahoney, anymore, she wondered? She thought Declan would win in the end. She would be another statistic. A story on the late news. But he didn't win. Declan would never hurt her again.

Sheila Mahoney was another story. Declan's crazy mother was surely still lurking around the streets of Blessington. You couldn't avoid the nutter if you wanted to.

She blamed Dory for Declan's death, even though it was an accident. She hurled accusations at the graveside ceremony Dory forced herself to attend, just to see his body go into the ground. Believe he was dead. Sheila's histrionic carrying on and incessant keening made Dory want give her a good shove and land her into the gaping hole that awaited her son.

Dory couldn't have tuned her out that day if she'd been Mother Teresa. The woman was relentless. *"My Dekkie! You bitch, you murdered my son. Drove him to the whores. To the drink. To his grave. You wanted him to die. You should die."*

Was it Orleigh or her sisters who finally shut Sheila's mouth? Dory couldn't remember. It could have been Da. He wouldn't stand for his daughter to be demeaned that way, grieving mother or not. Maybe it was Mam who silenced Sheila Mahoney? *Shite, I want to remember.* Well bless them whoever put a sock in her mouth that awful day.

Someone had put their arm around Dory and led her away from the grave and the lunatic mother. That she remembered, the leaving. She felt nothing but cold when they handed her a whiskey in the pub later. She drank them down one after the other, obediently. Then burst into tears, surprising everyone. Surely she wasn't that upset about losing Declan, people wondered? "He was the worst sort of shite to her," they whispered. "Nothing to miss in him. Sure he's not worth the tears. Have another whisky, love."

Dory wasn't crying for her dead husband. She wept for her babies. For them she mourned alone. Fiona knew. And Orleigh. Both would take that secret to their graves. It was Orleigh who helped her through it. Orleigh who watched as Dory passed three fragmented lifeless fetuses out of her warm womb and into the tepid bath. *My wee babies.* Three girls who never had the chance to grow and thrive within her. Become her daughters. Let her love them. As she had tried to love their father. The father who killed them. *You murdered my babies, Declan. I will never forgive you. Or your mother.*

191

It had taken an ocean between her and the past to put her mind to rights again. For a time Dory thought she'd wind up like the poor vacant eyed crathers up in the asylum on the Wicklow road. *I am as mad as them. Why am I still allowed to walk around freely? I'm no saner than they are. How could I be when I live with him? Why do I let him treat me like yesterday's rubbage? Why do I stay with him after he killed my babies?*

Dory's rebirth in America was the second half of her reentrance to the living. Orleigh was her first step back from the depths of self-loathing. Doc and Orleigh. Her saviors. If there was any luck about it, then they were hers in spades. She longed to see Orleigh. Her beautiful face. Her generous hugs. Their unspoken kinship that went beyond blood. If only Orleigh could make Sheila Mahoney disappear. That would be one feckin' day to celebrate. *I'm going home and Sheila Mahoney can shit in her hat, paint her arse black and go stark raving madder than she already is for all I care.*

"Now," Dory said out loud, "I feel so much better." She told Fee her very thoughts the next day. Fiona agreed.

"That's the spirit. You do know there are far more people back home who will be watching your back, not that shite Sheila Mahoney's. Unless they're wondering where to stick the knife."

"Good point," Dory said, smiling. "What about you? What do you miss?"

"I can't wait to wrap my legs around one of my da's new studs." Fiona had a wicked smile on her face.

"You little slapper, you."

"*Horses.* Where's your dirty mind, sham?"

"In the gutter, where else?"

"Right. Not that a grand ride from the human kind wouldn't be welcome. Just that the four legged ones are so much less complicated, know what I mean?"

"Don't look at me for an argument there."

Chapter Thirty-Four

Dory blew by the sign for Blessington. She caught Fiona's eye in the rearview mirror. Fiona winked. *Orleigh's first,* they silently agreed. A perfect place to buy some time. Neither was ready to face her parents just yet. Dory stepped on the gas heading for the Glen. Mae was silently drinking in the scenery. Dory didn't know her to ever be this quiet for so long.

"You right, Mae?"

"Um hmm. Where are you taking us, hon? The Garden of Eden? It's beautiful, but I really need to pee."

Dory laughed. "Sorry. I was anxious to get to Orleigh's. I'll get off at the next exit and we'll pee and get a drink, okay?"

"Thanks." Mae continued to look out the window. It was exactly like every coffee table book she'd pored over in the Heights bookstore. Pictures of Ireland came to life. The reality as vivid as the dream. Mae was pleased. Normally places didn't live up to their press. People tend to romanticize their travel. No need to here, she thought. Lush pea green splendor speckled with lazy grazing cows and painted sheep. Mae knew the large red, green and blue X's painted on the sheep's backs signified to which farmer they belonged. She had read about that in her Irish research. Maybe him, she thought, waving to an old fellow in a sweater riding past on a bicycle.

"He's the genuine article. Your one on the bicycle," Dory told her.

"Yeah, if he'd have smiled he would have shown you the two teeth he owned," Fiona laughed.

Dory pulled into a petrol station and Mae headed for the loo. Fiona bought three orange sodas and they were back on the road in a matter of minutes.

"Nearly there now," Dory said. "You're smack dab in the middle of County Wicklow, the Garden of Ireland. Famous for its breathtaking vistas," Dory rolled her tongue.

"Feast your eyes, darlin," Fiona said, "the mountain will take your breath away. Look over to your right. Castle ruins. The pride of our ancient kings and queens. Can you not hear the wail of the pipes? They play like a siren's song from the sea. Listen. Don't you feel the thundering hoof beats of grand stallions mounted by Celtic goddesses and alchemists journeying to their stone circles, the dewy mist enshrouding their sacred rituals?"

"Holy shit. I had no idea you were so poetic." Mae looked back at her.

"Ah, I get all mushy gushy when I'm on the auld sod."

"They don't call her Lady Gregory for nothing," Dory said.

"Fuck off, sham. Don't mind her."

"I feel like I've stepped into a fairytale. Yeats' girlfriend or not."

Dory and Fiona cracked up. "She's got it sussed, Dor."

"She does and all. You're a card, Mae. A feckin' card. Brace yourself, darlin', the storybook has only just opened. We're about to enter The Glen Of Imaal, Orleigh's little piece of heaven. The best place on earth. But we're biased, of course. You judge for yourself."

Another emerald meadow opened up alongside them. More plump sheep and cows dotted the landscape, framed in periwinkle heather. There was something else apparent besides the obvious lush beauty. A sense of peace. That was ironic, Mae thought, for all the blood that was shed here long ago. And only too recently in the North. But right here the scar of violent history and oppression was absent. It was a perfect picture postcard. As lushly green as bolts of freshly cut velvet. Visible to the naked eye so clearly one minute and mysteriously curtained in mist the next. The seemingly magical vapor seeping down the Glen, its huge mountain looming in the distance. They hadn't seen another car for miles. The tranquility was intoxicating.

"It's called The Lug," Dory said, pronouncing it Loog. "The mountain. Short for Luquinella. Grand no? Orleigh treasures her privacy. She has that here."

"Right. Our very own biddy, witch of the Glen," Fiona said.

Mae looked back at her. "You're taking the piss out of me, right?"

Fiona and Dory hooted. "Listen to your one, will you?" Fiona said.

"I read The Van and The Snapper. *And* Angela's Ashes," Mae said proudly.

"Roddy Doyle *and* Frank McCourt? Ah sure you're well schooled then."

"Did you say *witch?*" Mae looked at Fiona.

"I did. Dory told you Orleigh was a writer, I presume? Well she's also the resident witch. Healer, shaman, whichever you like. Semantics."

Mae had her mouth open to say something when Dory quickly took a sharp turn up a dirt path. Mae held on to her seat. The path came out of nowhere, very overgrown and dark. Her eyes adjusted as the light came through. They went in further. Finally Dory slowed down. What had to be Orleigh's cottage was in front of them. "Okay, now I am smack dab in a fairytale," Mae thought.

The charming house was whitewashed limestone with cornflower blue shutters framing small paned red-framed windows. Rose of Sharon spilled out of window boxes on two levels. The roof was thatch. Smoke peeled from the chimney and the fragrance of burning peat filled their noses. An arched front door was painted a brilliant hue of vermillion. You couldn't do it justice by calling it red. A brass knocker gleamed at its center. Was it in the shape of a woman? Mae couldn't tell for sure from where she stood. She walked closer, following her friends.

195

The cottage bowled her over. It was everything she had read and dreamed about. Quintessentially Ireland. The place Sister Devora sang of so lovingly. *Sister, I'm actually here.* Sister Devora would jump for pure joy if she knew.

The front door flew open and through it came the most enchanting woman Mae had ever seen in real time. Her hair matched the color of the door and caught the sunlight creating a halo around her face.

"My God, it's Mary Magdalene," Mae said.

Fiona howled. Dory screamed, "Cooeee, we're here…."

The woman, clearly the infamous Orleigh, not the lover and disciple of Jesus, came running down the stone path, flaming tendrils flying behind her. "Wow." Mae was stunned.

Orleigh fell into Dory's embrace and they stay locked together for several minutes as if they'd been parted for centuries. Fiona was next in line to receive this goddess's affection. Mae could not stop staring. Orleigh was walking towards her. No way, she can't be real, Mae thought. Nobody looks like that. Maybe she works for a reenactment company.

"Welcome to my Glen," Orleigh spoke in a voice so melodic Mae could have sworn she was singing. Her smile was radiant. She took Mae's hands in her own.

"Orleigh Maeve Teelon at your service. You would be Mae West, of course. I've heard all about you."

Mae felt a pleasant wave go through her entire body. Orleigh was still holding her hands.

"Um, hi. Happy to meet you." Mae was so nervous she was shaking. *She's just a woman. Not some mystical creature you dreamed up. Get a grip.* The self-talk did no good. Mae was enraptured.

"Make yourself at home. Your wish is my pleasure to conjure." Orleigh winked. Mae was speechless, her eyes glued to Orleigh's ageless face and virescent eyes.

"Sorry, I'm normally chattier," Mae apologized. "It's just that you're so incredibly beautiful."

Orleigh laughed. It was the sweetest sound. Babies giggling. A fountain splashing. The first notes of a flute.

"Why thank you. Aren't you the most fetching wood nymph I ever laid eyes on?"

"Thanks." Mae was still staring even though it was impolite.

Dory interrupted them. "I told you she was the real thing."

Both Mae and Orleigh looked at her. She could have been talking to either one.

"Let's go inside," Orleigh said, "You must be bursting for a pee. I know my cousin in the car, rushing to get here. Starving are you? Come in."

Mae and Fiona followed Orleigh and Dory up the path. "I'd eat a child's arse through the back of a chair now," Dory said, her arm around Orleigh.

"Nothing's changed there so," Orleigh laughed. When they reached the top step, Orleigh turned back towards the woods and clapped. "Come to me, Jesus," she called out, then whistled. "Jeeesus, we've company…."

Mae watched the trees blow in the soft breeze. If a longhaired man with sandals walks through the clearing now, I'm toast, she thought. Only barks were heard in response. The cutest little dog came scampering up the path and jumped up and down at Dory's feet. "Well Jaysus, you haven't forgotten me." Dory cooed to the precious dog, leaning down to let him lick her face.

"He's a Glen terrier, isn't he?" Mae bent down to pet Jesus.

Orleigh was impressed. "Yes. He's a Glen of Imaal terrier. How did you know that?"

"There's no flies on your one," Dory said.

"I read about them," Mae said. "They're very popular. Friendly too."

"Brilliant. Jesus is lovable all right. Himself and yourself will get along famously."

"Fancy his name?" Dory asked.

197

"Fitting. Which way is the loo, hon?"

Orleigh clapped her hands laughing, "Aren't you are as charming, Mae West? Up the stairs and to your right."

The three women were deep in conversation when Mae returned. She could hear from the hallway, their animated brogues blending like one voice. Mae envied their shared history and loyalty. She didn't have old friends like that. Only Sister Devora from the orphanage.

"There you are." Orleigh was in the hallway. "Have yourself a gawk around the cottage. Then join us so I can feed you."

"Thanks, I will." Mae walked through the turquoise kitchen archway leading to a sitting room. Celtic knots in deft blue embellished the white molding around the top of the room. Straight ahead a small black tiled fireplace beckoned warmly. A gentle peat fire glowed within. Mae's attention was drawn to the mantle of polished oak covered in seven-day candles burning brightly in thick glass jars. To the right of the fireplace sat a plump chaise covered in a quilted fabric the color of Irish oatmeal. A book of fairytales lay in wait on top of a sky blue chenille throw. Mae was tempted to ignore her stomach's rumblings and take a nap there.

Her eyes kept moving. There was so much to look at she didn't know what to focus on first. Celtic artifacts hung on the sage green walls. A life-size statue of the Goddess Brigit stood regally under a window. The sun lit her face making her seem alive. Mae remembered Sister Devora showing her a tiny version she kept in her room. *Brigit, the Goddess of divinity. My granny gave her to me. There's nothing wrong with having all the women on our side, Mae. Mary herself is the Supreme Goddess, of course.*

Across from Brigit stood a Queen Anne chair of olive green velvet. On a small mahogany tea table next to it was a book of poetry. "Bog Wild," was the title. Now that sounds interesting, she thought. A half full Balleek china teacup and saucer explained where Orleigh preferred to sit. Mae could picture her there, sovereign, yet sexy in a velvet verdant gown. Her hair fiery spirals cascading majestically around her. Emeralds at her throat. A Celtic queen. Morgan. No, Maeve. Didn't Orleigh mention that was her middle name?

Mae continued her walkabout. She pushed open the door at the far end of the sitting room and stepped inside. A pleasant fragrance surrounded her. Bergamot. Orleigh was wearing it. The room was welcoming and warm. The last of the day's sunlight shone on butter yellow walls. On first glance it appeared to be a library. Books lined the wooden shelves than ran the perimeter of the room. An old wooden farm table with bench took up the center. Small glass bottles of cobalt blue were lined up on a metal tray. A glass bowl of cork stoppers sat next to them. *Potions?* On a large wooden lazy susan, labels and recipes lay in organized piles, weighted down by flat stones. *Spells?* Above the long table hung fragrant bundles of herbs and dried flowers. Mae inhaled a potpourri of aromas. Lemon, lavender, rosehip, vanilla, mint, sage, valerian, yarrow. *Magic teas?* Orleigh the witch?

Mae walked over to the intricately carved desk in one corner of the room. Piles of pages sat on top, a cracked coffee mug full of pens, a laptop and a good reading lamp. Orleigh the writer. The stained glass window behind it cast prisms of color across the walls. Celtic knots danced around a triad of fairies. Inspiration undoubtedly flowed in this room. An old fashioned physician's cabinet across from the desk caught her eye. It was filled with a collection of colored bottles. They looked like carrier oils and essential oils next to them. She read the labels: camphor, clary sage, dragon's blood (*definitely witch*), myrr, frankincense, geranium, mandarin, marjoram, pine, patchouli. Orleigh the healer. Like Doc, only of the body. Mae imagined Orleigh took her work seriously. *Wouldn't she and Doc make a spectacular team?*

Another fireplace smoldered in the room with more candles above it. A zaftig stone fertility goddess stood fireside, keeping vigil over hearth and home. Mae sat down next to her in a blood red club chair. She pictured Orleigh sitting there reading her spell/recipe cards and concocting new aromatherapy healing potions. So far this was Mae's favorite room. Did Orleigh really practice magic? The thought excited her more than a little. She followed laughing voices back to the kitchen.

Here was the true hub of the cottage. A peat fire burned in a large old stone hearth. Jesus dozed nearby on a green flannel pillow bordered with Celtic knots. He was the picture of contentment. Lucky dog. Dory, Fiona and Orleigh were seated at a round oak pedestal table covered in Irish lace and set for a grand tea. A china dish was piled high with freshly baked scones. A loaf of brown bread waited to be sliced on a wooden board. Sister Devora's favorite. Creamy butter, the color of daffodils, in a small dish sat next to it. Sister would be in heaven here. Was that fresh ham? Mae's mouth was watering. A tray of cheeses and fruit completed the gourmet delights awaiting her. And she didn't miss the dessert tray on the counter, not where chocolate was concerned. Brownies and chocolate biscuits. The scent of chocolate was making her high. The china was Balleek, matching the large teapot that sat importantly at the center of the table. Sugar cubes in a dainty crystal bowl stood next to it.

"Have a seat, Mae, let me pour you a hot cuppa." Orleigh touched her back gently as she filled her cup. Mae felt a pleasant quiver up and down her spine. She looked up at Orleigh.

"Thanks. This is some feast. And some cottage. Wow."

"Welcome home," Orleigh whispered. Only Mae could hear her. What a strange thing to say, Mae thought. Yet in an odd way she felt as if she had come home. Not that the word ever had much meaning for her. *Home. Shome.*

"Mind if I move in?" Mae said, in between bites of her second chocolate biscuit. These babies put the old Schoolboys to shame. And Mae always thought they weren't half bad for store bought cookies. Of course Sister Beatrice's baking was another thing altogether.

"You like my baking that much is it?" Orleigh smiled and passed Mae the plate of cookies.

"Fabulous, hon. And I consider myself a chocolate expert. But no, I was thinking that I've never felt like this before. Except in dreams, you know? I feel like I'm visiting a real-life fairy queen in her storybook cottage. Oh, now I'm rambling. Please don't take offense. I don't mean that in a condescending American isn't it all so quaint way."

Fiona laughed. "Didn't I tell you that part? Orleigh is a fairy queen. She can be wicked though, be careful. Some people think she cooked up a couple of kiddies in the Aga. Someone wrote a book about her. What was it again? Hansel and somebody."

"Don't mind them. They're just jealous. Hotsy totsy city dwellers are you now, shams? Grand you feel at home, Mae. I'm thinking you and I could do interesting magic."

Mae drank the rest of her tea in one gulp. She wanted to ask Orleigh if she was taking the piss out of her, but she didn't want to be rude. *Real magic?*

"Cousin, you're likely to scare the girl right out of the Jaysus Glen sure. Talking about magic and all."

"Mae doesn't scare easily, sure you don't?" Orleigh asked her.

"No, hon. Reality is much scarier if you ask me."

"Brilliantly put. Besides, anyone with an appetite like yourself, bless you, a little of the Craft is not about to give you the jitters."

Mae put her biscuit down and looked at Orleigh. "I wish I'd met you years ago. I could have used a spell or two. Eye of newt and all that. No disrespect meant."

"None taken." Orleigh studied her guests. She was over the moon to have Dory back in her life. Fiona as well. It had been too long. And wasn't Mae West a pure delight?

"You are aware that I practice no harm? 'Tis only the healing and such. Nothing black, you understand."

"Oh sure. I meant like a protection spell."

Dory and Fiona were a little surprised at Mae's candor. She must really feel relaxed to be so open with Orleigh. They couldn't have been happier. Coming home was a good decision. So far. But they were still in the Glen. Miles away from Blessington.

Orleigh touched Mae's hand. "Someone *did* protect you. Did she not?"

"You mean Sister Devora?"

"Yes." Orleigh saw the innocent child Mae once was for a fleeting moment in time. There's not a hell raging hot enough for the likes of someone who could hurt a wee thing like her, Orleigh thought. She felt the familiar rage well up deep within her that never quite went away.

"Now can I interrupt you witches for a moment?" Dory asked.

"Mind your tongue, cousin," Orleigh scolded her playfully. "The magic hasn't hurt you a'tall. Sure you're here aren't you? Credit yourself alone for that brilliant idea?"

Dory looked closely at her cousin. Her smile widened. "Why you feckin' biddy. You did it again didn't you? Is it any wonder I couldn't sleep for nights on end? I thought day and night only of coming home. No wonder. 'Twas yourself all along."

"I love you, too. Madly."

"I love the shite out of this woman," Dory said, "No jewel or treasure could I love more than her. Not in all the world."

"Oh brother," Fiona rolled her eyes. "You are no less a poet. Yeats and Joyce are worried so, both doing cartwheels in their graves."

Mae burst out laughing. "Good one, hon."

Mae was suddenly tired. The flight, the drive and the good food and sweets she'd stuffed herself with were taking their toll. Worth every bite, she thought.

"Where do you put it?" Orleigh asked her.

"Tapeworm." It was Mae's standard answer for years. Sounded better than saying she had a speedy metabolism. Or lucky genes. Genes shmeens.

Orleigh loved it. "You are priceless, you are, Mae."

"So I've heard, hon. That and a buck fifty will get me on the subway."

Orleigh howled again. She liked that one even better.

Mae tried to stifle a yawn but it was no use. Orleigh caught it. "Why not have yourself a lie-down? Lads, you must be knackered from the flight. Go on up so. The beds are ready."

Mae stood up, carrying plates to the sink. "Sounds good to me. I am sleepy." She yawned again.

"Grand than. Leave those dishes to me. Get your cases from the car. Dory show Mae her room. You and I will share mine. Fiona can take the front bedroom."

"Aye, aye, Captain," Dory saluted Orleigh who gave her the backwards peace sign in response. Mae followed Fiona out to the car. She stopped back in the kitchen.

"Just a little something for having me here. Hope you like it." Mae handed Orleigh a shopping bag.

"Ah, aren't you as sweet. Totally unnecessary. But thank you. I do love a pressie." Orleigh wiped her wet hands on a tea towel and sat at the table.

"Hurry hon, I can't stand the suspense." Mae was like a child at Christmas.

"You do know what's inside?"

"Of course. But you don't."

"Good point." Orleigh ripped off the ribbon and paper and lifted the lid of the box. She gasped as she lifted the stone figure and held it up to the light. "Oh Mae, wasn't I ever right about you?" Orleigh smiled.

Mae was so pleased with herself she couldn't help grinning back. Orleigh looked closely at the angel. It was her double. Save the halo of Celtic knots. They shared the same amazing copper curls and flawless milky complexion. One porcelain, one flesh and blood. The eyes clinched it. Right down to the authentic auburn lashes. Orleigh stared into the very same intense bottle green eyes as her own. The angel wore a deep green velvet gown. Her wings majestically dipped in gold leaf. At her throat, an amulet of the Goddess Brigit.

"I'm deeply touched, Mae. Thank you."

She had underestimated Mae West. She couldn't take her eyes off the angel in her hands.

"She's you, hon," Mae said, matter of factly.

" 'Tis. Yet how could you know? Unless Dory showed you photos?"

"Nope. No pictures. Dory never takes her stuff from the past out of the attic at the Brownstone. None of us do."

"Then it was Divine Order," Orleigh said, hugging her tightly. Mae could feel her good energy.

"Thanks very much, Mae."

"Your welcome. I'm glad you like it."

"I adore her. My twin. Come with me. I know just where she belongs."

Mae stepped inside Orleigh's workroom for the second time that day. "I take it you like this room?" Orleigh asked her, turning back from the mantle where she cleared a space for the angel.

"It's gorgeous. Smells great too. She looks happy there." Side by side Orla and her stone cast double did indeed look like twins.

"Now sleep is in order, what do you say?"

"Sweet dreams?"

Orleigh laughed. "I could get used to you."

Dory appeared around the corner by the stairs. "Are you right? Ready for Freddy?"

"Who?" Mae rubbed her eyes.

"Sleep, sham." Dory led the way upstairs.

Mae hadn't seen the bedrooms. Dory opened a door at the top of the stairs. It was arched just like the front door. Made of the same beautifully carved wood. Dory switched on the bedside lamp and the room came to life. Mae's breath caught in her throat. So far Ireland was leaving her breathless. A mural of angels in flight filled the entire wall across from the big wrought iron bed. A ring of trees in a lush forest surrounded the angels.

"Does Orleigh *paint* too?"

"If I told you it was your one below, would you believe me?"

"Fiona did this? What the hell is she doing waitressing?"

Dory laughed. "You can tell her that when you wake up. She'll be pleased. I suspect you'll be learning a lot more about us both while you're here. In the meantime, will you be able to sleep?"

"Like a baby, hon." Mae kicked off her shoes, threw off her jeans and crawled under the thick colorful patchwork quilt. Dory tucked her in.

"Codladh samh."

"Hmm?" Mae asked, already dozing off.

"Sleep well," Dory translated her Irish, closing the door.

Chapter Thirty-Five

Dory found Orleigh in her sitting room. She looked up from her reading. "I thought I heard the loo. Can't sleep?"

"Not a wink. Too wound up. Besides, I wanted you all to myself," Dory said, taking a cozy seat by the fire. "Is that coffee I smell? 'Tis brilliant."

" 'Tis. Go help yourself to a cuppa than we'll dish the dirt like we used to...."

Dory returned with a large mug of coffee with cream and a refill for Orleigh. "Right. About Mam and Da? They know I'm here I suppose?" Dory stared into the fire.

"Aye, They do of course. 'Tis fine, sham. No worries. Didn't they know you would come here first? Seriously, they don't care a sheep's arse about the past. Only that you're home. Your sisters are thrilled to bits."

Dory felt relieved. What was she expecting? They were her family no matter what. But there would be questions. *Why did you have to leave? Why let that miserable wretch run you out of town? Out of the country for pity's sake. Just what in God's name did Declan do to you?"*

"Cooee...you're away with the fairies. What's up?" Orleigh's voice snapped her out of it. Doc called it monkey mind, the endless chatter in our heads.

"Sorry. I was as you say, dwelling. Tell me about your work. What's your latest book about? Wasn't it fairytales and healers or something?"

"Brilliant memory, as usual. I'm reviving traditional fairytales with stories of Irish women healers. Folklore, remedies and beautiful illustrations, hopefully by your one above if she'll agree."

"Finoa?"

"Any better suggestions?"

"No, you're dead on with her. Knowing Fiona she'll want to develop a new design line from it. You know, Folklore Chic. The Biddy Early Boudoir."

Orleigh laughed. "Could do worse."

"Did I say how much I've missed you?"

"Once or twice. Likewise. But it sounds like you have a nice place over. The Brownstone and all. The big city across the ocean. Grand shopping. Cities are useful."

"It's not the Glen, though. Brooklyn is lovely. Doc is a gem. And Rooney is gas. You've seen Mae for yourself. But I hadn't realized how much this place is in my blood."

Orleigh clapped her hands. "I'm delighted you haven't forgotten. Calls for a proper drink. Back in a wink." She headed for the kitchen and Dory stirred the fire and tried hard not to remember her past.

Orleigh put a snifter of port in Dory's hand and sat down across from her. "To your return, cousin. Slainte, Bean Sidhe." *Ban Shee. Fairy girl.* They clinked glasses.

"Slainte, Banrion Sidhe." *Bonreen Shee. Fairy Queen.* The names Orleigh gave them years ago. There were some good memories in there, if you sorted through the nightmares.

"Okay, spill it." Orleigh swirled her wine and drank.

"Spill what? Okay, you win. Can't fool you for shite. How's he keeping? Happy now, witch?"

Orleigh laughed. "Delighted. Ah yes, the one that got away. Kieran is still a fine thing. Unattached, you might be interested to know. He'll be beside himself seeing you again. Purely beside himself."

"Don't know if I'm ready for that. So much time has passed. So much I can't undo."

"Nonsense. Dust your fanny off and get back on the horse. 'Tis the best cure. How long has it been, by the way? How about some potcheen?" Orleigh suggested. "Back in a wink." She returned with a bottle of whiskey in her hand and that familiar look in her eyes.

"Ah, truth serum, is it? Okay, but just a drop, I'm already buzzed from the Port."

"Lightweight."

"Sadly, yes. And by the way, if it's any of your business, which it isn't, my sex life is just fine, thank you very much." Dory sipped her whiskey.

"I see." Orleigh swirled her glass of Teelings in the firelight. "That long? Sure I suppose that's what rechargeable batteries are for."

"You do not have one of those?"

"A vibrator? You can say it, sham. Lovely invention that. And don't be shocked. We've chewing gum in Ireland now too. You have been away from the bog too long."

Dory snorted, "Very funny. Where is Rory these days? Surely you haven't traded him in for your mechanical friend?"

"Not a chance. He's up to Dublin on a book jaunt. There's his latest." She motioned with her foot toward the book of poems on the table.

Dory picked it up. "Bog Wild, poems by Rory DuShane. Sounds hot."

" 'Tis. Have a gawk. Rory will be chuffed you read it. Might want to dig out your little friend if you brought him. I've a brand new one if not. There's extra batteries in the press."

"That good, huh?" Dory flipped through the pages, shaking her hands as if she'd burned herself. Orleigh laughed.

"Only thing better would be himself reciting them. The man has a magic tongue I tell you." Orleigh threw her head back and fanned herself. Dory drained her glass of whiskey. She felt her cheeks. They were warm and flushed.

"Mercy, where is that huntsman in yonder woods when we need him?" Dory kicked her legs up in the air.

"There's my girl. That's more like it."

"I believe I could use a bit of a lie down." Dory stood to go upstairs, sat down again. She felt a tad woozy. *Lightweight is right. You better get your drinking shoes on, Dor.* She could just hear her sisters. She looked down at the book of poetry.

"Take it with you," Orleigh said. "But keep your moaning down to a roar, there's people above sleeping."

"Fuck off, witch." Dory blew her a kiss from the stairs.

"Ah now there's the dirty talk I love," Orleigh teased, blowing her a kiss back.

"Don't you have a cauldron that needs stirring?"

"Cute. Skip to the third poem. You won't be disappointed." Orleigh waved her off and turned to stir the fire.

Chapter Thirty-Six

Fiona was the first one to surface after their naps. Mae was sound asleep with the angels. Dory was snoozing like a contented cat in Orleigh's four poster bed. The scent of bergamot oil lingered in the lamp lit hallway. Somebody had a glorious soak, Fiona thought, inhaling the orange fragrance coming from the loo. She needed coffee at once. Strains of Mary Black came from Orleigh's workroom. Not wanting to disturb her, Fiona foraged around in the kitchen press until she found a bag of coffee. "Ah, you're only heaven," she stuck her nose in the bag, closed her eyes and sniffed.

" 'Tis the truth, isn't it just?"

Fiona spun around. Orleigh was standing in the doorway.

"Jaysus, you do walk on cat feet. I never heard you."

Orleigh smiled. "I was finishing some oils below. I could use a cuppa myself."

"In the sacristy, were you? I heard the music. Didn't want to bother you." Fiona spooned coffee into a metal basket. She covered the percolator and set it on the Aga.

"You know you're always welcome at my altar, sham. Sleep well?" Orleigh took a tin of biscuits out of the pantry.

"Like a child. I never have a problem here. I've missed this place. And you." Fiona helped herself to a chocolate biscuit.

"And you've been missed. Your sisters pop down now and again. Last trip they brought me that fabulous slipcover for the chaise. Neeve's design. Lovely, no?"

" 'Tis. I've missed her. Oona too, oddly enough. Speaking of Oona, did you swear her to secrecy about me coming home? Put a muzzle on her?" Fiona loved her sister, but Oona couldn't keep a secret if she was being asked by the President of Ireland herself.

"I did. Not the muzzle bit though. But than you know Oona, so I can't promise anything. Anyway if the Teelons know Dory is home don't you think your parents know you're with her?"

"You're right. A surprise wasn't a good idea anyway. Mam needed time to prepare. To roll out the royal carpet. Shine the good silver. Alert the bugle corps and pipes. God, it feels damn good to be home. I didn't think I missed the place that much. Another life, you know?"

"So New York and all its excitement didn't make you forget the auld sod than?"

"Not a chance. No comparison. Chalk and cheese. Home is Ireland. Don't get me wrong; I adore the Brownstone. Doc is a class act. And your one Rooney, she's a bog girl deep down. And there's Mae of course. Now if we only had you there, what else could we want sure?"

"I'm thinking maybe a man? A good one. Didn't find one galloping around Central Park?"

"You read too many novels. Or write them. The answer is no. But Doc and Rooney got hitched."

"That's grand. So now you have two real live men living in the Brownstone is it?"

Fiona laughed. "Ahm, not exactly... they married each other."

"Grand for them."

"You aren't shocked?"

"Why should I be? We have lesbians in Ireland. Along with chewing gum and vibrators."

Fiona burst out laughing. "What are you like?"

"Seriously, how are you, Fee? It was a long time ago... All work and no play, really?"

Fiona drank her coffee. Stalled. Toyed with another biscuit. Put it down.

"I swore off the shites, remember? Too complicated. Selfish. Demanding. Possessive."

"That's someone in particular you're describing. I know you have scars, but all men are not the devil."

211

"How profound. So tell me, does your man, gorgeous Rory, poet and *lova* extraordinaire, have a brother then?" Better to indulge Orleigh, she wasn't about to give up.

"That's my girl." She was glad Fiona hadn't turned bitter. It wasn't her nature. The feckin' Irish Svengali had done quite a number on her. Wouldn't she be pleased to know he was on a very short leash these days? His new wife made sure of that. She'd spare Fiona the information. Why dredge up the past? It was a pleasant thought just the same. Grayson O'Leary tethered. Orleigh just hoped your one had it grand and tight around the fucker's neck.

"Yoo hoo? I asked you if Rory had a brother?"

"He does as a matter of fact. Cillian. Fine thing. Lives in Galway. Single as it happens. Straight, for your information. A very gifted musician. Fab singer. Plays a lot over on Inishmore."

"Brilliant. What does he play?"

"The cittern, for one. Strums that pear-shaped guitar like he's stroking a worshipped woman."

"Is that right? Perhaps we need a wee skip over to Inishmore."

"A grand walk on the quay would do you a world of good."

"I'm in. Nothing like an auld hot whiskey to warm the cockles. It would be great craic. We could all go."

"Fine with me. Rory will be back tomorrow. I'll mention it to him."

Fiona yawned. "I'm still tired. A bit peckish too. All this sex talk makes me hungry."

"Deprivation can do that." Orleigh smiled. "Can I interest you in a toasted cheese? Or would you rather a vibrator and a dirty book like your one above?"

"I wouldn't say no to one of your famous cheese and tomato sandwiches. And my fanny is fine at the moment, thanks. What were you and Dory talking about anyway?"

"The usual shite. Heat the griddle so while I slice the cheese?"

212

"You got it."

"It's like old times, isn't it?" They were seated by the fire in the kitchen chomping on their toasted *samiches* and chatting away like neither of them had ever left.

"I feel transported to my childhood. Back in Marnie's kitchen. Her burning fag in the ashtray and there you have it, the scent of my childhood," Fiona smiled.

"Yours and every other Irish child's. You could do worse."

"Much." Fiona instantly thought about Mae.

" 'Tis the new families we create that save us. Yourself and Dory have grand big hearts bringing her here. Ah, she was meant to come sure."

"Mae? How do you know about... Never mind." Fiona took a big bite of her sandwich and relished the moment.

"You *have* been away for a long time. Welcome home." Orleigh toasted her with her coffee.

"Ta," Fiona said. *Enjoy it while you can sham*, she told herself, *you may have changed, but home surely has not.*

Chapter Thirty-Seven

Daylight streamed into Mae's room, illuminating the angels dancing on the wall in front of her. She smiled and stretched, remembering where she was. Voices and laughter came from downstairs. How late had she slept? There wasn't a clock in the bedroom and Mae never wore a watch. She threw back the covers and walked over to the window. No dream, she was in Ireland.

A lush green valley greeted her. Sheep. Cows. Above it all the mountain Dory called, what was it, the Lug? Loog. It loomed like a watchful shepherd keeping its eyes on the flock. Soft Irish sunlight beamed through fine lace curtains warming her face. Orleigh's adorable terrier came running out into the field. Mae opened the window wide and stuck her head out. "Good morning, Jesus," she called, cracking herself up. She threw on some sweats and headed for the loo.

Orleigh greeted her at the bottom of the stairs. "Well good day to you, our wood nymph is up I see. Sleep well, did you?"

Mae was once again taken by Orleigh's beauty. Otherworldly.

"Like a baby, hon. Your angel room is beautiful."

"Thanks very much. That's Fiona's work. Talented lot those Monahan women."

"Ah, there you are. Come meet my sisters," Dory beamed. "Nory, Jury, say hello to Mae West."

Mae could swear she was seeing double. Triple with Dory thrown into the mix. She looked from one to the other.

"Nice to meet you. Wow, you all have the same face."

" 'Tis a bit off-putting I suppose," Jury said, "Lovely to meet you, Mae." At least Mae thought it was Jury. She had Dory's red hair and they all shared the same apple cheeks and creamy skin. Except Nory's hair was dark. Raven waves fell down her back. The contrast was stunning. The eyes had it.

Three pairs of aquamarine eyes stared back at her. Mae liked them on sight even if they hadn't also shared Dory's warm smile and contagious laugh.

"You're all so beautiful." Mae was gushing but she couldn't help herself.

Nory laughed, "You're as sweet. Look who's talking? You're very like that actress, Winona Ryder. Same great short haircut and tremendously sexy brown eyes. Surely you have been told that?"

Mae laughed. "No, actually I never have. Thanks though. That's quite a compliment."

" 'Tis true of course." Nory said. Dory and Jury shook their heads in agreement.

Mae imagined these three were quite the handful growing up. Must be nice to have sisters. There's safety in numbers. Allies at least.

"Okay lads, let the girl eat now. Mae, what'll you have? Anything in particular? Otherwise I have an Irish breakfast here with your name on it if you're able for it."

"If it's anything like your tea yesterday, bring it on," Mae said, grinning.

Fiona laughed. "She means it too. She could put a lumber jack to shame. We still don't know where she puts it. Never gains a feckin' ounce."

"Tapeworm," Orleigh said.

Mae laughed. Orleigh set a full plate in front of her and a pot of tea. Mae smiled at her. "Thank you."

"My pleasure. I've more bangers if you fancy them."

Mae looked up from her plate, raised her eyebrows and did her best Groucho Marx, "Now there's an offer I don't get every day." She speared a sausage and took a healthy bite. Everyone laughed.

"You're gonna fit like a glove around here," Jury said.

"Thanks, hon."

Mae gave her generous breakfast her full attention. Perfectly poached eggs, Irish sausage (bangers) Irish bacon

215

(rashers) and toasted brown bread with fresh butter and marmalade. IHOP eat your heart out. Mae took a good swallow of strong Irish tea. She really was in heaven.

"So what's on the agenda for today, lads?" Orleigh asked her guests.

"Blessington to Mam and Da," Dory said. "Fee, are you going to stay up here for a bit?"

"I am. Orleigh and I can show Mae around the Glen."

"Perfect. We'll meet up at Pipers later for a pint so," Nory said.

"That suit you, Mae?" Dory asked.

"Peachy. I can always have a romp with Jesus. I'll need to work off this giant breakfast." Mae sat back and rubbed her belly that didn't exist.

Fiona shook her head. "You're a prize package. One of a feckin' kind."

"That's me. An original."

"Are we right so, lads?" Jury stood up. "Cheers."

"Thanks very much, Orleigh. See you at Pipers." Nory echoed her sister's voice in tone and expression. It was Dory's voice. Identical. Bet they drove some guys fairly wild once upon a time, Mae thought.

Orleigh walked the triplets to the front door. Fiona poured herself another cup of tea, took it with her into Orleigh's sitting room. Mae stood in front of the kitchen hearth. "Turf," she said out loud, liking the sound of it and its pungent aroma. She was about to start collecting tea cups and plates when she heard Fiona's voice from the other room. At least it sounded like Fiona. But the language was certainly not English.

" 'Tis Irish," Orleigh explained, seeing Mae's face. "She speaks it when she's here sometimes. Communing with the ancestors, reacquainting herself with home."

"Do you speak it too?"

"Aye. One never forgets their Irish. Especially during the rituals. Now I haven't spooked you a'tall, sure I haven't?"

216

"Me? Not a chance." She could smell sage burning in the sitting room. "Now there's a familiar aroma. We burn our fair share of it at the Brownstone."

Orleigh laughed, "You are a kindred spirit. I wouldn't be surprised if there wasn't more than a wee drop of Irish blood in you."

"Couldn't tell you. If there is, it's probably a tinker's in my case."

Orleigh laughed again, "Ah now, aren't you indeed a prize package?"

"Are we to the sightseeing tour or wha'?" Fiona waltzed into the kitchen all misty eyed and peaceful. Mae guessed her Irish agreed with her.

"Aye. Get your hiking boots on, Mae. We're going into the hills." Orleigh threw the tea towel on the counter and headed upstairs.

Chapter Thirty-Eight

"You're so lucky to live here," Mae said, as they walked a path around the Glen called the Ring Of Imaal. Huge trees formed a majestic canopy. Mae recognized certain wildflowers. Red poppies, blue forget-me-nots. Others, though strange, were still a visual feast. Orleigh pointed to each one as they passed. "Flaxen lady's bedstraw, lavender spotted orchid, red clover, meadow buttercups, scarlet flax. They walked on and she kept going, the names rolling off her tongue as if she were calling her children. "Deep purple tufted vetch, white dog roses, baby blue eyes, yellow archangel, sunny bog asphodel, violet devil's bit and that's climbing wild thyme you see just about everywhere."

"Gorgeous. How *did* you find this place?"

"I lived in Blessington, like the lads. For awhile. My parents were travelers, gypsies. When I came back to Ireland later I fell in love with the Glen. I knew it would be my home. I figure I'm in very good company. The High Kings of Ireland, the Leinster Kings, chose the Glen Of Imaal as their seat of power, back around 500BC. Imaal means 'lands of the descendants of Mal, High King of Leinster province.' What we know now as County Wicklow."

"So you live in an ancient royal kingdom? Very romantic."

Orleigh laughed. " 'Tis. That's what appealed to me. Besides the obvious beauty of nature. Speaking of which, there's a fairy fort now." Orleigh pointed ahead to a circle of trees. "Not an actual fort, but rather a fairy dwelling. Bad luck to cut the trees if you have such a ring on your property. People respect that. Even today. The Druids considered these rings sacred. More so if the trees were oak, ash, or hawthorn. They would listen to the rustling leaves for a wren's song giving them divine messages."

"You're serious? About the fairies?"

"I am." Pretty pink flowers at the base of the tree hung like bells on a blanket of red. "That's foxglove and valerian, both useful in remedies. You might have heard of valerian for inducing sleep?"

"Yep. Doc keeps a bottle in the Brownstone, better than those over the counter pills that make you feel exhausted the next day." She threw a stick for Jesus to fetch.

Orleigh looked over at Fiona. "You've been very quiet."

"Just taking it all in again so. I forgot how calming it is here. I almost feel sedated. Or is that your magical voice?"

"It's the valerian, sham," Orleigh said with a smile. "Sometimes just the smell of it can make you sleepy. Jesus, come here to me, boy." The little dog was barking at the fairy fort. "He probably sees a fairy or two, gets him very excited."

Mae looked sideways at Orleigh. "Okay, now you *are* taking the piss out of me."

"No, darlin', I swear I'm not. I take my Glen and the fairy realm very seriously. Don't mind Fiona. She likes to pretend she doesn't believe in pishogues and banshees."

"Superstitions and fairies?" Mae asked. She gave Fiona a gentle nudge in the ribs when Orleigh nodded.

"Exactly. You *are* well read. I for one am delighted. You won't be bored with my tour so."

Mae found herself staring at what looked like a movie set. Lord Of The Rings or Rob Roy. Round stone huts about eight feet high stood in a circle inside a wooden fence. "Is this one of those wilderness B&B's?"

Orleigh chuckled, "Cute. Actually it's a recreation of an ancient Celtic ring fort or rath. These sites are built on the actual dwelling places of our ancestors. As such they're outdoor museums. Climb in one and have a gawk."

Mae climbed down a ladder of one of the huts. Inside on the earthen floor were animal bones, very clean ones, and there was barely room to stand up. Outside at the center of huts was a large iron cauldron over an unlit pile of turf. Crude cooking instruments hung on a metal frame. The ancient kitchen and gathering place.

"It's charming," Mae said, when she came out. "No coincidence it's a circle?"

"None a'tall. You see the ancients believed that the life force within was fire, the spiritual. Surrounded by the portals of land, sea, and sky. Hence the circle, the sacred symbol of ancient Ireland. Way before the Celtic cross. And the shamrock, by the way."

"How about this, Mae? What do you think? Will we order one for the Brownstone?" Fiona called from up ahead. She was standing behind a large boulder with her head stuck through a hole.

"Nice. Maybe Rooney could put her shampoo basin on the other side."

"Legend has it that if the ailing person sticks their head through, as demonstrated, their headache will vanish instantly," Fiona spoke in a proper tour guide's voice.

" 'Tis called St. Brigit's Stone. Take a turn, lads, no pushing now, queue up, take your photographs..."

Mae giggled. "Does it work?"

"Apparently. Look at all the gifts left here by thankful migraine sufferers. Have a go."

Mae walked over, careful not to step on the coins, candles, medals and pictures gathered at the base of the Stone. She stuck her head through. "Does it do anything for you if you don't have a headache?"

"No, but it's good for a laugh. Where's the camera when you need it?"

"I left it in my suitcase," Mae said, dead serious. "I like committing certain things to memory instead."

"Come, lads," Orleigh said, urging them ahead. "As you have seen, the Glen is steeped in history. Years after the ancients reigned, a new thief came to wreck savagery on our people. England. But a famous Irish independence fighter, a Wicklow chieftain who lived in this very Glen, led the rebellion against our foe. The year was 1798 and his name was Michael Dwyer. His comrade in arms was one Robert Emmet, school chum of the poet Thomas Moore."

"Don't tell me," Mae said, "There's got to be a woman involved?"

"Aye. At the heart of all good men. She was called Anne Devlin. A more dedicated lass you would be hard pressed to find. Loyal to the cause and the man. They tortured her for information. Poor crather was half hung and stabbed repeatedly with British bayonets. Still she refused to disclose Robert Emmet's whereabouts. We're almost to his cottage now. The ruins of it, anyway. Many come here to pay homage to such fearless devotion to Ireland. Not to mention, love."

Orleigh's expression spoke volumes about how she felt about her history. Ireland was enchanting, yes, but Mae was learning something else. In the soft rain she felt the weeping of a people divided by an unwanted foreign intruder. The romantic notions of leprechauns and pots of gold took a backseat as a deeper story emerged. An Irish story. Ancient. Devastating.

Fiona was on her knees.

"Now what?" Mae asked. Fiona was not the religious type. "Praying for us heathens?" Mae walked up to the long flat stone where Fiona was kneeling. "What are *these* for? More cures?" Mae ran her hands on the indentations in the stone. Like carved shallow bowls. "Foot wash? Ancient pedicure station?"

Orleigh laughed. "Not exactly. Something a little more practical. It's called a Bullin or Holy Stone. Used for grinding grain. And ore. Herbs for rituals. Used as well for prayers and curses. Legend says the unjustified curse will rebound onto the curser."

"Are you praying or cursing?" Mae asked.

"Wouldn't you like to know?" Fiona smiled wickedly. They walked on. Orleigh stopped at a stone circle.

"Another fairy ring? The Flintstone's version?" Mae asked, standing on one.

"Pipers Stones," Orleigh said, "The ancients of the Bronze Age would gather to worship the sun." She held her hands up to the sky. Jesus curled up on his own stone for a rest. They all laughed. "What do you say, lads, we head back to the cottage, get the car and drive to the Vale of Avoca?"

"Grand, lead the way," Fiona said.

"The veil of what?" Mae asked.

"A valley. Avoca is the tiny village there. It's about 20 miles south. There's a meeting of two rivers and a valley joining them. The Vale of Avoca. 'Tis the literal Irish translation."

They walked on as Orleigh continued. "The valley was carved by glaciers right into the heart of the Wicklow Mountains. One of Mother Nature's masterpieces."

"I bet there's more. A fairy kingdom, right? Mystic happenings? Don't keep me in suspense."

Orleigh looked at Mae. "No flies on you, smart girl. As it happens, The Vale of Avoca was home to the Holy Wells of the Tuatha De Danann. The people of the Goddess Danu, Mother of the Irish gods. The Tuatha would bathe their fallen warriors and restore them to life. Sadly, copper and lead mining has marred some of the beauty. Goldsmiths dug the area for treasures. There are local hand weavers and a wool mill. The Vale is also the birthplace of Charles Stewart Parnell, famous Irish patriot. Some call him the uncrowned King of Ireland."

"Popular guy." Mae said.

"You could say that. Many a cup of tea was shared under his roof in the Vale, discussing plans for Ireland's Home Rule, freedom from the British. That's the story of the Vale so," Orleigh stamped her feet on the mat outside the cottage.

"Aren't you forgetting someone?" Fiona asked, "The famous poet...."

They followed Orleigh inside. "Oh right. Thomas Moore, of course. Grab his book in my study, will you, Fee? I'll be down in a flash, lads, I'm bursting for a pee."

"You're a poet yourself, hon," Mae laughed, following her up the stairs. "I'm getting my camera for the rest of the tour."

"Come on, boy, let's get ourselves a drink," Fiona walked into the kitchen with Jesus on her heels.

Chapter Thirty-Nine

Mary Black serenaded them on the way to the Vale of Avoca. Orleigh blasted the haunting singer's CD and they sang along, seated comfortably in Orleigh's classic mint green Moris Minor. Orleigh kept her promise; the view was magnificent. The valley hung like an emerald jewel on a liquid necklace of moving sapphire. The proud mountains above in reflection, complimenting the trinity of earth, water, and sky. Mae felt the past here just as she had in the Glen. She imagined secret pacts being sworn under secluded oaks. Forbidden love consummated on the edge of a swelling river. And death. Men fighting for freedom, their spirits reborn in the fertile soil that was their birthright.

"Are you right, Mae?" Fiona asked, "Grand place for daydreaming, hmm?"

"Yeah. If these trees could talk…."

"Ah now there's a girl who would appreciate Thomas Moore's poetry."

"Don't keep us waiting," Mae said, skimming a stone in the river.

"Right." Orleigh took out the book she'd stuck in her backpack. "It's called The Meeting Of The Waters."

There is not in the wide world a valley so sweet
As that vale in whose bosom the bright waters meet
Oh the last rays of feeling and life must depart
Ere the bloom of that valley shall fade from my heart
Ere the bloom of that valley shall fade from my heart
Yet it was not of that nature had shed o'er the scene
Her ourest of crystal and brightness of green
'Twas not her soft magic of streamlet or hill
Oh No 'twas something more exquisite still
Oh No 'twas something more exquisite still
'Twas that friends, the beloved of my bosom were near
Who made every scene of enchantment more dear

And who felt how the best charms of nature improve
When we see them reflected from looks that we love
Sweet vale of hearts, how calm could I rest
In thy bosom of shade, with the friends I love best
Where the storms that we feel in this cold world should cease
And in our hearts, like the waters, be mingled in peace.

Mae and Fiona applauded. "I love that," Mae said.

"Brilliant reading, sham," Fiona added. "Thomas Moore certainly had a gift."

Orleigh nodded. "A velvet tongue."

"The truth in cotton wool." Mae tossed another stone in the river.

"Now that's not an American saying."

"One of Sister Devora's gems. I always liked it."

"Lovely. This Sister had quite an effect on you."

"She saved my life."

"Bless her heart. She sounds like a wise woman."

"Now lads, are we going to get all mushy?" Fiona shook her head and made a face.

"What would you rather? A sordid story? Grand, I have just the thing. Your man Parnell dipping his wick with Kitty O'Shea. Is that a good enough one?"

Fiona laughed, "Don't forget Miss Kitty was very married to one Captain O'Shea at the time."

Mae clapped her hands. "Go on, don't leave me hanging."

Orleigh began, "Once upon a time now the talk was vicious. Kitty O'Shea a married woman and himself a well known respected political big shot. The pair of them fawning and writhing in this very valley. 'Tis said they would refer to one another as King and Queen. Now we know a standing prick has no conscience, however another man's woman run amuck was heady fodder for the gossip. In the end they married each other after Kitty's husband, the Captain, granted her a divorce. Scandalous. Highly unusual for holy Ireland. And not without its consequences. Parnell lost his career in

225

government. Herself? Kitty O'Shea goes down in history, no pun intended lads, as the loose woman who slept with the patriot Charles Stewart Parnell."

"What's with you?" Mae asked Fiona. "Didn't you like the story?"

Orleigh smiled. "Ah now, Fiona is a wee bit sensitive on the subject of wanton women."

"Fuck off." Fiona didn't look amused but Mae knew she wasn't really angry either.

"Sorry, Orleigh. Being home stirs up the settled bits, if you know what I mean."

"I know. Settled and buried too. I was just coddin' you. Uncalled for perhaps. Sorry, Fee." Orleigh had forgotten how well Fiona had disguised her pain in the past. Coming home peeled off the mask.

"No dramas, no worries. We gullible whores have to stick together. Right on, Kitty." Fiona raised her fist in the air and stuck out her breasts. Mae fell over laughing.

"You hardly know me is it? Shocked?" Fiona asked.

"I don't get shocked, hon. Still, I would have never taken you for a tramp." Mae ran off down the riverbank and Fiona screamed running after her. They were both in fits of laughter when they got back. Orleigh was gazing into the water.

"See anything interesting, witch?" Fiona asked. "A pair of Kitty's knickers? Maybe your own lost thong?"

"Oh wad some power the giftie gie us, to see oursels as ithirs see us."

"Now that ain't Thomas Moore," Mae said.
Orleigh laughed as they splashed each other, a new friendship baptized in the vale.

Chapter Forty

Dory

The sign above the bakery boasted a fresh coat of blue paint. Teelons Baked Goods, established 1966. Dory took a deep breath and looked back at her sisters.

"Do you want us to go in with you?" Jury offered.

"No thanks, lads, I'll be fine so. Butterflies is all. Feckin' nauseous. Seriously, no worries, off you go." Dory smiled and got out of the car and waved them off. And then she saw her. Mam. Standing at the counter pulling string out of the holder hanging from the ceiling, tying up a neat white box for a customer. Something fresh and delectable Da baked that morning. Dory's mouth watered, quenching her dry nerves a little. She opened the bakery door. Bells jangled announcing her presence. She breathed in deeply. An infusion of familiar smells greeted her. Vanilla, cinnamon, apples. Da's apple tart in the oven. *I'm home.*

Finn Teelon looked up from her work. "Dory, sweet Jaysus, 'tis you. Thanks be to God, my girl is home." Mam shoved the box at the woman and ran out from behind the counter.

"Hello, Mam." Dory braced herself. Her mother smothered her with hugs and kisses.

"Dory, Dory," Mam said over and over, holding her back now to get a proper look. *I'm home.*

"You look brilliant, so you do. The very picture of the big city woman. Where have your curls gone?" Mam smoothed her hands through Dory's stick straight red hair. "Like pure silk, 'tis…" Mam hugged her again.

Dory felt relieved. *Maybe this won't be so hard. We can talk about hair and clothes and New York. Shallow talk. Safe talk.*

"You do it with a flatiron and straightening gel. Where's Da, in the back?"

Mam nodded. "Eamon, come out here, we've a visitor."

Eamon Teelon came through a swinging door, wiping floury hands on the front of his apron. His whole face lit up when he set eyes on his daughter's face. Dory's heart swelled at the sight of him. Her da never changed. Handsome as ever. Ready with a smile for one and all. Her parents, two peas in a pod. Dyed in the wool solid folk whose triplets never ceased to be the light of their life.

"Come here to me, Dory girl, I've missed you something fierce." Her father held out his arms and Dory walked into his embrace. That did it. Mam was bawling.

"Ah now, Finn. 'Tis a happy day sure. She's home, is she not? Ochh, now you'll get the buns all salty with your tears, there, there."

Dory was touched as she watched her da comforting her mam, handing her his handkerchief. The bells tinkled and they all looked towards the door.

"Bridie, will you look who's come home from America, my Dory!" Finn Teelon wiped her tears, her voice elated. Dory recognized their old neighbor. *Here we go.*

"Howyeh, Bridie?"

"Fine sure, no use complaining. Grand to see you, Dory. You've already shed some tears have you, Finn? Eamon, I won't ask how you are today. Brilliant, the pair of you." Bridie laughed and gave Dory a big hug. Rosewater, Bridie Morgan's signature scent. Dory hated it. It reeked of funeral parlors and dead flowers.

"She's nothing but skin and bones now, Finn. Dory, you're like those fashion models on the television. Need a good feed now you're home. Still gorgeous just the same. Where are your curls? The new look I suppose. Smashing on you."

"Thanks, Bridie." Home sweet home. Bursting with love and questions. Thankfully Mam took Bridie over to the counter to choose a cake. Dory followed her da into the back of the shop. Not before shouting a goodbye to Bridie Morgan.

Must not forget our manners. "Lovely to see you again, Bridie. Say hello to everyone for me."

"Ah sure you'll say it yourself down to the pub. And do stop in for tea, anytime. I go nowhere but the shops and home."

Right. So you can grill me. No thanks.

"Where did you leave your sisters?" Da asked, "I thought Nory said she and Jury were going to call in to Orleigh."

"Aye, they did. Had some errands to do. They'll be back for dinner."

"Dinner is it? No more tea so? You're all Americanized. Bound to happen, I suppose." Her father kissed her cheek.

"Not a'tall, Da. Believe me, when Fiona and I talk, people think we're right off the paddy boat sure. Quaint little Irish serving maids...." Dory almost choked on her words. "Ahm, I'm kidding. We're still developing our decorating line, no worries. But the waitressing money is brilliant, over." *Big mouth. Good job.*

Eamon Teelon smiled a proud smile. "Right so. Just be sure you don't forget how many of these apple tarts I had to sell to put you girls through college."

"I won't ever forget your sacrifice, Da. Ta." Dory watched him work.

"Forget that shite. I'm just glad you came home, girl." Her father closed the oven door and gave her another one of his famous bear hugs. " Twas' like missing a limb ..." Eamon Teelon wiped a tear from his crinkly blue eyes. Dory touched his ruddy cheek. Da remained a mushpot.

"Now there's a Kodak moment." Mam walked into the kitchen. "Grand to see our girl, isn't it? Now what do you say we have a cuppa and get you settled?" Mam took off her apron and reached for her coat by the back door.

"The two of ye go. I'll be over when I've finished frosting the cakes so."

"See you later." Dory pecked him on the cheek.

"Ah you will, love," he said, whistling as he set a hot apple tart to cool on a baker's rack.

Dory followed her mother along the cobbled path that led from the bakery directly to the Teelon house. Home. It stood ahead beckoning Dory like an old friend. Had it shrunk? Or was she so used to the Brownstone? The old house was as charming as ever, immaculate whitewash gleaming pristinely. Coal black shutters in stark contrast against it. Mam had painted the door a sunny yellow. The trusty old black iron ring latch was as big and bold as ever. *Do you girls have to bang that knocker so? Wake the dead, you will.* Mam had planted geraniums in a ruby red milk can at the entry way. Creamy white daisies waved in the gentle breeze from ebony window boxes.

"Ah, it's lovely. Where do you find the time to keep it up? What with the bakery, the Rosary Society, etcetera...."

"Ah you know me, not a spare moment do I have that there isn't something I forgot to do. It makes me smile to see the flowers at the end of a long day. Worth the work so." Mam opened the front door, "Let's go meet the girls."

A plump calico meowed around Dory's leg. She bent down to stroke her. "Now who would you be?"

"That's Cara," Mam said, walking into the sitting room. "She's the affectionate one. The other two are more stand-offish." Two more fat cats dozed lazily on the window seat. "Meet Dara, the white and Tara, pure black."

Dory laughed. Rhyming names, of course.

"I swear it's like you and your sisters again, what with their different personalities. Cara as you see is the friendly one. Dara's a bit of a prima donna. And Tara is as moody as Jury, I swear."

Which one am I? Dory looked around the parlor. Time had stood still here. Her memories in this house were good ones. It was in the leaving that her troubles had begun. *How can I possibly go back, Fee? Mam will look me in the eye and I'll be done for.* Avoid home at all costs. That had been Dory's stance for five years. And it worked well in a

Brownstone an ocean away from her previous life. Today was a whole new ballgame, as Doc's Uncle Carmine would say. *Madonna mia.*

Mam stuck the kettle on the Aga. How many times had she done that one simple act in her lifetime? The veritable answer to everything. Can't sleep? Stick the kettle on. Neighbor having a crisis? Come in, I'll stick the kettle on. Tired? Hung over? Soaked to the skin? Stick the kettle on. Black sheep returns home, stick the kettle on. Tea cured a multitude of ills.

"Dory? You're away in dreamland, love. Would you light the fire? I've a wee chill in me bones. Reacquaint yourself with the turf."

"Sorry? Right, the fire...." Dory reached for the box of wooden matches on the shelf over the sink. She arranged blocks of turf in the kitchen hearth and lit them, the old ritual mooring her back home.

"Missed the auld place, hmm?" Mam was talking to her. Her voice sounded miles away. Dory continued to stare into the glowing fire.

"Guess I hadn't counted on how much," Dory said dreamily.

"You know the door is always open for you. I knew 'twasn't forever you'd stay away. No matter how high the heels, 'tis the bog you'll always have under your feet. I know you thought Ireland your jail. Maybe now you can let it be your sanctuary instead. You have the blood of your ancestors coursing through your veins, love. You've an Irish soul, no matter the distance you travel."

"Ancestral blood? I thought 'twas the Guinness you put in our baby bottles."

"Very funny, sham." The kettle screeched. Her mother shut it off. "I did no such thing. No harm for you to have a pint or two while you're home. Fill out those apples in your cheeks so. You're awfully thin." Mam filled a ceramic teapot and carried it to the table.

Yeah, Dory, you're home. Where they either want to fatten you up or tell you to give the sweets a rest. Are we ever just right as we are?

"Now that's a grand fire, love. I'm warmed to my cockles so I am." Mam slid a box of Kimberlys across the table and poured the tea.

"You always did know my weakness." Dory bit into the chocolate covered graham cake and closed her eyes in ecstasy. Mam laughed, the lines around her soft blue eyes creasing. Her face had a healthy glow to it. Sure she never sat still. Busy bee that she was. *Idle hands....*

"I've longed for this day. To sit here and drink a cuppa with my daughter again."

Dory concentrated on drinking her tea. If she looked at Mam it could be dangerous. The look. Tears welling up in Mam's eyes. *Got to avoid the drama.* It was this kitchen. The fire, the table, the goddamn tea. It made people talk. *There's no escape.* She stuck another Kimberly in her mouth. All she heard was Declan's voice playing in her head. *Keep your fucking mouth shut, Dory. I'm warning you. One word to your parents and you'll be sorry. Dead sorry.*

Dory had listened back than. It was easier than another beating. Now it all seemed insane. She didn't know herself when she was married to Declan Mahoney. *You were an eejit.* A romantic dreamer who thought she could save a cruel man who was missing a heart.

"Yoo hoo! You're away with the fairies, love." Mam's voice snapped her back to the present.

"Sorry. Nothing like a peat fire to send me right off."

"Aye. I see you grew out your fringe? Your hair suits you this way, I think."

"Thanks," Dory said, realizing her scar was now in full view. Hiding under a full head of bangs was necessary once. Or had she only fooled herself? She bit the bullet and looked at her mam.

"I was unhappy for a long time, Mam. Very unhappy." Mam looked away. And in that gesture Dory remembered why she never told her the truth. Mam couldn't handle it. The guilt alone would have killed her. She'd failed her little girl. That just wasn't on. *Now what were the shallow topics again?*

"You won't believe who I saw down the town yesterday," Mam said.

That's right, Mam, change the subject. Very wise.

"Sheila Mahoney, of all people. She's gone daft I tell you."

So much for shallow topics. Was her mam actually going to discuss Sheila Mahoney with her?

"Och, the genuine article she is. Ranting and raving. Dresses only in black. Hair like a rat's nest. Desperate. She didn't know me from Christ, imagine. Or she was acting the whole time, who knows? Didn't she make a right show of herself dancing and weeping in the middle of the grocery? I was half embarrassed for her. Och, she brought it all on herself, did she not? Raising that evil son of a...."

"Mam! Are you seriously going to go on about Sheila feckin' Mahoney?" Dory pushed away from the table and walked over to the sink. She hit the tap with the back of her hand and stuck the kettle underneath, banging it noisily. *Your mother brings up your dead husband's lunatic mother; make tea.*

Mam didn't say a word. That didn't make Dory feel like screaming any less. She took a few deep breaths instead, "cleansing breaths," Doc called them. Hah, Dory thought, there isn't enough oxygen on earth. She had no right to come home and raise hell. But why did Mam have to mention Sheila Mahoney? It was like a match thrown on gasoline. There was bound to be an explosion.

"I'm so sorry, Dory. That was insensitive of me. I have such guilt over those years you were with Declan. I tried to get you to come home. To leave him. And I'm sure I never knew the half of it. Your life with him was so secretive. But I could see he was killing your spirit. You stopped smiling. And we rarely saw you. You told me and your da to stay out

233

of it. Insisted on it. Or he wouldn't let us see you a'tall. We felt so helpless. I know there was serious damage done. And it's more than what your fringe was hiding. God forgive me for not doing something. Och, I don't forgive myself."

If Mam starts wringing her hands and blessing herself, I'm jumping out the goddamn window. Dory's head was spinning. She was pacing back and forth, nervous as a cat. She started rummaging through the kitchen drawers. *I know you're in here. Where were Mam's fags?*

"In the top press, behind the peas." Mam's voice was oddly calm and soothing. Dory opened the cabinet and shoved aside the tin of peas. She found her mother's stash. Silk Cut cigarettes, red package. Good, the strong ones. Dory shook one out and lit it with the matches in the front of the packet. She took the pack with her over to the hearth. She kept her eyes on the burning turf and blew out a stream of blue smoke. *In for a penny, in for a pound.*

"I never wanted you to know, what had become of my life. It was like being under a dark spell. I couldn't get out. Away from him. He wasn't going to let me leave him. Nothing was normal. Like some sick routine. Me trying to save him from destruction. From himself. Him destroying me. In the beginning, it was different. Before... he was reckless sure, but fun. Sexy. Rebellious. And he wanted me in the worst way. It was like a drug to be needed like that. He was so seductive. Little boy lost. A fine thing to look at. Everybody wanted him. And he wanted *me*. Just me. Well, until we got married.

I can't say for certain when it changed. It was kind of subtle at first. Rough sex games were his thing. That I could deal with. Then herself started making up stories. Sheila told him I was doing things with other men. All lies. He punished me to shut his mother up. He couldn't tell your feckin' evil one to stop. No, he was under his mammy's thumb. I didn't know how badly.

One night he'd had too much to drink, let it slip that he wouldn't be alone in a room with the bitch. She *wanted*

234

him. I didn't understand. Who would? Suddenly it dawned on me what he was implying. Pure sicko. She ruined him for other women. When she would come to our house, that's when he was the most vicious. When she left, he'd call me names. I'd trapped him, he said. That's a laugh. Control freak he was. Anyway, it was all her doing. 'Twas herself talking. Eerie, the hold she had on him. He barely had an original thought anymore. He wanted to hate her, but he couldn't. I told him we should leave town, get miles away from her. He didn't need her. That's when he nearly killed me.

She had nobody, only him, he said. How could he leave her all alone? What kind of a person deserts their own mother? What kind of son? 'Twas her words in his mouth. I should have run then and there. He needed mental help. A strong dose. I couldn't see that ever happening sure, so what was left? I wasn't about to give him any ultimatums. Right, go to the asylum, you're sick, love. Hah. I'd be the one pushing up daisies now. Every so often I would think things were okay. Well, not okay. Just sort of normal, for a crazy house. He would be nice for a short while. To get me in bed. Not that I ever refused him. I only wanted him to be a bit gentle. Less angry. He couldn't be. And there was *nothing* I wouldn't do, by the way. Nothing.

He would not be kind. No sooner had we rolled around like animals, he'd be up and dressed, headed for the pub. He'd enjoy telling me later how the sluts were throwing themselves at him. I went and got tested. Who knows what diseases he exposed me to? Sorry. I can't stop it coming out now, Mam. Have a fag if you need one.

To him, sex was like washing his teeth. No meaning in it. He actually relished telling me about his escapades, the cruel prick. I wanted to stab him every time. Was never near the knife drawer at the time. Pity. Anyway, I had nothing left to fight back with. I'd lost my mind, my nerve, and my self-respect. I lost everything because of him. Everything. He took my *babies*."

235

Dory heard her own voice. *Are you mad?* Had she actually said it? *You are mad.* She talked about what she'd swore she never would. *Oh my God.* She clamped her hand over her mouth. Mam was staring back at her. Strangely. Right through her. Catatonic like. And she'd gone a frightening shade of pale. *Good work, Dory. Brilliant. Now you did it. Gave her a stroke.*

"Mam? Shite. Talk to me…" Her mother said nothing. *I've killed her. Oh, God, please let her be alright. You and your stupid confession. Good work, Dory girl. Brilliant feckin' work.* She prayed her da wouldn't walk in at that moment. She poured a glass of water and carried it over to her mother. "Drink, Mam, please…" Mam took the glass and sipped. *Thank you, God. Don't punish Mam, I'm the pagan.* Mam's color was returning. She was pointing.

"In the top of the press, Dory, get the Bushmills."

Dory got the bottle of whiskey and poured two neat glasses. She handed one to Mam. "There's a girl, now. Pour, Dory, don't be shy a'tall." They drank, forgoing a toast. This was medicinal. "There 'tis," Finn Teelon said, "Now pass us a fag like a good girl." She patted Dory's hand. Dory lit Mam's cigarette. And one for herself. They smoked in silence.

"Now that tastes gorgeous. Pour us a wee tot more now, love."

Shite, Dory thought, they'd both be in their cups when Da walked in. Won't that be grand? *Sorry Da, no dinner for you, I've got Mam stewed to the gills.*

"No worries. We can celebrate your homecoming sure. 'Tis adult women we are." *You are, Mam. I'm an eejit.*

"Right." Dory poured another round. Added a few ice cubes this time. She walked over to the hearth and stirred the fire. They drank in silence. Baring one's soul is overrated. What earthly purpose was served in dredging up ghosts? Small talk is much more accommodating. Pleasant. Benign. *Nice outfit. Thanks. New shoes? Gorgeous.*

Finn Teelon looked over at her daughter. Guilt is natural for a mother. But what good did it serve really? Only gives you ulcers. Heals nothing. *Fuck all, really. Excuse the language, God.* Self-flagellation was ridiculous. She drank her drink. Dory deserved better and her mother aimed to fix that right now.

"Darlin', listen to me for a minute, hmm?"

Dory nodded. The conversation couldn't possibly deteriorate.

"At the bottom of it, you loved him. I know that. We don't pick and choose love. It chooses us sometimes. However, you are not to blame for Declan's crimes. The way that he hurt you is unforgiveable. As God as my witness, he is lucky he's already dead or I'd be on my way over to end his life this very minute. Catholic or not, right or wrong, I wouldn't have a second thought. Och, I am so sorry you had to endure his cruelty and assaults, and you all alone in it. No one on earth should have to bear that heartache and misery. Certainly not a daughter of mine. Please forgive me."

"It wasn't your fault. And I wasn't alone. Orleigh and Fiona knew. I'm sorry if that hurts your feelings but I could hardly come to you and Da with it." *I talked, Declan. You can do nothing to me about that now.*

"My feelings are not important. You did what you thought best at the time. You paid a terrible price. I could have lived and died without knowing the awful truth. They were my grandbabies, God rest their wee souls." Finn Teelon's voice cracked but she cleared her throat and went on. "This is not about me. Or your da. We're just grateful you came home a'tall. And I do understand your having to leave when you did. Please forgive your old mam for being so blind. And for telling you girls all that flowery shite about marriage and being good wives. No help twas that."

Dory was amazed at her mother's words. She wasn't finished. Dory stayed quiet and listened.

"I never thought any one of you would be treated without proper respect. And to be beaten? Och, wouldn't I gladly take all your bruises if I could erase that memory for you? One last thing and I need you to hear this. Perhaps my time would have been better spent paying attention to you grown girls than what Mass was happening in the church. Fine for the priest to stand up there and tell us to forgive and forget. Quite another when he'll never have a daughter someone tried to kill and succeeded in murdering her babies. My God. I won't hide behind the cross ever again, Dory. 'Twas a fatal mistake. I am so very sorry. Can you ever forgive me?"

Dory took a deep breath and finished her whiskey. Talk about enlightening. *Holy shite.* Mam had never spoken so candidly before. Frankly it was a little weird. And very damn nice to hear.

"Mam, don't be too hard on yourself. I forgive you, of course. You were brainwashed by the church a long time ago." *This is one time you get away with that remark.* "I didn't buy the fairytale marriage bit anyway. I knew it wasn't meant to be a romance novel. But not a horror show either. I played my Joan of Arc role. 'Tis over. He did me one big favor, dying. I never have to look over my shoulder again. Except for his crazy mother."

"Never mind about that auld bitch. I'll hang her myself by that mop of snakes she calls hair. Feckin' wretch. She won't be able for the wrath of me, I swear to Jaysus on the cross."

Dory laughed. "Watch out, Rocky, Finn Teelon is in the house."

"Of course I'm in the house, sure where else would I be if I'm here talking to you?"

"It's American slang," Dory laughed. Mam was an original all right.

"Lovely. Is that what why we sent you to college? Now how about I get the dinner started. Your da won't be pleased with Kimberleys and Bushmills for his tea. Of course with his Dory girl home, he'd eat cardboard, so he would." Mam stood up and gave Dory a tight hug. "I love you, Dory Glory."

"I love you too. Is that bacon and cabbage I saw in the fridge?"

" 'Tis. And I've Golden Wonder spuds. That suit you?" Mam turned on the oven and got a large roasting pan out of the drawer in the Aga.

"Bring it on." Dory started clearing the table. Her mother shook her head.

"More American slang is it? You came home just in time I'm thinking."

Dory's sisters appeared at the kitchen door.

"Dory, quick, put that whiskey back in the press, Mam whispered, "Your sisters will think we're having a party. You go down to Pipers with them now and let me cook in peace. They're as nosy."

Dory wasn't quick enough.

"Having a piss-up without us?" Nory asked.

"Never mind, sham," Mam said, peeling potatoes with a vengeance. "Tisn't every day your sister comes home. Take her down to Pipers for a pint and we'll have the dinner at half six so."

"Aye, aye, captain," Jury saluted, giving her mother a kiss on the cheek. "About face, lads." Jury marched in place.

Mam shook her head. " 'Tis a circus I'm running here."

Dory put on her coat and as they headed out the door, Mam's voice followed them. *"Sonny don't go away, I'm here all alone. Your daddy's a sailor, never comes home…"*

Chapter Forty-One

"Well if it isn't my favorite triplets. That third one there is a sight for sore eyes now. Come here to me, Dory, I need to give you a grand hug."

"Howyeh, Nolan?"

"Grand sure, but the hell with me, look at yourself, beautiful as ever."

The burly barman came out from behind the bar. Dory felt honored. Nolan only left his post for two reasons. To sit in with the band or to throw out some wanker who had too many pints. He had an ear to ear grin on his meaty face. He captured her in a bear hug.

"You can let me go, Nolan, I promise not to leave."

He laughed, "Ah, you're twice as beautiful as when you left so. America agrees with you, apparently. Sure they don't feed you well, aren't you wasting away? Let's get a good dark pint into you now." He released her and walked back behind the bar.

"They feed me fine, over. New York is brilliant. But I must say I missed your face, sham. And your lovely establishment. And the Guinness, well now doesn't that go without saying?"

"Ah Dory, go'way with your flattery. The pints are on me now, darlin.' If you're looking for your cousin and friends now, they're in the back. That little one is smashing. A regular wood nymph come to life, isn't she just? Sure I've already asked her to marry me. I believe she said yes. We'll be eloping tonight so." Nolan looked as serious as a priest on Sunday.

Dory hooted. "That'd go over real well with Mrs. Nolan."

Nolan laughed. "You got me there."

Dory walked further into the pub, following the familiar voices and laughter. Her little crowd was nestled in one corner. Orleigh, Fiona and Jury were deep in conversation. *Love to be a fly on that wall*. Mae and Nory were chatting with two men. Very cozy. Mae seemed right at home. They loved her already. Mae the grown-up pixie who tugged at your heart. Her big doe eyes the color of espresso grabbed you and wouldn't let go, the tiny child behind them pleading for deliverance.

Mae grinned at her. "Dory, we've been waiting for you." Her face was flushed from the Guinness.

"I see that. And the waiting's done you good." Dory laughed, "Howyeh, Aiden?" she asked the handsome man next to Mae.

"Grand, Dory. So you didn't forget us after all. Wasn't I just saying that to Kieran?" He kicked his brother's foot under the table and stood up. He gave Dory a generous hug and kiss. Dory laughed, catching her breath. *Siblings. Can't live with 'em, can't kill 'em.*

Kieran. Dory felt her heart skip hearing his name again. He was walking towards her now.

"Sit down, little bro," he said to Aiden, "Let me show you how it's done." He swept Dory into his arms and planted a particularly passionate kiss on her lips. Apparently public displays of affection were all the rage in Ireland now. Dory blushed six shades of red. She recovered. Just barely.

"Well, you always were a grand kisser, Kieran. I see some things haven't changed. On behalf of the women of Blessington, we can be grateful for that sure." Dory smiled, thinking she handled that quite well. In stride. *Right. In stride, me arse.* Kieran appeared unruffled. *Playing it cool, is it, Mr. O'Rourke?*

"So howyeh, Dory? You taste grand and by the looks of you, you're only fantastic sure. Look like a million bucks so. We're only honored a fancy city girl like yourself has graced us country bumpkins with her presence."

"You're knee deep in it now, sham, but thanks very much. I can see you're just fine yourself. Full of it as usual like." Everyone laughed and she sat down in the chair he held out for her.

241

"Things have definitely improved around here very recently," Kieran said, leaning in close to her.

What a day so far. Mam drunk thanks to loose lips. Old flame still flickering. What next?

Dory caught Orleigh's wink. She was eating it up. Dory and Kieran, like old times, she was thinking, bless her little witch heart. She always wanted Dory to end up with Kieran. Not even Orleigh's clairvoyance could help Dory's mind back than. She tried to focus on her sisters now but the scent of Kieran was distracting her big time. Jaysus, aren't you pathetic? she thought. A wee whiff of male pheromones and you're all but panting. *Maybe I should have given Orleigh's mechanical friend a go back in the Glen. Released some pent-up emotion.*

She indulged herself and inhaled. Sandalwood. She remembered it very well. She met his eyes for a second. She never could quite decide the color of them. A perfect shade of blue-green. Like the ocean meeting the forest. Depending on the light. Silky chestnut hair, short enough to be manly, long enough to be damn sexy. Dory was trying hard to listen to Mae but with Kieran's face in her line of vision it was all but impossible. Aiden distracted Mae for a moment. Dory studied Kieran. An Aran jumper and jeans always did it for her. The simple trappings of the Irish male. A nice change after the garden variety tee shirts worn everywhere by American men. Dory took a healthy sip of Guinness and silently applauded herself for coming home.

"So New York suits you then?" Kieran was talking to her. She watched his full lips move. *Have mercy.* Why didn't she answer him? She was being rude. *Wake up, Dory. The man is making small talk. Your turn.*

"Aye, it's grand. Lots of people. Ahm, shops, buses." *Buses? Brilliant, Dory. What are you like?* Her mind was seriously blank. Well that was a lie. Plenty was going on in there. All of it inappropriate for mixed company. Now if she could make this crowd disappear she could speak her mind. Her dirty filthy mind.

242

"Aye, Kieran, I love The Big Apple, the Brownstone is brilliant, lots of friends, good job, yada yada, as they say over." *But right now all I can think about is your fine body naked.*

Kieran looked at her. "Okaay."

Orleigh saved the day. "What do you say, lads, let's hear some music so," she slapped her hand on the table. "These O'Rourke boys are not only good looking, Mae. They're quite talented. Show us your stuff, lads."

Dory nearly spit out her mouthful of Guinness. Her mind was still in the gutter. Fiona piped up as if reading it verbatim.

"Right, lads, do. We're starved for a man that touches a fiddle like yourself, Kieran, aren't we Dory? And Aiden, we're all a bit envious of the way you wrap those lips around that tin whistle, aren't we girls? I don't know what else to say."

Dory thought nothing was spot on. Chance would be a good thing.

"Hang on to your knickers, Mae," Orleigh said, "You're about to witness your first Irish session."

Mae clapped her hands as she watched the men situate themselves on a bench near the fireplace. There was no stage in the pub. It was all very informal and intimate. Mae eagerly awaited the first note.

Nolan tapped out the first ones with a short wooden stick. His big solid hands came down in perfect rhythm on a thin handheld drum.

" 'Tis a bodhron," Orleigh said, "Like the ancients."

Mae nodded and smiled, her feet keeping time with the throbbing pulse of the drumbeat. Kieran's fiddle jumped in rambunctious and animated, chords leaping out beneath very long and practiced fingers. A weathered man with a white beard and sea worn cap fingered an acoustic guitar completing the instrumental harmony. Aiden's voice, strong and melodic, brought The Fields Of Athenrye right into the middle of Piper's Pub. Everyone was singing along. Mae

243

didn't know the words but she was enjoying the passion and energy surrounding her. Tribal. A ritual as old as time.

The musicians switched to a rousing rendition of Finnegan's Wake. Mae clapped and stomped with the crowd, applauding wildly at the end. She found herself shouting out a request before she knew it. "Play The Wild Rover!"

Aiden winked at her and Nolan came over and kissed her cheek. Mae giggled. Dory and Fiona looked at her. She was having the time of her life. "Good craic, hon," Mae said to them, making them laugh. Orleigh rubbed her back and said, "Good on ya,' Mae."

Mae looked around the pub. Normal people. Lovers, families, singles, everyone gathered for the fun. She wondered if anyone there had a dirty little secret.

Do you love me, Mama?

Stop with your silly questions, Mae. Get under the covers now.

Mama, can't you read me a story tonight? I promise not to talk, Mama. It's too dark.

Is that my little Mae waiting to be tucked in?

No, Daddy. Mama's here.

Hush, now, little Mae. Your mama has things to do.

Mama, please don't leave...

Shhh, Daddy's little Mae. There's my good girl.

Mae shook her head and concentrated on the music. The tin whistle was haunting. She felt a strange yet delightful current pass through her body. She realized Aiden was staring at her. She lowered her eyes, took a gulp of Guinness. The music got faster, louder, and there was stomping and clapping and singing. It felt like chanting. Mae was caught up in the fever. She felt free and exposed at the same time. Her cheeks were hot and her eyes were tearing. It was incredible. She hadn't felt music as intense as this before. Drawing her out of herself. A feeling of belonging. She was on her feet now giving the musicians a standing ovation. Aiden couldn't take his eyes away from her.

The pub went quiet for a moment as a stocky well dressed older gentleman walked over and sat next to the musicians. He nodded to them once and they nodded back. He set his full pint on the table nearby and stood up. The musicians immediately hit the first notes and the entire pub was on its feet. *We'll sing a song, a soldier's song...* They sang in unison. The Irish national anthem. Mae had seen it in a movie. The gentleman sang the loudest, keeping his eye on Dory the whole time. At the end there were howls and cheers and clapping. As quickly as the man appeared, he was gone, vanishing somewhere towards the back of the pub. People resumed their low hum of chatter while the musicians took a short break. The front door of the pub slammed shut. People looked towards it. A hush came over the crowd.

Slovenly was the only word Mae could think of when she saw the woman. No spring chicken came to mind, for what she was wearing. Mae couldn't decide exactly what she was going for. Flimsy chic? Or was she actually wearing a nightgown? And over it, a gaudy knitted filthy grayish shawl. Was she a beggar? A tinker? The red patent leather fuck me heels and torn black stockings suggested something else. Completing the bizarre outfit was a black hat left over from Mardi Gras. The woman's hair was like a tangled nest of black seaweed. She walked, teetered was more like it, further into the pub. She stopped and pointed a long red chipped fingernail. God help whomever that's aimed at. Mae shivered.

Oh my God, beggar woman was screaming at Dory. Through her cracked lips and smeared red lipstick she hurled filthy insults. Dory looked frightened out of her wits. Terrorized. Who the hell was this horrible woman standing shamelessly in the lamplight, breasts illuminated like hanging eggplants, yelling at her friend? Beggar woman sashayed back and forth, like she was for sale, grinning at the men with her stained brown teeth. They all turned away, uninterested. She continued to scream at Dory, who didn't move.

"You! How dare you show your face back here. Where's my boy? Feckin' hussy, what have you done with him? You killed him; you whore. I'll see *you* dead this time, not my Deckie. Ahhhhhh…." She wailed like a tortured cat.

Mae cringed at the sound. It was diabolical.

No one moved. Poor Dory looked as if she'd seen a ghost. Kieran walked towards crazy woman, Dory's sisters on his heels. He stepped out of their way. Nory and Jury pushed the woman against a wall, away from Dory.

"How dare you come here, you disgusting feckin' horror," Nory spat. "Don't speak another word to my sister, Sheila. Not one feckin' word."

"Your Declan is dead. Stone dead. Now take your sorry ass the hell out of here." Jury added.

The sisters with an edge stared her down. They were incensed on Dory's behalf. It was awesome to watch, Mae thought. People, kin standing up for you. She loved it.

Nory wasn't finished. She pointed a finger down the woman's sharp nose. "*You* killed your son, Sheila. Not Dory. He drove his hateful bollocks off a cliff. End of story."

Jury pulled her sister back and stood in her place. "Right. Dory was too good for the likes of him and you are a poor excuse for anyone's mother. Now get out. Never speak to any of us again, you despicable bitch."

If any of their words registered was a mystery. Sheila Mahoney responded with a silent empty gaze. Was she certifiable? Mae wondered. Or was this mother-in law of Dory's a first class actress? Orleigh pulled both Teelon sisters back gently, before blood was shed. She calmly walked towards Sheila and stood eye to eye with her cousin's nemesis. Orleigh spoke in a low clear voice that commanded attention and vowed reckoning.

"Mind me now. You stay miles away from my cousin. You will fail in any attempt to harm her and the end will not be good for you. Not good a'tall." Orleigh didn't say another word. She didn't have to. Sheila Mahoney moved away as if struck, covering her eyes.

"Don't look at me, witch," she shrieked, "Witch of the Glen. I want my Deckie! Aieee… Aieee…"

Nolan flew out like a shot from behind the bar. He stopped short of Sheila Mahoney and put one large arm on a man's shoulder at the bar. "Fergus, take the oul bitch home now. I'll not have the likes of her in my pub terrorizing my friends and customers. Enough of her shaggin' antics. Keep her the hell locked up. Och, she's done enough damage."

People clapped and cheered. "Drown the oul cunt. She can be with her wanker of a son once and for all," someone shouted. "Shoulda' stuck with being a whore, Sheila. Vengeance for that waster son of yours has turned you into a freak show," a man yelled out. And there were whispers. "Hard to imagine your one almost blew the bullocks off me one night," one man said. His friend nodded. "Right. Fine mouth she had once. Look at the state of her now. Wouldn't touch her with your cock." The two men roared, drinking off their tarnished memories.

Fergus Mahoney drained his pint and walked over to his sister in law, head down, ashamed. He grabbed her arm and steered her towards the door.

"But, Fergus, I have to make the tea," she whined, "Deckie will be home. I give him his bath on Mondays. Fine strapping lad he is now. God blessed him there. 'Tis a waste of time on that little whore," she spat back at Dory.

"Shut your mouth, Sheila," Fergus said through clenched teeth. Would he ever be free of her?

"Sheila's your best ride, isn't that so? Deckie knew it too." She touched his cheek. He pushed her hand away.

Before Fergus could get her completely out the front door, Sheila let loose a shrill insane laugh. The chilling primal scream echoed in the quiet pub. She pulled back from Fergus and turned to face the crowd, her eyes wild and her hands milking her bare pendulous breasts. "Anyone here I haven't shagged the bollocks off of?"

Fergus's pulled her out of the pub. For a few seconds there was nothing but dead silence. Sheila Mahoney's grimy presence had cast a poison atmosphere into the pub. You could almost touch the residue.

Nolan banged on the bar. "Enough, lads. Drinks are on the house. I'm pouring whiskeys here, take advantage. Play something, Kieran, will you? 'Tis a homecoming celebration not a feckin' wake."

People clapped and stomped and Kieran's sweet guitar notes floated through the pub creating a fresh atmosphere. Along with the music another face reappeared. The well dressed anthem man from earlier came and sat beside Dory.

"The devil be gone," he said, setting a shot of Bushmills in front of her. She looked at him and obligingly drank it down.

"Thanks very much, Mr...." she hesitated.

"Call me Liam," he said. "And don't ye worry about your one anymore. That dreadful Mahoney woman won't be bothering you again. I can assure you." He winked at Dory and before she could ask him why or how, he was gone. Swallowed up by the bowels of the pub.

Dory felt strangely calm. Almost relieved. Who was this Liam? She had no clue, but felt she owed him a debt of gratitude just the same. Kieran was playing Sweet Molly Malone, crooning softly and soulfully. Aiden joined in on flute, providing the proper essence, necessary and healing. Not that there was a quick cure to the previous disturbance, the dark mood Sheila Mahoney had created. But the edge was taken off considerably.

Mae swayed to the music and kept her eyes on Dory. She'd let family handle it. Their turf. Kin. She had been brought painfully up to speed on Dory's past. The hell she must have lived with married to Declan Mahoney. And to top that, his mother too. But Dory hid it well. Like Mae, she was a pro at masquerading. Keeping her secrets buried, until now.

Orleigh was at Dory's side. Consoling, comforting. Mae watched in admiration. Orleigh would obviously swing for Dory. She had her back. Mae could think of only one person from her own past like that.

Sister Devora, her steadfast champion. Her protector. Sister wouldn't let anyone within an inch of Mae if they meant her harm. She wouldn't have given anyone the chance to hurt little Mae again. It was the reason Mae's name had conveniently been left off the monthly available orphan adoption list. Sister Devora would have sacrificed her own job, her own life, to protect Mae. The child would never have to repeat the horror she endured with her father. Sometimes one had to take the power in one's own hands. Certain things could not be left up to Him. God would have to understand that. If not, Sister wasn't concerned. Her unwavering faith in her decision and her love for Mae overrode any threat to her eternal soul.

Orleigh was Dory's Sister Devora. People respected her in the same way, Mae could tell. Even a madwoman like Sheila Mahoney knew Orleigh meant business. Mae had seen fear in the disturbed woman's eyes regardless whether Orleigh practiced no harm or not. She was a healer first and foremost. Still, Mae wouldn't want to be the one who tangled with her just the same. Witch or not, Mae mused, the woman was a force to be reckoned with. Sheila Mahoney had seemingly gone too far. Mae had a gut feeling beggar woman was on borrowed time.

Chapter Forty-Two

Fiona

Fiona walked towards her parent's house reliving the scene with Sheila Mahoney down at Pipers. At least the crazy bitch didn't ambush Dory when she was on her own. Still it put a damper on their first day back in Blessington. Dory would be well taken care of by now. Back in her mam's kitchen with her sisters and her whole family cocooned around her. The Teelons would inevitably have a bit of craic. They were a fun bunch. No pretense, no airs. Things under the Monahan roof would be a whole lot quieter. Formal. Standing on ceremony. Just herself and her parents and their housekeeper rattling around the enormous house. She closed the big iron gate behind her and walked up the stone path to the front door. She read the inscription on the transom. "Capall Ri Sidhe," she recited in Irish. Horse King of the faeries. Granda Monahan's sense of humor. He took his horses seriously, himself less. "I miss you, Granda," Fiona whispered to the twinkling sky. "Siochan, Ard Ri." Peace, high king. She took a deep breath and lifted the brass horse door knocker. The prodigal daughter returns.

"Ah now, child, as I live and breathe." The most welcome voice swept over her as the door swung open wide. "Miss Fiona, you've been missed so."

"Marnie! Howyeh?" Fiona snuggled into the housekeeper's embrace. She inhaled a familiar scent, nestling into her plump neck. Honeysuckle soap. A fragrance from her childhood. Marnie's one indulgence. That and a tot of Bushmills every now and then. "Like any self-respecting Irishwoman," Marnie always said. Marnie smoothed Fiona's hair now.

"My pet, you stayed away far too long. Ah, howsever, grand you're back, Miss."

Fiona laughed and kissed her on both fat rosy cheeks.

"You better call me Fiona. We're both adults. Promise me now?"

Marnie laughed, "Anything you ask, as long as I get to lay me eyes on you again, sure I'm a happy woman so. I intend fattening you up. Jaysus you're emaciated. No decent spuds in America I suppose?"

"No decent *studs* either. I'm dying for a ride."

Marnie howled. "You're as cheeky as ever I see, Miss… I mean, Fiona."

"What are you like? I was only talking about horses sure. Where's your mind, Marnie McGovern?"

The housekeeper grabbed Fiona to her bosom again. "You need some good Irish milk. Put a few stone on you so." She kissed the top of Fiona's head.

"You don't plan on whipping out one of those grand tits, now do you?" Fiona teased.

"Twas good enough for you once. You suckled like a contented babe. You and your sisters. Hungry lot the three of you. Now you're all skin and bones."

"Ah now, you were the best wet nurse a girl could ask for, truly mother's milk as far as I was concerned. You're not going to cry? Ah now, there, there."

"Sorry, you always were my favorite. And don't let on I said so. Swear to me, now."

"I swear. Mum's the word. Speaking of which, where is the Queen of the Castle?"

As if on cue her mother's voice came from the upstairs landing. "Is that Fiona?" Brynn Monahan sang out from the top of the stairs. Mam always knew the importance of an entrance. She had definitely missed her calling.

"Aye, 'tis me, Mam," Fiona called up, watching her mother's graceful descent. She glided like a movie star in an old film, caressing the polished oak banister lightly like the heads of adoring fans on her way down. Glamour and class. That was Brynn Monahan. Gene Tierney in her prime had nothing on her. Entering the scene, capturing her audience with flashing jewel green eyes. Fiona could only hope she

251

was half as preserved at that age. No one would guess that her mother had just celebrated her sixty-fifth birthday. Brynn Monahan attributed her youthful skin tone to Irish milk and a vigorous ride each morning. She enjoyed people's reaction when she told them her beauty secret. She was merely referring to the horses she and Fiona's da bred. Though Fiona remembered a time when she overheard Mam telling Marnie "The man is insatiable." And Marnie had only smiled and said "Oh, Mrs.?" When Mam left the kitchen Fiona distinctively heard Marnie say, "Who are you telling like?"

"Fiona, darlin, come here and let me get a proper look at you so. You're as gorgeous. Isn't she just, Marnie? Nice and tight in the bum, too," her mother said, twirling her around. "So you've found a grand stallion to ride in the Heights of Brooklyn is it? Do tell, daughter of mine. You're skin is pure peaches and cream. Must be a man so." Her mother's hands were soft as a baby's bottom. Riding gloves. "Mustn't have the skin of a washerwoman, girls." Chanel Number 5 wafted under Fiona's nose.

"It's Brooklyn Heights. And no, there is no horse or man for that matter. Only thing I've been riding is a bike. Spinning."

"Well, what on earth? My daughter is now some kind of whirling dervish is it? A cycling one, no less? You must show us your moves if it has those results. What do you think, Marnie?" Her mother's laugh was like a melody. Her brogue a musical lilt.

Marnie laughed, her big bosom shaking. "Watch me whirl myself into the kitchen now, Mrs. 'Tis only a grand day now you're home, Fiona," Marnie smiled. Fiona was pleased Marnie had dropped the formality.

"Thanks very much, grand to be here." Fiona didn't miss her mother's raised eyebrows. She flashed her an identical prim smile, well learned. "Save a whiskey and chat for me, Marnie, will you?" she called back towards the kitchen.

"*Really*, Fiona, is that necessary?" Mam's disapproval. Another familiarity. *And I'm home what, five minutes?*

" 'Tis the new millennium, Mam. Get with it."

Her mother swatted her backside. "Never mind. Now let me tell Marnie we're having drinks in the parlor and I must ring your sisters and see what's keeping them. Go to your da. He's below watching the races. Probably has the telly on so loud he hasn't heard you come in."

Fiona walked down the hall to the parlor. She stopped at the large oak door and listened like she'd done as a child. She could hear the race being broadcast from the Curragh, the racecourse in Kildare. Fond memories. She and her sisters, Oona and Neeve, spent their whole childhood around the Curragh watching Granda Monahan's horses. The ponies, Granda told them, came from the island of Connemara where they ran wild until such a time came that they were needed for breeding. *The lifeblood of racehorses all over the world originates from Ireland, girls. Connemara wild ponies. The most beautiful you will ever lay your eyes on so.* Granda loved to talk about the horses, his eyes misty with pride.

Ah now girls, it's been told that the Spanish Armada sank off the coast of Connemara in the 16th century and the horses swam to shore. They bred with the native ponies running wild in the mountains. These horses survived out there on that rocky coast and became all the stronger for it. Remember that you have such blood coursing in your veins as well. Strong beauties you are. We Monahans are survivors. And like the ponies you must mind your wild edge.

Granda's legacy lived on in his son James and three granddaughters. Fiona turned the doorknob and walked into the parlor.

"Are we ahead Da, or wha'?" She snuck up behind him and put her arms around his neck. The sweet scent of Bay Rum enveloped her. She was home.

"Ah Fiona, come here to me, I want a proper look at my lovely daughter." James Monahan stood up. Fiona was drawn into his arms. Da was never stingy with his kisses.

"So like your mam you are. More beautiful with each passing day. Now sit down and tell your oul da how America is treating ye. What will you have to drink, love?" He walked over to the drinks tray at the end of the couch.

"Nothing a'tall. I'm just back from Pipers." Fiona plopped down on the plush sage green velvet couch. Of course Mam insisted on calling it *moss*. Fiona gave up trying to convince her otherwise. "I don't know how I functioned all these years not knowing the proper color of things," Mam said every time.

Fiona ran her hand along the soft fabric and let her eyes sweep the room. A turf fire burned pungently in the huge stone fireplace. The warm glow illuminated floor to ceiling windows across the room, the identical sage velvet draping their immense frames. A pair of buttery dark chocolate easy chairs sat cozily side by side next to the fireplace. An antique mahogany tea table between them, two hardback books on top. The fiction, Mam's. The book on racehorses, Da's.

Connemara ponies galloped freely in a gilt frame above the mantle. Below on a ledge, small antique frames boasted generations of Monahans on horseback. An enormous Celtic tapestry hung on one wall. Golden spirals encircled winged chestnut ponies soaring towards a stone castle on a background of bottle green. Not to be confused with sage *or* moss. Oona and Mam had a difference of opinion about their green palette. Oona liked to call it olive, just to piss her off. Neeve was always Switzerland.

"The room to your liking then?" Da was studying her, comfortably seated in a leather chair.

"Same as I left it," she smiled at her handsome father. He was for all the world like a mature cover of GQ. Trim and impeccably groomed in an Aran jumper over russet corduroy trousers. He crossed his leg revealing polished black boots. His silvery hair accentuated his indigo eyes and jet lashes.

"You look younger, Da. What's Mam been putting in your Wheatabix?"

Her father laughed. "Good one. Truth is your mam keeps me spry all right. And the horses, of course. You know your mother's old line…" His blue eyes twinkled when he smiled, Irish cheekbones prominent in his lightly tanned face.

"Who could forget?" Fiona said. She proceeded to fill Da in on her life in New York.

"And tell me, how is Dory keeping?" he asked. "Fair play to her for coming home. Grand girl. Tough break she had." Da always liked Dory. And he had no time for men who were bullies.

"Ah well she *was* fine. Until that nutter Sheila Mahoney dragged herself round to the pub, stirring up trouble. She's one horror show. You can't imagine the things that came out of her awful gob. Pure shite. She's evil."

Her father nodded. "The oul crather should be put down. Like a mad animal. She's no good to anyone. Her husband couldn't stick her. Only thing is he should have taken his boy with him. There's the tragedy. And poor Dory suffered for it the most. 'Tis a shame."

Truer words were never spoken, Fiona thought. No more were needed. Brynn Monahan breezed into the parlor like a gazelle.

"Now what's this? You look all serious like. Fiona, have you not been entertaining your da with tales of the Heights of Brooklyn?" She kissed her husband and sat down next to Fiona on the couch. The *moss* couch.

"We were just chatting," Fiona said.

"I'd love a glass of wine, James." She patted Fiona on the knee. "Will you have a glass of Chardonnay with me?"

"Sure."

Her mother crossed her long shapely legs. "Now I know you were on about something. Which of you is going to spill the beans so?" Her mother sipped her wine.

Fiona sighed. "Dory had the misfortune of meeting Sheila Mahoney down at Pipers. She made a spectacle of herself; I was just telling Da. She's desperate. Looks like an ould hag. In her nightie, no less, braless, teats hanging like a cow. Wailing like a banshee on crack." Fiona drank her wine.

Her mother shook her head. "My goodness. Poor Dory. That disgrace of a woman ruining her homecoming. Why Fergus hasn't committed the slapper to the sanitarium in Dublin is beyond me. She's a danger roaming the streets. When Eamon Teelon gets wind of this, he'll see something is done. Ah, poor Finn, she was so happy to have her daughter come home."

"Orleigh gave her quite a what for in the pub. Sheila's afraid of her life to piss *her* off."

"Well she'd be right there. My money's on Orleigh."

"Old Fergus hasn't been right since he stepped foot in Sheila's house," James Monahan said, sipping his Jamesons. "He told me once she was like poison he couldn't stop taking. Back in her prime she apparently had the jaw of a snake. Could ride like a bitch in heat."

Fiona laughed. Her mother did not.

"James, *really*!"

" 'Tis the truth, Brynn. I don't make these things up sure."

"Still it doesn't bear repeating, sure it doesn't?" Mam smoothed her skirt.

Time to change the subject, Fiona thought. "Da, do you know a man called Liam who comes into Pipers? Older man, well dressed. They stood for the anthem with him."

"Liam Casey," he said, "He's IRA, why?"

"He came over to Dory after your one made a scene. Told her she didn't have to worry about Sheila Mahoney anymore so. Gave her a whiskey and fucked off with himself."

"Fiona, is that necessary?" Mam hated the F word. Fiona always found that odd for an Irish woman.

"Sorry. He seemed to have vanished into thin air," Fiona smirked.

"That's from years of keeping a low profile so," Da said. "I'd say Declan Mahoney got himself in the thick of it a while back. Drugs, gambling. He had a big mouth, that boy. They don't abide that. Not a'tall. If he shared his tales with his mammy, they would be only too glad to shut her up permanently. Like they did him."

"Is *that* what happened to Declan? Really? It wasn't an accident?" Fiona's eyes were wide. "Wait till Dory hears about this."

"Now Fiona, there's no proof. And you are absolutely not to speak of it." Da refilled his glass. Her father was rarely that serious. He meant business.

"No worries, Da. My lips are sealed." *So Declan Mahoney had a little help driving off that cliff. Very interesting.*

Mam clapped her hands. "Enough of this unpleasantness. And we haven't had a proper toast to Fiona. James?"

"Right, my love. Welcome home, beautiful daughter of ours. Here's to having all my beauties under one roof tonight. Does my heart good. Slainte."

"Slainte," Fiona and her mother echoed. They drank in silence. Marnie knocked and walked into the parlor carrying a tray of canapés. She set it down on the low table in front of Fiona and her mother.

"Now eat something. A few stone wouldn't hurt you," her mother ordered.

"I thought you said I had a grand bum. Make up your mind, so." She took a salmon and cucumber thingie anyway. Home sweet home. Eat or be eaten.

"I think she looks fine, Brynn," Da said. "All the Monahan women are perfection so. Even our Marnie. Join us now. What'll you have?" he stood to pour Marnie a drink.

"I wouldn't say no to a wee tot of whiskey, Sir. If you don't mind. In Fiona's honor."

"That's the spirit, Marnie," Fiona said, delighted.

Mam gave her the high eyebrows. Fiona ignored her. Da handed Marnie a small glass of Bushmills. A certain look passed between them. Fiona caught it. It was the way she said "Sir, if you don't mind…."

Sir? If you don't mind… I'm just after putting the girls down for the night. Did you need me for something? Mrs. Monahan will be back quite late she said to tell you. I have a dinner below in the oven warming. Famished are you, Sir?

Fiona was supposed to be asleep. Not frozen behind her bedroom door listening to what she wasn't supposed to hear. Da had been into the whiskey that night. Fiona recognized the glare in his eyes. Granda had it too sometimes.

'Tis famished I am so. Come here to me, Marnie. Don't be shy, there's a pet. Marnie walked towards him. Da swept her in his arms. She didn't say a word.

Marnie, open your dress. There's a good woman. I long to suckle on those lovelies, like a wee babe. Brilliant. I won't be able to stand it much longer.

Fiona couldn't see the rest but she could hear sounds and moans that sounded like pleasure. She wasn't as shocked as she should have been. She'd been around stables all her life, seen her share of horses mating. People were no better than animals, she figured. Worse when they had a fair bit of whiskey in them. But Marnie had been stone sober. Maybe those tremendous tits of hers had her in a constant state of arousal. Fiona and her sisters had enjoyed suckling on them all right. Mam finally succeeded in weaning them off Marnie way past what she deemed a respectable stage. Or they'd have come home from school and run straight to their housekeeper's bosom rather than the milk and biscuits she had for their tea.

As for Marnie, she couldn't refuse Mr. Monahan. He was always nice to her. Respectful. It was a one off thing. She was sure of it. He'd forget about it tomorrow. Just like his father. The elder Mr. Monahan caught her a few times by surprise. Minding her business singing and kneading dough when hands would come around to her breasts. He would whisper for her to keep quiet while he lifted her dress and slid into her from behind. The loaves she served at tea that night would be extra high from her frantic kneading. All her life Marnie had been a lustful sight for men's eyes and appetites. She'd gotten used to it. Things could be worse sure. She could be walking the streets for a living. Or on the dole. She may not have been to the manner born, but she had been nicely compensated, more than comfortably housed, and brought to her crowning point by the lords themselves. Yes, things could be worse.

"Coo eee, Fiona? She's away with the fairies, Brynn."

"Sorry? Did you say something?"

Her father laughed. "Ah, you're ever the dreamer. I asked if you missed the horses?"

"Sure. Of course. I take it you are as involved as ever. No retirement for you, hmm?"

Her mother laughed. "He eats and breathes them sure. Same as always. My competition."

"Nonsense, Brynn. You smell much better."

"Come down to the Curragh tomorrow, Fee. See the new mares. They arrived from Wexford only yesterday. Gorgeous so they are." Da's face lit up. He loved his horses.

"I'd love to. Granda would be so proud of you. Continuing the tradition and all."

" 'Twas proud of you girls that's what he was. You were the light of the oul fella's eye."

Fiona knew that to be true. It was Granda Monahan who insisted his granddaughters not be sent away to boarding school. It wasn't a question of money. Monahan girls would learn about their heritage and the Connemara ponies and horse breeding firsthand. Every day. Do their studies locally and enjoy their childhood in the house their Granda built. They would be as comfortable in a stable as in the owners box at the Curragh. Well rounded women. Proud of their heritage.

Brynn Monahan luckily agreed with his logic. She was a horsewoman herself. And a lady. Her daughters would follow suit. Good breeding in people had little to do with money and everything to do with integrity and grace, she believed. Like wholesome Irish cream rising to the top. Fiona wondered if her mother had known the truth about herself and Grayson O'Leary would her high regard for her daughter have changed? She also knew she was more a disappointment to herself than anyone else. Still, better they never knew that she had sacrificed her better judgment for pleasure. And pain.

A sophisticated love affair was so appealing back then. So cosmopolitan. Without the bind of marriage. Grayson was her client. Fiona, an enthusiastic interior designer fresh out of Art College. He contracted her to refurbish his cottage in the country. Fiona was flattered and eager for the work. Grayson acted the gentleman the entire length of the project. At its completion he invited Fiona to bed. She had already fallen for him. She was too distracted to ask any questions. Or maybe she didn't want to know the answers.

The cottage became their love nest. Sometimes Grayson would call her mid week to meet him in the city. He couldn't wait for the two weekends a month he spent in the country. Fiona knew he lived in Dublin and was a very busy man. A solicitor with high paying clients of his own. He was besotted with her. And she with him. He was an adventurous lover. He knew fine wines and enjoyed good food. He kept horses. Fiona couldn't have created a more perfect man if she had sketched him up in her drawing pad, listed his qualities and sent her intention out to the universe. But she hadn't had to. Her luck. He simply came with the job.

She'd never before had a man so devoted to her. It was heady stuff. He called her on her mobile during the day. Left messages for her at her flat in Dublin. A few times they met in a hotel for a quickie. Sometimes Grayson just fancied oral sex. Fiona obliged. She couldn't blame him, she was good at it. She would return to work afterwards and feel desired. On the surface. She didn't look within or she would have realized how selfish Grayson could be. How it was all about him. His pleasure. His orgasm. But then he'd call her and invite her for a romantic weekend at the cottage, careful to stock all her favorite foods and delicacies, fresh flowers, plenty of candles. They would stay in bed all weekend. Grayson was the one who always did the planning. Fiona hadn't found that odd. He was a successful businessman; he liked to be in charge. She didn't want a daily life with a husband anyway. The drudgery of mundane tasks, shared bills and the inevitability of marital boredom on the horizon. A houseful of brats? No thanks. Grayson was exciting. That was enough.

Stupid is not a strong enough word for how Fiona felt when he told her he was married. She felt knocked off the horse and stomped to death. He presented himself so much *not* the marrying kind. Didn't he? She almost disbelieved him.

"You're married? I didn't see that coming."

"No worries, pet. I'm not breaking it off or anything," he said.

That wasn't the reason for his sudden bout of honesty. He was merely setting parameters for their relationship. Fiona had suggested a different weekend to meet than the pre-arranged one. That wasn't on, he'd told her. He was very busy and his leisure time was carefully doled out in a very organized fashion. Fiona pressed him. After all she had a busy professional life too. He wasn't supporting her and she never expected him to. She was independent. But she started to feel put upon. If she didn't answer to his beck and call he would get annoyed with her. Impatient. Abrupt. But the pre-arranged cottage weekends were written in stone. Unless Grayson changed them.

The sex got rougher than she enjoyed. Bordering on cruel. Like he was punishing her. It wasn't fun anymore. There was something vague she couldn't quite put her finger on creeping in amongst them. Than his confession. *I'm*

261

married, Fiona. Really? Grayson was never one to have long chats by the fire. "Delving into one's soul and all that shite, such a waste of time."

Fiona wasn't looking for therapy sessions. She had sisters. She had girlfriends. But she wasn't interested in dating a liar.

"I didn't lie, Fiona," he swore, "I merely omitted something that wasn't your business. Nothing to do with us." How do you omit a wife? Fiona wondered. Practice, she guessed. Lots of practice.

She expressed her shock with tears and anger. He smoothed over her hissy fit with jewelry. She mentioned ending their relationship. He filled the stable with horses for her. She barely rode them. Mostly she was saddle sore from riding Grayson all weekend. When she started to doubt the whole *affair*, (how Fiona despised that word, now they were a cliché), he'd tell her she was beautiful. How lonely he was in his other life, unsatisfied, bored.

She had a gift, he told her. It would be cruel if she denied him her body. He called her daring and spirited. Willing to try new things. Bondage, spankings. Something his wife would never consent to. Fiona pouted and tried to deny him his jollies. He gave her left handed compliments. "Yes, you're a grand decorator sure, but you'd make a lot more money with your body, than splashing paint on a wall, love. Not that I'm suggesting you make a trade out of it. I'm far too jealous."

Fiona couldn't end it. She was as addicted to Grayson as he was to her arse. She no longer looked herself in the eye. She was less than proud she was denying her own self respect. Why was she with someone who had no real respect for her?

"Face it Fiona, you are what you are. You enjoy sex. You weren't cut out to be anyone's wife or mammy. I didn't choose you to drink tea with, that was clear from the beginning. Don't make it about hon and dearie and playing house. I already have a wife."

Fiona should have been insulted. People hear what they want to hear. Women love to transform bastards for some reason. Fiona was no different. She would prove Grayson O'Leary wrong if it was the last thing she did. He was that enamored with her body? Good, she thought. I have the upper hand. The rest would be a piece of cake. He needed her. He was ravenous for her. Grand. Men left their wives all the time. Every day of the week. She'd been too agreeable. Time to tip the balance of power, she decided. Time to ante up, Grayson.

When she saw the emerald dress in the window of a Dublin boutique, she knew the time was now. She went into the dressing room and slipped the gorgeous satin material over her head and zipped it up. It was a bit formal and they never went anywhere but the damn cottage or out to dinner. But it clung to her in all the right places, tastefully and classically brushing the floor in grand style. Her auburn curls would be swept up like a princess. No, a queen. She'd wear the diamond and emerald studs that Grayson bought for her. Underneath, the lingerie he loved. Grayson would go out of his mind with desire. But that wouldn't be the focus for once. She was painting a new portrait of herself. Showing him he could have the whole package with her. Great sex and hearth and home. She would cook for him. Like Marnie had taught her. Good wholesome Irish food. No man could resist that. Grayson was in for a big surprise.

That weekend at the cottage, Fiona put her plan into action. She brought ground meat from the market. Cans of Guinness. Grayson had his share of fancy food all week. She would make him Shepherd's Pie. A special pudding to follow. Whiskey by the fire. Not that 300 year old brandy Grayson ordered when they were out. Simple food. Served with elegance. He would forget all about having a wife.

Fiona soaked in a luxurious bath surrounded by candles. She sipped a glass of Sauvignon Blanc for courage and imagined how the evening would play out. Grayson would be so happy. First at how elegant she looked. Second that she knew her way around the kitchen. Cooking something besides egg and toast for their breakfast. Tonight would be the night he admitted he was wrong. He'd tell her he was leaving his wife. He didn't love her and he badly wanted Fiona. At his table and in his bed every day and night. Yes, the tides would turn tonight. Fiona could barely contain her excitement.

She dressed and went inside to arrange the drinks tray in the sitting room. She lit the fire and put on Kind of Blue, Grayson's favorite Miles Davis CD. She had already set the table in the cozy kitchen. There was nothing to do but wait. She poured herself another splash of wine and stood by the fireplace practicing her most demure pose. Finally she heard his key in the lock. My prince arrives, she thought. Let the fairytale unfold….

She knew he was crossing the room to her. She could smell his cologne as he got closer. She kept her eyes shut in the candlelit room. She was Sleeping Beauty about to be awakened by her prince. She could almost feel his kiss. *Now, Grayson, now…*

She nearly bit her tongue the slap was so hard. It sent her reeling. She held her cheek and spoke through choked tears. "Why, Grayson? Why?"

Grayson helped her to her feet and stepped back. Away from her. His eyes were steel. Unkind. Why had she never seen that?

"Is there something you didn't understand, Fiona? What are you playing at? High society lady of the manner is it? Go put on a nice short dress, preferably with some cleavage showing. You're the mistress. Not the feckin' Mrs. of the manor. That role is already taken." He poured himself a whiskey and sat down by the fire.

"Why are you standing there?" He shook his head and laughed at her. "Come now, pet, be a good girl and change."

Fiona didn't move. She met his eyes and glared at him, eyes wet, makeup ruined. She couldn't have felt any more like shite if she tried.

"Right. Mr. O'Leary. It'll be 500 pounds a go. Extra for the blowjob. Another 500 up the arse. I'd like to be paid in full beforehand." She kept her voice business-like, as if they were discussing draperies or what color to paint the walls. She wanted to vomit. But she refused to give him the satisfaction of seeing her weak.

He got up from his chair and walked over to her.

"What's this? You're going to charge me is it? Cute. Since you didn't understand the first time, let me make myself perfectly clear." He reached into the bodice of her dress and cupped one of her breasts. "I can't see the lingerie I bought you," he whispered, coming close to her ear. She shuddered.

Fight him, Fiona. Have some feckin' spine, sham.

"Not yet Grayson, let me go…."

"Too late," he said. He let go of her breast and tore at the dress, ripping the beautiful expensive silk. "That's better," he said, unzipping his pants. "Now do what you do best." He held her by the hair, pulling out her carefully arranged French twist. "You really are asking for it, Fiona. But you're going to have to wait. Now do what you're told, pet."

Fiona's mind shut off. She had hoped. Big mistake that. Now she was crushed with disappointment. They could have had it all. If he had only thought more of her. An iota less of himself.

"I don't feel anything…" Grayson barked.

"Oh, sorry, baby, I'll do what you like now," some voice coming from her mouth meekly replied. She took him in her mouth. Well, not exactly.

Grayson screamed in agony. He held his bleeding bollocks in one hand and hauled off to punch her but she ducked out of the way. He kept looking at his dick, disbelieving. "How could you do this to me?" he screamed, "You miserable cunt!"

And once you thought me magnificent. Biting your John Thomas was easy. How could you not love me?

"Bitch! Look what you did. I'll beat the living shite out of you for this" he screamed. He sat there tending his bits and pieces, making idle threats.

Now that'll keep you out of commission for awhile, asshole. Fiona threw him a tea towel on her way back from the bedroom where she'd gone to change behind a locked door with a sharp pair of scissors for company.

"Mind the carpet, Grayson. Blood can stain something fierce," she said, coming into the living room. She put on her coat.

"Where are you going? You can't seriously leave me like this?"

Fiona ignored him. Grabbed her purse and keys.

"Sure I suppose you could say a dog bit you. Though the teeth marks wouldn't match up, would they? The Mrs. isn't much for the oral sure she's not? Won't even notice. Well, it's been fun, Grayson. Don't ring me. Ever. I'd say go fuck yourself, but you won't be doing much fucking any time soon, now will you?"

Grayson didn't say a word. He was sitting on the floor cradling his balls. Moaning in an awful way, the tea towel turning a deep red.

"Maybe I should ring the guarda? They can take you to hospital. Good laugh they'll have at the cop shop
afterwards, I reckon. Or shall I ring Mrs. O'Leary?" Fiona lit a cigarette and sat on the arm of the chair closest to the door. She was strangely enjoying herself.

"Don't you fucking dare," Grayson managed through clenched teeth. "Just get me some shagging ice."

Fiona didn't move. "Still the boss? Even in that position? You really ought to learn some manners."

"Please…" he begged.

She sighed, rubbing her own swollen cheek.

"Well, I guess I could do that before I leave." She strolled into the kitchen. Strolled back out. She carried the ice bucket to where he was sitting and poured it in his lap. He screamed.

"You cunt! I meant in a towel!"

Fiona left him fucking and blinding and slammed the door on her way out.

She punched in a Dublin number on her cell in the car. A woman answered. "Hello? Mrs. O'Leary is it? Right, just wanted to let you know that your husband had a bit of an, ahm, accident. He's at the cottage."

"Sorry? An accident? Who is this?"

"You might say his precious pet turned on him. One good thing though, his bollocks will be out of service for a good bit."

"Sorry? His pet? Did you say a dog bit him? But he doesn't have the dog with him. The dog is here. I don't know who you are but if this is some sick joke...."

"Ahm, no dear, no joke I assure you. I'm the housekeeper, but it wasn't proper for me to do anything for him but ring you, you understand." Fiona wanted to burst out laughing.

"My God, of course not. Did you ring for an ambulance?"

"No. He won't bleed out that quickly."

"God, I should hope not. I better hang up so and go see to him. Thank you."

"Not a'tall. Stitched up, he'll be right as rain in no time, no worries."

"I wasn't worried, believe me. You have no idea."

"Oh I do, Mrs. O'Leary. I do. A very good idea. Suffer from the TMJ a'tall, do you? Grayson being so well hung and constantly erect. I'm not telling you anything new, sure I'm not?"

"What? How dare you! I thought you said you were the housekeeper?"

"Did I say that? Pardon me for lying, Mrs. O'Leary. No, I'm the whore your husband has been sticking his business in every other weekend sure. And twice during the week, hungry fucker. He said you weren't much for the blowjobs. Useless, I believe is how he put it. Well, I'm through with him. He's all yours, love. Anyway, better hurry now. He's ruining a perfectly good carpet bleeding like a stuck pig."

Fiona clicked off her phone and threw it on the passenger seat, and turned onto the path to Orleigh's cottage. She badly needed a drink.

Chapter Forty-Three

"I'd say the turf has gone to her head." Oona nudged her sister with her knee. "Coo eee, Fee, you in there?"

Fiona looked up into emerald eyes identical to her mother's.

"Oona. How long are ye standing there?" She rubbed her eyes and looked over at her other sister, Neeve, her mirror image.

"Twas away with the fairies you were, sham," Neeve smiled, her blue eyes twinkling. "Get up and hug us properly so."

Fiona melted in the arms of her kin. She curled Neeve's red curls around her finger and smoothed Oona's shiny black tresses.

"I've missed you, lads," she said, her eyes teary.

"Now don't start bawling, we'll all be in puddles. I'm just after paying a fortune for this new eye liner," Oona said.

Fiona laughed, "Grand so, it must be waterproof."

The three sisters held hands. Oona gave her long lost sister the once over. "You're as fit. Have you been running the streets of Brooklyn? Or is it a fine stallion? Do tell."

"I spin, and the other is none of your damn business."

Neeve laughed. "You tell her. But *don't* tell her. She'll have an ad taken out in the Irish Times."

Fiona shrugged. "Nothing to report, trust me."

Oona let it go. For now.

"Dinner is served," Marnie called out at the door. The sisters followed their parents into the dining room. James Monahan was chuffed to have his three daughters gathered around his table. Four chatty females didn't faze him in the least. To another man it might prove daunting. Not James Monahan. He was in his glory surrounded by the beautiful women he loved. Having them all together was a rare treat.

Neeve and Oona were hard to pin down with their popular interior design business. They were constantly hopping back and forth from their Dublin base to all points hither and yon. They were in high demand all over Ireland. Their father was so proud of them. Their magic touch could transform an ordinary house into a smashing designer home without draining the owners of their savings. Yet they were savvy enough businesswomen to take advantage of what the market would bear. The only thing missing from The Sisters Monahan Designs was the third sister.

Brynn Monahan watched her daughters. She silently congratulated herself for doing a fine job rearing them. They were beautiful, smart, interesting women. They knew how to dress and keep their lovely shapes. A credit to herself. She taught them well. They were as comfortable at a cocktail party dressed to the nines as they were in dungarees getting themselves dirty painting a room, refinishing a piece of furniture or mucking out a stable. Well-rounded girls made grand women. Brynn had raised three.

She would have loved grandchildren to spoil like Granda Monahan had spoiled her girls. Marriage and family were not on her daughters' agenda so far. Oona and Neeve had men in their lives but they preferred to keep their own flats and not formalize the relationships. Fiona was more of a mystery. Brynn was aware that something happened to her daughter to make her move to America without a glance back. Fiona remained tight lipped about it. One day, hopefully, her daughter would feel she could share it with her. Marnie might have known. God knows she wouldn't break a promise to Fiona no matter who asked her. That stuck in Brynn's craw. But she'd be damned if she'd let on. I wouldn't give the old cow the satisfaction, she thought. 'Tis a pity daughters don't realize their mothers were young once, Brynn thought.

Marnie appeared from the kitchen carrying the dessert tray. She set down Waterford crystal plates of gorgeous raspberries and fresh cream and a pedestal dish of perfect chocolate madeleines from Teelon's Bakery. She proceeded to pour coffee. Fiona gave her a kiss on the cheek when she came to her. Marnie smiled. "Does my heart good to see you at the table again…." she hesitated.

"Say it, Marnie. *Fiona*. 'Tis fine, sure," Fiona assured her, taking a cookie and raising her eyes at her mother.

"Grand, call her whatever she likes," Brynn Monahan said, surrendering. "I'm beyond telling my daughters what to do at this stage."

Marnie didn't know what to say, so she said nothing, just gave a subservient nod in the Mrs.' direction. James Monahan found it amusing. He gave his wife a pat on the leg and a wink. Marnie came over with a plate of raspberries and cream for each of them. One heavy breast brushed Brynn's arm. Marnie apologized. Brynn waved her off, scooping up a single plump raspberry and a dollop of cream with her spoon. *Good Lord, if I'd had to nurse three hungry babies, one year after the next, my lovely breasts would be hanging like a field cow.* She shuddered. *Thank heaven I didn't have the milk that Marnie had in her enormous dairy of a bosom. 'Tis a shame Marnie lost her own babies. Wasn't meant to be. The coincidence of their pregnancies worked to Brynn's advantage. Yet she often wondered how Marnie managed to get herself pregnant three times when she barely left the Monahan home. Further speculation Brynn did not engage in. It only gave one wrinkles from worrying.* She caught her husband stealing a peek down the ravine of Marnie's mountainous cleavage. She admonished him with her eyes. *Men. Ye are so transparent.*

When all three sisters had given their dessert a fair go, they pushed back from the table stuffed and groaning. There was always an hour at the gym or a hard ride in the morning.

"Are you girls trying to convince your sister to come home and join you again?" James Monahan asked out of the blue.

"We're trying, Da," Oona said, "She's a tough sell. She likes her Brownstone and her mates there. But seriously, you can't wait tables forever."

Fiona glared at her sister. *Bitch.* Oona just had to go there. Mam was perfectly satisfied with vague information as to what she was doing to support herself in America. Until now. Neeve quickly tried to smooth it over.

"But you only do the *gourmet* café in between planning your new decorating ideas, isn't that right?" Neeve smiled at Fiona, glared at Oona.

"Right." *Good save, Neeve.* " 'Tis mail order. Shanty Chic I'm calling it. A spin-off of the Shabby Chic over. Like it?" The trick was to keep talking and ignore the trouble Oona could stir up at a moment's notice.

"That's lovely," Mam said. Brynn was hardly oblivious to what Oona was doing. *She could instigate a row from her pram, that one.* "Why don't you get an export thing going? People will love it. I know you miss the designing, Fiona. And by the way, Oona, you aren't telling me what I don't already know. Your sister always liked to pretend she was a scullery maid, helping Marnie in the kitchen when she should have been practicing her piano."

Fiona forced a laugh. Mam had a way of getting her digs in one way or the other. Fiona didn't take it to heart. She treasured every moment she spent with Marnie. Their talks and their confidences over the years were precious to Fiona. Marnie never judged her. Not even when she felt so ashamed she would rather have died than ever let anyone know the humiliation she suffered at Grayson's hand. Marnie was not shocked in the least. *Men can be as cruel, Miss Fiona. You must try to keep the healthy appetite you have for a good roll in the hay separate from allowing any man to mistreat you. You are worth so much more. Remember that always. If need be, I'll carve the bollocks off the shite meself!*

James Monahan stood up. "What do you beauties say to an after dinner tot?" He took his wife's hand and led her from the dining room. The sisters followed, continuing their conversation about interior design. "Look at them, Brynn. Fierce planning going on in those three beautiful heads,"

James Monahan said, pouring a Bailey's for the women and a whiskey for himself.

"Yes," his wife agreed, "Even when they were bent over their mud pies, there was endless chatting and plotting the whole time."

"More in those tree wee heads than a comb would take out sure." Fiona and her sisters recited Granda Monahan's words verbatim. Their parents laughed.

"We need another toast, James," Brynn Monahan insisted.

"Right. Welcome home, Fiona. Here's to the four loveliest women in the whole of Ireland and the world sure. Slainte."

"Slainte," the Monahan women replied in one sweet voice.

Their parents excused themselves to bed and left Fiona and her sisters to enjoy the glowing fire and their nightcaps.

"So...." Oona began, "Did you ever hear a word from your man? Did he know you were moving to the States?" Oona blew the smoke from her cigarette into the fireplace.

Fiona nearly choked on her Bailey's. "Sorry?"

She knew exactly to whom Oona was referring. *Your man, my arse.* Oona was violating the sister code and Fiona was instantly annoyed with her. Oona knew good and well that certain topics were not up for discussion. Grayson O'Leary being one of them. Top of the feckin' list.

"Leave it alone, Oona," Neeve said quietly, discouraging her inquisitive sister. Damn her, Neeve thought, Oona had been a Nosy Morgan from birth.

"Ah now, come on," Oona waved her cigarette in the air, unaffected. "Don't be stuffy, Neeve. She can handle it sure."

"Listen to this, Fee. We show up at this la di da flat in Dublin on a referral. The client's second name was a different name to his, you see he hadn't hired us a'tall. His wifey did. Well who shows up one day in the middle of the

273

project? Your man. So we tacked on an additional cost for the hell of it. Fuck the bastard. And wasn't he leering at Neeve? Drooling practically. Like he'd seen a ghost. One he wanted to put his slimy hands on."

Fiona stood and poured herself a Jameson's. The conversation was beyond Bailey's. She took a stiff drink and said rather nervously, "Right. Like he'd ever get the chance."

Neeve said nothing. Not the time to clam up, Neeve, Fiona thought, grinding her teeth. Oona stared into the fire. Fiona felt the anger rise up in her gut. *Not my sister, Grayson.*

"Give me a fag," she said. Oona held up an empty crushed pack of cigarettes. Fiona wanted to slap her.

"No worries pet, I've more in the car." Oona shot out of the room like it was on fire. *Typical Oona. Stir the shite and disappear.*

Fiona tapped her fingers on her glass. Neeve's silence was a bad sign. Fiona couldn't stand it another second. She moved closer so she was facing her sister dead on.

"Look at me, sham, and don't bother denying it. Sure it's written all over your face. And why *wouldn't* he go after you? Nothing would give the gobshite more pleasure than shagging the sister of his former mistress. Now where in hell has Oona gone for the smokes, back to Dublin?" Fiona took another sip of whiskey. She let out a loud sigh. "Seriously, Neeve, how could you? Never mind, I know Grayson."

Neeve was crying. She looked truly mortified. She never wanted Fiona to know. It was all a very bad mistake on her part.

"Fee, please don't hate me. It only happened the one time. I made it quite clear that if he rang me or bothered me again, I'd go straight to his wife. You see she was the one who hired us. Apparently she didn't know about you. Well, your name anyway. I was weak, Fee. Stupid. Oona was in Athlone on business. I was alone working at the flat. His wife was in the country. He said how beautiful I was, how like you, and how sorry he was for hurting you. He even shed a tear or two. I missed you so much. I don't know why I believed him, but I did. And than he was, um well… and I…"

"Christ. Spare me the feckin' details, if you don't mind." She heard the front door close. "Finally, Oona, I thought you got lost." Oona handed her a fresh packet of Silk Cuts. Fiona shook out a cigarette and lit it with a shaky hand. God, I am thoroughly pissed with you Oona, she thought. *You're a right bitch.* She concentrated on smoking while she gathered herself. *My feckin' sister, Grayson?* Fiona felt like screaming. *Goddamn you, Grayson.*

She looked at Neeve. "Right. So you shagged his brains out, the little he has like. Notice any scar when you were down there? Teeth marks? Hope you enjoyed yourself. Did he have the decency to get you to *come*? Grayson can be so damn selfish."

Neeve's face was beet red. "God, Fee, please. I'm so damn sorry. And no, I didn't enjoy it. Actually it was a bit painful. The fucker isn't normal, sure he's not? If you think I put that thing in my mouth, forget it. I told him that wasn't on. He said that was where myself and my sister parted company. He said you had that bit down pat. Oh God, I'm sorry, what am I after saying? I'm so sorry, please believe me, Fee. I was temporarily insane. Still, no excuse for my behavior."

"Relax, Neeve. I'm not mad at you. You didn't know why I left home, how bad it got with him. I was ashamed of myself, disappointed in my own behavior. And done with men. You didn't know. Only Orleigh knew, and later Dory. Let's forget it. Put it to bed, so to speak," she flicked an ash into the fire.

Neeve nodded, relieved. "Thanks. Really. I was sick over you ever finding out. I never thought you would." Neeve glared at Oona.

"What?" Oona said defensively, "She was bound to find out. You forgive me too, don't you, Fee? You know I can't keep a secret to save my life. Be a pet now, don't be angry."

"Always with an excuse? Some things never change around here. Anyway, I forgive you both. I wouldn't give Grayson O'Leary the satisfaction of thinking he could come between us. Fuck him and the horse he rode in on."

"That's the spirit," Oona laughed. "Besides, Neeve had more fun with the Magic Tongue you sent her for Christmas than with your man."

Neeve spit out her drink. "You feckin' don't know when to shut up, sure you don't? Christ, you're hopeless."

Fiona laughed. "It's okay. Glad you enjoyed it. Great invention that."

Neeve laughed, finally relaxing. "I still am, sister dear. When my honey's out of town, 'tis a lifesaver." They all roared laughing.

Fiona cut a sharp look at Oona. "What about you, sham? Have any deep dark secrets to purge?" *I'll fucking kill you where you sit if you tell me you shagged himself. You're too wide for his antics.* Fiona waited. She helped herself to another cigarette. *Talk, Oona. And then I'll murder you.*

"I'm not a fan of the Tongue but I did like the vibrator," Oona smirked.

"Grand. Now talk." Fiona wasn't amused.

Oona waved both hands in surrender. "Okay, okay. I swear to you, I did not shag your man, a'tall a'tall, thank you very much. Not a peck or a feel did he get from me. I think he could hear me hiss when he got too close. Besides, I like my men low maintenance. A constant salute is too much work. Give me a man with an average sex drive and I'm happier than a pig in shite." Oona raised her glass and drank. "And I am sorry. Truly I am, for bringing it up. Pardon the pun."

Fiona laughed, more out of relief than anything. Oona must take after Mam. Fiona and Neeve always did enjoy a good go at themselves. Oona couldn't be bothered. *You should give your fannies a rest so,* she'd tell them. *Clean your rooms. Do some drawing. You're liable to get a rash."* They would crack up and continue. Silly Oona, they'd think, she didn't know what she was missing.

"What do you say? Think the craic is still happening at Teelons?" Oona asked.

"I'd say a session is well under way. Are we for it so?" Neeve looked at her sister. Fiona met her eyes. She was forgiven.

"Right as rain, lads, let's go," Fiona said. The sisters locked arms and headed out into the cool Irish night.

Chapter Forty-Four

The Teelon kitchen was abuzz. A veritable female hive. Finn Teelon orchestrating the whole lot. Dory on washing up detail. Nory and Jury drying and putting away. Jury's sixteen year old twins Nicola and Noreen brewing coffee. Orleigh and Mae covering every square inch of the kitchen table with what had to be all the sinful desserts on earth. Mae was salivating as she inhaled rich fragrant chocolate from a cake as shiny as a fat round patent leather purse. There was blackberry cobbler, lemon teacakes, toffee bars, lace cookies, brownies and an incredible meringue that Mrs. Teelon proudly called Burnt Orange. If you hadn't a sweet tooth, Mae thought, you might just develop one instantly. A sweet feast.

Kieran stuck his head around the corner startling Mae. "Scared you did I? Both hands in the cookie jar is it?"

Mae laughed. He was adorable. "Guess I do, hon."

"Never mind flirting with the girls now, sham. Here's something you can do," Dory called over to him as she flung a bag of garbage at him.

"You're only too kind to me, love. I'm nothing but a lucky man so." He walked outside, the trash slung over his back.

"Not yet you're not, but the odds are in your favor," Dory said under her breath.

Nory hit her across her rear with a tea towel. "You little slut, hardly back in the country."

Dory flicked her with some water. They both cracked up.

"Ah now girls. Don't go getting me nice desserts wet now." Finn Teelon admonished her daughters in a playful manner. She was delighted she had them all in her kitchen again. Her eyes rested on Dory. She wished she could erase every horror the poor child suffered in that horrid marriage. Ah, to see her smile, she thought, a true gift. A mother feels her child's pain. *You can't go back, Finn, you can't go back.* She followed Dory's gaze now. *Ah, the road not taken….*

Kieran appeared at the kitchen door arms full of Monahans. "Look what I'm after finding out by the gate." He was grinning like a fool. One who'd stepped in shite, Dory thought. She threw a sponge at his head. "Hey!" he ducked too late. Soapsuds dripped down his forehead. Fiona and her sisters howled.

"Grand shot. You haven't lost your touch," Oona said.

"We'll see about that later, so we will," Kieran mumbled, eyes twinkling at Dory. She laughed. He went in to join the men in the sitting room.

"I said the sink couldn't get any cleaner," Neeve repeated, over Dory's shoulder.

"Aye. I suppose you're right so," Dory dropped the sponge. "Howyeh, Neeve?" She gave her best friend's sister a tight hug.

"Grand."

"You're Fiona's twin, I swear you are," Dory remarked.

"Could be worse sure, I could take after Oona."

Oona heard her and mouthed, "Fuck off." Dory and Neeve roared laughing.

"You reckon the marching bands ever looking like this, mate?" Aiden said to Jury's husband Johnny as the women pranced into the room in a line.

"Some things are worth waiting for so." He gave Jury a nod of approval and played a few high notes on his accordion as she swung her hips suggestively at him. Eamon Teelon strummed his guitar to the tune of Danny Boy. Aiden added the necessary melancholy notes on his tin whistle. A full scale session was underway.

Dory's da began to sing, his strong tenor voice backed up by Kieran who harmonized an octave lower. Finn Teelon dabbed at her eyes with a hanky. At the end they didn't pause. Kieran tapped out the beat on his bodhron as the others joined in singing Whiskey In The Jar, Orleigh belting out the lead. Jury's twins laced up their step dancing shoes for the next song, an instrumental jig. Their feet flew as if unattached as the notes danced around the room. The girls clicked down again and again on the wooden floor in perfect rhythmic precision to the clapping and drumbeats.

Mae was impressed. The girls were wholesomely beautiful with genuine smiles and sparkling eyes. Much like Doc's nieces at the Brownstone wedding. She watched Johnny, Jury's husband, admiring his girls. He looked proud. He squeezed his wife's waist. Mae was moved. So that's what a normal father-daughter relationship looks like, she thought. Mae envied the twins. She wouldn't wish her early childhood on her worst enemy. Mae was thankfully distracted by Fiona's voice.

"Let's have it now, lads, please," she shouted, "The Hills of Connemara, for my Granda."

Kieran picked up a fiddle and Eamon Teelon traded his guitar for a banjo. Aiden sang with them, his eyes fixed on Mae the entire song. She couldn't decide which brother was better looking. Either way, the heat was on. *Have mercy.*

Mae tried to keep her gaze steady on the Monahan sisters as they sang. Her cheeks were flushed she could feel it. She felt Aiden looking at her. She boldly met his eyes, lingering there for a few seconds. She felt the good in them. Honest. Safe. That appealed to her. God, he was sexy. *He won't hurt you, Mae.* She heard Orleigh's voice in her ear, though she was sitting across the room. *He'll treasure you, as you were meant to be.* Mae looked at her. *So you are a witch.*

"Can you play Purple Heather?" Mae had no idea where that came from, but it was her own voice shouting it out. Aiden began the song. Mae's memory of it came rushing back. Sister Devora would sit Mae next to her at the piano and play. She listened to the words now and realized it was an odd choice for a nun. An Irish love song. Mae knew there was more in Sister's hair under that veil than a comb would take out. She smiled to herself and concentrated on Aiden's voice.

I will build my love a tower... by the cool crystal waters...and we'll go together to pick wild mountain thyme all along the purple heather...will ye go lassie go? Mae was singing along with Aiden as if it were the most natural thing in the world. And didn't Orleigh look pleased with herself? Definitely *witch.* The song was over. Mae was embarrassed.

"Now where did you learn that song, child?" Finn Teelon asked her, patting Mae's hand.

"From a friend, a long long time ago. It was her favorite."

" 'Tis as sweet as sugar you are, Mae West," Eamon Teelon said, "Isn't she just, Finn?"

"Aye," his wife answered, giving Mae a peck on the cheek, "You are as lovely, Mae."

The kindness in their eyes touched Mae's heart. "Thank you," she managed, keeping her emotions under control. Good luck, in this room, she thought.

Dory came over and rescued her. "Look at you, a brilliant singer and all. Who knew? You've been holding out on us so."

Mae laughed. "Right, hon, after how many Guinness? Besides, everybody here sings."

Dory shook her head. "Not like *that.*"

"Fancy a cuppa?" Aiden was standing in front of her, looking hopeful.

"Sure. And anything chocolate." Mae followed him into the kitchen. She scanned the table.

"Spoiled for choice?" Aiden laughed, setting down the coffee pot.

"That's the problem all right. The brownies are calling me. Hear them? The toffee bars look way too good. And what's this Burnt Orange? Never heard of it. To die for, am I right?" Mae wanted everything on the table. And him.

Aiden laughed and handed her a cup of coffee. "You are priceless, Mae West."

"Am I? Like a diamond you mean? Right, that's me. No, maybe an emerald. Really I'm more like an old penny.

281

The kind you find on the ground and put on the railroad tracks."

She sipped her coffee after adding cream and sugar. Aiden leaned next to her at the counter. He smelled like freshly cut Christmas trees. Imagine finding him wrapped up in your stocking? Bring on the mistletoe.

"Mae?" Aiden was talking to her.

"Hmm?"

"No way, darlin. Old penny? Not a'tall. You've been misinformed. You are definitely a jewel. Let's see... An opal? No. An onyx. Yes, that's it. Onyx, beautiful and mysterious." He bit into a brownie.

Mae wanted to lick the chocolate crumb off his lip. *Good Lord.*

"Yes, that's me, to a tee. How'd you know? So are you full of the blarney with all the girls?" She cut herself a healthy wedge of Burnt Orange, slipped it onto a plate and dug in. He was staring.

"What? Do I have meringue on my face?" Mae asked. If his brother was adorable than he was off the charts. No wonder Sister Devora was singing Irish love songs. *Saints preserve us, indeed.*

"No blarney in your case, I promise. A beautiful wood nymph like yourself couldn't be fooled anyway. If you are to be my undoing, than I'll die a happy man."

"Your undoing? You mean there'll be women throwing themselves off bridges if you're not there to charm them?"

"What are you like? No other lass concerns me anymore, a'tall, a'tall. I've been bewitched by you, Mae West. I leave myself in your hands. Disappointed?"

"Do I look disappointed, hon? Very smooth by the way. Can you say that a'tall bit again? I like the way it sounds."

Before he could oblige her, she offered him a bite of her Burnt Orange. He leaned in to take it. Instead he put his lips on hers and kissed her softly. She was too busy savoring the taste of him to be taken aback.

"Delicious," he said, "No, not an old penny, a'tall, a'tall."

Mae giggled, delighted. Dory walked into the kitchen. They were nearly caught. Dory smiled.

"Grand playing, Aiden. Find any sweet to your liking so?" Guilty as sin, she thought, looking at the pair of them.

"I'd recommend the Burnt Orange." Aiden said, "Purely heaven." He winked at Mae before he left the kitchen.

"You throw a great party, hon," Mae said pouring herself another coffee and one for Dory.

"Changing the subject, sham?" Dory took the cup Mae handed her and a toffee bar. She munched and watched Mae squirm. She was cute when she was caught.

"Was there one?" Mae asked. She did innocent very well. Academy Award material, Dory thought.

"Burnt kisses...ahm, I mean Burnt Orange, I believe 'twas." Dory smirked, enjoying herself.

"Dory, he kissed *me*. I didn't expect... I mean, I liked it, don't get me wrong. Who wouldn't? But it was nothing. He's a big flirt is all. Right? And I'm not looking to...."

Poor Mae. She was charming.

"Relax, darlin,' you're on holiday. Enjoy yourself so. And actually, no, he's not a big flirt. Gorgeous, yes. But sincere. He likes you. Big time, I reckon. He's all moony-eyed. And don't worry. Aiden wouldn't hurt a fly. Bank on that. He knows I'd break his bollocks. Kieran would as well. He thinks you're the very thing his brother needs."

"What's that, hon? A love-starved American tourist? A good shagging?"

Dory laughed. "No, just yourself. Your humor, your honesty, your impish face. You. The whole package. The entire woman. You just don't know how appealing that is do you? If I were a man I'd fancy you as well."

"Now who's full of blarney? You'd fancy me? Wow. I love you too, but not like that. Besides we already have our lesbian quota met at the Brownstone. You do have beautiful tits, though," Mae giggled. Dory just shook her head.

"I agree with that wholeheartedly," Kieran said, walking into the kitchen. I couldn't have timed that better, he thought, grinning at Dory.

Mae giggled and excused herself. There was a man in the next room with her name on his lips. And her friend's seal of approval on his very nice ass.

Chapter Forty-Five

Dory slept like the dead. Waking in her old room was surreal but comforting. She was home. In Ireland. She rubbed her eyes and stretched her body like a cat. Throwing on her fleece bathrobe at the foot of the bed, she strolled over to the window and looked out at her old view. The field behind the house was covered in mist. The day was grey and damp. You don't come to Ireland for the weather. She stood transfixed as the mist danced across to the neighbor's field like a large woman in a gossamer dress. There was the low stone wall where she and her sisters sat on Sunday mornings eating sticky buns Da gave them from the bakery after Mass. Mam would sing from the window. *Three pairs of maryjanes swinging to and fro. Three little moppets sitting in a row.* A simple time. Babes in the woods. Something shot across her line of vision. She could have sworn someone moved out near one of the trees. Dory leaned in close to the glass to get a better look but the mist hid whoever it was. Probably an old farmer looking for a stray sheep. She let the lace curtain fall back into place. She needed coffee. Pronto. And a few aspirin wouldn't do any harm.

The house was quiet. Last night's hooley a memory. Her parents were already well into their day at the bakery. Bless their hearts, Dory thought, slipping her feet into thick wool socks while she waited for the kettle to boil. She went into the sitting room. Was there actually a session here last night? You'd never know it. Everything was clean as a whistle. No flies on Mam. Unlike her three cats who dozed lazily on the window seat.

"You have the life now girls, do you not?" Dory said to them. They went back to their naps ignoring her. The kettle screeched. Dory padded into the kitchen.

She spooned two heaping teaspoons of coffee into her cup and reached for the kettle. Inhaling the brew, she anticipated her first sip. Something hit the kitchen door. She jumped, her arm knocking over the coffee. "Shite," she said, grabbing a tea towel to wipe up the mess. She reached for the kettle and started again. She stirred the strong coffee and added a healthy drop of cream. "Umm, that's better."

Something hit the door again. "What in the Jaysus? Doesn't anyone know how to knock properly?" Dory left her coffee on the counter and walked over to the door. She swung it open and stuck her head out. Nobody there. Must have been birds or maybe a squirrel. She stood out in the yard and stretched. Held her robe close against the morning chill. At least there wasn't an unforgiving sun to glare on her aching head. She turned to go inside. Then she saw them.

A pile of stones. Pebbles really. Odd. She looked out towards the field. There was something on the low wall. It didn't move though it looked like it had feathers. Grand, a dead bird is all I need this morning, she thought, walking over to it. She froze. It was no bird, dead or alive. Dory stared at the hat and cursed the day and the woman who ruined it.

"Bitch!" she shouted. "You just won't leave me be, will you? Now you've gone too far and come too damn close, Sheila. But you won't win, you demented hag." Dory shook her head. Now I'm crazy, she thought. Talking to a hat. An ugly black crow-like fringed monstrosity of a feckin' hat. But a hat nonetheless. There was no one there. Vanished. Yet the woman who left it behind was the one person she wanted to make disappear for good.

Dory went inside and continued muttering to herself as she sliced bread for toast and popped two aspirin washed down with her lukewarm coffee. She ate a corner of leftover brownie and lit the turf in the kitchen hearth. "I refuse to let the bitch get to me, simple as that," she announced to no one. Her toast sprang up. She buttered it generously and put a layer of marmalade over that. The kettle screamed. She made herself another coffee, propped her feet up on the hearth ledge and sipped and chewed, thoughtfully planning Sheila Mahoney's imaginary demise.

286

She heard footsteps outside the door. It didn't startle her as much as piss her off. "Now what? Is there no peace this morning or what?" She stood and grabbed the bread knife off the cutting board and waited. The door handle jiggled. "Make my day, Sheila," she thought. The doorknob turned. Dory walked towards her visitor, her adrenaline pumping.

"Holy shite, it's only you, Mam."

"Of course it's me. Who were you expecting? The Blessington Strangler? What in the name of God? Put that knife down, child. You're making me nervous. Is this what big city living is like so? You greet your guests with a serrated blade? We've no real crime in Blessington, love. What's up with you?"

Dory burst out laughing, relieved. Secretly disappointed though. She had pictured herself stabbing Sheila Mahoney. Over and over.

"*She* was here. I knew I saw someone out there earlier from the upstairs window. Had to be her. She threw stones at the door. Than left her feckin' calling card. Bitch." Dory lit a cigarette and got another cup down out of the press and stuck the kettle back on. Mam sat down at the table.

"Slow down now. Are you telling me that Sheila Mahoney was *here*? I'm guessing she was long gone before you saw her. What was it she left? A *card*?"

"Her hat. She always leaves her feckin' hat."

"Her hat? I don't know what that's about but imagine the cheek of her coming to my house. This is not on. Wait'll I tell your da. He won't have it. Not a'tall. What's this about a hat will you tell me?"

Dory was calm now. "Long story." Dory turned towards the fire.

"Sure where am I going? Only to do the washing and that can wait. That crazy whore has gone too far, Dory. Lucky I wasn't here. I'd have stabbed her myself, no questions asked. Grand you're okay so." Mam squeezed her around the waist as she poured her tea. Dory put two sticky buns on a plate from the bag Mam brought in with her.

"I'm fine. No harm done. Only an old hag's crow hat out there on the wall."

Mam looked at her. She set her cup down, got up and walked outside. Dory followed her, with the knife. Just in case. Finn Teelon put on her gardening gloves and picked up the filthy hat, holding it away from her body like a diseased animal. They walked back to the house in silence.

"Um, why do you want that thing in the house?" Dory shook her head, disgusted.

Finn Teelon held onto the hat and looked at her daughter. "For evidence, sham. For the guarda. I'll stick it in a trash bag so."

Dory watched as she shoved the hideous thing into a plastic bag, tied a knot at the top and put it under the sink. She wanted to laugh but Mam took her solutions seriously.

"Now. Are we right, love? Imagine, all this falderal before a person's had a decent breakfast."

"You're asking me if I've I gone psycho myself? No worries. She just riles me still, after all this time." Dory looked out the window. *Fuck you, Sheila.*

"Remember the song?" Mam asked. For all the world her grown daughter was still her little Dory girl at heart. Sticky icing on her lips and little patent leather shoes swinging. She began to sing. *Three pairs of maryjanes swinging to and fro… Three little moppets sitting in a row. Where is your da, girls? Driving a big lorry? What are your names, girls? Dory, Nory, Jury!*

Dory clapped and gave her mother a hug.

"Thanks, Mam. And you're not to worry about your one, Miss Gobshite Horror Story."

"Is that so? And that's because you'll sort the whore out? Do you plan on carrying that bread knife around all day? I have a small but very sharp pair of sewing scissors that might interest you."

They both laughed. No point in letting Sheila Mahoney ruin their day. The phone rang interrupting their talk of murder weapons.

"Hello. Ah, Kieran, you're more than welcome. 'Twas great craic. She's here sure. Bye. All the best." Mam covered the mouthpiece. "That good looking O'Rourke fella is on the line. Surely you're not interested?" Mam had a wide grin on her face. Dory stuck her tongue out. "Aren't you as fresh? I've a mind to hang up."

Dory practically jumped across the floor and grabbed the phone. Mam had a satisfied look on her face as she left the room.

"Grand. And yourself?" Dory lied, leaning against the kitchen wall.

"Fine is it? You don't sound fine. Not feeling the Mae West? A wee bit hung over?" They both cracked up at his choice of words. "Guess that saying is out while your one's here sure. I said the same thing to Aiden this morning and he nearly ate the head off me."

Dory laughed. "Safe to say he's smitten than?"

"No doubt about it. He's got it bad for your wood nymph, so he does. But enough about them. What do you say to a tour of the B&B this morning?"

"Oh is Aiden running those again?" Dory couldn't resist egging him on.

"No, Miss Wise Knickers. Yours truly at your service, I'm afraid."

"Guess I could go slumming." Dory smiled.

"Good one, sham. I'll pick you up in an hour."

Dory went in search of Mam. She found her pegging out the wash. Dory handed her the last of the tea towels.

"I'm going over to O'Rourkes in a bit. Need me to do anything before I go?" Like she'd let me, Dory thought. Mam was a perfectionist.

"Not a thing, love, thanks. Have a good time. Your da will take care of that other unpleasant business. He'll ring the guarda, just as a precaution. Take a box of scones with you to O'Rourkes. Eamon Teelon is after baking enough to feed the country after the famine."

289

By the time Dory had showered and dressed and come back downstairs, Mam was gone. She'd left a note on the kitchen table.

Dory, brought lunch over for your da. Fiona rang. She'll drop Mae at the B&B later on. Don't forget the scones. Enjoy yourself!
I love you, Mam.

Dory grabbed her purse and hummed the old tune taking the path to the bakery. *Three little maryjanes sitting in a row...*

Chapter Forty-Six

A feeling of déjà vu came over Dory on the way to the B&B. *I was here before. Before the secrets and shame that swallowed my voice.* What was it like for Kieran watching me choose Declan over him? She wondered. He warned me against it, she remembered. *Declan Mahoney's not some stray you take home and love the wildness out of. He's bad. He'll destroy you. I won't hang around to watch. If you change your mind, Aiden will know where to contact me. I love you Dory. But you've made the wrong choice.*

Dory didn't see Kieran for years. He left Blessington and her behind. Now he was in her life again. *Just as a friend, mind. You blew it, sham. Who's to say he forgives you at all?*

Attraction was one thing. But how could Kieran want her after she'd been Declan Mahoney's wife? That tarnish would never come off. Dory could only imagine what Kieran had heard about the goings on of herself and Declan. The stories would still be gaining momentum. The fishwives love to flap their jaws. Gossip couldn't hold a candle to what actually happened. Will I ever feel clean again? Dory wondered. Confident in my own self-worth? Never mind what people see on the outside. A funny girl. That was just veneer. Pretty polish. No one really wants the ugly truth. If she repeated the affirmations of self-love that Doc taught her, every minute of the day, "Out the yin yang," as Mae liked to say, that wouldn't even cut it. When do the bad feelings go away for good? And what man on earth was up for that job?

"Can anybody join in or is that a private party you have going on inside your head?" Kieran took his eyes from the road and Dory realized she'd been ignoring him.

"Oh, sorry. I've been useless company. Forgive me?"

"Don't I always? So are you ever gonna smile today? What's up with you? The coming back thing I suppose, aye? Relax love. No one's here to dig up the dead."

No? That's what you think. She felt like crying. She sucked it up. "Why do you do it? Forgive me?" Dory never could leave well enough alone.

"Are you coddin' me? Oh, you're serious, I see. Okay, well if memory serves me right, you're a fine ride. The stuff dreams are made of sure." Kieran kept his eyes on the road and two hands firmly on the wheel. Just in case she hits me a good belt, he thought. He wanted to laugh but forced himself not to. He kept his face as serious as an undertaker. A man has to hold on to some semblance of pride.

Dory was speechless. A rare event. She knew Kieran was enjoying himself and didn't mean any harm. She opened her mouth to say something, and then stayed quiet. There were no words for the moment. Besides, she decided, Kieran deserved a little fun at her expense.

"I haven't even gotten to the good bits, I could go on and on. Some things a man just doesn't forget. Your spectacular arse for instance, astride my…"

"Kieran! Really? Jaysus." Dory couldn't take it as well as she gave it, she realized. Or was the talk quite frankly turning her the hell on? She shifted in her seat and looked out the window.

"Have I offended your sensibility? I remember you being made of stronger stuff. Earthy, if the truth be told."

Now it was her turn to laugh. "Okay, Mr. Memory, you win. But were you planning on committing those good bits strictly to your archives like? Or is there a hands-on part to this conversation?"

You never did get over him, did you, Dory? For the love of Pete, shag him already. Bob's your uncle, girl, go for it. Shut up, Orleigh.

"Now you're talking." Kieran stepped on the gas. "And imagine me not even having me Lucky Charms for breakfast," he spoke with an exaggerated brogue cracking her up. He took the next left at the signpost. O'Rourke's B&B.

"Here we are so. O'Rourke's at your service. Hot tay, warm fires, featherbeds, private loos, claw foot tubs, with bubbles, piped in Irish music 24-7, and all the chocolate bickies you desire. All served with a smile by your enthusiastic innkeepers who by the way do *not* wear kilts."

Dory laughed. She put on her best American accent. "Wow. Sounds awesome. But no kilts? Bummer. I thought you guys all played bagpipes and wore those plaid skirts and nothing underneath? Like in the parades."

"Ah no, Miss. That would be the Scots. You're tinkin' Mel Gibson in Braveheart. Or your man Liam Neeson in Rob Roy, whom I'm told had to get an extra *long* kilt if you take my meaning."

Dory giggled, made her eyes wide. "Yeah? For real? You mean like because of his big…."

"Hung like a Connemara stallion so he is, darlin."

"But isn't Liam Neeson like, Irish?"

"I rest me case, lass. Now would you be wanting a room so?" They both roared laughing their way up to the house.

Everything on the outside was exactly as Dory remembered it. She'd always loved the O'Rourke house. It was a classic stone beauty. Coal black shutters and crisp Irish lace at the long windows. Hazel and rowan trees surrounded the property that went back generations. Flowers bloomed in front of a low stone wall that wrapped itself around and beyond the house leading to a path into the woods at the back. Dory could smell honeysuckle. Bluebells were always her favorite. They spread across the lush grass like a huge periwinkle blanket. Primrose and violets with cascading ivy in two huge stone urns stood at the front entrance. She felt as welcomed as if Mrs. O'Rourke had been there herself to greet her. Or Mr. O'Rourke and his singing all the time.

Kieran's parents were gone now. His parents had been pleasant, hard-working people all their living days. Their presence could still be felt in the beautiful state of the house. Their sons had seen to that. They treated the B&B as a cherished heirloom, which in a way it was. Guests would feel at home now as they had been made to feel when the elder

O'Rourkes were innkeepers. Their handsome sons didn't hurt the presentation one bit. Kilts or not, the O'Rourke brothers could charm the skin off a selkie.

"Shall we go in? You're away with the fairies again."

"Sorry. Oh, Kieran, the place looks smashing. Better than I remember it so."

"Thanks. 'Tis nothing, though. You haven't seen the inside. But first impressions are important; Mam always stressed that. Lure them in with gorgeous surroundings and all, she'd say."

"You miss her, don't you? She was a wise woman, your mam."

"I do. But she's redecorating heaven no doubt. Fattening up the angels with her tea cakes." Kieran smiled, opening the front door. "She'd have loved seeing your face again."

Would she? I broke her son's heart. I can barely forgive myself.

They stepped into a large foyer and Dory was hit with the delicious aroma of baking apples, cinnamon and cloves. A baker's daughter knows her smells.

"Who's cooking these days? Aiden hasn't gone Julia Child has he?"

"Hah. No chance of that happening. We're useless in the kitchen, the pair of us. That would be your old neighbor, Maire Morgan, Bridie's daughter. She does all the cooking and baking. We don't want to poison the guests. Come say hello, she'll be delighted to see you."

Dory followed Kieran through the front parlor. She recognized the antique occasional tables and paintings. They had belonged to Kieran's grandparents. The reupholstered couches and chairs were lovely and they had an all too familiar stamp on them. As if Fiona had snuck back home and redecorated the room herself. Kieran looked amused watching her.

"Fiona's sisters sure. We hire only the best. You approve, I take it?"

"Wholeheartedly. 'Tis grand. I would expect nothing less." Dory smiled.

"I thought I heard voices in here…" Maire Morgan walked into the dining room, wiping her hands on a tea towel. She had a regal yet inviting air about her. She'd always reminded Dory of the model in the old Ralph Lauren ads. A stunning brunette with radiant skin and an athletic body with curves. Honest sea blue eyes and long black lashes.

"Dory, grand to see you. Mam told me you were back. Howyeh' keeping? You look smashing."

"Thanks, Maire. I'm grand. And yourself, as gorgeous as ever." Dory accepted the woman's generous hug. She smelled fresh, like citrus. Probably wearing that English perfume, Jo Malone. Maire always had style. Her own. Dory liked Maire. She had class. Most of all, she minded her own business. A rare thing, especially in a small town like Blessington. Somebody's gob was always flapping about someone's misfortune. Good news never traveled that fast.

"How's Sinaid?" Dory asked. "Tell her I was asking after her, will you? We should all have a pint one night. What are you cooking, besides the apple tart?"

Maire laughed. "You have a nose for the baking, of course. Sinaid is well, thanks for asking." Her face lit up when she said her name. "She's teaching yoga these days."

If Dory hadn't known the truth she'd have competition right under Kieran's roof from this beauty. But Maire had no interest in either one of the O'Rourke brothers. Now if they'd had a sister…. Life hadn't been a cakewalk for Maire Morgan. Beautiful lesbians were not something Ireland was famous for.

"I've been cooking your lunch as a matter of fact. The boss ordered something special," she grinned at Kieran. "I have a roast in the oven and a pot of potato leek soup simmering. A bit of brown bread. I hope you're hungry." Maire adjusted a cup on the large oak table that was set for tea.

"Have you ever known me not to be, Maire? I'm sure you outdid yourself. Oh, here, Mam sent these scones," Dory handed Maire the bakery box.

"Thanks very much. Tell your mam for me. They smell grand. I'll have one with my tea."

Belleek china and Waterford Chrystal covered a leaf green satin runner draped diagonally over an antique creamy lace tablecloth. Plush sage green velvet wingback chairs accented soft rose walls. A polished oak sideboard held serving platters and a large earthenware soup tureen. Fresh daisies sprang out of a robins egg blue crockery vase in the center of the table. Four places were set. For herself and Kieran, Aiden and Mae. Cozy.

"I remember yourself and your sisters eating cinnamon buns on the stone wall behind the house," Maire was saying. "Like it was yesterday sure. If we could have captured that simplicity forever...." She had a wistful look on her face.

"True enough. But life has a way of becoming pear shaped before you know it."

Maire nodded. "We've both had our trials, no doubt. And we're grand in spite of it."

"We are. Good on us. 'Tis lovely to see you again, Maire."

" Always a pleasure. Will you have a cuppa now?"

"I'd love to chat, but Kieran promised me the fifty cent tour."

"You go on then, I'll see you later." Maire whistled her way back into the kitchen.

Dory followed Kieran through the downstairs. He stopped at the staircase.

"After you, madam..." Kieran said, with a sweep of his hand.

"Such a gentleman. Or is it that you want to watch my arse?"

"Couldn't blame me now, could you? 'Tis a fine thing."

They reached the landing. "Go to your right, Miss, may I present the Blue Room. Or as Neeve corrects me, the Periwinkle Room," he exaggerated the syllables.

Dory laughed. "Get your colors straight, sham. Your *palette* to be precise."

"Right. I'm only an ignorant man sure. Well, what do you think? I mean about the room?"

Dory was speechless. The walls were the exact color of her favorite crayon as a child. Painted shutters in glossy white framed the windows, their handles opaque blue glass, as if washed in the sea. Milky pima cotton curtains flowed to the floor. An old brick fireplace painted black with a border of Delft tiles, lay stacked with turf waiting to be lit. The mantle held tall white pillar candles in Delft saucers covered with glass sconces. A queen size sleigh bed in distressed white was adorned with plump white pillows and a downy periwinkle quilt. It invited a midday nap or a romantic romp and the sweetest of dreams.

The bed was so high that a crackled white step stool served as a quaint and useful touch. A snowy white chest of drawers sat to the right of the fireplace, snug against the wall. Its drawer pulls were black iron Celtic knots. A lapis glass vase bursting with purple heather graced the top. An overstuffed chaise in cerulean chintz lazed to the left fireside. On a small white nightstand sat a whimsical cornflower blue ceramic teapot fragrant with purple freesia. Several novels were stacked invitingly next to the flowers. Edna O'Brian, Nuala O'Faolain, Roddy Doyle, Brendan O'Carroll. Dory's favorites. She was tempted to choose one and crawl directly under the covers for the remainder of the day. After she lit the turf and stripped down to her bare skin.

"You like it, I take it? You're as quiet...." Kieran was standing against the door frame watching her.

"I just want to get into the bed." Too late, her big mouth was ahead of her as usual. "Ah, what I mean is, I love the room. It's just the most inviting place. Perfect." She felt the heat rise to her cheeks. Dammit. She'd have to get some herbs from Orleigh. Maybe it was the peri-menopause. Right, she thought, fat chance.

Kieran was loving every minute of her flustered state. He had the cat that ate the canary look on his face. "Anytime, the room is yours. Provided we don't have guests, of course. Which we don't at the moment. Did I mention we serve breakfast in bed?"

"In your kilt, sir? A girl can only dream."

"No need for that, the dreaming bit." Kieran stepped inside and gently swung the door closed with his foot. He walked over to Dory. Before she could feign disinterest, his mouth was on hers, soft and hungry. All she had to do was lean back and they'd be on the bed setting the sheets on fire, rekindling old memories.

Do it.

She pulled away. "Hang on, sham. Your one is down below cooking lunch for us. Besides, you said before I was a grand ride is all. Is that what I am to you? The memorable shag that broke your heart?" *You had to go for the drama, Dory, didn't you? Ejit.*

Kieran held her shoulders and looked into her eyes. "We were inevitable. Eventually... and here we are. Bad timing and all in between. You're here, aren't you? I've always loved you, ejit."

"Now there's a term of endearment if I ever heard one." Dory pulled a face. Secretly, she was over the moon. *He loved her? Still? How was that possible?* If she said the words back to him right now, she would have to make love to him. Immediately. Flying bra and knickers, tearing at each other hungrily, sweating, moaning, the whole bit. Not a bad thing. But she didn't want a quick ride. A quick explosion of lust. That was too easy and they'd waited so long anyway. She wanted to linger languidly in Kieran's arms. Go slowly. Savor every second of pleasure. She could wait. Even if it killed her. And it just might.

"The tour, Kieran, ahm, let's have the rest of it, please. The day is young."

He looked very disappointed. Shot down. "Right. You do know Maire's a romantic herself? She wouldn't be a'tall bothered if the chandelier below shook and all."

"Good try, sham. Now the tour." She felt his pain. Discomfort even, she imagined. She hated herself for resisting when all she could think about was Kieran's naked body all over her own. However, she thought. Time and place.

He led the way through the rest of the upstairs. The other rooms were equally lovely. Rose Red, Forest, and Thistle. Neeve's sense of humor at work no doubt. She would have to tell Fiona's sisters they did a remarkable job. The Periwinkle Room alone was a showstopper. She'd like to book it for a month.

"Do you remember the cottage in the woods?" Kieran asked her.

"I do, why? You put guests there as well? The storybook Irish experience?"

"Nope. The cottage is mine. Interested in seeing it?"

"No, really I'd rather watch Maire bake bread. Are you serious? But what about Aiden?"

Kieran looked surprised. "I didn't know you were into threesomes these days. It *has* been awhile. Should I go find him? And Mae too? Have you gone orgy is it?"

Dory laughed. "Of course, that's it. What I meant was, is Aiden *sharing* the cottage with you?"

"Not a'tall. 'Tis all mine. Being the oldest has advantages. I got first dibs. Aiden's happy in the master bedroom with its private garden. Plus he can mooch around the kitchen in the middle of the night and see what goodies Maire left for the guests. One more thing before we go over there. Follow me." Kieran led the way down the hallway through a door and up another flight of stairs.

"Sex in the attic?" Dory felt totally at ease with him now. And her mouth was getting ahead of her once again. He grinned wickedly over his shoulder.

"If you like. We aim to please here at O'Rourke's."

299

I'll just bet you do. Her breath caught in her throat when they'd reached the top of the winding staircase.

"Oh Kieran, I didn't expect this."

"You like it then?" He had envisioned her here.

"Spectacular. Your idea I'm guessing?" Kieran had talked about building Dory a library someday, back when they were only kids. In this very house. She'd always had her head in a book and he wanted to give her all the books in the world. Fate. It sucks, sometimes, Dory thought, shaking her head. But she was here now.

"Better late than never." He winked at her.

She didn't have one word at the moment. Not a single vowel. She let her eyes travel around the room. Floor to ceiling shelves held volumes of books. Sliding polished wood ladders ran along a brass rail on umber walls. A mocha couch and two easy chairs in butterscotch leather were gathered near the stone fireplace. The cozy reading/conversation area was lit by two large white hobnail hurricane lamps with brass key switches perched on a long mahogany table behind the couch. A smaller version sat on a low tea table between the chairs. Reproductions of old lantern sconces hung on all the walls, illuminating the bookcases. But the piece de resistance was in front of her.

Hand carved oak French doors led out to a balcony. Kieran opened the doors. Magical, was all Dory could think, stepping outside. A scrolled wrought iron balustrade wrapped around the perimeter of a granite widows walk revealing a view that was straight out of the movies. Green fields for miles in all directions, the standard sheep and cows now in miniature. The heaven-kissing Wicklow Mountains stared back at her while Blessington Lakes glistened below like a royal blue gazing ball in the sunlight. In the distant east lie Bray Head and the sea. Dory felt the breeze on her cheeks. It was unusually warm for an Irish fall. She closed her eyes and smelled freshly mowed grass and burning turf. The combination left her intoxicated.

"Mam always liked the romantic notion of the sea captain's wife watching from her widow's walk for her sailor to return from the sea. Pity we didn't build it sooner."

Dory was touched by the love he had for his late mother.

"She would have loved this, Kieran. And she'd be happy her boys are enjoying it. Keepers of the castle, you are. The King and the Prince.

"Aye. Castle O'Rourke. King Kieran doesn't have the proper ring to it, sure it doesn't? Just call me your royal highness."

Dory laughed. "I will in my shite."

Kieran pulled a face. "You could be my fair maiden. The nymph in the Waterhouse painting, you know the one? Beautiful and barefoot, meeting her knight in the woods for secret trysts. He's putty in her hands. No mercy."

"Got it. Knight is it now? I thought you said king? And by the way, where's the queen while this is happening, the nymph thing?"

"Ah, that's the thing, love, there is no queen. Search though the tireless king does, he cannot find one suitable. For him there has been only one. He longs to take your one home to make her his queen, but alas the stubborn nymph will not put a pair of shoes on her lovely feet."

"How sad. Maybe she prefers the rough outdoors. Earthy nymph that she is and all. So, when do I see your secret cottage, King?"

"Right now too soon? After you my lady," Kieran bowed, grandly sweeping his arm.

Dory laughed and stepped inside the library. "I love this room, Kieran. I do. You outdid yourself."

"Thanks very much. Again though, it wasn't my doing alone. And you know who decorated it. That's obvious. Did I mention we serve high tea?"

"Cute." Dory touched a row of books. Such a beautiful room, she thought. *It could have been yours.*

"You're serious? Tea? All the way up here like?" She made a face. "Come on."

"I'm dead serious, sham. 'Tis a bit of a climb all right but we take turns bringing the trays. The Americans love it. Afternoon tea is quaint to them. They soak it up like mother's milk. Soon enough they'll be back standing in ques drinking their lukewarm crickets piss out of take away cups."

Dory laughed. "True. How did you know? Now you see why I was homesick."

"And all the time I thought it was me you missed," Kieran looked disappointed. "Guess I'll have to remind you exactly what you were missing. Follow me, lass, to yonder woods...." Kieran started down the attic stairs.

"Lead on wicked Prince. Ahm, I mean King."

"You sure now? I notice you didn't refuse that wet one Aiden planted on you in the pub."

"I can't help the O'Rourke obsession with wood nymphs now, can I? But for the record, the Prince can't hold a candle to the King, sham."

"Good answer, Queen."

Chapter Forty-Seven

They slowed their pace when they reached the footpath, walking in comfortable silence half the time and then chatting easily about safe topics. Dory's life in New York and Kieran's role as innkeeper since his parents died. Catching up like old friends. Which they used to be. As well as young lovers. Before Declan Mahoney cured the chance they could become anything more. Dory had chosen the storm over the stable. Danger over kindness. Kieran's simple life was too predictable back then. She didn't want the life her parents had. Back then, she longed for a bit of living on the edge. It was exciting, seductive. Be careful what you wish for, she thought wryly now. Mam and Da had quite a nice life together, she realized.

She looked at Kieran. "Sorry? What did you say? I was doing it again, I know."

"I actually didn't say anything this time. But you were lost in your head again. Coming home can do that. No worries. I don't require a constant chat."

"You don't? You're not telling me you've become the strong silent type?"

"If you like. As I said before, we aim to please. Not that I ever understood that Quiet Man routine. Women don't actually find that attractive, do they? It was a movie. Full of shite like, reinforcing the Irish stereotype, dumb thick headed paddys, the lot of us."

"Aren't you?" Dory laughed. "You'd be surprised what some women like. I call it the Heathcliff syndrome. The fantasy of the brooding hunk. Poor Heathcliff would be searching for the Holy Grail trying to find a virginal Cathy on any moors."

" 'Tis the sad truth. Whatever happened to the good old days of yearning and pent-up frustration? Today they'll ride you for a pint. Even buy the damn Guinness for you." He shook his head.

"Ah, poor pet. My heart bleeds for you, sham. 'Tis the same over. And you get your spirits served to you in plastic cups. Like we've all arrived at some child's party. And then there's the *bottled* Guinness...."

"Stop, that's going too far. Sacrilege!"

They both laughed harder than either of them had in a long time.

"Here we are, home sweet cottage," Kieran announced. "Sorry no drawbridge, no drum and pipes, just a mere humble abode."

Dory stood stone still. The years came rushing back like a tidal wave. She and Kieran playing here as children. The two of them later clumsily discovering love and each other's bodies. She ran her fingers over the wooden creatures on either side of the front door and smiled.

"Griffins. Guardians of the gold. I remember the story your mam read to us. We had a picnic and it started to rain. We made a fire inside and ate Kimberleys and drank tea. One of my favorite days."

"You're a sentimental fool, Dory Teelon." He smiled and his eyes told her that he remembered that day too. He opened the door and they stepped inside. The cottage had changed some. Dory approved. The original charm was still there. She panned the room. This could be the very model for her and Fiona's Irish Cottage design, she thought. She was about to say so when her eyes landed on an oak chest in front of the couch. *No, it couldn't be. Not here.* She blinked but the image remained.

A black fringed hat sat on top of the chest. An ugly uninvited specter to spoil their day. Dory felt the blood drain from her face as her knees buckled. She felt Kieran grab her arm, supporting her.

"What's wrong? You look like you've just seen a ghost. Or did you forget to eat this morning?" When she didn't answer him he followed her gaze. "What in the Jaysus is that?" He walked over and picked up the hat. "Why does this look familiar will you tell me? Talk to me, love."

Dory's voice came out raspy. Somewhere from the bottom of her disappointment. She sank down in a chair, her exuberance and nostalgia punctured like the air out of a party balloon.

"It's *hers*. That crazy bitch. She's trying to drive me mad. I swear to God, she is. I'll never be free of them. I shouldn't have come home. I'm cursed since I married that loser. I thought it was over but Sheila just won't leave me alone."

"Sheila Mahoney? This is her doing? She didn't do enough yesterday in Pipers? Stalking you now, is it?" Kieran threw the hat in the corner. "What is her game? How did she even know I lived in the cottage? She didn't break in; I must have left the door unlocked. Still, this is not on. I'm calling the guards. Someone has to stop the nutter cold."

Dory looked at him, then at the hat he had thrown in the corner. "The guards will do nothing, Kieran. She hasn't committed any crime. And make no mistake; Sheila knows everything she needs to know. You're with me, so you're not safe either."

"What do you mean? This is breaking and entering. That's legal all of a sudden?"

"The door was unlocked. You said so yourself. Besides she's crackers, a loony tune. She gets bouts of amnesia she'll say, the whore. Ah, she's too cute for the guards, probably shagged half of them once upon a time. Welcome to my nightmare."

"What do you propose we do then? Nothing? You have to let me at least try to frighten the oul hag." Kieran was hell bent on being Dory's avenger. She was flattered. Yet scaring Sheila was not going to cut it. Sheila had to be stopped once and for all. Dory wasn't sure what that meant just yet but the germ of a very good idea was coming to her.

"I want to ring Noel at Pipers. You have your mobile with you?"

"Noel? What's he got to do with it? You lost me."

"I'll fill you in, in a minute. I promise. Just let me ring him first."

While Dory spoke to Noel, Kieran took the opportunity to have a good look around the rest of the cottage without alarming her. So far everything looked to be just as he'd left it. Still, he didn't feel a bit relieved knowing *that* woman had been inside nosing around his home. He wondered if she actually was harmless. Just messing with Dory's head or a real threat? A kook or dangerously insane? He bent down to look under the bed. Nothing. He could hear Dory talking. He peeked out at her. She was fine. He was about to go in to her when he had an inclination to check the bedroom closet.

He pulled back the door quickly and pulled the light chain. No crazy woman hiding there. He stepped inside and pushed the rack of clothes with one hand. Intact. His foot hit something on the floor. "What the bloody hell…."

He grabbed a shirt off its hanger and picked up the large knife on the floor. It was recently sharpened and there was a smell of paint off it. No, not paint, nail varnish, he thought, examining it closer. He turned the blade over. A chill passed through him. Scrawled across the blade: *Dory dies*. He wrapped the knife in the shirt and slipped it into a dresser drawer. He went back inside to Dory.

"So? Did Noel have a solution for you?"

"Not exactly. But remember your man in Pipers yesterday? When we all sang the anthem? Kieran? Are you listening to me? What's wrong?" Dory thought he looked like the one who'd seen the ghost.

"Nothing. I'm just creeped out by her being in the cottage, that's all. Go on."

"Well your man in the pub yesterday, Anthem Guy, he told me I needn't worry about Sheila anymore. I didn't know what he meant by it. Maybe nothing. But now that I think of it, it sounded quite ominous. He seemed to know Sheila. Turns out he's IRA. Interesting, right? His name is

Liam Casey. Anyway, I wanted to see if Noel had seen him at the pub again."

"And why would that be? You suppose he'll shoot the oul bitch for you like? Smashing idea, don't get me wrong. I just didn't know the IRA were for hire for the average citizen. Are they in the business of knocking off wackjobs now?"

The expression on Dory's face didn't ease his mind one bit. She was dead serious. Uh oh, he thought. Trouble.

"Okay, give me the plan, sham, go ahead. I can smell the wood burning. It's the fire brigade I'll be calling soon."

Dory was all business. Kieran gave her his full attention. Like he had a choice. Mata Hari was at work. Dory started to pace and talk.

"First of all, Sheila is a first class actress. Aside from hating my guts, she has no intention of doing anything drastic. She's all talk and histrionics. That's her M.O. Declan was her dirty deed doer. Without him, she's just a raving nut bird. Besides, 'tis only a stupid hat. Big feckin' deal. However, and this is the good bit, I do think Sheila has something belonging to your man, Liam. Something her son took for instance and she hid perhaps. Or spent. Like their money, maybe. Now possibly we know what really happened to Declan."

Declan Mahoney. The fucker wouldn't stay dead. Kieran certainly hadn't wanted that name brought up in his house. But there was nothing he could do about it under the circumstances. Bless the IRA if they did get rid of him. Bless them twice if they took care of Sheila Mahoney as well. He was starting to cotton to the idea and he was no violent man himself.

"Right so. Out of our hands, is it? That's fine by me," he lied. Dory didn't know about the knife or she wouldn't be so calm. Not a'tall, he thought.

"Good. Glad you agree with me, Kieran. Are we out of here so? The mood's been affected and all."

"You think? Thank your one for that." He was going to pursue the question of Declan's *accident* as it had always been known, but he didn't want to hear that name mentioned one more time. He'd ring the guards about the knife, back at the main house when Dory was occupied with Aiden and Mae. She didn't need to know why. Not now. He'd handle it. For her. Dory deserved a medal for putting up with that lot for years.

"Ready?" he held the door open and waited.

"Right. Lock the door." Dory waited while he did and they walked back down the path together to the B&B.

Aiden and Mae were in the kitchen with Maire. The three were thick in a discussion. They turned quiet when Dory and Kieran walked in.

"Somebody die? You're as serious as undertakers," Dory said.

Pot calling the kettle, Kieran thought, looking at her.

"Dory could use a strong cuppa, Maire. She's after having a bit of a shock." He was about to go into the other room to ring the guards when Aiden held up his hand.

"Hang on, bro. We've unfortunately got a shockeroo of our own for you."

Dory sat down at the table. "So tell us, Aiden, what is it? Tell us yours, we'll tell you ours."

"Sheila Mahoney is dead, darlin. Orleigh's just after ringing. I was just coming to find you. You right, love?" Aiden touched her arm. Kieran came around to her other side. Put his hand on her shoulder.

"She's dead?" Kieran asked his brother. "Stone dead?" Before Aiden could answer, Dory interrupted.

"They killed her? Already?"

Aiden gave her a strange look. "What do you mean *already*? And I didn't say she was murdered. You obviously know something we don't?" Aiden looked to his brother. Kieran shook his head. It was Dory's call, not his.

"Give it to me so," she said, "all the details. Leave nothing out. Was she strangled? Stabbed? Multiple times?

Bludgeoned? Shot between the eyes? Driven off a cliff like her son? Of course she was murdered sham. What do you think; she died peacefully in her sleep? Not that evil bitch. She wouldn't have the decency to simply die and leave me alone. No, she had to be encouraged. Well, that was quick."

It was Aiden's turn to be shocked. Not so much at Dory's reaction to Sheila Mahoney's death, that part made perfect sense. But what was with all this murder talk? What was that about, he wondered? Dory made it sound as if she knew it would happen. *Already*, she'd said. *What the hell did she mean by that?*

"She was at the cottage, man," Kieran told him. "She left her hat there to torment Dory. She left something else too. A feckin' carving knife." He looked at Dory. She opened her mouth to give him a piece of her mind, shut it again. It was moot now. Sheila was dead. *Dead*. Case closed.

"Sorry," he said, "But I didn't want you worrying anymore than you already were. Turns out she *was* dangerous after all. Not the harmless nutter we thought. But she didn't win. Not in the end. They took care of her for you. You were right about that."

"What are you two going on about, lads?" Aiden was still lost. "They *who* took care of her?"

"IRA," Dory blurted out, then nonchalantly sipped her coffee. "Same as her shite bag son."

"Are you coddin' me?" Aiden couldn't believe it. "The feckin' IRA? *Both* of them? They killed Declan?"

"Yep," Dory chewed on a chocolate biscuit. She felt like celebrating and saw no irreverence in that. Sheila wasn't her mother-in-law like normal people might have. No, she was her nemesis. Her competition. Her pain and suffering for years. But no more. She would lie in the cold ground with her son. The pair of them rotting together for eternity.

Dory felt all eyes on her now as she walked over to the Aga to pour herself some coffee. She could do with another biscuit. Suddenly she was famished.

"Excuse me for asking," Maire said, "But how is it you know all this? I mean the IRA involvement and all? Wouldn't you be in danger yourself? Just by knowing?"

"Not really, Maire. You see, I just found out myself, yesterday. When your man came into the pub. Like a guardian angel. Now everything makes perfect sense."

The three of them looked at her.

"Sense?" Maire asked, cradling her own coffee in her hands, waiting for Dory to continue. There hadn't been this much excitement in Blessington since that strangler escaped from the mental hospital in Dublin years ago. Thankfully he was caught. "Go on, Dory," Maire said calmly.

"Yes. You see Declan was sneaky. He never told me where he was going or how he had money when he was on the dole half the time. There must have been secret meetings. I asked no questions. I had enough beatings without spying. He had loads of money at one point. Not that I saw a dime of it. I figured he was selling drugs. Or maybe he'd stolen it. I was going to ring the guards. Then out of the blue he tells me Sheila gave it to him. It was a good amount, I know that much. Supposedly sent to him by his long lost da, he said. Guilt money for leaving. I believed him. It was easier that way. If it wasn't true, I'd be the last to know. If he stole it, with any luck the guarda would show up at the door and lock him up. I only wished. That never happened, as you know. That's as much as I ever knew. All his special secrets were told to Sheila. I was only the *wife*. She was his...well...let's just say, pillow talk is powerful stuff, lads."

"What?" a chorus of three asked the question.

"What are you saying?" Aiden asked.

"Are you serious?" Maire added, putting her coffee down. "His own *mother*?"

Kieran shook his head in disgust. Only Mae was beyond being shocked by Dory's implication.

"Wow, hon, this is like a movie," she said. "Psycho, anyone? Sorry. Don't mind me, go on."

"No worries. 'Tis unreal, I suppose. Welcome to my nightmare." Dory turned back to Aiden. "By the way, who found her?"

"Fergus. Who else goes near her place anymore, but him?"

"Poor crather," Kieran said. "He deserved better than Sheila. She had him by the short and curlies for years."

Dory nodded. "Yes, poor Fergus. Besotted with her once, when she had her looks. But Declan was it for her. Her boyo. Her man. Her regular stiffie."

All eyes were on her. Incest was a show stopper. Only Mae remained unfazed, and Dory knew why.

"Her special mammy's boy was Declan Mahoney," she went on. "Ah sure, he hated Sheila, but loved her too. In a sick way. He couldn't stay away from her. Needed her approval, her opinion, and it drove him to be meaner and angrier. The oul crone knew what she was doing to him. Ah, she did sure. She had to know it was wrong, twisted. He must have too, at some stage. She didn't care. He turned purely mean from it. I got the results of that. No more could he have done to me. She told him what to do I swear it. Oh he was his mammy's boy allright. He did whatever she said. She was always behind it. Basically, she wouldn't share him. Demonic woman. Sure what else would you call someone who tells her son to murder her own grandchildren?"

Oh Christ, was that my voice out loud? Oh sweet Jesus, I'm not able for this twice.

Dory went white and dropped her coffee cup on the floor. She stared at the pieces. Poor Kieran, he looked ready to punch something. Or someone. *You can't beat up the dead, sham.*

"I don't know about you, lads, but I could use a whiskey and a smoke, if someone would be so kind." Dory rubbed her cold hands together and stood to pick up the broken cup.

"Leave it, Dory," Maire said. "Someone get the Bushmills. My smokes are on the counter, Aiden." Maire touched Dory's arm. "Sit down, love, you're as pale as a corpse. Christ, what am I after saying? Just sit. There you are, drink now. It's all right."

Dory nodded obediently, sipping the whiskey. *Good, kind Maire.*

Maire put her arm around Dory. "Let it out, darlin."

Dory nodded and let the tears come.

Chapter Forty-Eight

There was no procession down the streets of Blessington following the coffin of Sheila Mahoney. Fergus was her sole living relation through marriage. He plodded alongside the old priest in the rain. The hunch in his shoulders seemingly disappearing overnight. He was finally relieved of his burden. Remembering his brother's words caused him a twinge of pain even now.

Watch my boy, Fergus. I canna' stay a minute longer. Herself will be the death of me, man. Och, I'm tired of the fight, I am. I'll kill her with my own bare hands if I stay. She's ruining the lad and there's fuck all I can do about it. I sent him away to school, didn't I? More than that I canna' do. He has to come home on his holidays. He won't talk to me, Fergus, and there's no proof, you see. He thinks his mammy walks on water. Yet he looks tormented sometimes when he doesn't know anyone's watching. He's angry, Fergus. Boy's got my temper, no doubt. 'Course his mother's no saint either. But it's more than that sure. Unnatural is what 'tis. Her behavior towards the lad. Och, I'm done. Be my eyes, Fergus. Don't let Sheila destroy him. And Fergus? Be wide, man. She's ferocious. You have no idea, the bitch will destroy us all.

Fergus couldn't get his mind around what Sean was going on about that day before he left town for good. He'd pushed Sean to explain. *How do you mean ruining the lad, Sean?*

Can you not cop on to what I'm telling you? Something's not right with her. The way she looks at him. I've got no proof. Sheila's a minx. Be careful, Fergus. Watch my Declan.

"Unnatural." That was the word Sean used that stuck in Fergus's mind. A heavy accusation. What the hell was going on with Sheila and his nephew? Was there anything to it or was Sean imagining it? Out of jealousy perhaps? Was it just a drunken man's ravings? Whatever the case, Fergus advised Sean to take his son with him if he really was the concerned father. *The boy can go to school anywhere, Sean. If you're truly worried about him, how can you leave him behind, man? He's your son.*

Fergus' plea fell on deaf ears. Sean was gone by morning. Fergus deemed him a coward. How could he do a runner on his family? He should have stayed and faced the music and fought for his son. He was ashamed of Sean. Poor Sheila was distraught when Sean left. Convincingly bereft. Bewildered when Fergus related his conversation with Sean to her. Sheila told him Sean had a vile temper and was "constantly giving out to myself and Declan." She was afraid of him, she said. As was Declan. If they banded together it was due to their common fear. How could Fergus argue with that?

"How could Sean send my son away? And blame me for his leaving us?" Sheila seemed genuinely shocked, he remembered.

Fergus remembered the expression on her face. He felt sorry for her. To send Sheila's only son away from home against her wishes had been cruel. Any mother would find that hard. An Irish mother? Might as well stick a knife though her heart.

His brother was a drunk. A hothead. A bit of a waster. Sheila was right about that. But still, Fergus wondered, why would Sean leave his son in danger at the end of the day? No, Sean must have exaggerated the problem. Fergus took Sheila's side. Would a woman cry if she was glad her husband was gone? No, surely Sheila was not the villain here. The drink can often drive a man mad. Make him prone to paranoia.

Fergus knew his brother's marriage was not a calm loving affair. Sheila was a handful. A hellcat. She could give as good as she got. No demure flower was she. And Sheila believed the son rose and set out of her son's arse. That was it, he thought, Sean couldn't stick it. Declan was the cock of

314

the walk in Sheila's eyes, not Sean. Fergus had no idea how close to the truth he actually was. Boiling hot. But a man doesn't see when he doesn't like the picture. Fergus was no exception. Blind as the next man when it came to women. Sheila Mahoney was not your average woman.

" 'Tis simple. I'll be there for her," he told himself. How strange that Sean had not asked him to look after his wife. See that she was all right financially at least. For Declan's sake, if nothing more. He hadn't mentioned a word about her welfare. His only concern had been Declan.

"See to the boy," he'd said.

Grand, Fergus thought, I will. But Sheila was the task at hand in his mind. She clung to him in a way he couldn't refuse. "Help me, Fergus," she'd moan in a sensuous voice that grabbed him in his loins and wouldn't let go.

"Ah now, Sheila, you'll be all right," he told her at first. His resolve was short-lived. Sheila obviously needed him. What could a man do? He was in her bed before he realized he knew better. "Och, why not?" he asked himself. Sean was clearly not intending to come home. And Sheila was not the monster Sean portrayed her to be in his parting speech. She was beautiful. Sexy. And very lonely. She craved a real man. Not a drunk with brewers droop. Not a selfish rager. Fergus loved his brother but the truth was the damn truth.

Sean was dead wrong about Sheila and Fergus intended to pick up the pieces. It was the least he could do. Her sadness was seductive. She was quite skilled at lovemaking. Fergus hadn't paid for better. And he'd paid for the best. His mission, and he was the man for it, he decided, was keeping Sheila satisfied. He damned Sean less and less each time he lay down with his brother's wife. Sheila was nothing less than grateful every time, thanking him in ways most men only dream about. Fergus was addicted to her. His mind consumed with thoughts of her astride him. He stopped meeting the lads for a pint. The craic in the pub couldn't compete with Sheila. A veritable pig in shite I am, Fergus told himself. *'Tis only heaven I'm in.*

Sheila never spoke of Sean. Rarely of Declan. Not to Fergus anyway. She wrote her son letters. Fergus heard her cry out in her sleep. Not for her husband. For Declan. *Ah, God love her. Thinking of her son with no father.* Fergus's heart went out to her. A loving mother missing her only child. Sheila was sure to be worried what his reaction would be to the loss of his father, bad and all that he was. Poor Sheila. Poor Declan.

Fergus didn't dwell on it any longer. Sheila didn't ask his opinion either way. He figured the relationship between mother and son was a private one. Fergus himself had no children. He couldn't imagine leaving them if he had. Or a wife, if he'd been married, which he never was. Now he had Sheila. He always did fancy her. But of course she had been off-limits once Sean staked his claim. Now the fates had intervened. Given him a gift. A gift of the most excitement he had in years. And he had a fair amount when he traveled the continent. Women galore. No simple paddy was he.

Lately his pleasure didn't come from books and bought women. His one thought at the start and finish of every day and all through the hours he worked were one and the same. Going to bed with Sheila. Twice a day and three times on Sunday. He could get hard just thinking about her wild mane of black hair thrown back like a wild animal. That low earthy growl she'd make before she took him in her mouth. If ignorance is bliss, Fergus was experiencing nirvana.

Sean popped into his head one night, uninvited. "Go'way," he thought. He could only pray his brother would stay gone. Declan would be better off without him. In the meantime there was Sheila. It's all about the here and now, he told himself, isn't that what they say? He could smell her as she moved up his body, teasing him as she slid over his hardness, climbing slowly. He could feel her wetness.

"Make me scream for mercy, Fergus. I'm aching for you," She purred.

He obliged, kneading her full breasts and clamping down on her spectacular nipples. "Come here to me darlin," Fergus demanded, all thoughts of Sean vanishing as Sheila straddled his head. She howled like a banshee when her sweetness met his tongue.

Chapter Forty-Nine

Christmas approached and with it the pending arrival of Declan. The atmosphere in Sheila's house underwent a sea change. She was manic. She snapped at Fergus for no apparent reason. A little bit of nothing set her off on a tear. Fergus didn't take it to heart. He tossed it up to nerves and anticipation. Naturally Sheila would be anxious. Her son was coming home for the holidays for the first time since Sean left. Still, Fergus felt something underneath all the fuss that he couldn't quite put his finger on.

Sheila seemed oddly distant. They were still fucking like demons. But Sheila was preoccupied, aside from the usual holiday season preparations. Fergus was not a man given to panic so he ignored his unease. No skin off his nose, he figured. Things would be a bit different for a short while, that's all. Sheila was turning back into a mammy. Can't fault the woman for her natural tendency.

Sheila gave him no less attention, rode him with no less enthusiasm. Lately it was more intense, more passionate, if that was possible. She'd wake in the night, reach for him, wanting more of him. Insatiable. I like my job, he thought, I won't bother making mountains out of molehills.

Sheila had been baking for days. As if the crowned prince himself was coming to stay. " 'Tis Betty Crocker, you are," he told her. She was at the dough board day and night.

"For my Deckie," she told Fergus. "It's the Christmas."

He humored her. Women. You can't go trying to figure them out, he reckoned. Sheila was a sight in the kitchen.

"Betty, are you in?" he'd call from the front door. Betty Crocker didn't dress like Sheila. Dress being a bit of an overstatement. There she was, in her frilly apron, not a stitch on underneath, standing in the kitchen stirring a mixing bowl. Her luscious breasts bouncing, dark silver dollar nipples sprinkled with flour. Good enough to eat, he thought. Bending over to get a tray of Christmas cookies out of the oven arse up in the air. She's no one's mother, Fergus thought, getting harder. Yet, she was. He felt a sneaking feeling like something was a little off in that house but he couldn't quite put his finger on it.

He'd forgot about it straightaway as he happily fucked Sheila on the lino, baking pans clanging, utensils flying. He'd give her a good spanking with the warm spatula until she screamed. She coated her favorite part of him with chocolate frosting, slowly licking him off. He poured warm milk on her delectable breasts and sucked them dry as Sheila laughed with delight, spreading her legs wide. Fergus lapped at her like a hungry kitten. She got up returning with a bowl of warm water and washed his cock, caressing him until he was hard again. He put her over his knee and spanked her playfully, this time with a whisk he found on the floor. For the grand finale, she'd make him tie her hands to the table leg while he entered her from behind. She said unmentionable things the whole time until they both came.

How could he not dread the boy's homecoming, nephew or not? It may have been selfish of Fergus, but who could blame him? He would have to hide his emotions while Declan was home. He hated that the most. Fergus was an affectionate man. He wanted to kiss Sheila whenever he fancied. Certainly he wanted to be in her bed every night. And anywhere else they wound up. And that was not going to happen with Declan home. *Sorry, lad, you have to cut your holidays short. Frankly, you're cramping our style. I'd explain what a fantastic ride your mammy is, but that wouldn't be proper a'tall a'tall. You see, lad, she's your mammy. You have no earthy idea of her talent.*

Fergus watched now as Sheila's coffin was lowered into the ground. Buried next to her Deckie. He couldn't help but think how this would have pleased Sheila immensely. Recalling his past awakening, the thought sickened him. *You are mocking me from the grave, Sheila, aren't you? Och, it could have been so different. Normal. But could it have been?*

Sean had been right after all. The damage was long done. Beyond any rational man. Betraying all decency. *You were a monster, Sheila.* God forgive me for speaking ill of the dead, he thought. He shivered. Not from the bone chilling rain. But from what had gone horribly wrong in that house.

The unspeakable had happened right under his nose. Short of killing the pair of them, poor Fergus knew it was out of his hands in the end. Sean had run from it, never to return. Fergus would have liked to drown in a vat of whiskey rather than face what he had that night.

He had only had the best intentions concerning Sheila. And his nephew. He would not desert them the way Sean had. He was devoted to Sheila. Respectfully giving her space and privacy when Declan returned. He hardly expected the lad to embrace him with open arms. He was just Uncle Fergus. He remained so while his nephew was home. Soon Declan would be back at school and he could be Sheila's lover again. He could wait. Give his John Thomas a holiday. He went back to meeting the lads at the pub and caught up with the usual gossip and complaining.

He moved back into his own house, only coming over when Sheila invited him. Christmas Eve, they were a family, the three of them. They all had a grand night. Declan was in good form. The lad was growing up, Fergus surmised. When Declan went out for a pint with his friends, Fergus took Sheila home to his own bed. She was as pleasing as always. Giddy with happiness over having her son home again. She hoped Fergus understood her need to spend time alone with Declan. He said he did, of course.

Fergus swept Sheila's wild hair away from her face with his hands. He stroked her milky white back. He was appalled at the mean red scratches he found there. Not his doing. He would never hurt Sheila that way. But someone obviously had. He felt a rage well up inside him. *Ah, Sheila, how could you? If you were that horny even in the middle of*

320

the night, surely you could have come to me. Why would you go elsewhere? He rubbed Sheila's back over the scratches.

"Hurt yourself, love?" he asked, as calmly as he could.

"Ah now you won't believe it, Fergus when I tell you," she forced a laugh.

"Don't tell me, you fell into the brambles, weeding naked again were you?" *Make it good, Sheila. Make me believe you.*

"No, silly goose. I was in changing the sheets on Deckie's bed. The cat was dozing there and I chased her away. And didn't she go for me as I reached for the pillow like? Clawed my back before I could move, the little bitch."

"What were you wearing? I mean for her to do such damage?" Fergus wanted to scream. Punch something. Did the woman take him for a complete idiot?

"Well obviously I was naked, Fergus," she started to stroke his spent penis.

He moved her hand away. "You have a young lad in the house, Sheila. You can't be prancing around in the buff. Where was Declan when this happened with the ahm…cat?" Fergus reached for a smoke on the night table. *Liar.*

"He's not that young anymore." Sheila took his cigarette and inhaled a good drag. Blew out a cool stream of smoke. "He's old enough to have a few pints, love. Grand strong muscles he has, haven't you noticed? Anyway, he was out with his mates. What's the matter? Are you actually jealous of my Deckie? Ah now, you know I love you." She popped her engorged nipple into Fergus' mouth before he could refuse. He sucked away like a baby.

"There 'tis. Nobody better than Sheila. So hungry for it."

He couldn't have let it continue. How could he live with himself if he had? But why didn't he ring her first? Why had he been so hell bent on popping over that night, unannounced? He could have easily invited them to supper over the phone. Things would have remained the same. He

321

would never have known. But Fergus wasn't built like that. He knew deep down Sheila had something to hide. An ugly shameful truth. As ugly as it gets. He knocked on the door. No one answered. It was open so he let himself in.

"Sheila? Declan?" he called. Nothing. He went towards the kitchen. It was dark. He turned on the lamp and reached for the kettle to make tea while he waited. She must have gone out paying a Christmas visit or doing a grocery shop maybe. Sheila was cooking up a storm these days. He grabbed a cup from the press. That's when he heard Sheila's laugh. Loud and lusty. It didn't come from outside. Maybe she was watching a movie in her room. Let that be it, Fergus thought. He walked down the hallway to Sheila's bedroom. Stood outside the door. Listened.

There it was. Her unmistakable growl, the sexy teasing laugh. Someone else was moaning. A man. Don't do this to me, Sheila. *For fuck sake*. Fergus felt the anger rising in his stomach. The cheek of her to bring someone home with Declan here on his holidays, he thought. Never mind the fact that she was shagging someone behind Fergus's back. *Indecent bitch. Whore. Have you such a burning you couldn't spare a minute to ring me? Say hurry, Fergus, I need you. Sure you're well able to say that every other time? Are you fucking your man from the creamery? Did you seduce the mailman? You just couldn't wait, is it?*

The moaning continued. Slapping of flesh against flesh. The picture in his mind was eating at him. Fergus leaned in and put his ear to the door. "There 'tis," Sheila said to her lover. "Such a man, so hungry for it. Nobody better than Sheila, is there, love?" Furious, Fergus turned the knob.

"You bitch!" he screamed, bursting through the door in a blind rage. He suddenly froze. *Kill me now. God strike me dead on this spot.* He wanted to tear out his own eyes. Bile rose up in his throat. He swallowed it back. "Noooo…" came his voice low and wounded like an animal's cry. "Noooo…"

He didn't remember removing his belt. He watched someone else outside himself strike the leather again and again across Sheila's bare back and buttocks. "Fergus... agghh..." The moans belonged to Sheila now. High pitched wailing sounds begging for mercy. Fergus finally stopped when he met her lover's eyes. He stared back at Fergus. Half brazen and half like an animal snared in a trap. *Kill me, God. I beg you.*

"Please, Uncle Fergus. Stop."

Fergus hung his head, defeated. He put on his belt, ignoring Sheila's incessant sobbing. She hadn't even the decency to get off Declan. What could Fergus possibly say to her now? She was the devil incarnate. This was the most repulsive consummation he'd ever encountered and he was no sheltered man. *Declan? How can this be?* He was no child she was overtaking. He was a man.

Fergus walked in a daze through the house and out the front door. *God help you, Sheila. You'll burn in hell's eternal fires. You are evil. We can never come back from this.* Fergus shuddered, wondering how long Sheila had been shagging her own son before he vomited in the street.

Chapter Fifty

Fergus sat in the early light of his small kitchen letting the strong tea work on his pounding headache. The aspirin tablets he took weren't doing the job. He hadn't slept, that was the problem. The nightmare at Sheila's house yesterday would keep him awake nights for days. *If only it had been a nightmare.*

Fergus was not hung over. He wished he was. He'd had a few pints with the boys last night when he finally could stomach swallowing anything. He didn't want to be alone, didn't trust his rage at Sheila. He felt like someone he'd seen in a documentary on the television telling how they witnessed human sacrifice or cannibalism. The look on their faces telling the story. Horror. Disgust. Tortured missionaries they were. All Fergus knew was what he'd witnessed himself was no less an abomination. And not for love nor money or the grace of God, would he ever be the same again.

A slice of bread popped up in the toaster. He stared at it disinterested and finished his tea and cigarette. It's all on you, man, he told himself. *Nobody to save the lad but you. 'Tis a crime what's after happening. A crime.* He stamped out his smoke in the ashtray and carried his cup over to the sink. He was stalling. Plotting out some kind of plan in his head. He scrubbed the brown tea stains meticulously, leaving the porcelain cup as good as new. Virginal white. Pity we can't sprinkle bleaching powder on people and scour their sins away, he thought. There wouldn't be enough in all the world for Sheila. *Och, there are mistakes human beings make, fair enough. And then there are atrocities demons commit that fester in the corners of our darkened souls forever.* Sheila, he deemed the later. *Unredeemable. Doomed.*

Fergus took his sweater from the hook on the wall and grabbed his smokes off the table. Thank Christ it was the Christmas week, he thought. No work. No mates to face and feign jolliness or expect a slagging from about Sheila. How the pair of them were going for the sex record. One for the books and all that. He shook his head. No, the lads wouldn't be able for this truth. Fergus wished he didn't have to be.

He walked with a heavy heart down the road towards Sheila's, the usual spring in his step gone. He prayed she was out on her usual morning errands so he could speak to his nephew alone. In peace. Or some semblance of it anyway. Declan wouldn't give him a hard time. Dreading the task at hand but resigned to it, he lit a smoke, and turned up the path to her house.

Declan answered the door. "Uncle Fergus..." he looked away for a second, seemingly unsure of what to expect. He looked back and met Fergus' eyes, dead on. Was that defiance? It chilled Fergus to the bone. *Ah, the damage, Sean. Where the fuck were you all those years?* Fergus cleared his throat.

"Can I come in? Your mother, has she gone out?" *Praise God, let her be nowhere I can see her.*

Declan stepped back. "Yeah, she's out. Come in. Have you had breakfast? I've started a fry-up." Declan walked back to the kitchen, boots dragging on the wooden floor. Fergus followed him and the greasy smell of rashers and eggs. His stomach grumbled. He hadn't eaten, not even a bit of dry toast could he swallow this morning. The strange thing was this was an ordinary day to this lot. Shag your mother and cook your brekkie in the morning. Go down the town and do the grocery shopping. That was more disturbing than the hideous business in the bedroom. Am I mad or do the pair of them consider this a normal life?

Fergus was nauseous. He thought of Sean and what his brother had been trying to tell him that day before he left town. The warning. The pathetic cry for help. Coupled with his cowardice and drunken guilt. So he escaped, miles away from his life. *Damn you, Sean. This was your job, man. She's your feckin' wife. I just tried to love her.*

"I'm not hungry," Fergus said, "Just coffee, Dec, if you have it made."

"Right," Declan muttered, grabbing a cup out of the drain board.

Fergus poured milk and sugar into his cup and watched Declan devour his breakfast. Usually the sight would give him great pride. The lad's healthy appetite. Today he wanted to reach across the table and knock him off his chair. Had he been a child it would be a different matter. He'd have carried him away from this evil house. Soothed him. Had him seen to. Removed him from his mother for good. But he was no child.

Declan sat there bold as bollocks drinking coffee and smoking a fag like he hadn't been underneath Sheila last night a'tall, Fergus thought, anger boiling in his gut. The cheek of Declan.

"Och," Fergus said, out loud, disgusted by his thoughts.

"Uncle Fergus? You all right? Coffee too strong?"
Fergus lit another cigarette and looked at his nephew.

"No, coffee's fine. Here 'tis, Dec. What happened here last night…ahm…'twas a sin against everything right and decent. Against God and man and your soul." Fergus took a swallow of coffee. Declan had the common sense not to interrupt him. Smart lad. He knew a thing or two about survival. He started to fidget though which pissed Fergus the hell off. Declan tipped his chair back, blowing smoke rings to the ceiling. Fergus fought hard not to lose his patience. *Don't fuck with me, lad. I'm not your da.*

"Hear me out. Now I can't blame you. You were the minor in the situation here. I am presuming this ahm... kind of thing began some time ago. Your da hinted at something before he left. I didn't cop on until last night. That's neither here nor there. You have to leave, Dec. Today. Soon as you get packed like. I'll drive you to the train or back to school early or to your mate's house. Wherever you like. Point is you can't stay here. You following me? I'll handle Sheila. No worries. She needs serious help. I'll see she gets that. And you should seek some kind of counseling yourself back at

326

school. You cannot come home again until you have a place of your own, preferably with a wife. Until that day comes, stay away. If you're at loose ends after school finishes, do some traveling. Get yourself a job out of town. Everything here has changed. There's no other way for this to go. Surely you see that?"

Declan continued to smoke. He was studying Fergus with a look not easily read. Was it relief? Gratefulness? Contempt? *Talk, Declan. Now.*

"Right. I'll go to Danny O'Leary's. He lives out the Wicklow Road. He can come for me. I'll ring him straightaway. We're organizing a band. He has a brilliant guitar collection." *Was the lad serious? Guitars?* Fergus was flabbergasted. Either Declan was a first class actor like his mother or the Mahoneys had a sociopath on their hands.

"Why don't you pack now, Dec? I'll do the washing up, go ahead, no worries."

Fergus was relieved when the lad left the room. *Holy shite. It was fucking eerie is what it was. Cold as ice, was Declan. Or was he so twisted in his mind from his wacko mother that he didn't know right from wrong?*

Fergus scrubbed the iron frying pan like a man possessed. Everything in this house now felt grimy and sordid. He had so much anger towards Sheila. Sean too for that matter. He could hardly contain his emotions. Even the fun days and nights he had with Sheila thanks to Sean's leaving didn't make up for this feckin' movie of the week he was in now.

Declan stood in the kitchen doorway. He had a duffel bag over his shoulder. "Danny should be here soon," he said, looking out the window, preoccupied. Bored even.

"You need a few bob than?" Fergus walked over to him, drying his hands on a tea towel. He reached into his pocket pulling out whatever cash he had on him. Money was the least of it, he thought.

327

"Sure, I could do with some money. Mam was going to… well whatever." Declan blew out a stream of smoke. Looked down at his boots.

Christ, Fergus thought. Christ Almighty. Mammy indeed. He handed Declan a wad of bills. "Take it. Be wide now, Dec. Stay gone. I mean it. I'll tell Sheila you had to go with the band and all. I'll contact you at school. Keep in touch. And you are not to ring your mother a'tall, you hear? I'll see she doesn't bother you. Save yourself, lad. You have a future ahead of you. One day we'll talk about your da. The rest is best forgotten."

Declan pushed his hair out of his eyes. Again the icy stare. "My da was a loser. A fucking drunk. Couldn't even get it up. So there's nothing we need to chat about like. Look, I'm out of here. Thanks for the money." He grabbed his guitar off the dining room chair.

Fergus opened the front door. "Take care of yourself, Dec. Let me know how you're getting on."

His nephew looked back at him. "Tell Mam…"

Fergus swallowed hard. *Mam* was a fucking stretch. He nodded. "Right. Right, no worries. Off you go." Fergus forced a smile for sanity's sake.

Declan met his eyes. For a second Fergus could swear he saw a small innocent boy there. Declan blinked and the boy was gone. A smugness in its place. He smirked at Fergus.

"Take it slow, Uncle Fergus." He walked out to his friend's car and waved Fergus off. *Uncle Fergus, you couldn't wait to get me out of the house could you? Have your Sheila all to yourself, old man? You're already too late for her first session of the day.*

Twenty minutes and half a pack of cigarettes later, Sheila returned. Fergus was sitting in the kitchen drinking coffee.

"Fergus, what are you doing here? Come for tea? Where's Deckie?" She let Fergus take the groceries. He set them on the counter.

"There's fresh coffee. The lad's gone to his mate's. Something about band practice. Thing is, Declan won't be coming back, Sheila."

She looked at him quizzically. Took off her coat and hung it on the back of a chair.

"What are you on about? Of course he'll be home for his dinner." Sheila sipped at the coffee Fergus put in front of her and nervously lit a cigarette.

"You're only playing with me, aren't you, pet? That's not funny. Are you trying to make me mad?" she laughed. "You're a bad boy, Fergus."

"I sent him away. What went on in this house last night is finished. Done. The lad cannot be here alone with you. 'Tis criminal what you've done to that boy. Did you honestly think life would go on as such? Surely you can't be that daft, woman."

Sheila tapped her cigarette in the ashtray and looked up at Fergus. "You don't understand. I had to be more than a mother to Deckie. Sean was useless. He taught him nothing but how to drink and be abusive. Certainly didn't teach him how to love. Useless he was in that area. A lad has to know certain things. He'll be a fine lover to a young one someday. Taught by the best. Ah now, don't be so holy Catholic Ireland provincial. You never had better sex than in this house. Get off your high feckin' horse."

"That has nothing to do with you interfering with Declan. We're consenting adults. He's your child!"

"You're so naïve, Fergus. Keep your sanctimonious crap off me."

Fergus's head was spinning. "Sheila, I don't know where you got your ideas, but it's dead wrong. You want to teach your son about sex, you buy him a book. You're his mother. Christ. Had you sent him to a whorehouse, that wouldn't even be anything near as bad as this. But you don't elect yourself for the job. You were shagging your own son! Can you cop on to fuck or what?"

"And your point is? No, I'm not crazy; so don't give me that look. Listen to me. I love Deckie the most and he knows it. I never forced him. It was never like that. He comes to my bed willingly. He was precocious. Curious. He has a very healthy sexual appetite. Gifted he is. I barely had to instruct him. Who better to show him what I know best? He's well able to be a real man with the young ones now. You see the way they look at him. He'll be a fine lover. He's skilled. Not a clumsy oaf like the rest of those sheep shaggers. Why must you make everything dirty?"

"I'm not the one who walks around naked. Did you torment that poor boy when he was only impressionable? How could you? Why not shag someone from the pub? You fucked half the village. What's the matter, you got shy all of a sudden? Decided to become a pedophile? That's what it's called, you know, seducing a minor. You're a pariah. Despicable. This business didn't start yesterday, did it? You should be locked up. Sent to an asylum at least. You're a danger to humanity. Och, I curse the day we met."

"Drama, drama. Save it. You going to call the guarda on me? Look at you on your high horse. Wasn't that you who took your pleasure from me? Did I seduce you, Fergus? Poor helpless man. I didn't hear you complain. Not once. Aren't we relations, Fergus? I am still married to your brother. Did you forget that? Sure you had no problem putting it out of your mind while you had the best sex of your life. Don't go judging me, sham, don't you dare."

Fergus was losing his rag. "Sheila, for Christ sakes, I'm not your blood. Besides, Declan is your son. That's the crime. Immoral. Unnatural. We're not living in some uncivilized village without rules where we run naked and shag anything that moves." Fergus lit a cigarette and paced the kitchen. He stopped and leaned against the counter. *God help me. I'm in the nuthouse here. With the queen of the nutters herself.*

"Uncivilized is it? Please. Blessington isn't exactly Paris, France. And maybe we don't run bare arsed through the streets but have you seen the men in the pubs? Leering buggers. They'll shag whatever sits still long enough to listen to their shite. Right here in the arsehole of Ireland. Grow up, Fergus. You're just jealous someone else was poking in your Sheila's whiskers. It's okay; I'm flattered, really. And I forgive you for the outburst. Forget the high and mighty shite, though. You can make it all better now. Come on, don't be all uptight so. Take me to bed...or right here... I know what you need..." Sheila stared him down. *Don't fuck with me, Fergus. You have no idea. A determined woman can fuel the Queen Mary with the power in her cunt. You haven't got a prayer, sham.*

Fergus wanted to bolt from the room. But he couldn't move. He had passed from reality into an alternate universe. He was dumbstruck as Sheila unbuttoned her blouse and unhooked her bra. She rubbed her big bare breasts slowly and licked her lips. Sliding out of her skirt she removed her panties. Fergus was a captive audience. He didn't want to hurt her. He couldn't if he tried now. He was hypnotized.

She was naked as Eve and moving towards him. He could smell her. Soaking wet, he imagined. He was rock hard and all he wanted was Sheila. She smiled knowingly and kissed his forehead, teasing him with her breasts brushing his sweater and neck. "Fergus, pet...." she purred, taking his hand and sliding two fingers inside her. She moved against him, sliding out with a moan, she brought them to his lips. He let her unzip his pants and take him out. She straddled him in the chair and rode him as he held her bouncing breasts. She pumped and squeezed his hardness tight in a steady rhythm. He was dizzy with her. She was moaning his name. He lifted her up and down, grabbing her ass. She rode harder. "Fergus, spank me, I've been bad, love." She was breathless and Fergus was beside himself.

She lay astride him, Fergus inside her. His hand came down again and again on her bare bottom. She screamed with pleasure. "Yes, Fergus, yes!" Just as he was about to explode, she climbed off. Kneeling on the floor, she took him into her mouth. He cried out her name. He came, screaming for mercy. She wouldn't let him think. Or stop. She pulled him to the floor with her and opened her legs for him. He gave her his tongue until she climaxed, letting out a banshee's wail.

They smoked, lying on the bare floor in front of the Aga. "Say it, Fergus. I want to hear it," she cooed.

"There's nobody like Sheila, The best. Take me to hell with you."

Chapter Fifty-One

Fergus found himself in Pipers after the funeral. He accepted the pint Nolan pulled for him.

"Sorry for your troubles, Fergus. You did your best, man."

"Thanks very much, Nolan. Och, 'tis over now sure."

"There's timing for you...." Nolan motioned his head towards the door. Dory and Kieran walked in. Fergus felt the guilt and shame wash over him.

Dory came and sat on the stool beside him. "Ah, poor Fergus. Sorry for your troubles. I know you loved the evil bitch, God help you. Neither of them deserved us."

Fergus looked at the kind young woman next to him. Dory Teelon had not had an easy time of it. He knew that like he knew his own name.

"Have a drink with me, love. Ah Jaysus, what can I say? I'm sorry for what you went through back then. That's no excuse; I'm a weak man. 'Tis a terrible curse. I wasn't able for her. I would have killed her myself if I knew she was going to hurt you. And Declan should never have come back. I was too ashamed to tell anyone. But you had a right to know. Och, the damage. Can you ever forgive me?"

"I do, Fergus. I'd never have believed you. Who would have, really? Anyway, it's finally over. We both survived them. I have a second chance now." She looked in Kieran's direction. He was chatting away with Nolan. Fergus nodded.

"Right. He's a good lad, that one. You deserve to be happy. Ah, you will, love, you will."

Dory patted his rough wrinkled hand. A tear fell down his ruddy cheek.

"To us, Fergus. To the rest of our lives. Be well. Do it for spite, in the very least." Dory raised her glass.

Fergus smiled, revealing tobacco stained teeth. "An angel is what you are, Dory Teelon. You've a forgiving heart.

Slainte. All the best to you now." They drank in silence. Fergus smoked and sighed. Dory excused herself and went to join Kieran at the end of the bar.

"Poor fucker is in bits, is he?"

"His misfortune was to be related in any way to that miserable woman. Look at all the lives she ruined. Still, I never thought I'd be coming home to her funeral. Ah, howsever, the door is shut now. For good."

Kieran kissed her. "You are a true survivor, and a beautiful one at that. And how lucky am I will you tell me? Your own knight in shining armor."

"Right. That's you in spades," Dory laughed.

"To us."

They clinked glasses and drank.

"Any chance I can keep you here for awhile, love?"

Dory breathed deeply. "For what?" she teased, "You need help around the B&B? I am a terrific waitress, I'll have you know."

Kieran laughed. "No doubt you are. But no I was thinking in more personal terms."

"You could visit me over, couldn't you? We've plenty of room at the Brownstone. Bring Aiden. Mae would be delighted."

"Speak of the devil...."

Aiden and Mae walked into the pub, arm in arm, as thick as thieves.

"Well now, look who's graced my establishment once again, 'tis the lovely Mae West." Nolan beamed at her.

She gave him her winning smile. "Howyeh, Nolan?"

The barman cracked up. "Ah, you're as sweet. If this yabbo doesn't marry you, you come see old Nolan, you hear?"

Mae laughed. "You've got a deal, hon."

"Thanks for the vote of confidence, man." Aiden said, "Planning on moving to Utah is it? Or is Mrs. Nolan booting your arse out?"

"Ah, can't a man have a wee bit of a fantasy now? Two pints is it? Fergus is buying, lads."

Aiden ordered them pints of Guinness and nodded to Fergus down the bar. "Thanks, mate. Sorry for your troubles." Fergus nodded back.

Mae came over to Dory. "Are you okay, hon? A lot going on in your small town. Wow."

Dory hugged her friend. "That's an understatement sure. I'm fine. Not such a sleepy little place so, is it? Hope we haven't scared you away."

"Are you kidding? I'm having the most incredible time." Mae's face lit up as Aiden joined them. He put his arm around Mae. She beamed.

"So how do you suppose we're going to get your one here on the plane?"

"Kicking and screaming I'm thinking, Aiden," Dory laughed.

"Well it's all your fault," Mae said, looking at Aiden. "Yours too." She looked at Dory. "Enchanting a poor girl with fairy forts and magic cottages and gorgeous men with sexy accents."

Aiden was eating it up. "Go on..." he leaned in to kiss her.

"Oh brother," Dory said.

"Did someone call?" Kieran was behind her like a shot. "So I suppose you're sick and tired of the place, Mae? No interest in seeing Inishmore and hearing about the selkies, I guess. I can understand that sure. You've seen one castle you've seen them all." Kieran winked at Dory.

"Don't even think you're not taking me there, hon. When?" Mae looked at Aiden. She wanted to jump up and down for joy.

"Is he *serious*? There *are* selkies, right?"

Aiden kissed her. "There are, of course, love. If we weren't in public..." he whispered.

Mae smiled. "We are though, so behave. For now."

335

"No flies on this girl," Dory said, "Inishmore 'tis. Sign us up, lads."

A familiar laugh came from the back of the pub.

"Having all the craic without me?" Orleigh appeared seemingly out of nowhere. She gave Dory a tight hug.

"I was just wondering where you were, witch," Dory said.

"Upstairs. Delivering an herbal tonic to Nolan's lovely wife. He's in for a grand ride tonight, I reckon." She touched Dory's face. "You right, love? You look okay, despite everything."

" 'Tis over. Kieran was with me. She never would have gotten that close. Let's just try to forget it."

"Right. Good idea. I see the poor bastard who slept with the devil is recovering, in his own way." Orleigh looked over at Fergus. "Finally putting that bitch in the ground has added a few years to his life, has it not?" Orleigh signaled to Nolan and ordered a glass of wine.

Dory nodded. "True. Enough said on that subject. We're planning a trip to Inishmore tomorrow. Are you for it?"

Mae came to sit next to Orleigh. "You're going with us, aren't you?"

"Wouldn't miss it. Don't tell me, Mae, you've read The People Of The Sea as well, have you?"

"Yep. *And* The Secret Of Roan Inish."

"Brilliant." Orleigh smiled warmly.

A handsome hunk of a man came walking down the bar to stand next them. He leaned in and gave Orleigh a very friendly kiss on the lips. Mae realized she was staring. "Wow," she mouthed to Dory.

"The poet?" Dory whispered to Orleigh.

"Tis. Rory, meet Dory Teelon. And the lovely Mae West from America. You know the infamous O'Rourke brothers, of course."

The brothers shook hands with Rory.

"Howyeh, Kieran, Aiden?" Rory extended a hand to both women. "Dory, my pleasure. I see beauty runs in the Teelon line. And aren't you the very picture of a wood nymph, Mae West? You are as lovely as Orleigh said you were."

Neither woman could seem to find her vocal cords. Orleigh laughed, seeing Dory speechless. Mae too, she was a talker.

"Uh oh, it seems you rendered them speechless, love. Good thing I'm not the jealous type."

It was Dory's turn to laugh. "Hah, no need to be when you can conjure up a dose of the crabs."

Mae couldn't take her eyes off Rory's eyes. Black as night and perfectly round and long lashed and flecked with gold.

"Dory's wide to you," Rory's voice resonated in the pub. Deep and hypnotic. Orleigh laughed. A sexy musical compliment. What a pair, Mae thought. Good looking, sensual and a dash of the mystical. Very interesting couple. If Mae hadn't been to Orleigh's cottage she would find it hard to imagine either of them doing anything mundane. Like taking out the trash. They appeared to float above the ordinary.

"So if you'll release the spell on our women, Rory, we can get back to the business of Inishmore," Kieran teased him.

Rory roared with laughter. Mae giggled. They weren't gold flecks in Rory's eyes at all, she realized. They were *stars*. Tiny gold stars. Oh boy, she getting was way too used to the Guinness. Coupled with her wild imagination. Would she ever be the same after Ireland?

"Mae is anxious for a selkie story, Orleigh," Aiden said, "If you wouldn't mind, of course. Nobody tells it better."

Orleigh sipped her wine and set the glass down on the bar. "Right, lads. Now wasn't my own Great Granny Bridget Early, a selkie herself? 'Tis my great granda who found her one lovely spring day off Inishmore. In the very same spot he passed every day where the seals basked themselves on the sun-kissed rocks. My granny was standing near the shore singing a haunting chantey. Great Granda was quite taken with her. She was a raven haired breathtaking beauty I'm told. Jet black eyes as shiny as onyx. They were married that very summer and lived happily away in a small stone cottage that still stands on the island today. Bridget kept her selkie pelt in a hope chest in the attic. She never had the need to put it on again. She had no regrets about her life on land with her husband. Fiercely in love, the pair of them. Bridget gave birth to twin girls. One was Grainne, named for the pirate queen of Celtic legend. The other poor wee child was stillborn. They called her Sela. Heartbroken, the couple wrapped their tiny daughter in a bunting and Granda built her wee coffin himself. They sailed over to the far side of the island and buried Sela. All the selkies came in close to shore that day, singing their sad song for the wee babe. Grainne never did settle after her twin died. Ah, she was only an infant herself. 'Twas powerful the time they shared in Bridget's womb. 'Tis said twins are linked forever."

"The sea lured Grainne. Not a day passed that she didn't toddle down to the water's edge seemingly looking for something she had misplaced. Her dark sad eyes looked across the water searching, calling in her singsong child's sweet voice. "Deirfiur, deirfiur." Sister, sister. The sadness never left her. One could see it in her eyes. I saw it myself sure years later. Grainne was my Gran, married to my Granda Teelon. She told me the story of her mam, my Great Granny Bridget and her poor wee daughter, Sela. I never tired of hearing it."

Mae waited, digesting all she'd heard. "Is it for real, hon? The pelt too?"

"Aye. Though some believe it to be legend. I'd peg you for a true believer myself. Would I be right?" Orleigh's green eyes were as warm and soothing as her lilting voice.

Mae nodded. "You've got my number. I loved it."

"Thank you." Orleigh sipped her wine.

"I did have one question. You said your great grandfather's name was Early? Any relation to Biddy Early, the healer from Clare?"

Orleigh smiled. "Very good. You are well read so. She was Great Granda's sister. I have her red hair and her eyes. And her gift, of course. Biddy didn't take after the selkie line as far as the dark looks."

"Wow. Imagine meeting one of Biddy Early's relatives. Dory didn't tell me. She's full of surprises." Mae looked at her friend.

"Sorry, had I known you were such a fan of Irish folklore, I would have. But isn't it more fun finding out this way?"

"Loads. Much more craic."

Everyone laughed. "You are priceless, Mae. Is she not, Orleigh?"

"She is. Aiden, you are one lucky man, meeting this one."

"Don't I know it. Now can we steer away from the selkies for a moment and finish planning the Inishmore jaunt? I'll be needing my beauty sleep."

"A lot I'm thinking, bro," Kieran slagged him.

"Right, lads. Why don't we meet at the B&B in the morning? Brekkie for everyone," Aiden suggested.

"Would that be with or without kilts?" Dory teased.

"What are you like, Dory Teelon?" Aiden looked at her.

"Private joke," Kieran said to his brother and winked at Dory.

"I suppose you're staying at the B&B tonight, Mae?" Dory whispered to her.

"That all right, hon?"

"Of course. You're a big girl. We don't want Aiden throwing pebbles at the windows in the middle of the night. Da might go out and brain him with a shovel."

Mae laughed. "Have you seen The Forest Room?"

"I have. You're blushing. I'm guessing you had the upgraded tour?"

Chapter Fifty-Two

Breakfast at O'Rourke's B&B was nothing short of a feast. Maire Morgan outdid herself serving the full Irish fare. As if heaps of rashers, plump sausages, perfectly fried eggs and delicious homemade brown bread with creamery butter and marmalade weren't enough, there was a platter filled with sticky buns and scones. All was being devoured by the motley crew gathered in the dining room. Two ceramic teapots made another go 'round as the kettle whistled promising more strong Irish tea.

The regular B&B guests were fed and long gone, touring for the day. Kieran and Aiden had their old and new friends all to themselves. Kieran watched his brother with Mae. Aiden looked happy. Fair play to him, Kieran thought, he deserves it. He had taken their parents' death very hard. He was different than Kieran. Aiden was more of a homebody. He didn't share Kieran's wanderlust. He was a simple guy. A voracious reader since he was a child, Aiden journeyed to exotic locales through his books. He was content to go down to Pipers for the odd pint and a game of billiards but the pub scene wasn't Aiden's thing. He was well aware of the local talent; he was a normal red-blooded male after all. But try as they might, and the women tried, Aiden remained non-committed. No one thus far had any luck pinning him down. After he saw what love did to his brother, he stayed miles away from it. Kept things casual and carefree. Mae West might have just thrown a spanner in the works, Kieran mused. Good on ya' Mae, he thought, my brother could do with a dose of the genuine article.

"Penny for them…." Dory said, looking at Kieran.

"Just thinking there's a lot of passion at this table. Pity Mam and Da aren't here to see it. Especially Aiden, doing something other than working and reading. I've never seen him so taken with anyone before. For more than a night.

341

Maybe he's been waiting all this time for Mae West to show up. What do you think? Crazy is it?"

"Not a'tall. And Mae's radar has certainly improved. I know she feels that Aiden wouldn't hurt her. And he better not. He does seem different around her. Not so much at arm's length like I remember him. Mae's very special. Aiden would be more than lucky."

"Who are you telling? I'm all for it. You know I'm a sucker for a happy ending." Kieran winked.

"Please, sir, this is a respectable B&B." Dory pulled a face.

"Get your mind out of the gutter, girl. I meant and they lived happily ever after."

"Right. Of course you did. And that's not a tea cosy over there, a'tall. Why it's a caravan for leprechauns sure. Oh look, there goes one now, hopping across the plate of scones in his wee boots."

Kieran burst out laughing. The conversation at the table stopped.

"Dory, are you after telling Kieran your latest dirty joke?" Fiona teased.

"Actually, we were talking about the new line of knickers you designed to go with the suites of furniture." Dory kept a straight face. "Wasn't it moss velvet thongs for the River Collection?"

"You know it was sage," Fiona shot back with a smirk.

Rory had remained quiet during breakfast, preferring to listen to everyone and get a good flavor of Orleigh's cousin Dory and her friends. They were certainly entertaining. He spoke up now. "So lads, as Orleigh may have mentioned, my brother Cillian is over on Inishmore as it happens. His band will be playing tonight."

"What's he like, your brother?" Mae asked, squeezing Fiona's leg. Rory didn't miss it.

"Let's see… I'd say Cillian is quieter. But that wouldn't be hard," he laughed. "He's easy on the eyes, but not obnoxious or vain. Grand musician. If he wasn't my brother, I wouldn't mind him as a friend. Would you agree, love?" he turned to Orleigh.

"I would. All of that, except you are more handsome." She gave him a kiss.

"Thanks, love. Orleigh's prejudiced, lads. Anyway, Cillian sings as well. He's played all over Ireland and visited the States a few times. His band plays mostly the traditional Irish music and some contemporary tunes as well. They're brilliant. As for the, ahem, more important information...." he winked at Fiona. She nearly choked on her tea. *Here we go.*

"Cillian *is* single. Partly due to his nomadic lifestyle. Plus the fact that he hasn't met the right woman. Imagine the types he meets in bars. Not exactly high quality women, if you get my meaning. He could do with a fresh face now."

He was staring at her. Fiona could feel the heat from across the table. *Does your brother have those incredible see into my soul nowhere to hide eyes and dark good looks? Holy Hannah.* She wanted to speak but the words were stuck in her throat.

Orleigh saved her. "Ah, he will, love. Find the right woman." *Perhaps sooner than he thinks.* Orleigh winked.

"Bring him on," Fiona said, surprising even herself and temporarily forgetting that she was off men. Nice, Fee, really subtle. Why not wear a sign around your neck, Desperate Single Woman?

Rory laughed, a sexy booming sound. I'm in deep trouble, Fiona thought, if Cillian DuShane is even half his brother.

Everyone helped Maire clear the dishes but she refused help with the washing up. They packed the car and headed out in two cars to Galway. From there they would catch the ferry to Inishmore. Mae was as excited as a schoolgirl, anticipating everything she'd read about the Aran Islands. Psyched with Orleigh's tale of the selkies, she was primed for anything romantic and adventurous. Aiden beside her was no harm.

343

"Awfully glad I came to Ireland, hon."

Aiden smiled at her, his blue eyes twinkling. "Ah, Mae West, not as glad as myself sure. Where you've been all me life, well I don't know."

"On the wrong side of the ocean, apparently."

They both laughed.

Fiona was having a fierce chat with Orleigh and Rory. Normally she'd have felt like a fifth wheel. Or was it a seventh in this case? Orleigh and Rory made her feel like her presence was not only wanted but also necessary to the success of their time on Inishmore. She felt she already knew Cillian DuShane though she'd not laid eyes on him yet. Just from Rory's description and obvious fondness for his brother. Yet Fiona couldn't help but remind herself what a royal pain men could be. She convinced herself she would take nothing serious. Just check out the eye candy and enjoy the craic. This is a mere holiday not a Hallmark movie. Love in Ireland; give me a break.

They finally arrived at the ferry crossing in Rossavael. Galway Bay was calm, the sapphire water beckoning the coromonts overhead as they swooped down for a drink. Rory was entertaining them with a history lesson on the Aran Islands. Mae hung on his every word.

"The last outpost of Irish civilization. Our culture has endured. Much the same as the old fishing methods, taking small wooden handmade boats called curraghs out on the sea in all kinds of weather. Inishmore is the largest of the three islands, Mae. Inishman, the middle island, Inisheer, the south island."

Mae watched the tall cliffs looming ahead facing out to sea. Large Celtic crosses came into view on the shore. Standing relics of Christianity, their metal pitted unmercifully by the relentless wind. She inhaled the salty air as Rory spoke about monasteries from the Middle Ages.

"In particular, the ruins of Dun Aengus and Dun Duchathair, which we'll soon see."

"What about castles?" Mae knew Rory was going to be the ultimate tour guide. Her head was spinning with visions of towers and dungeons. And bagpipes.

"Ah, without a doubt, love. Arhin's castle, erected in 1587 by a lad called John Rawson. 'Twas granted the land by Queen Elizabeth. During the 17th Century occupation by the British. Have you had enough to digest for now?"

"Yep, thanks," Mae said dreamily. She could have listened to Rory all day. His voice was hypnotic. Deep as the sea that surrounded them. Mae imagined he and Orleigh as a Celtic king and queen. Or maybe sorcerer and goddess was more apropos.

The Aran Flyer sailed into Kilronan Harbor. Mae drank in the sights recording it all on her trusty old Nikon. Canoe type boats were moored in the shallow water. Ruddy faced fisherman in thick woolen sweaters and caps stood on the beach repairing nets and filleting fish. Time truly stood still here.

Rory explained how the curraghs were still made in the old way, stretching fabric (before that, animal skins) over a wooden boat frame. The art of thatching a roof was also passed down according to tradition. The simplicity of Aran life was very inviting. Yet with it, came hard work and sturdy dispositions. Especially if the sea earned you a living. And if separateness from the rest of a stressful fast paced society suited you and you didn't mind the cold, this was the place. Heaven on earth. Simplicity.

Mae watched a fisherman clean his catch.

" 'Tis called plaice," Orleigh told her, "Delicious. We'll order some for lunch. You do like fish?"

"Love it, hon. And cockles and mussels…" she sang.

"Alive alive oh," Orleigh sang back. They laughed their way off the ferry and stepped onto Inishmore.

Mae could see the entire village from the pier. Thatched roofs covered small shops built of weathered limestone. Horse drawn carts tooled around the Island carrying tourists while hearty villagers in thick sweaters and

345

woolen caps walked or cycled about their daily life. Orleigh pointed out a woolen shop. "We'll have a gawk later. Find you a nice warm jumper. A sweater, I mean."

"I *know*, hon."

"Right. Angela's Ashes and the lot," Orleigh laughed, giving Mae's arm a squeeze.

The group wandered down a cobbled road leading out of the village. Rory booked them into a B&B for the night. Mae was quiet, drinking in the scenery and enjoying the soft salty breeze on her face. Low stone walls zigzagged, winding in and out of the village and down to the sea. She knew from her reading that the walls protected the gardens from the strong winds. She noticed beautiful wildflowers sprouting out of the rocky landscape. Extraordinary. Flowers growing out of what was a virtual limestone desert. And yet there was no lack of green fields dotted with the usual cows and plenty of sheep to keep the woolen shops in business and export the treasured souvenir, a genuine Irish jumper.

They passed signposts painted in black and white. Undecipherable to Mae. Not only was Irish the spoken language on the island, but the unspoken as well. The history. Mae found it charming. The contrast of gentle pastoral beauty against a wild churning sea and craggy rocks all existing in some kind of ancient harmony. There wasn't a car in sight. They were forbidden on the island. A horse and cart, a bicycle or your own feet got you around. The past was more evident here than anywhere else in Ireland. You could see it. Feel it. She could easily understand why most of the inhabitants never left Inishmore.

"They have everything they need right here, Mae. Mostly the tranquility the rest of the world is busy searching for."

"Right lads, here we are," Rory announced. The group stopped behind him. Mae read the sign in front of the house. Coneely's B&B: warm rooms, hot baths, and full Irish breakfast. It was a beautiful two level limestone cottage with thatched roof and creamy yellow shutters framing tiny paned windows. Red painted window boxes brimmed with ox-eye daisies and purple mountain thyme. Violet flowers lined the path up to the house.

"Self-heal, they're called," Orleigh said, "Lovely, no?"

Mae nodded her head noticing the blood red centers surrounded by deep purple petals. "Doc would love these for the Brownstone."

"We'll see you get some seeds to take back, darlin."

Rory was already charming the proprietress of the B&B while they were admiring flowers. No doubt he had arranged for the best creature comforts available. They piled into a sitting room where a glowing fire welcomed them. The low table in front of a plump tapestry couch was laid out for tea.

"Come lads, let me show ye to your rooms, then ye can wrap your hands around a nice hot cuppa." Mrs. Coneely led them through the hallway and up the carpeted staircase. "How was the ferry crossing? Not rough a'tall today, sure it wasn't? Ye brought lovely weather with ye." The stairs creaked. "Don't mind me old bones, now."

Everyone laughed.

Rory said something to her in Irish and she laughed again, her crisp blue eyes crinkling shut. "No one's called me beautiful in ages, Mr. DuShane. Ah now if I was younger, sure…. 'Tis an honor having yourself and Miss Teelon here. I'm a big fan of your poetry and her fairytales." She smiled at Orleigh.

"Thanks very much, Mrs. Coneely. You're as sweet to say so. And please, call me Orleigh."

The elderly woman was plain yet attractive in an earthy way. More in that long plait of silver hair than a comb would take out, Orleigh guessed. In her day, Mrs. Coneely was probably quite the ride. Brace yourself, Brendan.

"By the way, Orleigh, ye wouldn't have brought any of those herbs with you? I've a pain in me back that won't quit sure."

Orleigh smiled, considering her thoughts of a young Mrs. Coneely. "What do you say after tea we have a little chat? I wouldn't be surprised now if I have the very thing you need."

"Grand. I knew you wouldn't mind me asking. Oh and how could I forget?" Mrs. Coneely said, after opening the last of the rooms for the group, "Mr. DuShane, your brother is playing down the American Bar. I presume ye will be there for the craic later?"

Rory nodded. "Ah we will. You should join us. Do you a world of good. And do call me Rory."

She smiled at Rory and blushed. He was the kind of man women of all ages had crushes on. "I'm afraid me dancing shoes are rusty at this stage."

"No worries. 'Tis only like cycling sure. Comes right back to you." Rory winked at the old woman. For a brief moment she felt twenty again. Full of the carnal lust, she thought. What she could have taught Rory DuShane back then.

Orleigh smiled a knowing smile at the old woman. Their eyes met. Mrs. Coneely lost her train of thought.

"Now make yourselves to home, lads," she managed, "The tea is there for ye." She meandered down the flight of stairs a lot quicker than she'd climbed them.

Chapter Fifty-Three

Fortified with a strong cup of tea and a chocolate bickie or two, the group headed out for a walk into the village. The weather cooperated nicely, the afternoon sunny with a soft breeze. Light jacket weather. First stop on the road to Kilronan was an old church. They all went inside the dark stone building and the women lit candles in front of a saint Mae had never heard of before. St. Sooney.

"Better than later, I reckon," Aiden kidded.

Rory told them how the early saints lived as hermits on Inishmore. Some later rejoined the popular civilization in cities like Dublin. Churches here were erected in their honor. Back outside the modest building, they bumped into a friendly old salt who introduced himself.

"Martine O'Donnell, at your service, lads," he said. He was the real thing, down to his worn woolen jumper, sun leathered skin and brogue thick as Irish stew. He was eager for a chat. "By the way, I could do with a pint," he made no bones about mentioning. Rory told him he would be more than happy to buy him one later at the pub. Martine promised to tell them all about his days of "Whispering fairytales to the blondes…." He winked at Mae. "I'll be down to the pub tonight and ready for the ould jig, lass. Tomorrow I'll be washing me legs for the Sunday mass."

Mae giggled. "Okay, hon."

Martine turned and headed on his way. He stopped and looked back at Mae. "Dontcha' forget about me. Unless ye're as stupid as a day old chicken." He laughed a phlegmy cackle, baring the only three teeth in his head. They stood out like brown weathered pickets on a neglected fence. He continued on his way holding his gnarly hand up in a wave and singing about beautiful women that came to him in whiskey laden dreams.

"There you have it, Mae," Aiden said, when the old man was well out of earshot. "A shining example of Irish sex appeal. We never outgrow it seemingly."

"Don't worry, hon. I'll make sure you keep all your teeth." Mae looked very serious.

"Good woman," Aiden laughed, revealing a full set of pearly whites. "

Small bells tinkled as they pushed open the door of The Aran Woolen Shoppe. The harmonic voices of Mary and Frances Black greeted them like old friends. Mae looked at Orleigh. It was the same CD they'd sung along to in the car on the way to the Vale of Avoca. *"Only a woman's heart can be. When restless eyes reveal my troubled soul and memories flood my weary heart. I mourn for my dreams, I mourn for my wasted love, and while I know that I'll survive alone...."*

Orleigh smiled back at her over a pile of Aran sweaters. "What do you think? Fancy the cream color or do you prefer the black wool?" Orleigh held up one of each.

"I've always related to the black sheep," Mae walked over and slipped on the darker cardigan that Orleigh helped her into. She modeled for her friends, sweeping up the soft wide collar dramatically as if warding off the cold wind. She fingered the wooden toggles and made a few twirls around the store.

"That one, no argument," Fiona said, admiring the deep grey against Mae's jet black hair and fair skin. "You're as gorgeous. Hold back the paddys."

"Someone call me?" Aiden came over. He took one look at Mae and let out a whistle. "The cover of Irish Vogue, you are. You mustn't ever take off that jumper."

"*Never*? Not even in the bathtub?"

"Now you've gone and given me that visual. How's a man to control himself will you tell me?"

Mae giggled and struck an innocent pose. Aiden covered her mouth with his and the whole store applauded.

"Sold," Aiden said, coming up for air and racing Mae to the cash register. "My treat," he insisted.

Mae was more then touched. "Thank you. I really didn't expect you to pay."

"I know. That's what makes it all the more fun. Please allow me to spoil you a little."

"Thank you. I don't think I will take this sweater, umm, I mean jumper off. Ever."

They all met up outside the shop each with their purchases to share. Mae wearing hers, of course. Next stop was a jewelry and craft shop. The window display boasted Celtic silver rings gleaming on dark green velvet. Next to them Celtic crosses of gold hung from a dried tree branch. Colorful papier-mâché fairies held silver and gold bangle bracelets with Celtic knots and Irish inscriptions as if they were rolling hoops down the sand into waiting handcrafted Aran baskets. Books covering everything from Irish cooking to Celtic shamanism provided the backdrop of this first glimpse into the whimsical shop.

Mae was chomping at the bit to get inside. "Now we're talking my language." She made a bee line for the jewelry counter. She noticed something that wasn't in the window. Small flat white stones hung on leather cords in front of her. Each stone was imprinted with black lines.

" 'Tis the ancient Ogam alphabet," the pretty raven haired saleswoman explained. "A sacred way the Druids communicated."

Mae chose two with the woman's help. For Doc and Rooney, representing their initials. She was off in search of new reading material next. She opened a beautifully illustrated coffee table book. Sacred Fairytales From The Glen by Orleigh Teelon. Mae shrieked.

"You right?" Dory looked up from the row of baskets she was studying.

Mae shook her head. "It's Orleigh's book!" Mae held it high. "Now it's mine." She flipped through the pages. She couldn't wait to read it properly.

"Grand. That's her first. She'll be chuffed you bought it. Come over here for a minute." Dory called her to another display. She and Fiona were trying on silver rings. Fiona moved her hand into the lamplight. She had on three different rings.

"The spirals, hon," Mae said matter of factly.

"That's what I was thinking," Fiona said, touching the band with three small Celtic spirals across it. "They signify earth, sea and sky. The three dimensions. You pick one for yourself, Mae. So we each have one. Dory has the double spiral one. Dory held up her hand. Two ornate spiral designs were carved into a larger ring.

"Nice. What does it mean?"

"Beltaine and Samhain. Summer and winter. Birth and death. The magic within the two gates."

Mae nodded. "Perfect. New beginnings."

"Aren't you the little witch?" Fiona laughed.

"Your turn to choose one," Dory said.

Mae tried a few rings on and then took all of them off. Except one. It slid on the middle finger of her right hand and she felt like she had it on forever. The image itself she wasn't quite sure about.

"It symbolizes deep intuition and freedom," the saleswoman told her.

Mae turned to Dory. "But a *wolf*?"

"Why not? You're as fearless as one. A bit of a Biddy like your one. You're small, but you're powerful."

Mae bought the ring. The three friends hugged, delighted with their purchases. Where was Orleigh? She had a habit of disappearing. Suddenly, she snuck up behind them.

"Ah, you've chosen lovely rings, lads."

"Where did you run off to?" Dory asked her.

"Just stepped out for a wee breath of air. Grand to be missed so." She turned as Rory came to stand next to her.

"Are we for the ring forts then, ladies? Or do you fancy the castle ruins?"

"The castle, please," Mae bubbled, looking around for Aiden. The two brothers had made themselves scarce when the girls took the jewelry shop by storm. Probably went off for a pint or a walk on the pier. Mae took out her camera and took a few impromptu shots of her friends while they waited for Kieran and Aiden. Just then a horse drawn buggy pulled up in front of the shop.

"How adorable," Mae squealed, snapping away. A handsome face came into focus. "What are you doing up there?"

"Your chariot awaits, Miss. Hop aboard." Aiden held out his hand so Mae could climb up. Orleigh and Rory joined them. Kieran came up behind in another one. Dory sat next to him and Fiona on the seat across. They were off to the ruins.

The horses click clacked along the well traveled road. Dun Aengus was in front of them. Mae could see a stone structure, what was once was a castle, overlooking the sea.

"A beautiful nine hundred meters uphill," Rory announced, as they stood on the ground looking up.

"A climb anyway you slice it, love," Orleigh added.

Red faced and breathless, they reached the top of the steps. The view was magnificent. Perched on a cliff 300 feet above the Atlantic, this former majestic fortress or what was left of it stood as proud as a warrior. Mae wandered the ruins of Dun Aengus with her friends wondering what stories the remaining slabs of rock could reveal. She imagined the sound of clinking armor as knights raced up these very steps with messages for the King.

They climbed to the tower room. Mae peered out the windowless opening to the sea below. Ships would have sailed to this faraway shore to wreak havoc on a peaceful people. Pagans who revered goddesses would be challenged and silenced forever. A forced unforgiving faith crammed down their throats. People versed in music and poetry, craftsmanship and healing would be judged and sentenced for crimes they did not commit. Hated for their gifts of wisdom and intuitiveness. Rory spoke of the violation of his ancestors by Vikings, English and Moors as if he himself had lived it. Or died for it.

353

Mae was moved by his passion for Ireland. "You would have made a formidable king yourself, no doubt."

Rory laughed. "Thanks very much darlin', but I'm no Brian Boru, I'll tell you that. What I wouldn't give to have sat upon the throne at the Hill Of Tara. I'm chuffed you appreciate our history. We Irish can wax nostalgic in a heartbeat. Or get morose, I'm afraid. It's in our DNA."

"I didn't come here to kiss the Blarney Stone. I'm intrigued. I love it all."

Rory laughed. "An original you are, Mae West."

Mae thought Rory could have ruled several kingdoms. They started their descent down the steps.

"Next stop on the tour," Rory called out sounding very official, "The world of shamans, mystics and alchemists. The sacred wells."

"Heavenly," Mae said. They all laughed.

"The water here was considered holy," Rory said, as they stood around the site of what had been one of the many sacred wells scattered across Ireland. "A source of healing to those who came to drink from it. Blessed by the gods and goddesses who bestowed their wisdom. Up there on the hill stood at one time an ancient monastery. St. Ciaran's. Its ruins are a reminder of how the rise of Christianity destroyed the sacred Celtic practices of a devoted tribe of people. 'Tis ironic how the very rituals in the Catholic Church, not to mention all the holidays, derived from pagan origins."

"I said something like that to one of the nuns when I was in secondary school," Fiona said. "I can vividly remember the sting of the slap she landed across my face. 'Aren't you just the brazen little article Fiona Monahan, let God please forgive your blasphemy.' Sister Ignatius the Cruel we called her. The ould bitch."

"Dead on, Fee. I remember her," Dory said.
"Desperate. We didn't deserve any of it. How did we ever survive?"

"Ah, but you did sure," Orleigh said. "Ignorance and blind faith are dangerous partners, lads. Grand you knew better than to believe half the ridiculous shite they fed you."

"I guess I was saved from all that," Mae piped up. "The Sisters at the orphanage were kind. I was lucky. Maybe they were a compassionate order. What about you, Orleigh? Do you have a nun story? I thought everyone in Ireland went to Catholic school?"

"I was spared, thank the Goddess. Mam and Da were travelers. Musicians. Brilliant voices, the pair of them. We went all over the country in a caravan. Like gypsies. It was fun times, mostly."

"Sounds good to me," Mae said.

"Ah, it would I suppose. But it was hardly glamorous. We fell on some hard times on the road. They wanted to protect me from it. They did their best. We do pull through in spite of our childhoods. Grace gets us there, I reckon. And one day we find our voice and there is no turning back."

Mae couldn't have agreed more. "That and a lot of chocolate and wine and a superhero or two."

Everyone laughed. "Spot on, Mae," Rory said.

Dory and Fiona locked eyes. Gave each other the thumbs up. Bringing Mae to Ireland was one of their better decisions.

"I want to hear more about the ancient ways," Mae said.

Rory clapped his hands, took a seat on a large rock.

"Right. Now those who believed in the old Celtic ways celebrated and revered nature and their relationship with her, Mother Earth. Healing ceremonies and rituals coincided with the moons, the Solstices, the changing seasons. Without a man-made dogma to adhere to there was a balance to the whole thing. Peace however was another goal. Granted, some fierce warriors were bred on this very soil. Undeniable. Defending Ireland and our Celtic traditions was of dire necessity to our survival. With organized religion came violence. One God or else. Minds were brainwashed. Fear ruled the day. Our own country was divided over it. Turned brother against brother. Against everything our ancestors lived and died for. Had we all stuck to the old ways there would be no need for any division a'tall. Problem is someone always wants to be right.

One day people will realize that the ancients had it sussed out already. We are fighting someone else's war. Shedding blood over religion has never been the answer. Look back to the Crusades. Disaster. The soul of Ireland had always been her roots of music, poetry, and healing. The gift of intuition so many possessed. In today's society, the overload of media and instant gratification has done us all more harm than good. We are not as kind, patient or capable of staying quiet. We constantly look to the outside to fix us. The ancients knew everything lies within. Surrender is a dirty word because we don't understand its true meaning. We'd rather spin our wheels in the mud. We're uncomfortable just to *be*. Well that's my sermon for today, lads. One thing remains the same. An Irishman with an audience finds it nearly impossible to shut up. Please forgive me if I've bored you to tears, Mae. The lads are used to my rantings."

"Frankly, hon, I could listen to you all day. I'm a sucker for the brogue for one. I know, how cliché of me. But seriously, I do love a good history lesson. And a rant."

"You are too kind. Thanks very much. I'm flattered as it comes from such a lovely lass such as yourself."

"Jaysus, will someone get me the wellies, we're knee deep in it now," Kieran said.

"Listen. Does anyone hear that rumbling?" Dory asked. "No it's not the knights of yore. It's my stomach crying to be fed. I'm starving like Marvin, lads."

"Better feed her, Kieran," Mae said. "She'll eat a child's arse through a chair and all that."

Chapter Fifty-Four

Inside the Aran Fisherman over steaming bowls of chowder and fried plaice, the conversation drifted back to selkies. Mae could never hear enough about them and Orleigh was only too willing to indulge her. Shaking malt vinegar over a plate of fish and chips, Orleigh waited for Rory to sit down before digging in. He had excused himself to make a phone call.

"Are you right, love?"

"Grand. Cillian will join us for dinner tonight. He's anxious to meet you, lads," he said to the group.

Orleigh squeezed his leg. "Lovely. We're in for a magical musical evening so." She smiled at Fiona.

"If you say so," Fiona said, stuffing a salty chip in her mouth. No expectations, no regrets, she thought.

"About the selkies…." Mae said, looking at Orleigh.

"Right. Selkies 'tis." Orleigh began.

"On this very island of Inishmore, a man called Johnny O'Reardon met his young bride. She came seemingly from parts unknown, stood on that very pier one day." Orleigh pointed out the window of the restaurant. "Aye, she was a rare beauty she was. Dressed in long brown silk, wavy tresses black as night, flowing down her back. Not a boot nor shoe did she have on her lovely feet. Poor thing was drenched to the bone without so much as a shawl to protect her from the cold Aran winds. 'Twas a mystery how Johnny came to find her that October day, on the eve of Samhain, All Hallows Eve.

The woman seemed to be glued to the pier, her dark eyes searching the sea. Johnny tied up his curragh and carried his catch to the dock. Setting his fishing basket down, he approached her. The pier was deserted. Johnny had been late getting in that day. His mates would be on their second pints by now or gone home to sit by a warm fire. Johnny removed his wool jumper and wrapped it around the woman's shoulders. She said something to him in Irish. Johnny understood her words all right yet they made no sense a'tall.

He met her eyes. Did he know her? He didn't think so, but there was something about her eyes that haunted him. The lone seal he saw only the day before oddly enough had the very same eyes. It had followed him back into the harbor. But what did that have to do with this woman? Johnny didn't know. Now he was well versed in selkie legends. Everyone on the island knew the tales. But this woman was standing before him now. She was real. Johnny couldn't help remembering how the seal yesterday had hung around his boat. It did not attempt to eat his fish nor distract him from his work. It seemed to merely keep him company. He'd paid it little mind. Until now.

'A cuppa and a good fire is what you need, lass,' Johnny told her. She nodded and followed him to his cottage. Not a soul witnessed them walking down the road in the dusky light. Once inside and out of the unforgiving wind, Johnny led the lovely creature to the hearth and lit the turf. He filled the kettle and set it to boil on the Aga. When he turned to see if the woman was still there and not some figment of his imagination, he nearly dropped the teacups in his hands. The lass was there all right. She stood facing the fire, nary a stitch of clothing left on her back. Johnny took a deep breath. She faced him, her jet hair gleaming in the firelight. Her womanly body a sculptor's dream. She was radiant. Otherworldly. 'Och, I'm going off the deep end so I am,' he told himself. He could not move. Nor take his eyes from her.

'I am Marina,' she said, her Irish musical and eloquent. Johnny put the teacups on the small kitchen table and walked towards the fire. 'Perhaps I am having one of those visions people talk about,' he told himself. Johnny had been so lonely since his wife died five years ago to the day. True he'd been no stranger to the whiskey since. But today he was stone cold sober.

'I am Marina,' she repeated.

Okay, he thought, vision or not, I can't be rude. 'Johnny O'Reardon, Miss,' he said, feeling like a right ejit. 'Have ye no second name yourself?'

'Marina, is what I am called,' she repeated, in Irish, her eyes never leaving him for long.

'Right so. Marina 'tis. Ahm, let's see about finding you something to wear.' Johnny handed her one of his shirts hanging on a peg by the door. Thankfully she put it on. He needed to concentrate for a minute. You're a fool, Johnny O'Reardon; he chided himself as he made the tea. There's a naked woman by your fire and you haven't taken her to bed straightaway. Too long at sea, man. Too long at sea.

'Come, Marina, have a cuppa now and a bite to eat.' Johnny placed a sandwich in front of her as she took a seat. 'Fancy a wee dram of whiskey to warm you, love?'

She looked up at him. 'Ta.'

'Grand.' Johnny poured each of them a short glass of Jamesons. 'To warm the very cockles of your heart, Marina. Slainte.' Johnny raised his glass to her.

'Slainte,' Marina drank the whiskey down.

'Well now you're a girl after me own heart, so you are,' Johnny laughed, finishing his own whiskey. Marina just stared at him. Then turned her gaze to the window to stare at the water.

'Tell me have you lost someone? Your family is it? Did you fall overboard?' Johnny reckoned there had to be a logical explanation for her appearance. Beautiful abandoned women do not arrive on the pier every day. Not in his life.

'No. I came here for ye.' She touched his hand. He searched her eyes.

'What? For me? How do you mean? Did you follow me yesterday?' Johnny decided to play along. Perhaps she was a bit disturbed, beautiful creature. 'Ah, right, you were the selkie I saw out in my boat. And you decided to come to land and be with me. 'Tis lovely.' Johnny was enjoying the game.

359

'Are you not pleased to see me?' Marina looked painfully sad. She came over to him, reached for him to stand. He could smell vanilla and the sea. 'Do you not believe I came here for ye? You saw me yesterday. You talked to me.'

Johnny scratched his head. Had he actually talked to a seal? What had he said? That he was a lonely broken man since Maeve O'Reardon was ripped from his life. Was the legend true? Did selkies come to land in human form at the plea of drunken fishermen who believed in fairy stories about magical seals? He reached for the bottle. Marina touched his hand and brought it to her face. Porcelain skin. Not slimy a'tall. She was no seal. Ah now you're cracking up man, he laughed at himself.

'The answer isn't in there,' Marina said, corking the whiskey bottle. 'I am real, Johnny O'Reardon. And you are not alone anymore.'

How badly Johnny wanted to believe her. Was it that simple? What had he to lose?

'Is it you, Maeve? Some kind of divine intervention perhaps?' What was he on about? He believed in none of that. It would be just like Maeve, to have the last word. His late wife always did have a sense of humor. She would kid him, 'If you find someone after I'm gone, Johnny, she'd better be a selkie. Or I'll haunt the bitch for the rest of your days, love. 'Tis only in the sea you had better find her.'

Johnny's head was spinning. Did his Maeve of the flaming red hair and green eyes and jealous nature replace herself with a seal? Selkie, he corrected himself. 'Thanks very much, Maeve. You're a grand girl. I have your blessing so? Me and the selkie like?'

'Who are you talking to?' Marina asked him.

'What? Thinking out loud. Ahm, where are your people? Have you no husband? No children?'

'You are my people. A chuisle.'

Johnny blinked back the tears filling his eyes. 'A chuisle. My love. My heart.' The very words Maeve spoke to him in Irish every night in bed. Now Johnny believed. He truly believed.

Marina kissed his cheeks where his tears had fallen. She unbuttoned the shirt she wore and let it fall to the floor. 'The selkies and Maeve sent me here to love you.'

Johnny surrendered, taking her in his arms and meeting her mouth with his own.

That was the first night of many that Johnny O'Reardon of Kilronan, Inishmore, made love to his selkie bride by their turf fire. Marina never returned to the sea. And wasn't Johnny the luckiest and most envied man on the island? Such good fortune did not happen every day. If anyone deserved it, Johnny did. He was a good man. The kind of man a shipwrecked woman might find after losing everyone she loved.

'Poor lass washed ashore on our very own Inishmore,' people said. 'And Johnny the lucky one to find her.' Only Johnny and his Marina knew the truth. 'Twas a selkie he loved by the fire for the rest of his life.'

Mae clapped. "Great story. It is just a story, right?"

Orleigh took a swallow of tea. "Is it, love? That's for you to decide. Some believe it as such. Others believe it to be true. You want to know if Johnny O'Reardon is a real person?"

"Is he?" Mae could barely stand the suspense.

"He was, yes. Long gone now, as is his sweet Marina. They did have children though. They would be very old or passed on themselves, I imagine. We could pick Mrs. Coneely's brain. She ought to know something sure."

Mae was tickled pink. "Thank you. No one since Sister Devora has indulged my fascination with fairies and leprechauns and now selkies."

Orleigh laughed. "You're very welcome. I'm only delighted you have such a keen interest in all of it."

"What about it, selkie fans, will we head back to the B&B for forty winks before the craic tonight?" Aiden suggested.

361

"You go on, lads," Rory said, "I'll settle the bill. No arguments. I'm after signing a grand book deal." Rory drained his pint of Guinness.

"Congratulations, mate. Cheers," Kieran said. The others echoed his praise.

Mae was staring out at the pier when they were back outside.

"Looking for your one in the brown silk?" Aiden asked, his arms around her snugly.

"Are you taking the piss out of me now?"

He laughed. "Not for a second, darlin. I take my wood nymph very serious. I'll show you just how serious if we hurry back to the B&B."

"Race ya," Mae said, taking off down the road with Aiden fast behind her.

Chapter Fifty-Five

Fiona spotted him straightaway. Demurely sipping her Shiraz at the bar, she happened to turn her head at the precise moment he walked into Mac's Pub. She wasn't the only female to take notice. But this fine thing was walking right in her direction.

"Ah, sham, there you are," he said to someone at the bar. Fiona nearly lost her balance on the stool and did a header at his feet. That voice. Pure sex. She felt her cheeks go hot. Get a feckin' grip, he's only a man. Purely gorgeous was beside the point. Ah, you've been there before. Bought the feckin' tee shirt. Fiona took another sip of her wine.

"Hey bro, we've been waiting on you," Rory said. Good Christ. Sexy Voice was his brother? And she'd been boring holes in him with her eyes.

"Rory, howyeh, grand to see you," Sexy Voice said. "Orleigh, darlin', you look as ravishing as ever."

Oh this one was a right charmer.

"Thanks very much, Cillian. You're no slouch yourself," Orleigh smiled warmly at her boyfriend's brother. Fiona watched them, riveted. These three could set a house afire. Combustible sensuality. Holy shite. Mae seemed to agree. She was making high eyebows and mouthing 'Wow!' to Fiona, who wanted to burst out laughing, but was too mesmerized to move.

"Let me properly introduce you, lads," Rory's voice boomed. He looked to Fiona first. Fiona froze. Did she reapply lip gloss? That was all she could think at the moment. Shallow gal. But seriously, did she?

"This lovely woman is Fiona Monahan. Fiona, my brother, Cillian."

Fiona swallowed her sip of wine and set her glass on the bar. Steady as you go, Fee. Don't sound like an ejit schoolgirl now. She smiled at Cillian. Their eyes locked. Trouble, this one, guaranteed. Pure sexy trouble.

363

"Fiona. A pleasure." It was the way his top teeth brushed his full bottom lip when he said her name. She wanted to be the teeth rubbing his full bottom lip. Maybe he just looks like a heartbreaker. Still this brother of Rory's was no country bumpkin from the arsehole of Ireland. He looked like a model, dressed in his upscale trendy clothes. No starving musician was he. Be wide, Fiona. The devil in herringbone and all that.

"Hello, nice to meet you, Cillian."

"Have we met before?" Sexy Voice was talking to her. "There's something very familiar about you." He smiled with his perfect teeth. Dead giveaway. This man had been well off the isle of Eierran. Fiona composed herself, pushing her hair back. A subtle gesture that didn't go unnoticed by your man.

"I'm positive we haven't met. Faces and names stay with me. Yours I would have remembered." Fiona was no stranger to flirting. It took more than a gorgeous man to undo her. She met his dark brooding eyes. But it was his mouth that kept her attention. Make-out session lips, she and Dory used to call them. Cillian asked her something, forcing her to abandon her fantasy. Concentrate.

"I'm from Blessington. I lived in Dublin after that. Seems ages ago. I'm on holiday from America at the moment. New York City. Brooklyn, actually. You're very like your brother. 'Tis the voice mostly. And the eyes. Rory's been giving us the 50 cent tour. I take it you're the icing on the cake?" What the hell was she saying? Icing on the cake? Jaysus. Her mind was going X-rated again so she turned to take a ladylike sip of wine. Dory stood behind Cillian giving Fiona the high eyebrows.

"You've probably met her sisters," Dory said. "The Monahan Sisters Interior Designs? Fiona was one. Now she's the ex-Paddy. Both of us."

"I do know them. Nice to meet you too, Dory. I understand completely about leaving. I escaped the ould sod myself for a time. Big world out there. Grand to be back, though. Howyeh, lads," Cillian shook hands with Kieran and Aiden.

"Howyeh, Cillian. Still as ugly as ever I see," Kieran said.

"Tommy O' Hilfiger is it?" Aiden teased him.

Cillian laughed. "Funny, the pair of ye. You boyos up for a session? Or did you need some clothing tips? I could loan you some boots that haven't got the smell of the bog off them." Cillian jabbed Kieran in the ribs.

"Fuck off with your Ralph Lauren shitkickers, sham. The bog's in your feckin' soul, man."

"Cillian Calvin Klein, meet Mae West from America. Mae, meet Cillian. Local farm boy turned fashionista." Aiden cracked up.

"Very funny. Lovely to meet you, Mae West. If you aren't a vision out of the fairytales, a regular wood nymph come to life."

Mae blushed. "So I've been told."

Their table was ready so the group walked into the dining room. Cillian held back for his pint while Fiona excused herself to the loo. She was surprised to see him still standing at the bar when she returned.

"Neeve. Your twin, right? She and your other sister, who is also stunning as I recall, designed a friend's flat in Dublin. Smashing job." Cillian was rarely unnerved and he was used to women fawning over him. The modeling gig. The band gig. He never took it seriously. Fiona was different. He also knew some fucker had broken her heart. Badly. Something in her eyes. A guarded look. He would have to prove he was one of the good guys. If she ever gave him the chance.

"Neeve and I aren't twins, actually. Thanks though, I'll be sure to tell them your friend was pleased with their work." Fiona wondered if it was a female friend?

Cillian handed her a fresh glass of wine. "So you don't miss the designing then? Or do you have a business in New York?"

"Dory and I are working on a cottage business. At the moment we're waiting tables to finance the project. The tips are grand. Upscale café and all." Fiona inhaled his cologne. Citrus. Fresh. Like after a shower. Bare arsed nak…. Get a grip. "Sorry? Yes, we all live together. Dory, Mae and myself. At the Brownstone."

"The Brownstone? Do you rent rooms there?"

"Sort of. Our friend Doc owns it. We're all her boarders. Doc's a therapist and we help her run the place. We're like a family. 'Tis grand."

"Sounds so. A houseful of women couldn't be a bad thing for sure. I do hope you aren't running back to your Brownstone soon?"

Well. He was actually listening to her. And keeping his eyes more north than south. But can you be trusted, Cillian DuShane?

"I've a few more days at home. Shall we join the others?"

Cillian nodded. He was going to have to step up his game for Fiona Monahan. Something told him she was worth it.

"My brother's bending your ear I see," Rory said, as Cillian held a chair out for Fiona.

"Not a'tall. 'Twas a mutual gabfest." Fiona smiled. She'd have to have a word with Orleigh privately. Get the real deal about Cillian DuShane.

Rory's voice resonated around the table. The man was a natural storyteller. They were all engrossed. Except herself and Cillian, who were more enthralled with each other at the moment.

"So tell me about your music," Fiona said, "Rory tells us your band plays the traditional stuff? You don't look like the typical Irish musician."

Cillian laughed. "Whatever that means. I can bang a bodhron with the best of them."

"I'm sure you can. You look more like a writer, like your brother. And a model, yes I see that sure. The clothes, the face, the perfect teeth. Dead giveaway."

"I'm not ashamed of it. I took my share of slagging from the lads as you could imagine. Pretty boy and all that shite. But it paid the bills at college and I got to do my music. I teach in Galway at the University. Surprised? Thought I was a jetsetter, didn't you? Brainless piece of playboy arse and all that."

"Don't knock the arse bit," Fiona laughed. "But I am impressed. A professor? Proves the saying that you can't judge a book by its cover, even if in your case it's GQ."

He laughed. "True enough, never assume. If that was the case, you would have lived centuries ago. Holding court as a ravishing Celtic queen. Fighting off suitors left and right."

"Hah, royalty is it? If only. Instead I'm just a lowly peasant eeking out wages from arrogant trust fund brats who don't eat enough to fill a thimble. Sometimes I'm desperate for home."

"But that's just a temporary gig. You have your designs, no?"

"I do. 'Tis my passion. Something you are very familiar with coming from such a talented family yourself."

"Touché," Cillian raised his glass to her.

"To sisters and brothers," Fiona toasted.

Stuffed with good food and drink, they all took a leisurely stroll down the road to The American Bar, where Cillian and his band would be playing later. Mae and Aiden held back from the crowd, lingering by the pier. Mae drank in the village by moonlight feeling very relaxed from the wine. It was charming by night, the warm light from the pub across the way, the smell of peat burning inside and the odd light of a passing boat, the cool sea air. The street was quieter with the fishermen and tourists cozily ensconced in the pubs or tucked into their cozy cottage rooms.

367

Aiden was pensive, looking out at the water. He took her hand and put a small wrapped box into it.

"For me?" Mae was secretly delighted.

"Open it. I can't stand the suspense…"

Mae eagerly ripped off the ribbon and tore through the wrapping. She held a green velvet box in her palm. She looked at Aiden. Lifted the lid and gasped.

"Oh, Aiden," Mae's voice cracked and tears welled in her eyes. He was moved. She was so damn beautiful. Did she not know it? He looked into her huge dark eyes, as luscious as new Cadbury's chocolate. He would be willing to spend the rest of his life telling Mae how beautiful and amazing she was, he thought.

Mae's hands were shaking as she stared at the ring. "Aiden…." She suddenly closed the box and handed it back to him. "Let's catch up with the others, okay?" Mae couldn't look at him.

"What's wrong? It's a gift. I didn't mean to scare you off. But the truth is, I'm in love with you."

"What? You can't be. You don't even know me."

"I know enough. What are you afraid of? I'm not going to hurt you, I promise."

"Don't make promises. I don't need…"

"What? Love? Another bollocks messing up your life? I'm not them. Give me a chance."

"I know you're different. You certainly sound different. Sorry. I didn't mean it like that. But how many times have you fallen in love? Dozens? I'm sure you get your fair share of American tourists at the B&B. And why wouldn't you fall in love often? I just thought we were having a good time."

"I see. That's quite a bite you have. As a matter of fact I did fall in love. Recently. With a beautiful American. Funny, smart, interesting, lovely. The whole package."

"See? And you'll fall in love again. Maybe that smart funny American woman will return to the B&B. You never know."

"You're right. She might."

"Where did she live?"

"In the Brownstone, that's all I know. In New York."

"You mean *a* brownstone. A lot of people live in them."

"No. Where she lives is called the Brownstone."

"Are you…?"

"Taking the piss out of you? No, I'm not. But you don't need… What was it you didn't need again? Right. Another bloke breaking your heart. Got it."

"I trusted people. Men. And they… They disappointed me. Badly."

"I know. So you're done is it? Finished with the love bit? Grand. Good luck with that. You're here for a quick shag on your holidays, that's fine. It's a turn of the tables we have here. Don't worry about me. I'll be fine. I made an ejit out of myself, but I'll get over it."

"Now you're mad at me."

"I'm not mad at you. I am mad as hell at the fuckers who broke your heart, I'll tell you that. But I had you pegged for stronger stuff."

"What does that mean? You calling me a chicken?"

"Yep."

"Cheap shot. You don't know what I had to… Oh never mind. I'll have you know that I do love."

"Right. Of course you do. You love your mates, the Brownstone, those nuns. I heard you. That's not the same."

"I *love.*"

"Grand, I heard you. Ready for the pub so?"

"I love, Aiden."

"That's grand, Mae. You win. Can we go now?"

"I want you to hear me."

"I heard you. Loud and clear. Have I not been standing here?"

"I love Aiden O'Rourke. Did you hear that?"

"Heard it. You love your mates, etc."

"I love you."

369

"You love me is it? But you can't be in love with me. Am I understanding you now? Maybe I'm crazy, but you are driving me stone mad, woman."

"I'm trying to tell you that I'm in love with you."

"Did I miss something? No one ever accused me of brilliance, but…"

"Listen, it turns out you were right. I am afraid. Well, I was. I've decided not to be anymore. I'm taking myself back from the begrudgers, as Dory says. They don't win. I win."

"Now you're talking. And can we be done talking? For now anyway?"

"We can."

Aiden needed no more encouragement. He covered her mouth with his and held her close to him. He would never let another soul hurt this woman he was lucky enough to meet. He would forever be indebted to Dory and Fiona for bringing Mae West home with them. Tokens of love were not as important he realized, as the feelings one had inside for the person he was truly in love with. 'Every day's a school day, Aiden.' If his mam were alive, she would have said those very words to him.

"Can I look at the ring again?"

"You can, of course. A woman's prerogative is to change her mind."

His mam would have agreed. He took the box out of his pocket and gave it to Mae. She opened it and took out the ring, turning it around in her hand. It was beautiful. Celtic knots danced around a single black onyx on a band of sterling silver. Aiden slipped the ring on the third finger of her left hand.

"A direct line to the heart. That's what they say."

Mae let the tears come. "It's amazing."

"It's a ring. You're amazing."

Mae listened to Aiden describing the ring. "A lover's knot 'tis. Some call it a Josephine knot. Named for the Empress Josephine. Napoleon enjoyed Irish music and employed Irishmen in his army. I thought it suited you. Your

370

innocence in the simple knot work and your unique beauty in the onyx. I meant it when I said you were a gem."

"Oh God, I can barely breathe. I've never felt this special before. And there's something else. I feel safe with you and that is the best feeling in the universe to me. You might say I've waited my whole life to find it. I don't take that lightly. I am in with love you and I don't want to leave you or Ireland." Mae was crying again. Aiden held her in his arms.

"Darlin', I'm not going anywhere and neither are you at the moment. As for the future, I don't plan on there being one without you in it."

Mae opened her mouth to speak but instead she pressed her lips to Aiden's. They could say so much more than mere words.

Chapter Fifty-Six

If nights could go on forever then Dory wished this one would. Her cherished friends and the man she loved, having the time of their lives. Even her sisters showed up. Nory and Jury were only too glad to hop the ferry and join them. Having them close again reinforced the feeling that they'd always had more than just good craic. The sisters fed one another's souls. Dory felt bad that she had waited so long to come home. Nothing and nobody would interfere with her life again. No man would ever separate her from her family.

She watched Fiona watching Cillian play the cittern. He had her best friend's rapt attention. Ah, Fiona. Good on ye, she thought. For ages Fiona had kept her armor up. No man could penetrate that wall. Now she looked as tough as a plate of mashed spuds. Dory smiled. Was that a spark of light in Fiona's eyes? Brilliant.

The music got livelier and Orleigh and Rory were dancing a rousing jig in the middle of the floor. Aiden and Mae joined them. "Mae, you're a bleedin' fairy yourself," Dory laughed. If Aiden had anything to do with it, and apparently he did, Mae was all through with looking for love in all the wrong places. This man was as solid as the Rock Of Cashel. Dory was a bit prejudiced there, seeing as she was stone mad about his brother. 'The O'Rourke's are a good lot,' Mam would say. Dory had to admit her mother was right all along. Is it pure defiance when we travel down the dodgy path instead? Live and learn.

Kieran was on stage doing a set with Cillian's band.

"I love you," Dory mouthed to him when they locked eyes. He smiled, singing his heart out on the last notes of the song. He was about to begin another when the music stopped.

"Lads, if I could have your attention for a moment," he shouted out.

What in the world? Dory felt her stomach do a flip flop. Don't be daft, she told herself; he's only announcing the winner of the soccer match.

"Right. Thanks lads," he said when it quieted down.

"We lost to fuck. Play the feckin' music," someone shouted.

Kieran laughed. "I will in a minute, sham. Stay quiet, will you? Now sitting over there 'tis the most beautiful woman in Ireland, lads. And she loves me, imagine." The crowd laughed and cheered.

"You lucky bollocks," someone shouted. "When she gets sick of you, I'll show her the moon and the stars sure."

Kieran laughed. Dory was embarrassed. She felt her face go beet red. Kieran was on his knees at the front of the stage. Oh Christ. I'm not able for this, she thought.

"Dory, will you marry me?"

All Dory could hear were hoots from the crowd as she stared at Kieran. People were moving away in slow motion. Only herself and Kieran in the world. Cillian's band playing softly, but Dory could hear no sound.

"Dory?" Kieran was talking to her. He jumped off the stage and came to her. "I've been waiting my whole life for this moment. Will you marry me?" He opened a box he took out of his shirt pocket. Dory's eyes moved from the shimmering diamond back to Kieran's face.

"Marry you?"

"Well I just thought you might want to make up for lost time and all that. However if you're not interested...." Kieran looked genuinely disappointed.

"Of course I'll marry you, sham. Dory O'Rourke. Has a nice ring to it sure." Dory threw her arms around him. He spun her around and around. When they stopped he slipped the ring on her finger. The crowd cheered and there were offers of drinks for everyone.

Aiden was the first to congratulate them. "You have no idea how long my brother has waited for this day. Cheers. Best to you both. Welcome to the family, finally."

"Thanks, Aiden. Believe me, if only I could turn back time…."

"No worries. The look on Kieran's face tells me you were well worth waiting for."

Dory was mesmerized by the gem on her finger and the man who had just proposed marriage. So this is the way it was supposed to be. Happy tears. She blinked the past away remembering she had long ago forgiven herself an almost fatal mistake. She had a second chance to be happy. Too bad babies would not be part of it too. Chin up, Dory, you have a man who loves you. And you him. You'll be dedicated to one another with no bother of nappies and sleepless nights around cots and the like. Nothing wrong with that.

"Like it then? The ring?" Kieran's voice snapped her out of her head once again.

"I love it. It's beautiful." She focused on the gold band and the triple spirals surrounding the crystal clear diamond. The trinity of truth, nature and knowledge. She smiled at the man she'd always loved. "It's perfect, love," she said, with tears in her eyes. How is this possible, she kept thinking? How?

"Look inside, Dory. There's an inscription. And by the way, no people were killed for the diamond. I checked."

Dory smiled and took the ring off reluctantly. She never wanted to remove it. Ever. She read the words in spite of the tears clouding her vision. 'A cuisle, Dory. Always, Kieran.' The most beautiful words in all the world. Dory couldn't speak. Kieran helped her slip the ring back on her finger.

"You *are* the very beating of my heart, sham," he whispered, his serious blue green eyes twinkling. "I simply wouldn't write you off. Something kept telling me you would come back. Though it appears I've turned you mute in the process." They both laughed.

"We know that couldn't last for long," Dory said, coming down to earth. She stroked his cheek. "I am so touched. Still in shock here. You always were a romantic."

Dory touched the ring again. She looked up at him. "And you are *my* love. Always." She laid a lip lock on Kieran that he would not soon forget, disregarding the crowd that watched them. She couldn't care less anymore. Let them have a grand gawk. She felt unabashed and truly free. For the first time in her life. "Mind if I break away and show off my ring?" Dory's arms were still entwined around Kieran's neck.

"Do, love. And don't ever feel you need my permission to do anything. That lot is over. This is your night. First of many. Enjoy yourself."

Dory kissed him one more time for good measure and turned toward her sisters. They were ready to land hugs and shrills of delight on her. Kieran accepted a whiskey from Aiden who clapped him on the back.

"Well done, bro." Dory heard him say.

The women formed a circle around Dory, oohing and ahhing over the ring. They all beamed. Happiness was contagious. Heck, it beat a sharp stick in the eye. Cillian's voice was resonating through the pub; Galway Girl was always a crowd pleaser. Fiona was googly eyed next to Dory, watching Cillian watch her clap to the beat.

Mae was total mush by now. What with Aiden declaring his love for her and Dory getting engaged all in one day, it was almost too much for a person to digest. Mae was ecstatic. Dory was her champion and vice versa. All of them had a common bond. But Dory and Fiona had given her Ireland. And Aiden. For that she would be eternally grateful. She never thought in a million years….

Rory joined in with his brother. Their two voices blending as naturally and complimentary as birdsong. Deeper. Sensual. As soothing to the ear as the hot whiskey Dory sipped, warming her whole body. Or was that Kieran? She looked over at him with the lads. My fiancé. There was a word she'd never spoken. Bliss. There was another. Get used to it, sham, she thought. Kieran winked at her. She winked back. Bless his heart. He is a keeper.

Dory chuckled to herself and watched her sisters. Nory and Jury were all lovey-dovey with their husbands. Engagements had that effect on people. Love was contagious. You couldn't help but feel good around it. Her sisters had already started planning the wedding. Dory didn't mind. She loved their excitement. Without saying the words she could read their minds. Their triplet code. "You've had the wham bam, now we're going to give you the wow." She loved them for that. What till Da hears, Dory thought. He'll be delirious with joy. He always thought the world of Kieran.

Dory suddenly thought of Doc and Rooney. They won't believe what's after happening. As for Orleigh, she probably knew all along, the bleedin' witch. Speaking of Orleigh…. Dory didn't see her with Rory, or anywhere else in the pub. She was there earlier, after Kieran pulled off his fabulous stunt. She had congratulated them. Dory hadn't seen her since.

Cillian was calling for the crowd's attention. Now seriously, Dory thought. Twice in one night? What could he be announcing? That he'd fathered several children on his last tour across Ireland? Dory realized that was not a bit nice. But he *was* too damn good looking for words. Woman be wise. Fiona beware.

She looked at Fiona. She just held up her hands. She had no earthly idea what he could be up to either.

"Lads, may I have your attention, please," Cillian said into the microphone. "Now, would you provide a warm welcome to some special friends of a beautiful lady I've had the pleasure of meeting tonight. Fiona, I presume you know these lovely women?"

Fiona turned to where Cillian pointed and the whole pub was looking. Dory screamed first.

"Jaysus in the manger, what are *you* doing here?"

Fiona clapped her hands. " 'Tis feckin' priceless, no?" she said to Dory and laughed, shaking her head.

Rooney McNeil strutted forward as the crowd parted.

"We heard y'all agreed to get hitched. Reckon we'd better check this dude out for ourselves."

Dory pointed to Kieran.

"Whoo hoo!" Rooney hooted. "We think y'all did just fine, darlin'."

"I second that emotion," Doc came over and hugged Dory. A third person suspiciously brought up the rear. Orleigh.

"The plot thickens," Fiona said.

"No shit, Sherlock," Dory replied, laughing. "Now when did you get here, Doc? I thought you were on your honeymoon? Leave it to Orleigh to conjure this up. I couldn't believe my eyes, the two of you, walking into the pub. This calls for a proper drink. What'll you have, lads? 'Tis feckin' gas. I'm pure delighted." Dory was breathless with excitement.

Orleigh walked up and Dory nearly knocked her over with the hug she landed on her. "You are very welcome, cousin. Slainte. You deserve all this and more. Now let's get these fine women a drink. Play us a grand reel, will you now, boys?"

Dancing ensued with Cillian's fiddle taking the lead. Sweeney's Buttermilk never sounded better. The pub was rocked to the rafters, people well in their cups by now, not a trace of inhibition in their flying feet. Then the band switched over to a Van Morrison tune and the couples slipped into slow dance mode. When the dance ended Dory went in search of her friends. Rooney gave her the low down on how they ended up on Inishmore.

"It was a secret mission. Doc and I loved the mystery and drama of the whole thing. Orleigh is a peach. We got on like biscuits and gravy. Now how 'bout that man of yours? You've been holding out on us. Y'all are as starry eyed as a virgin."

"I know, I'm toast. Seriously, he is the real thing. I've known Kieran my whole life. No surprises. He's one of the good guys. Now tell me about the honeymoon. London agreed with you, it seems. Are you more in love than before?" Typical Dory shining the spotlight on her friends.

"It was plum lovely," Rooney laughed. "And I couldn't love her anymore than I do, that's a fact. But this here's your night, darlin. You're positively glowing."

Doc walked over and sat down, having been given all the introductions by Fiona.

"I imagine you're waiting to wake up from a dream, Dory. Does that about sum it up?"

"Doc, you hit it slam on the head. Fate's a strange thing."

"You've waited a long time to be happy. Orleigh told us about your ex-mother in law. How bizarre and frightening."

"She never really stood a chance to do anymore harm. I had Kieran with me this time. And Mam and Da and my sisters. Any one of them would have been thrilled to have a go at her. Sheila got her comeuppance in the end."

"Karma. Don't discount it."

"Listen to her," Rooney said. "Karma gets 'em every time." Rooney clapped her hands and shouted out to the band, "What say we take this hooley up a notch or two?"

Orleigh seconded the motion. "Right, boys, let's have it."

Dory looked at Rooney. "Where did you hear that?"

"Hooley? You forget my last name's McNeil? C'mon, let's show 'em how it's done, girl."

Orleigh came off the dance floor and took a breather with Doc.

"So Rain, are you enjoying yourself? What do you think of our girl's news?"

"It's wonderful. I've never seen her this happy."

"You can take credit for that sure. Dory came home in much better form than when she left. Your healing shows."

"Thank you. That's quite a compliment, considering you saved her life."

Orleigh smiled. "How about this? Dory has two fairy godmothers."

Rain laughed. "Agreed." She sipped her wine and waited.

"Right. Where does that leave us so?" Orleigh asked.

"Declan and his mother. Done and done."

"Clyde Farrow and that other wanker Sonny, ditto."

"A four-bagger. Cheers."

"Cheers, B.C. To Haight Ashbury. Brilliant place."

Rain raised her glass. "To the only witch I ever met in a Frisco coffeehouse. Even if she gave me an espresso bath."

"Ha ha. That was fate. And you don't mean the only witch. Don't forget the one in the mirror."

Chapter Fifty-Seven

Dory watched her friends sleep. Their tears had long since dried. Their flight to New York was well underway. Like Mae and Fiona, Dory too had difficulty saying goodbye to Ireland. It turned out to be so much more than a holiday. Now it would be the five of them again, in their Brownstone beds, dreaming about a green and magical place, where nightmares were finally laid to rest and a promising future conceived.

Dory looked down at her left hand and smiled. Kieran. In her life again. How did she get this lucky? Her life hardly a cartoon where the character gets squished by a lorry and simply peels himself off the ground and skips merrily away in the end. Loving Declan had been like being hit by a truck. A Mack truck. How she ever survived was a mystery. Perhaps a miracle. She thought of Orleigh while she looked at her friends. They were all survivors. Each woman's story unique. Each thread identical. There is no upside to a violent man. Except surviving.

She bit into a chocolate biscuit and took a sip of tea. Mae stirred next to her and went right on dreaming. She had survived the worst. Now she had Aiden. Mae would never feel small again. She also had a new friend in Orleigh. Orleigh understood. She had been down the pike herself and found her way back. No one would have taken her for a victim. She exuded strength. Her mystical aura seemingly shielded her from the ugly side of life. Dory knew that wasn't always the case.

Orleigh's parents had left her with an uncle in England. To get her a formal education. Life on the road was hard enough for them, much harder on a child. The uncle became not her guardian as her parents intended, but rather a predator. In his guise as local landowner and pillar of the community, he hid his crime of rape and child abuse. This brat of his sister's was nothing to him. A child of Travelers, she was an embarrassment to his proper English blood. But he enjoyed breaking her in. His little Irish whore in the making. Orleigh was his to use every night. He took her to his bed and showed her how to service him. He would educate her in the one trade she could actually make a good living from. Or perhaps he would keep her just for himself. She was proving to be an apt pupil. By the time she was old enough to escape, Orleigh got the terrible news that her parents were burned to death in a caravan fire. She had been secretly saving whatever money she could from a meager allowance the uncle gave her for sweets and personal items. She planned to take the boat to Ireland and find her father's relations. She had to escape her uncle.

Dory remembered when Orleigh came to them. Dory was only about five or six herself, while Orleigh was a worldly teenager with flowing red curls and porcelain skin. Knowing green eyes, the color of Absinthe. Orleigh *was* ethereal, even then. She worked hard in the Teelon's bakery and Dory's mam and da adored her. She babysat for the triplets and stayed miles away from trouble. In other words, men. She saved every penny she earned besides the few bob she put aside each week to take the triplets for ice cream. She loved to spoil them. They would be as good as gold so she would tell them fairytales every night before bed. Stories about magical fairy women who could heal the sick and make people fall in love. She made each of them an amulet before she left for America when she turned 21. Dory still had hers somewhere in a box in the Brownstone attic.

Orleigh eventually got homesick for Ireland and her adopted family. She later found her private refuge in the Glen. People said she led a charmed life. No husband to take care of, no kids to feed. Behind her back they were not so kind. "Kook, gypsy, tinker, witch," they called her. A woman living alone in the forest. But they came to her for cures and tonics just the same. People were two-faced. "Why do you bother?" Dory asked her once.

"Sticks and stones, cousin. There's what we know to be true and what people assume. A world of difference. Being blessed is not the same as being charmed. One is seductive while the other is sacred. I know how I got here even if they choose to believe harmful gossip. Smart people know better. Stupid people are inconsequential. Ignore them. They're gnats."

That was pure Orleigh. Putting everything into perspective, protecting herself. Dory closed her eyes. In a few hours they would be landing at Kennedy. Bittersweet. Kieran and her family an ocean away again. But not forever. She was marrying a man who loved her. Good love. The kind that gave you goose bumps, not hives. Lovely 'organisms,' as Mam would say. Dory only had one sad fact to conquer regarding marrying Kieran. It was her own shortcoming. He didn't mind one bit that they'd never have children. Dory could see from his face when she told him, how hurt he was. For her, not himself. Like he wanted to dig Declan up out of his grave and beat his bones. Dory sighed. They could always adopt, couldn't they?

Dory slipped on her wool cardigan and snuggled under the thin airline blanket. She felt something lumpy in the pocket of her sweater. She looked at the little tissue paper package and smiled. A gift from Orleigh. She opened it and held the pendant up to the light. On a leather cord hung a small stone figure. Dory laughed to herself. The tiny sheela-na-gig stared back at her with her pendulous breasts and exposed vulva. You had to love Orleigh's wry sense of humor. She slipped the Celtic fertility symbol around her neck.

Chapter Fifty-Eight

Back at the Brownstone, routine took over their lives. Familiar tasks easing the transition back to reality for Rain's boarders. It seemed inappropriate now to refer to her friends that way. Boarders. Rooney was her wife, after all. All five women had shared one another's secrets. No longer were they merely boarders. Were they ever only that, she wondered? They certainly had evolved into so much more. Something she treasured. Particularly the one who still insisted on calling her "Doc." Rooney was stubborn that way and Rain loved her madly.

"Why, hell, Doc, seems to me we oughta' remember where we came from. We walked through the mire to arrive on your doorstep. We were mighty proud to be your boarders, darlin.' Nothing wrong in that."

Rain's Friday night support group, SAGAS, was thriving. A good and bad sign. Women were coming for help. Men were still beating women. They wanted the guy but not the violence. Sometimes that is an impossible wish. Might as well hope to be queen of the world. Some men do not deserve you. Be discerning and true to yourself was a message that still needed to be heard. Rain felt privileged to break bread with her boarders every night. All four glowed with beautiful possibility. All four could have wound up dead, had they stayed in abusive relationships. But they did not. Those kind of female balls were admirable. You don't need a scrotum to walk away. You need courage. Reinventing yourself takes gumption. Rain knew a little bit about that.

A tribute was in order. A celebration. A gratitude fest. For her boarders. And the Brownstone. It wasn't just a building anymore. Nor merely a house. It was an icon of survival. A mecca of metamorphosis. Her boarders were butterflies. Caterpillars no more. And they loved a party and were not shy around a good margarita or double chocolate cake. Rain was on a mission.

She found Mae at the kitchen table furiously tapping away on her laptop, Shamus dozing at her feet. Rain inhaled the heady aroma of Irish stew. She helped herself to a fresh cup of coffee and sat down. Shamus woke up and greeted his mistress with one large paw plopped in her lap. "There's my good boy," she cooed, brushing his furry coat.

"What's up, Doc?" Mae asked. They both laughed. Mae's face was lit like sunshine.

"Busy, I see. Love letter?"

"Yeah, hon. Real mushy gushy too. I'm pathetic, am I not?"

Rain laughed. "Not a bit. Mushy gushy suits you. I see you've got the cuisine *and* the lingo down pat, hmmm? You're more Irish than imp these days."

Mae smiled. "Not a bad thing. Maire sent me her recipe for stew. Something on your mind?" Mae sipped her coffee.

"I was wondering if you would whip up one of your famous chocolate cakes for tonight? If it's not too much work. I know you've already cooked."

"For you, hon? No trouble. Someone's birthday I forgot?"

"No. It's the anniversary of the day I bought the Brownstone. Cause for celebration, don't you think? Are you already baking too? What is that delicious smell?"

"Brown bread. Goes with the stew." She looked at Rain, wide eyed.

"You're a gem."

Mae laughed. "That's what Aiden says."

"Smart man. Keep him."

"I intend to. And if I am any kind of gem, that's thanks to you. And Sister Devora."

Rain's heart went out to the tiny five year old girl she could still see in those big brown eyes. She prayed there was a painful karmic lesson for the man who never deserved to call himself her father.

"Sister Devora and I were the lucky ones. Look in the mirror more often. Your strength is ravishing. And very underrated."

Mae blushed. She was humble too. A rare quality for sure. "Wow, I don't know what to say. I mean, thanks a lot. I'll get to that cake in a minute."

"The flattery wasn't for the favor. I meant every word. Have a gawk at your gob, as Dory would say."

Mae cracked up. "What are you like, Doc?"

Rain smiled at her. She had lived with these women long enough to know which questions required answers and which did not. She walked out of the kitchen down to her office with Shamus on her tail.

Epilogue

"Pressies! I love pressies!" Dory sang out when Rain passed around small wrapped packages just as Mae swung through the kitchen door with dessert. She set her chocolate cake in the middle of the table and sat down.

"What's the occasion?" Fiona asked.

Rain couldn't answer. She was dumbstruck by Mae's cake. That was an understatement. It was no ordinary chocolate layer cake. It was a chocolate house. The Brownstone. Complete with a stone path of brown M&M's leading up to the black licorice replica of the wrought iron gate. In each front window there was a colorful butterfly ready to take flight. On the cherry Nibs front stoop sat a china replica of Shamus. The front door was equally whimsical, flat banana taffy with a Red Hot for a doorknob. A Butterfinger chimney. Rain looked at Mae. The girl was a constant surprise.

"How did you *know*?"

"What do you mean? You asked me to bake a cake."

"I mean the *butterflies*."

"Oh. They're marzipan. It was easier than shaping women. Glad you like them."

"You have no idea how much."

Rooney touched her hand. "What's going on? With the butterflies and all?"

Rain smiled. "You'll see. Time to open your presents, everyone."

"Whoo hoo!" Rooney yelped as tissue and wrapping flew everywhere to Shamus's delight. He chased balls of paper around the table, tussling with bows and ribbons.

"*Now* I get it." Mae held up her bracelet. "Wow. The planets must be in alignment or something." Mae's butterfly had amethyst eyes.

"For protection and psychic growth," Rain said. "Which apparently you don't need...."

"It's beautiful, hon. Thank you." She slipped it on her slim wrist and admired it.

"Your welcome. The cake by the way is outstanding. I am so touched."

"A drop in the bucket, for you. Anyway I had fun doing it."

"Doc, you are a bit of a Biddy yourself," Dory was saying, over all the oohing and aahing. "I know that emeralds are about marriage." Dory put her bracelet on her freckled arm. "It's only gorgeous."

"I'm glad. Emeralds are also for fertility."

If Dory didn't know better she'd swear Doc and Orleigh were in cahoots. "Happy Anniversary, Doc. If we could take the Brownstone and transport it to Ireland, put it smack dab in the middle of Orleigh's Glen, there would be no need for heaven sure." Dory was choked up to say the least. She stared at her bracelet again.

"Thanks," Rain said. "That thought is unanimous, I think. I wish Orleigh were here."

"Okay, lapis lazuli for me. If I recall that's for harmony and understanding. Am I right?" Fiona asked. "Is there something I'm missing? And thank you. I'm mad about the bracelet."

"You're welcome. Yes, lapis is also for journeys or moves."

"Well if your man from Inishmore has anything to do with it, sign me up. You're as good as gold, Doc. I love you."

Things were getting very emotional, Rain thought. It was that kind of day. "Me too. I love you all," Rain managed.

"My turn! My turn!" Rooney was animated as usual. She turned her bracelet to catch the stone's brilliance in the candlelight. She was like a child with a new toy. A precious sight, Rain thought. "Let me guess. They ran out of rubies so you got one of each? The red's for love, right? What about the pink? That's for my girlish charm, I reckon?"

Rain laughed. "Close, but no cigar." She took Rooney's wrist in her hand. "Ruby is for your courage. The pink tourmaline is for our friendship first, and then our love. How's that?" There was only silence in the dining room. Rooney caught her breath as tears rolled down her cheeks. Rain fell in love with her all over again.

"You happy now? See what y'all have done? Reduced poor old me to a blubberin' fool. Which I am, for you. I love you, heart and soul, darlin,' heart and soul." Rooney was baring her vulnerable side. It was a huge step in how she'd healed. She leaned in and planted a bold kiss smack on Rain's lips.

"You'll excuse her," Rain said to the others. She's a tad shy."

Mae clapped her hands. "Awesome. This night rates up there as one of *the* best in this house. To Doc and the Brownstone, raise your glasses, come on."

"Doc and the Brownstone!" they all echoed and cheered.

Rain lifted her glass to her boarders. "To each of you. For enhancing my life. You are rare and intuitive women. Let me tell you what each of *you* have given *me*."

"Rooney, you were my first boarder in the Brownstone. Before your love, you gave me your charming Southern humor. Your dedicated friendship. Not to mention the sleepless nights wondering how you really felt about me. I love you."

Rooney touched her heart. "Back at you, Doc. You're my hero."

"Next to walk through my door was you, Mae. With your eternal optimism. Your sweet innocence. Yet such bravery. It's true. You stared down the wolf. In the end *you* won, he didn't."

Mae was crying. "You're too generous, hon. You forgave me so *much*. You let me stay. Gave me a real home. I never had that."

The tears were unanimous. They were all bawling like babies. Rain smiled at her and blew her a kiss across the table. Rain continued before they all drowned Mae's perfect cake.

"And then a soft Irish mist danced into my life. A double delight. Dory, your balls, and you do have them, are amazing and quite lovely. You stood tall when others in your shoes would have shrunk from such adversity. Not you. You are an outstanding role model. I am a lucky woman to know you."

Dory smiled, wiped her tears with her napkin. "Cheers. You may be right about the balls. I've been kicked in them enough to have a pair. Anyway, you are first rate in my book any day."

"Now, Fiona. The other half of the beautiful IRA of the Brownstone. Spunk and tenacity in a beautiful package. You're back in the game, girl. Surprised yourself, I know. You've no idea how extraordinary you are. I know. Shamus knows. He recognized your love for him immediately. If this Cillian chap is smart, he recognizes it too. Shamus has impeccable taste."

"Slainte,' Doc. We could nearly saddle this old boy up, couldn't we?" She rubbed Shamus's neck and he almost climbed into her lap. "In tribute to you and the home I found here, I think I'll create a new line called the Brownstone Design. What do you think, Dory?"

"Sounds grand. I can envision it already."

"I love the idea," Rain said. "Now there's one more thing. Last bit of show and tell." She reached into her pocket and took out her own bracelet.

"What color are your eyes, hon?" Mae was excited again.

"Orange. The stones are carnelian. For change. And here on the wings is each one of your stones. So I'll always have you with me. My dear Brownstone boarders. My family."

Her boarders were on their feet. "To Doc, you rock!" they cheered.

Rain was more than pleased with their celebration. The night was purely joyful. She couldn't imagine how it could get any better. No, she could never have imagined.

Dory remained standing. "I have a question for you."

"Ask away," Rain said, feeling positively euphoric. "I am in the best mood tonight."

"If she's a girl, and by the way, I *know* she is, I'd like to name her Rain. Rain O'Rourke. Lovely sounding, no? Any objection?"

Rain was speechless. Dory's face was lit like a Christmas tree. Rain didn't know who screamed louder. Her money was on Rooney. Fiona and Mae were a close second.

"I would be honored," she said at last, sending a mental kudos to Orleigh. *Go witch. We still got it.*

"Ah, sham, this is brilliant news." Fiona couldn't contain herself. "I'm delighted. Does Kieran know? What about Orleigh? Your mam and da? Neeve? Oona? Oh my God, if Oona knows the whole of Ireland knows by now." Fiona was going on at a pace, barely coming up for air. "Auntie Fiona. I love it!"

"Slow down, Fee. Kieran knows, yes. Orleigh, well in her way she must. Doesn't she always? No one else at home yet. Just her Brownstone aunties."

"We'll spoil her rotten. Try and stop us, sham. I better practice up on my Too Ra Loo Ra Loo Ra, hadn't I?" Fiona was overjoyed. A damn miracle 'twas, she thought. Or….

"Thanks all the same. But do you really think you should sing to the child?"

"Ah shut up, mammy. You do have a point, I suppose."

"Count me in for babysitting," Rooney piped up. "I know some 'ol Southern lullabies that'll guarantee sweet dreams for your baby girl. Way to go, whoo hoo! Go Dory glory!"

"Are you sure you didn't meet my mam while you were in Ireland?" Dory laughed.

"Why? She calls you that?"

"One of my many rhyming names. I reckon my wee daughter will succumb to the curse as well. There are worse things sure."

"So you're pretty confident she's a girl then?" Rain asked, finally getting a word in.

Mae answered for her. "If Dory says she's a girl, she's a girl. Congratulations, hon." Mae got up to give Dory a tight hug.

"I was worried there for a minute. You've stayed very quiet, Mae. What's up with you?"

"Just this dream I had. About a little girl."

Everyone stopped to listen.

"She was walking around the Brownstone. Not here in the Heights. Not in Brooklyn at all, on an island. There were castles and an alchemist. A woman with green eyes. Now this dream was a long time ago. When I first moved in here. It wasn't about me either. The little girl had your thick red curls. She was painting designs on the wall. I remember thinking they looked like intertwined teardrops. They were in groups of three. She was singing the same song over and over. Let's see, how did it go? Oh yeah, "Three little maryjanes sitting in a row...." Mae sang. "Oh God, hon. Are you alright? Dory? What have I done? She's gone pale, Doc. Do something!"

Dory didn't faint, thank heaven. But Mae felt awful until Dory's normal color returned.

"No worries, Mae. Orleigh was dead on though. You *are* a Biddy yourself. Orleigh knew it straightaway when she met you. Those were Celtic knots you saw on the wall. And Mam used to sing that song to myself and my sisters. That's gas. No harm done. 'Twas a grand dream. Ta."

"Your welcome, hon. I'd like to say one more thing... it's more of a toast, really."

"Raise your glasses, lads," Dory directed. Mae held her wineglass high with one hand and the other she rested on Dory's barely bump of a belly.

"To my family," Mae's voice was strong and clear. "My family here at this table. To the next generation of women at the Brownstone, let the banquet continue."